# The Best Seller

*A novel about codes, chromosomes, and conspiracy.*

# Dina Rae

Cover Art:
Michelle Crocker

http://mlcdesigns4you.weebly.com/

Publisher's Note:

This is a work of fiction. All names, characters, places, and events are the work of the author's imagination.

Any resemblance to real persons, places, or events is coincidental.

Solstice Publishing - www.solsticepublishing.com

# The Best Seller
## by Dina Rae

## Dedication

To Mike, Juju, and Bells-Love you!

# Chapter One

*Summer of 1947*

The general's most trusted airmen arrived at Broom Lake with four coffins from Roswell, New Mexico. The men knew what was inside of the coffins and now knew the location of the base's underground laboratory. They followed the general to the hidden entrance inside of the largest hangar and then entered the cargo elevator, descending one hundred feet into the earth. The doors opened into a secret world.

General Robert Andreas watched their poker faces and looked for fear, or worse, overwhelming excitement. *Were my men future blabbermouths? Would one of them be tempted to talk after too many drinks or discuss the Air Force base's secrets to family while on a deathbed? No*, he thought. *My men are loyal. We survived hell.* After Dachau, almost everything had lost its shock value.

Broom Lake was a sleepy, tiny airbase in Nevada. The site held three dirt runways. Its location and obscurity made it ideal for artillery and bomb practice. Pilots also used the base for aviation drills.

One enormous hangar sprawled out in the middle of the base and two smaller hangars were on the far south side of the lake. Andreas knew there would soon be expansion. The laboratory was new. More runways, hangars, and housing were in the works. He wondered what his new budget would be now that he was in possession of four aliens.

The general's airman set the coffins on the long table placed in the center of the laboratory. He would not take his dark eyes off of Jaeger. The doctor's beady, glacier blue eyes almost looked warm and kind. He laughed and smiled and then smiled and laughed, while pacing laps around the table.

"What in God's name? Sir, I mean General Andreas, are they like what I described? Like in Germany?" Doctor Jaeger asked. His English was flawless, but the general could still hear a faint trace of a German accent. He stared in ecstasy at the four child-sized coffins.

Jaeger was technically part of a post-World War II operation called *Paperclip*. Andreas brought the doctor back to the states, had his name changed, and then built him the laboratory. Six months later, Andreas finally got around to asking for permission. This bold move didn't endear him to the brass, but his ideas on how to use the doctor for America's advantage did. The doctor's expertise in genetics had ultimately swayed the higher-ups to grant the general possession of the alien bodies and space craft for research.

"These things inside the coffins…" The general paused and tapped on one of the coffins. "We found them outside of Roswell. Go ahead. Open them up. Let's see if they jog your memory."

"Ah, you give me too much credit, General." The doctor wiped his wireframe glasses with his shirt and put them back on his pasty face. He looked like an evil genius straight out of a comic book. "What did their craft look like? Are you bringing it here? Any pictures by chance?"

Andreas looked around the room at the five airmen and then looked at the doctor, indicating that he didn't want to talk about the craft. Jaeger nodded and dropped his questioning.

"General, can you tell me where you got the coffins? Does the Air Force keep them lying around?" asked the doctor.

Andreas didn't appreciate his snide tone, yet answered, "We confiscated them from a local funeral parlor. Probably not a good idea, but we needed something fast and something with a lock. Yes, rumors will circulate. We will deal with that later. We've only had them for sixteen hours and believe they are dead. There was no pulse or movement among any of them. But maybe you can use them in your study. Go ahead. Open one. My men are ready. They're prepared in case." The general nodded at the soldiers. The five men assumed a firing position.

Doctor Jaeger quickly put away his microscope and petri dishes. He then attempted to lift the lid of the coffin, but it wouldn't budge. "General, are these sealed?"

Andreas tried to read the doctor's thoughts, but the doctor's excitement abruptly ended and his usual stoic expression returned. "No, Doctor. They're latched shut. Try the other side."

Jaeger walked around the coffin and found the latches. He hesitated and then unlatched three of the locks and slowly lifted the cover. The airmen raised their hand guns.

"Ah, yes. I am familiar with this race. Do all of them look like this?" the doctor asked and the general nodded. "Back in Germany, well, there were times that I wasn't sure if I was seeing things. There were times when I doubted, but I never should have doubted. I should have believed. I am a believer now. This is a gift from the heavens and I will not disappoint you. Possibilities are endless!" The doctor smiled as he lovingly looked inside of the red velvet lined coffin. "Do they all wear this suit?" The doctor pointed at the metallic black jumpsuit with a black belt and small silver box clipped in the center. The jumpsuit fit the being like a second skin.

Andreas nodded. "You have seen these beings before, back in Germany?"

Jaeger answered, "Yes…" His voice trailed off and his eyes welled with tears. A moment passed. "I saw them from a distance. General, we are going to do great things to…" Before the doctor could finish his sentence, a black tentacle shot out of the small silver box that was clipped onto the being's belt. The doctor hit the floor, clutching the tentacle wrapped around his neck.

And then shots were fired.

# Chapter Two

My life changed completely after *The Master Race* was published. I went from invisibility to fame overnight. The book made me one of the most successful and famous American writers in the twenty-first century. I always loved to write, but never knew I had talent. There was a constant story going on inside of my head. The wilder the story, the more I would latch onto it, cultivate it, and even obsess about it. Science fiction had been my favorite genre since I could read.

The stories in my imagination never went anywhere until I met Eric O'Reilly. He hired me as a clerk in his book store in the Fashion Show Mall. He would always see me reading in between customers. Instead of getting mad, he would ask me about the book, my opinion, and how I would have made it better. I opened up, telling him details of each book that I would change, how the ending could have been more exciting, all of it.

I read pages almost as fast as the time it took to turn them. My favorite author was Jay McAllister. I read twenty-eight of his novels at least twice, some of them three or four times. He was a genius story-teller. His books were usually about the future, reading more like prophecy than fiction. He wrote about space and aliens in a believable way.

After telling Eric about Jay McCallister's latest novel *Naked in Niburu* which sat on the front table of the store, he smiled and said, "Blog about it. You've just been promoted to book reviewer at *TurnthePageBooks* blog. I created the blog this morning and want you to be the first to post."

Eric gave me the confidence to trust my instincts. Many customers would comment on the blog, usually in agreement with my suggestions. It was Eric who told me that I should practice what I preach, meaning if I criticized books all of the time, maybe I should write one.

Before fame and before fortune, I lived in a tiny one bedroom apartment in Las Vegas. My rent and bills prevented me from saving money, but at least I managed to avoid debt. At twenty-one years old, I was proud to live alone and support myself. I didn't have a car. My clothes, appliances, and furniture were all purchased from resale shops. I didn't have anything nice, but I had everything I needed.

My apartment building was questionable. There were numerous break-ins. I got scared enough to buy a gun off of my neighbor. I also bought a big knife that I kept underneath my pillow. Someday I hoped to move into a nice house with a husband and dog, maybe even kids. Out of loneliness I would have occasional company, usually a nameless face that I met in a bar. Sex was easy. Feelings were not.

After several weeks of blogging and then several more weeks of Eric's nagging, I set out to write a novel. Characters, various settings, and plot lines appeared out of nowhere when daydreaming. All I had to do was record the scenes that played inside of my head. On sleepless nights, I would often type in a frenzy as flashes of the story burned through my fingers like electricity.

I was extremely particular on my wording and chapter arrangement. The writing process became more of a task than coming up with the actual plot. When my laptop wasn't handy, I'd write on napkins, receipts, paper towels, or anything within reach. I took my scraps home and carefully added them into the story.

I did not have a printer. Two months after I started my novel I took my flash drive to the library and printed out the whole manuscript. I read it start to finish within a day. Strangely, I didn't remember many of the details. It was readable, maybe even good. I needed honest feedback before showing it to an agent or publisher.

I gave my manuscript to Eric. He was my only friend and the only opinion I valued. He was tall, skinny, and pasty with warm brown eyes and reddish brown hair. He wore Star Wars shirts and smoked e-cigs. He wasn't obviously attractive, but there was something about him that made me contemplate what it would be like to be with him.

I suspected that Eric was in love with me. Almost four years ago when I ran away from my last foster home he caught me in his store stealing a book. Instead of calling the police, he made me stock the shelves for three hours. He hired me by hour four. I was seventeen years old.

"This is probably the most stupid thing I've ever thought of, but do you need a job? Because I need a clerk," Eric said.

I readily agreed and went back to the flophouse where I was staying and cried. He showed me kindness when I deserved the opposite. The first few weeks of working for Eric my guard was up. All my life someone had always wanted something from me. All he wanted was an honest day's work. As the years passed, I'd catch him looking at me, but not with lust. It was a strange look, like I was someone special, like I should be placed on a pedestal.

Maybe it was fear that kept him from making his move. I know it was fear that kept me from making mine. I feared rejection and falling in love and getting dumped. We had a good thing going as friends and I couldn't withstand the thought of messing it all up.

I'm not sure if Eric was my type or even what my type was. He was by far a movie star, but then neither was I. We were reasonably in each other's league of prospects. I was short, slightly overweight, and had not got in touch with my inner "girl." My resale shop clothes were as exciting as Eric's old school t-shirts. My long, dull dark brown hair was never styled, nor was any make-up ever smeared on my face. I did not know my ethnicity. The nuns at the orphanage told me I was a mutt of sorts-part white and part Native American and maybe even part Mexican, but they were not certain.

Eric told me several times that I looked like an Indian squaw. "You've got to open a casino. Money, money, money and no taxes."

And I always replied, "You'd be my Rothstein." He and I once watched *Casino* together on his iPad when the book store was slow. We liked to recite lines from the movie.

I never corrected him about my culture or nationality. I didn't want to tell him about the orphanage and the nine foster homes I grew up in. He would pity me and I couldn't take one more pitiful gaze reminding me of the misery that I once knew.

I gave Eric my manuscript on a Tuesday morning.

By Wednesday early morning, Eric called. "Maya, I just finished it! I can't believe...I knew you had talent, but this, this is your first novel? I laughed, I cried. I can't remember being so absorbed, so on the edge of my seat. I am in the company of greatness."

"Eric, please. It's four o'clock in the morning. Love the praise, but haven't slept since I started this project," I said.

Eric apologized and hung up. The next day at the bookstore he approached me with a stack of writer magazines he took from the giant magazine rack in the back of the store. "Maya, you have to get published. There's a convention right here in Las Vegas a month from now. It's at the Bellagio, right down the street. You wouldn't have to pay for airfare or hotel. There will be big-shot agents who you can pitch your story to. It's only five hundred dollars. I'll pay. Call it an advance of sorts. You have to promise that my store will be your first signing. You've got to go!"

The advertisement in *Writer's World* read:

"Attention Writers—We've got dozens of publishers, agents, publicists, and famous authors who want to help YOU get published. The Bellagio presents Valentine's Day Writers' LoveFest. Learn how to write a novel or bring a manuscript to pitch to an agent."

Underneath the ad was a list of all who promised to come. The timing couldn't have been more convenient.

"Eric, I can't believe this. You are an angel! And look, Jay McCallister is scheduled to be there!"

"There you go. It's meant to be. Worst case scenario, you'll get him to autograph some of those books that you love so much. You better call and register. Hopefully it's not filled up."

I set the magazines down and hugged Eric as tight as I could. At that moment I probably would have fucked him if he would have made a move. I had exactly one month to reread, rewrite, and edit my manuscript. At that moment, I knew that LoveFest would change my life forever.

# Chapter Three

"Claude, you're working the convention whether you're sick or not. Quit the dramatics. That cough is fake. And your nose isn't bleeding because you're sick," Veronica Tatum said.

"Ronnie, I'm really sick. Don't know if it's a good idea to spread my germs. You want to be blamed for sending out your sickest agent and infecting...."

"Stop it, Claude. You haven't brought me a decent manuscript in, well, how long has it been? Definitely months, and I do believe that we've hit the year milestone a few weeks ago. Do your job and I'll get off of your case," Veronica interrupted.

Claude was like the boy who cried wolf when it came to playing sick. He held his job by a string, speculating minute by minute if Veronica or one of the other partners would pound the final nail in his coffin. *Just do it already*, he thought. Maybe he could get unemployment of some kind. He'd get nothing if he quit.

Claude always loved to read. It was one of the few things he was really good at. He read anything and everything with the kind of accuracy, speed, and comprehension of genius. It gave him an advantage that he desperately needed. His family had always taken short cuts. He had learned from the best in terms of just getting by without working. But poverty was not an option. He wanted so much more.

The day after graduating from U.C.L.A., Claude found his dream job at Tatum, Bayle, and Shapiro Literary Agency. He could actually get paid to read. Perfect.

Seven years later, Claude worked his way up from assistant to agent by reading every query, researching the market, and pursuing potential talent. His rise to a top agent was set at lightning speed, ultimately landing a client with a runaway bestseller. The commissions from one book alone tripled everything else. He enjoyed his cut of success.

Claude's specialty was nonfiction, but he dabbled in everything. His most profitable client to date was Doctor Benjamin Cloud. The doctor figured out a way to manipulate the human metabolism and lose weight while eating lots of food. The diet didn't work on everybody, but worked on enough. Millions of copies were sold. Doctor Cloud took Claude out of his dumpy, little Hollywood apartment and put him in swanky Silver Lake.

The good fortune enabled Claude to stop busting his ass and start enjoying the finer things of life. With his good looks, youth, and whopping cash flow, he became entrenched in the Los Angeles club scene. His expensive rent and car lease were only the beginning. Claude spent more money on restaurants and bar tabs than his actual bills.

Claude fell in with a Bohemian clique endowed with bottomless trust funds while frequenting the club scene. He was the hotshot agent who was signing million dollar advance deals for authors. But unlike his rich friends, his well soon went dry.

Shortly after a year of riding high on the best-selling diet book, good ol' Doctor Cloud found another agent who promised a lower commission and then published a second ground-breaking diet book that promised even better results. By year two the original diet book's success wandered off into oblivion, leaving Claude with a pile of bills.

Claude's new BMW was repossessed and his landlord filed for an eviction. He was forced to move in with his brother, Sam. He slept on the floor in the living room of Sam's one bedroom apartment. Roaches scurried and the plumbing constantly backed up. He was back to his beginning and more rancorous than ever.

Over the last six months, Claude begged for advances. Veronica was the only sympathetic partner of the agency. Now he was trapped into taking her shit and then eating it straight from her asshole. He even slept with her a few times despite the twenty-five year age difference. Claude didn't mind the sex. His boss was one hot fifty-four year old cougar. She had the body of a workout queen. Her long red hair and frozen smooth face made her look closer to forty years old. He could make her scream for hours.

Unfortunately, the sex wasn't enough to ensure more salary advances. Veronica soon tired of him and moved onto another booty call. From king of the hill to charity case/boy toy, and then finally ending up as the office lackey in less than two years. Elaine, the office secretary who was known for being a gossip and a flake, held a higher social standing within the office than he did. He was everyone's bestie when riding high with the doctor and the diet book. People were phony.

"Wouldn't Elaine be better at this kind of thing?" Claude asked, desperate to get out of going to the convention.

"Elaine? No doubt she would be better, more reliable, more prepared, more professional, more hard-working, but she isn't an agent, at least not yet. And all they want is an agent, especially an agent with success in competitive markets. None of my other agents want to go and you have nothing else going on. What's the problem? This is a fun assignment, a little work, a little pleasure. All of your food and beverages are included. It's at the Bellagio in Las Vegas," Veronica said.

Vegas was undoubtedly fun, but conventions were hard work with little down time. Claude looked at the itinerary for the first time and scoffed. "Ronnie, you expect me to run a class on how to write a query letter and then host a pitch fest? I don't know enough about either to give advice or tips. On Sunday, I'm supposed to show writers how to organize their sources for nonfiction? Now it's really getting comical. A class on teaching writers how to edit? If they don't know basic grammar by now…" Claude paused and leaned on her desk, giving her his best 'you're so hot, I got to have you' look. She pretended not to notice. He yelled, "Oh, c'mon! You're killing me! I'm expected to eat with the little eager-beavers? They're going to be blathering on about their pathetic novels that they've been working on for the last decade. Just fire me and be done!"

"I just might fire you, you little prick. Lord knows everyone who works here thinks you deserve to be fired. Who the hell do you think you are? After all I've done for you? There once was a time when you read through a hundred queries a day and hundreds, if not thousands of pages a week of manuscripts. You'd then sniff out the only one that would make money. Now you sit around and self-medicate yourself, feeling sorry about that damn doctor. Fuck him and fuck you. Show some gratitude. I just handed you a fun assignment and now you're going to sneer? You've got a few days to come up with some kind of a lecture for all of these subjects. See Elaine. She just graduated from Berkeley. She's the type that probably saved her syllabus. Go poach some notes, pack your bags, and oh, shut the fuck up unless you're about to say thank you."

Claude didn't like to be patronized. Veronica along with the rest of the agency had quickly forgotten that he made them more money in one year than most agents make in five years. But he played the obedient little boy routine, 'shut the fuck up,' talked with Elaine, and headed to Vegas. The trip could have a bright side. Maybe he'd get laid or even win some cash.

Claude arrived at the Bellagio around eleven o'clock Saturday morning, three hours late according to

Veronica's itinerary. He purposely missed his red-eye flight and the next two flights after that, preferring to drink with other regulars at Wino's Barstool until closing and then ignored his alarm clock.

The last time Claude had been to Vegas was three years ago. He took his little brother, Sam, to the strip to celebrate his twenty-first birthday. The weekend would never be forgotten. Claude splurged for an exclusive suite at the Venetian filled with drugs, booze, and women. Sam still talked about the birthday surprise with stars in his eyes. It was the only party anyone had ever thrown for him.

Claude looked out of the cab window as it slowly took him down the strip. Vegas looked more like an amusement park than a bank of hotels. His cab pulled up to the entrance of the Bellagio. He was pleasantly surprised.

The hotel was one of the few exceptions to the gaudy décor of the strip. It was grand and elegant. European fountains sprayed water in a large pool by the entrance. There must have been at least thirty floors with thousands of rooms. Although winter, gardens boasted endless waves of colors as if it were spring at an arboretum. *Maybe this wasn't so bad.*

The inside of the hotel matched the classy exterior. Soft neutral colors of marble, granite, and limestone gave the hotel an old world and modern look. The ceiling was the show stopper, dozens or maybe hundreds of colorful umbrellas were suspended in a dome. They gave off the illusion of flowers. The tourists failed to match the hotel's grandeur. Dozens of people clothed in flip flops, cut-offs, and t-shirts swarmed in and out of the entrance.

Claude checked into his room. The décor was modern and chic with neutrals and purple accents. The room was spacious. There was a desk and small couch, making it closer to a suite. It wasn't the Taj Mahal, but then it wasn't Sam's floor either. As far as he could see, there weren't any roaches.

Claude threw his suitcase on the bed and went into the bathroom. The size surprised him, spa-like and immense. He began to feel like a bigshot again. Maybe this convention was a second chance. Maybe Veronica truly believed he had an eye for talent.

He looked into the mirror and smiled. Despite his blood shot eyes and rumpled dress shirt and khakis, he looked more put together than most of the redneck schmucks in the lobby. His lifestyle was catching up to him. Claude was only twenty-nine years old, yet crow's feet framed his pale blue eyes and lines ran across his forehead. His face was still chiseled despite his growing alcohol dependence. Bloat hadn't taken over his lean, wiry physique. He was handsome in a rugged movie star kind of way and he knew it. He washed his face, brushed his teeth, and hopped in the elevator.

Claude landed on the main floor of the hotel and snaked his way through the halls, following the signs, and soon finding the Tower Ballroom. Embossed and gilded posters sat on easels in front of the entrance. He peeked inside.

The Tower Ballroom was immense and opulent like the hotel. Huge chandeliers cast a soft glow giving the ballroom a serene feel. A stage with red velvet draperies and gold fringe was currently vacant, but a grand piano and orchestra chairs were set up, suggesting there would be music later on. There were no dining tables, just rows and rows of long conference tables with cubical partitions that ran horizontally from the double door entrance. High-quality faux trees accented the ends of each row. Along the perimeter of the ballroom were decked-out booths filled with vendors and famous writers who peddled their newest masterpieces.

There were lines and lines of writers everywhere. He tried to calculate the turnout—five hundred? Maybe even a thousand writers minus the stragglers hanging out in the hallway.

A young woman, short and overweight with curly dyed blonde hair, zeroed in on him. She wore a business gray suit about two sizes too small and high heels that oozed out flab from the shoes' openings. She held a clipboard in her arm and smiled. "Hello. Can I help you? I'm Michelle Holichek, the event coordinator. You look lost."

"Not lost, just late. I'm Claude Kazinsky with Tatum, Bayle, and Shapiro. According to this itinerary, I'm supposed to …."

"Yes, Mr. Kazinsky. You missed the query writing class. No worries. The forty-two writers who sat there and waited for you were only just a little disappointed," she said. There was a hint of sarcasm mixed with flirtation in her voice.

"Sorry, my flight …"

"Yes, your flight was running on time. I called your agency and they double checked," she interrupted.

*Shit,* he thought. *Off to a bad start already.* "Yes, bit of an emergency. Personal. Well, I'm here now. Where do you want me to go?"

"I've got all kinds of ideas," Michelle said. Again, there was that hint of flirtation. Claude began to wonder if she'd be up for giving him a blow job later on. After a few dozen drinks, her squinty eyes and enormous girth wouldn't be so noticeable. "But I think we'll put you over there." She pointed to the center of the room where a couple of dozen booths were set up. "We have a pitch session next. I was beginning to doubt your attendance so I shifted some things around. You are listening to horror and science fiction pitches today."

"But I specialize in nonfiction," he protested.

"Not today. Listen, it's easy. The writers line-up and wait their turn. You signal a green light when it's time for one of them to sit in front of you. And then you switch it to red when you are busy during a pitch session. Repeat for each writer you see. The buzzer is set for three minutes. Each writer summarizes his or her story. You offer honest feedback, well maybe not too honest." Michelle laughed at her feeble joke. "Anyway, you might even want to represent one of them."

"Hah, I doubt it. I know jack shit about horror and science fiction. And I am well aware of what a pitch is, thank you. I think I can handle this." Michelle nodded and smiled. Her deep set eyes disappeared behind her fleshy cheeks. She handed him her revised schedule for the rest of Saturday and Sunday and then waddled away, leaving Claude alone with a small line already forming.

Claude slinked into his chair and practiced the off/on switch of the signal and then the on/off switch of the buzzer. Before committing to the "green" light of welcoming a new writer to sit down, he pulled out his phone. There were four messages from Veronica. She probably called to bitch about him being late. He had the event coordinator to thank for that. He then glanced at the new schedule—classes that taught elements of steampunk, paranormal romance and historical romance. *Oh great*, he thought, *I know nothing about this nor do I want to.* At least the Meet-and-Greet cocktail party promised an open bar. He reluctantly flicked on the green light and an old, thin man appeared in the chair across from him.

"Can I help you?" Claude asked.

The man wore a Star Trek t-shirt with a series of ears ending with Spock's pointy ear on the front side. 'Highly Logical Evolution' was underneath the picture. "I'm here to pitch you my novel."

Claude nodded and turned on the buzzer. "Go."

"It's about an astronaut who runs into a tribe of aliens somewhere around Saturn. He falls in love with one of the female aliens and then follows her back to the star that she came from. She then introduces him to her…"

Claude drifted off into daydream land at this point. He glanced at the buzzer. Only one minute had passed. It was going to be a long day. Finally the buzzer went off.

"So what do you think?" the man asked.

"Honestly, I am not sure. You have an active imagination and it's brimming with potential. Send my agency a copy once you are finished." Claude dug inside of his breast pocket for a stack of the agency's business cards and then handed the man one of them. He seemed happy and left.

Claude fine-tuned his brush-off speech for the next four writers, all white men and all over forty years old. Their ideas were way over the top and difficult to follow. He began losing faith in this so-called opportunity. Writer number five blathered on about The Grays attacking the United States for the gold in Fort Knox. He wished he had a bottle of vodka and a vile of cocaine to make the time go by faster. Maybe some marijuana as well. An altered state of mind might make the pitches entertaining. The man with the Gray alien story finished his pitch. Although Claude didn't like the story, it was the best one he'd heard since pitch fest began. "Yes, I think I see where you are going with this. I think I can sell it. Email me the manuscript direct. Let me write down my email. PDF please and I'll see what I can do."

The man smiled and practically floated away. Claude's afternoon improved. Science fiction and horror began to rub off. There were all kinds of new shows on television that discussed the possibility of aliens and vampires being real. Science fiction and horror could replace the commission of the diet doctor. He could hang another bestselling cover in his office. One of these books could be the basis for a new pilot or even a movie. For a moment, he felt the same excitement he had once felt at the onset of his career and got excited. Maybe this was why Veronica sent him here. He woke up from his daydream and began to take notes.

The first girl science fiction writer sat down in front of him. She was also the first of the dozen or so writers to be under forty. He guessed her to be somewhere in her early twenties. She was short and small with long dark brown hair and amber brown eyes. Her eyes were captivating. They were shaped like almonds and outlined with thick eyelashes. He wasn't sure about her race, maybe mixed or Hispanic or even Native American—definitely exotic. She was pretty in a self-conscious sort of a way. She wore no makeup, a plain black shirt, a crystal necklace, and jeans. There was something witchy and grungy about her, like she belonged in a novel about witchcraft.

"Okay, are you ready?" Claude asked. She nodded and he started the timer. Silence. "Let's start this again." She nodded but still would not speak. This was a first. Out of all of the windbags he listened to, she was the first to be tongue-tied. "Let's do this with no timer. Don't be nervous."

"I'm so sorry. I'll try this tomorrow," she said and then got up from her chair. Her eyes watered and her skin reddened.

"Miss, there is no sci-fi pitch fest tomorrow. Here, look at the schedule." Claude slid the itinerary her way before she walked off. "It's all paranormal and romance crap tomorrow." He got her to smile. "C'mon, sit down. Trust me, my opinion on this subject is meaningless. I specialize in diet books and nonfiction. I'm here because I was late. Try your pitch on me, I'm harmless."

She reddened again, embarrassed at something he must have said. Hotel workers entered the ballroom and began collapsing the cubicles, putting round tables in their space. He had a two hour reprieve and then it was cocktail time.

"They're kicking us out," the girl said. "Guess it wasn't meant to be."

"Let me assume you are coming to the cocktail hour." The girl nodded. "How about you drink up some false courage and then pitch me?" She smiled and nodded. Claude wouldn't mind taking her back to his room at the end of the night, but there was something more. She had his attention.

"I'll be here. I'll be ready then," she said.

*Yes, Vegas was getting better and better.*

# Chapter Four

The day of the Writers' LoveFest finally came. Bellagio
Hotel was only minutes away, but I couldn't sleep and rose
out of bed in the middle of the night. I reread my
manuscript for the twelfth time. By dawn I had to put it
down and get ready to leave. I must have changed my
clothes six times, eventually opting for the "I don't care
what I look like" look of a plain black tee and dark Levis. I
wore my green crystal necklace for good luck. It was one of
the few things that Sister Ruth from the orphanage gave
me. It supposedly belonged to my mother. I packed my
manuscript along with three hardbacks of Jay McCallister's
*Bent Timing* series and headed on foot for the strip. The
walk took forty minutes and gave me time to calm down
and reset.

Once I got on the strip I admired the eclectic variety
of hotels. As I headed north, I gazed at the mystery of the
Luxor and then New Orleans in the distance. As I came up
on the Bellagio, I noticed the hotel's beauty for the first
time. I had never been inside the hotel. Filled with
excitement, I picked up my step. If I had any money, I
would've gotten a room in the hotel just to feel the
experience of being a guest.

As I entered the hotel, I scanned for signs that led to
the conference. The opulence of the lobby had not deterred
me. I was on a mission to get published. Every connecting
hallway had some kind of sign. Was it my lucky day? I
found the LoveFest sign decked out with hearts pointing
down one corridor. I was still several minutes too early for
the convention. I thought about placing a wager. I played

craps once and burned through a week's paycheck. Maybe today would be different.

Eric was true to his word and paid for my LoveFest ticket. I wished he was with me. I had thirty dollars in my purse. The rent was paid until next month—what the hell, I thought. 'When you have nothing, you have nothing to lose' was my motto at the time.

I walked down another corridor into a new world of darkness with blinking colorful lights and fancy patterned carpeting. Bells, buzzers, and sirens sounded like a symphony. I saw the crap tables and kept walking. There were slot machines all over the place. I walked further, looking for the right machine. Finally, I found a slot with planets, constellations, and aliens. It was a sign, or so I thought at the time.

I inserted thirty dollars into the machine and then pressed the max bet which was fifteen dollars. I pressed the spinner. Nothing. The machine ate my credits. Maybe today was not my lucky day. I pumped myself up again and pressed the spin button to finish off the credits. *Go big or go home.* The machine lit up. I won two hundred and fifty dollars and then cashed out with my confidence restored. This was the sign I had been looking for. I was not leaving without a contract of some kind.

I weaved back through the corridors, eventually finding the signs for LoveFest. A short, blonde, heavy-set woman approached me.

"Maya Smock, oh yes. I'm Michelle Holichek, the event coordinator. Any questions, look for me. You're checked in. Here is an itinerary for today. You can attend any of these classes. Character Development is right around the corner and ready to start," Michelle said. She continued talking, but I didn't listen. There he was, my favorite author, the great Jay McCallister, only a few feet away. I didn't know then that he would become my friend.

There were at least twenty people in line who were waiting for his autograph and it wasn't even eight o'clock in the morning. That's fame. Based on the line, his fans were somewhat of a stereotype-male, nerd, and probably employed in some kind of occupation that used science and math. I was the only woman. As I waited, I took out three of his books from my backpack. Jay had stacks of his books on the table available for purchase, all expensive hardcovers. I was so glad I won my little jackpot. Once I got within fifteen feet of the man, I fixated on his words, gestures, breathing, expressions, and everything that I could absorb. I was in the presence of greatness and didn't want to miss a thing.

"Enjoy the book," Jay said to the middle-aged Asian man who was a few people in front of me. Jay was all business. He didn't look in the man's eyes or any of his fans' eyes for that matter. His hands shook when he signed the inside of the cover and his voice pulsed with nervousness. He was old. I didn't know how old, but at sixty years old, maybe seventy. His long hair was almost all white and tied back into a ponytail. His eyes were a washed-out pastel shade of green.

The man in front of me wasn't happy with just a signature. "Do you believe?" the fan asked the great author. Without waiting for a response, the fan asked, "Are they coming back? How long have we been lied to?"

Mister McCallister looked extremely uncomfortable. "Yes," he said and then paused. "Enjoy the book." The author's hands trembled as he handed the book to the man.

It was my turn and I didn't have anything intelligent to ask. I handed him three of his books. "I also want to buy *Planet X* and *Institute of Intelligence.*"

Mister McCallister looked at the books that I brought and then smiled. "I haven't seen these books in some years now. Most people know me by my *AI series.*"

"I know you by everything you ever wrote. You inspired me to be a writer. That's why I'm here. I want to get published." I handed him sixty dollars for the two additional books. He smelled like spearmint soap.

"Who do I make this out to?" he asked.

"Maya. Just Maya. You're a genius, Mister McCallister. Thank you so much," I gushed.

"No, just a conduit, my dear," he said as he handed me the three books that I brought with me along with the two books that I purchased. He looked at my necklace and his green eyes darkened to the color of seaweed. "Where did you get that?"

At first I wasn't sure what Jay McCallister was talking about and then he started pointing to my chest. "My mother, uh, are you okay, Mr. McCallister?"

"Where did your mother get it?" Jay yelled and sprang from his seat, reaching for my necklace. "You don't understand, child! I know that crystal. Your mother got it from them! They are here! Now!"

Before Jay could rip off my necklace, Michelle, the short, heavy-set woman who seemed to be running the convention, sandwiched herself in between Jay McCallister and me. A security guard was a few steps behind her. She pointed at my autographed books which were now on the floor and motioned for me to get them and go.

"Everyone, Jay McCallister needs a break right now. Please clear out. There are other authors to see and classes to attend to," she said.

A few more security guards appeared and escorted the great author out of the hallway.

"He's gone!" shouted the young man behind the event coordinator. "What did you do to set him off?"

"Nothing, I mean, he just went nuts and tried to grab my necklace," I answered.

"I got part of it on video and will post it later on," the young man said to me as he fiddled with his phone.

"The man's got a history of outbursts over the last few years. It might just be a publicity stunt to sell more books."

"Ah, don't post it. I kind of feel sorry for him. He's old and is working too hard," I said.

The young man shrugged and walked away. *Great, I thought. My first YouTube video with me setting off a famous author.*

I wondered why Jay McCallister kept on writing. He was one of the richest writers in the world. Critics said his new work seemed less like a novel and more like the splintering of his psyche.

Rumors of his crazy antics circled for years. Many cynics wrote Jay off as an actor trying to sell more books and stay in the limelight. Either way, the man was a genius. He and a friend were set on proving to the world the existence of aliens. Both had sunk millions of dollars into an institute somewhere in Nevada. Like most of Jay's fans, I wasn't sure if antics were for show or a passionate reaction to his lifelong beliefs. I didn't know it at the time, but Jay McCallister was very much part of my moment.

Later on that day I met Claude Kazinsky, another key figure in my moment. Claude was the agent who was stationed to hear my pitch. He was the best looking man I had ever seen outside of television or movies. His looks held my tongue hostage, taking away my opportunity to pitch my novel.

"You'll just have to pitch me during cocktail hour later tonight," Claude said.

The way he said it sounded almost as if he was flirting with me. But why would someone as good looking as he flirt with me? I was average, maybe cute if I put effort into my looks. He was the kind of man who should have been flirting with *Sports Illustrated* swimsuit models.

At the very least, I wanted to be heard. My dingy clothes weren't going to cut it during cocktail hour. I pissed away the remainder of my winnings at the women's boutique and acquired my first LBDR (that's an abbreviation for little black dress or at least that is what the sales lady had called it), along with my first pair of high heels, both on the clearance rack and both in my size.

The saleswoman threw in the nylons insisting that a lady always wears nylons when she wears a dress. I changed in the restroom and freshened up with an old, dull eyeliner pencil and a mauve lip stain which I also smeared on my cheeks to accent my cheekbones set high on my square face. I let my long hair loose. Looking in the mirror, I felt for the first time in my life empowered.

The giant conference room transformed into an elegant ballroom. An orchestra was playing classical music on the stage. The chandeliers barely dimmed the room and allowed candlelight to give off romantic ambience. Round tables replaced the cubicle rows of the afternoon with fresh flower arrangements as centerpieces.

There were long tables on each side of the room. Staff was setting up silver serving trays of food, plates, and silverware. In each corner was a medium sized bar with three bartenders filling bottomless cocktail glasses. Michelle, the event coordinator appeared, dressed in her own version of a LBD. I was hardly pin-thin, but she looked like ten pounds of shit stuffed into a five pound bag. Her dress had to be spandex or it would be splitting in the very near future. She had her clipboard out as if taking attendance amongst the agents and publishers who promised to attend. She stood in line by Claude and batted her false eyelashes as she checked him off of her clipboard. Claude seemed oblivious to her overt advances and turned away as if absorbed in line while waiting for a drink.

I felt wildly excited as if something bigger than the cosmos was about to happen. My stomach was too jittery to eat. I headed for the bar. Within minutes, the man who videotaped me earlier was standing behind me. He hadn't bothered to change and still wore the same grungy t-shirt and jeans from the afternoon.

"Hey, I know you. Were we in the query class together?" he asked.

"No." I didn't want to speak to him. He looked at my neck.

"The necklace, how could I forget? You're the girl who set him off. Hey, can I buy you a drink?" he asked.

"No. They are free," I said.

"Well, I …, guess they are. I'm sorry. I'm an idiot. My friends call me Moron or Ed, your pick."

"Well then, Moron, it's nice to meet you. My name is Maya or, as you call me, the girl who set off one of the most brilliant minds of this generation. If you want to portray Mr. McCallister as a senile, crazed old man, then go ahead and post that clip. I know it's not the first time he has been portrayed as looney tunes. I saw the interview with Katie Coural and I was also wondering if he secretly wore a tin hat. But the man is eccentric. All geniuses are."

Ed seemed happy that I was talking to him as we waited for drinks and then Claude approached me with a large fruity, icy drink with an umbrella.

"Excuse me, Moron. Maya never finished her pitch to me this afternoon. So scram," Claude said. And like that, Moron or Ed or whatever his name was turned away. He was smart enough to know that he could not compete with a handsome agent during a writer's conference. I took the colorful drink and followed Claude to a table.

"What was that about? I was surprised to learn Jay McCallister was still alive. Couldn't help but overhear that you set him off?" Claude asked and then smiled.

I wasn't sure at the time if he was teasing me or sincerely interested. "Yes, he is one of the reasons why I started writing. I love his work—so original, so believable. His characters are like my friends."

"What about me? Can I be your friend or is that just a bond you form with imaginary people?" Claude was definitely flirting with me and I blushed.

"If you get my book published, then I will be your friend," I said and then laughed. He laughed too. "So do you know him? Jay McCallister?"

"I've of course heard of him. Who hasn't, right? He is to science fiction as Stephen King is to horror. But there have been plenty of whispers, you know, about his mental stability. Some say it's all a publicity stunt—the misunderstood artiste, but who knows. What was that guy talking about?"

"He tried to grab me when I waited in line for him to sign the novels I brought with me. His people or security, not really sure, ended the book signing and I'm not sure if I'll get another chance to meet him."

"I heard he went all whack-a-doo. That was you? Small world. He probably just thought you were pretty and wasn't sure how to get your attention," Claude said. He then flashed his perfect white teeth. I blushed again. He was so gorgeous. I couldn't help but stare into his hypnotic blue eyes.

Claude's looks weren't all he had going for him. He had a way of making me feel as if I was the only one who mattered in a room filled with people. I suspected he was half in the bag as I spent almost an hour explaining my novel.

"It's kind of like *The Matrix* except there are no red or blue pills, just mind implants and our society is really just a caste system with reptilian aliens ruling. Democracy is an illusion meant to keep chaos levels down to a minimum but it no longer works. As humans evolve, so did their neuropaths. The implants aren't stopping higher levels of cognitive thinking. You know, writing is the only thing I want to do. It feels ….right."

Claude hung on every word. I told him about my dead-end job and how I had no idea of what I wanted to do with my life.

As I talked, Claude periodically told me to hold my thoughts and then fetched us more drinks. I didn't think I was drunk, but after five drinks within less than two hours I had to be. I leaned to the floor to give Claude my one copy of the manuscript and felt dizzy.

"Maya, I've got to be honest with you. I don't know much about science fiction, but I'm learning. And your work sounds so compelling. Our agency is looking to expand our genres. Maybe we could raid the mini-bar in my hotel room. You could tell me more about the book and how you plan on marketing it. Maybe I could even read a few chapters before it gets too late," he slurred and then rubbed my leg with his hand.

I should have been ecstatic that someone like Claude would even want to talk to me let alone be sexually attracted to me. But something deep inside would not be satisfied with a sexual adventure. I did not want to be someone's receptacle for the night. I wanted to be heard. Whether it was psychological or physical, some kind of change was swirling inside of me. My persona was replaced with someone who would do anything to make it to the top. Ambition was now my god and I would pray for power to manipulate instead of good-old fashioned luck. Something clicked on the way up the elevator. For the first time in my life I knew that I was in charge of my destiny instead of destiny being in charge of me.

By the time we made it to Claude's hotel room, he fondled my butt at least a dozen times. His message was clear. He wanted sex and the new me, the drunk me was prepared to give it to him, but I had wants, needs, and conditions that came before him. I had been used before, but not this time. Tonight I would take what I came here for.

Claude's hotel room was nice, but not the penthouse suite I had envisioned. Doubt reared its ugly head and I questioned if he had the ability to do anything for my novel.

He lunged at me and pushed me against the wall, grinding his manhood into my stomach. He was at least one foot taller than me and his size was intimidating. In desperation, I mumbled, "Claude, how about that drink?"

"Of course." He backed off of me and let me enter the room. I sat at the edge of the bed while he poured us both rum on the rocks and then opened a can of Coke from his pocket to mix.

I sipped the drink wondering if he remembered one word I said in the ballroom. "Claude, do you think your agency can sell my manuscript?"

"We don't do a lot of genre fiction, mostly biographies, diet books, that kind of thing, but I can sell anything. And you have what I think will be a best seller," he said as he resumed his position next to me on the bed. His hand cupped my breast and he began to lean into me, pushing me down onto the bed.

"What did you like most about the book?" I asked

"Everything," he mumbled as he fumbled for the back zipper of my dress.

"No, the story line I mean. Specifically, what did you like the most?"

"I will go over the whole book with you tomorrow over coffee and pancakes," he said as he took his free hand and ran it up my leg.

The new me did not like his answers but the new me was not about to let the night go to waste.

"I like the sound of that," I said. "I have an idea. Did you ever read that book *Fifty Shades of Gray?*" Claude stopped caressing me with his hands. I had his attention and was not about to let it go to waste.

"Never read it, but isn't it about S&M?"

"Yes. She ties up Christian Gray and blindfolds him. I always wanted to do that," I lied. I never read *Fifty Shades* or was ever interested in S&M, but Claude was about to have a night he'd never forget.

# Chapter Five

The LoveFest Convention was turning out to be a LoveFest for Claude. He met a sexy young writer who wanted to play S&M in bed. He assumed the conference would get him laid. Claude was handsome and knew how to seduce. Anywhere at any time got him laid.

Once back at the office, Claude planned to tell Veronica that he met some writers and then show her some manuscripts. At the end of the work day, he'd leave early and continue on with his self-destruction. He would leave out the tiny detail of being tied to a bed by one of the writers.

But his plan changed. Maya tied him up and stripped down to her bra and panties, but then started to read to him aloud.

"What the fuck?" he shouted. She then gagged him with a pair of his own underwear she took out of his suitcase.

In between chapters, she would take the underwear out of his mouth and quiz him. At first he listened out of fear. She was one crazy bitch and he didn't know what she'd do if he got the answer wrong. But somewhere around a third of the way through he listened out of interest. Her book was original, clever, and well written. He didn't know much about science fiction, but the way the book was worded he didn't have to know much. Fear suddenly was replaced with concentration. And concentration turned into visions of dollar signs.

Once she finished the book, somewhere around daybreak, she rewarded him with sex. Hours of sex. She nearly scared the shit out of him. Her tactics might have been illegal, but were wildly arousing. She liked to play with fire.

Claude blew off the rest of the convention. Maya didn't leave his hotel room until early Sunday afternoon and then he slept until Monday morning's plane. The bitch with the clipboard called his boss a few more times to report how he didn't show up for classes that he was assigned to teach.

Tuesday morning came and he slinked into work early, hoping to avoid Veronica but with no such luck.

"Well, if it isn't Claude Kazinsky, the only agent who didn't show up for almost the entire weekend of LoveFest. That's what the event coordinator said. Care to explain?" Veronica asked.

"Listen, I went to that damn convention. I even met a writer who I want to represent. I spent most of my time reading her novel."

"*Her*, huh?" Veronica asked. Her tone was sarcastic.

"Jealous?" Claude regretted the comment. He knew better, but was grasping at straws to keep his job. He was up to his eyeballs in advances and knew a nasty termination would brand a scarlet letter on him within the literary world. "I know you're not. Sorry. And yes, some of my obligations were not met. Just hear me out. This girl is new, but her novel is so original, so inspiring, like she has a special insight of the world. I couldn't put it down." *I couldn't pick it up either. She held me captive while she read it,* Claude thought. He mentally made a point of getting back to saving his ass with Veronica and hoped he wasn't overselling the novel.

"I'm listening. Pitch me."

Claude told her the basic story of how aliens used mind control to take over the world. The book would be forever ingrained in his memory. "Here. I brought the manuscript for you to read. I wanted your approval before I start banging on doors. Let me know what you think." He believed the gesture would buy him some time. Maybe he'd get lucky and find something else worth selling in his growing email queue.

"I'll read it. Haven't read a novel in years. Claude, I'm surprised. Diet books and bios to science fiction. You seem sincere about wanting a change." Veronica thumbed through the first few pages and then drifted away back to her office.

Claude only wished it was another diet book. Diet books made money. He sifted through the three hundred emails he hadn't read in weeks, deleting the ones that seemed the least important. His mind wandered off to Maya. Her address and phone number were typed on the manuscript. She mentioned the bookstore where she worked in Las Vegas. *No,* he thought. *She is one fucked up little bitch. What's done is done. No need to get involved.* But he couldn't stop thinking about her that day, night, and then week.

Claude read more of his queries and compared them to Maya's novel. *Master Race* was much more interesting than any of the emails he read. By Friday, his luck seemed to turn. A YA novel he had pitched to Ransom Day Press Publications was picked up, giving him a few thousand dollars in commission from the advance, just enough to cover the month's bills.

Claude almost called the bookstore, wanting to tell Maya that he can sell fiction, wanting to hear her voice. He already Googled the store at least thirty times. There was a "contact" widget that displayed four people's email addresses with Maya's address being one of them. He was tempted to at least tell her that his boss was reading her manuscript, yet fear held him back. She made him nervous.

Instead of going to the bars, trolling for action, he went to his brother's apartment where he had been staying. He took a couple of manuscripts he received in the mail.

The one that had the most potential was another diet book specifically for adults with ADD. He began reading it after finishing off a box of macaroni and cheese. Almost eight hours later, minutes before three in the morning, the phone rang. He secretly hoped it was Maya, but the caller ID showed Veronica's number. Booty call? Or did she want part of his commission? She had made it clear that his advances were just that—advances, and he was responsible for paying them back. He picked up the phone.

"Veronica, what can I do you for? You horny, lonely, hungry?"

"None of the above. Claude, you've really done it this time."

Being eternally in the doghouse, he wondered which one of his fuck-ups she was referring to. At this time of night she had to be infuriated, yet her voice sounded different, excited perhaps. "So what have I done?"

"You sober?" Veronica asked.

"Yes, imagine the odds. You call me at three in the morning and I am awake and sober. Please just spit it out. The suspense of your lecture is killing me."

Veronica laughed. "I guess you didn't check your email. I'm calling about Maya Smock. I started the manuscript yesterday and haven't put it down since. I don't even like science fiction, but this is something. It's a universal theme about powerlessness. Something about the story resonates with me. I think it's going to be a best seller. Hell, I can even see changing the ending and milking the story line into a trilogy. Pretty sure, if marketed properly, this could get sold off to Hollywood. Claude, I got to hand it to you, you've got a nose for talent. For all of your faults, you can spot a winner a mile away. I'm not calling to lecture you or put you down. I'm calling to tell you to forget about all of the advances. You don't have to pay them back. Concentrate on this girl. Get her signed immediately before she starts agent shopping. She could be the next J.K. Rowling."

Claude sat up in bed and stared at the ceiling. He was stunned. This was too much to process. His slump was broken. He was going to reinvent himself and be the hotshot agent again.

"Claude, are you there?" Veronica asked. Her voice sounded far away compared to the volume of his thoughts.

"Yes, I'm here. The girl is a little quirky, but I'll call her tomorrow morning at a decent time."

"There is something you're not telling me. Did you fuck this up already? Did you sleep with her? Does she hate you? Never mind. Forget those questions. I don't need to know." Her voice sounded angry. She paused and then said, "Just make it right. Get her signed or this is it, Claude. This is your last chance at this agency."

Claude's mind raced after Veronica hung up. Maya, the kinky dominatrix, or Maya, the callous author willing to do whatever it took to make it, or Maya, the treacherous man eater. Maybe he had her all wrong. He couldn't figure her out, but her mystique hadn't left him since Las Vegas. He now had a reason to call. He looked at the fading ligature marks on his wrists and smiled. He liked being tied up and hoped she would tie him up again. *She could be the next J.K. Rowling* echoed in his head.

Claude wasn't much of a dreamer when he slept, but that night he dreamt like crazy and woke up remembering. He dreamt of Maya in black leather whipping him bloody somewhere outside by the mountains. Something was burning but smelled different than campfire. Light kept flashing. He looked into her dark eyes and trembled.

*If you mess around with fire you eventually get burned*, he thought. *Was that night in Vegas going to stay in Vegas? Should I keep this relationship strictly professional? Would she expect more? Don't fuck this up and let her take the lead.*

# Chapter Six

General Robert Andreas nodded at his airmen. Shots rained from machine guns. A tentacle stemming from a silver box on the alien's belt was wrapped around Doctor Karl Jaeger's neck. The general enjoyed watching the strangulation of the doctor. Jaeger used to be Dr. Josef Handel, an obscure doctor that no one in the United States had ever heard of. He was perhaps one of the Nazi's biggest monstrosities of the war.

Andreas saw fragments of some of Handel's experiments. Jewish prisoners at Dachau were his guinea pig of choice. If the press got wind of who the doctor really was and what he had done, there would be a public outrage demanding the general's head on a silver platter. He was the asshole who saved Josef Handel. Not only did the doctor escape without justice, he was rewarded by coming to the States and continuing his work. Josef Handel was officially shot down during the liberation of Dachau, at least that was how the paperwork read.

The airmen's bullets either killed the alien or caused it to become dormant. The tentacle recoiled back into the silver box attached to the being's belt. Andreas wasn't sure if it was an appendage or part of the black uniform the being wore. The doctor coughed and gasped for several minutes before getting off of the floor. His pale skin turned ghost white.

"Sorry, Doctor. We need to be more careful. That was a foolish mistake by all of us and will not happen again. Were these things aggressive back in Germany?"

The doctor wiped his face with his forearm. "No, but then we were never this close. It felt threatened, that's all. Wouldn't you? They were kidnapped and then locked in the confining space of a coffin. No wonder they are angry."

The general felt a tinge of anger. The doctor had no reason to cast judgment. The soldiers involved did their best in the tiny time frame they were given. "It's all going to work out. We've got the press convinced the space craft was just a weather balloon. We paid a fortune for these coffins, obviously not in uniform. You'll have everything you need without any outside parties to question your methods," said Andreas.

"Can I have a word with you alone?" asked Dr. Jaeger.

"Major Lamphrey, excuse us for a moment." The recently promoted major and the other four men exited the laboratory. "Okay, Doctor, we have the privacy you requested."

"Thank you. I want to share a few things about these things as you call them. They have more intelligence in their fingers than all of New York City. We caught them watching us years ago. Who knows how long they watched us, maybe centuries. They learned our language, even the dialects of various regions. You need to build...I can't think of the word right now..."

"A cage, Doctor?"

"Yes, a cage. I don't know everything, but they consume a plant-based food that's more like a thick liquid. They drink water. There was something they had with them, a shiny drink in a clear bottle, perhaps metallic, but I'm not positive. They don't need to eat or drink every day like we do. We noticed they seemed to replenish once every few weeks or so. I really need to know more about the flying machine."

There was a long pause. The general knew the doctor was not telling him everything.

"The flying machine, or space craft as we call it, is classified, even for you," the general said.

"All right, you want to play. Go ahead. As you Americans say, 'show me yours and I'll show you mine.' You want to know what I was working on in Germany, don't you? I know you must have ideas."

"Obviously something with genetics, but you were way past dying brown eyes blue."

"Yes, I was," Doctor Jaeger said and then laughed. "I never shared my research with Mengele. Don't ever compare me to that simpleton. I knew of his work, as everyone did. He made sure of that—such a…showboat as you Americans say, but his work would never change the world like my work. Brown eyes or blue eyes—who cares? I know that goes against Hitler's Aryan dream, but I was dabbling with something much more profound. Did you ever hear of changing or modifying genes, General?"

"No, but I only know what most people know about genetics. It started with Mendel and his Punnett square. If I remember correctly, he figured out we have traits or genes and we pass our traits onto our offspring. If you are claiming to modify a gene, then you must be experimenting with changing one's genetic makeup. I believe you can do it with plants to some degree, but with animals? And people? Impossible."

"I was working on something so ground-breaking, so innovative. Making the impossible possible. Just imagine if, like plants, you can manipulate genes. Or how about destroy genes, genes that give off a disease? Maybe even insert a gene that can regenerate cells, making it possible for someone to walk again? Or live longer? Just think of the possibilities."

"So you're aiming for some kind of a humanitarian award? End disease and spinal injuries? How noble. Was that what Hitler wanted you to do? I remember your lab in Germany. Were you trying to cure cancer or create a new species?" The general paused, second-guessing why he risked his life and career over saving this psychopath.

Doctor Jaeger looked down at the floor. Andreas should have exposed him to the world along with the aliens. All of this change could not be good. But curiosity overruled logic and morals.

"Okay. Let's say you can make your own species? Are you going to cut up an alien gene and mix it with a human gene? Don't humans have to have sex to reproduce? Do these things even have male or female parts? How do you know if they aren't already manmade, possibly robots sent from another planet to watch us? Or maybe they duplicate themselves? Isn't there a word for that?"

"Yes. It's called cloning, or making an exact copy of a life form. And you're right. I don't know enough about them, but I can tell you this—I am very close to figuring it out and I will not rest until that day comes. We both know these things, or Advance Beings as I like to call them, are smarter than we are."

"Because they figured out how to get here before we figured out how to get to wherever they are from?"

"Yes, but there is much more to it. Maybe they are the reason that we are here. Maybe they somehow genetically modified themselves with the cavemen and came up with ….well, us. I'm saying they might be able to manipulate the speed of evolution or even evolution in itself. Think, General, if that advanced being is still alive after all of those gunshots, then they have figured out a way to be immortal."

"That thing attacked you. My men rained bullets into it. It's got to be dead. But if you're right, then these things will be too dangerous to study. We are like ants to them. This could be like opening up Pandora's box."

"If we find out their secrets, General…" Karl's pale blue eyes danced with glee. "Now I gave you an overview of my plans, how about you give me some details about their space craft?"

"Fair enough. Before the craft crashed into a zillion pieces, witnesses claimed it was round. I don't have exact measurements, but somewhere around fifty feet in diameter. They said it was not flat, but evenly raised on the top and bottom, maybe around ten feet high or so. Like a vertical oval intersecting with a horizontal disc. You follow?"

The doctor nodded and had yet to blink, clearly hanging on Andreas's every word.

"The craft dropped out of the sky like an asteroid and shattered into a zillion pieces of metal. One of these things or Advanced Beings was found under the heap, probably dead. Its body seemed unaffected by the crash. The other three were also unaffected, but found several yards away. We are not sure of how they got out. Possibly through the baby craft that was found a few hundred yards away. It was banged up. Maybe it was used as some kind of lifeboat for space. It might have been big enough to hold all of them. The baby craft must have been around eight feet tall, shaped like a bell. At the widest part of the craft it might have been six feet diameter. There might have been others on board that space craft, but we only found the four bodies. "

"Where are the two crafts now and who gets the honor of studying them? I would very much like to work with this team," said the doctor.

The general already regretted sharing the information. Jaeger had a cold, reptilian look of ambition that made the hair on the back of the general's neck stand up. "Doctor, that's all I can say for now. I shouldn't have told you that much. You'll have your cage built within the next week or two. It's top priority."

"In time, General, you will want to share more with me. The crafts and the beings are linked. I do have a small request, though." General nodded. "I need help with my observations. I trust the ones I worked with in Germany.

Let me give you a list. I doubt they are dead. We all had an exit plan in case. You persuaded me to come here."

"Persuaded, huh? Your only other option was to die," Andreas said, clearly annoyed.

"Yes, of course. Please, I need my team. Here is a list of their names." Doctor Jaeger scribbled on a sheet of scratch paper and handed it to Andreas. "I suggest you start your search in Buenos Aires."

General Andreas read the list of the five Nazis Jaeger requested. He was well aware of their reputations. Doctor Jaeger would soon have his team of monsters and together they would play God. Andreas felt lighter, as if his soul floated away. Hell was calling him.

# Chapter Seven

My first night with Claude got out of hand. I could have blamed it on the alcohol, but I knew exactly what I was doing—using sex to get what I wanted. I wanted him, but I wanted what he could do for me more. When he seemed more interested in sex than my manuscript, something inside of me roared like a tidal wave of anger with years of disappointment rolling to shore.

I've always been one of those girls who would rather put up with shit than stand up for myself. I feared confrontation, even when it came to sex. That night in Vegas, I was someone else. He could have called the cops and had me booked for rape. The next day, once the booze wore off, I apologized and went home. I assumed the whole weekend was in vain. I returned to *Turn the Page*, told Eric that no one was interested in my novel, and temporarily gave up writing. And then Claude called.

"Maya? It's Claude. I've got good news. Veronica, that's my boss, loved your manuscript even more than I did. We want you to sign a contract with us. We will get you top dollar for your novel. It's what my agency does best. I think we are also looking at possible movie rights."

Claude sounded glorious, but distant. I hardly knew him yet I ironically expected more warmth from someone I had just assaulted. He must have had worn his business mask. I should have been grateful. He believed in me. I longed to apologize to him and start fresh, but the timing didn't feel right.

"Claude, so glad you called. I'll sign whatever you think is fair," I said.

"Terrific!" The tone of his voice unthawed. "I'll email you the contract. Just print it off and sign, then send it back to me. I'll start making phone calls and getting it sold."

"Who do you think will buy it?" I asked.

"I have a few ideas, but don't want to say. Probably a subsidiary of one of the Big Six."

"Huh?" I asked.

"Basically there are six enormous publishers that publish almost everything available for brick and mortar stores and e-readers. There are smaller publishing houses and self-publishing too, but you'll make more money…"

"No, Claude, we'll make more money," I corrected. He laughed.

"Yes, we'll make more money."

"I'll go to the library this Sunday, my day off, and print the contract. I don't have a printer and have to work."

"You live not too far from Bellagio, right?" Claude asked and I confirmed. "How about I personally deliver you the contract and we can go printer shopping together? My treat. Then maybe dinner? You said Sunday is your day off?"

My heart stopped. At that moment I realized he wasn't too mad at my behavior in his hotel room and nearly dropped the phone. "Ah, yes." Those were the only two words that I could come up with. He didn't talk much longer and then hung up.

That Sunday I was Maya and he was Claude. He bought me my printer, took me to see Cirque du Soleil, and then made love to me all night in my apartment. He was different from other men I'd been with—handsome, charming, intelligent, educated, sophisticated, and so much more. My past conquests were none of those things, more like future residents of trailer parks or jail cells.

Claude was out of my league and we both knew it. How could I ever hold on to a man like him? I knew full well that I couldn't. I let the romance play out, content with the here and now instead of the inevitable.

Within a month, Claude delivered on his promise. He sold my manuscript for a twenty-five thousand dollar advance, unusual for a first novel. Life couldn't have been better. He convinced me to quit my job at Turn the Page.

I didn't tell Eric about Claude nor Claude about Eric, completely aware that both men would be jealous. Although Eric was a friend, the best friend I ever had, I didn't want him to know I had sort of a boyfriend. Looking back, I was still holding out for him. But he never made his move. Maybe I was permanently cast into his friend zone. I did tell Eric about my advance.

"Remember your promise—first signing is here at Turn the Page," Eric said.

With tears in my eyes, I replied, "That's a promise I plan to keep for every one of my new releases."

I gave Eric my two-weeks-notice and volunteered for hours up until my novel was released. With all of the good things going on in my life, I couldn't shake this uneasy feeling in my gut. I felt guilty about keeping Claude a secret from my best friend, but that was only a small part of it. The uneasy feeling morphed into something worse than guilt. Was it a sixth sense or some kind of omen? I couldn't say. Maybe it was women's intuition somehow warning me about a bad decision I was about to make. At first I ignored the feeling and then I even rationalized it. I convinced myself that I was just terrified of being happy. If Eric wasn't available, Claude was. I had a new novel, a new career, and a new man.

"I have an official release date now and have to do some work in order to create a buzz. I'm really going to miss working here," I said on my last day at Turn the Page.

"I hope you and me aren't over. You're quitting my book store, but you're not quitting our friendship, right? Are you moving away?" Eric asked. I shook my head and wiped away a tear that I couldn't hold back. "Good. I have a surprise." A few minutes later a van pulled up. Several bouquets of flowers were set on the counter—roses, carnations, lilies, daisies, and more flowers that I couldn't identify.

"Eric, you shouldn't have. This is too much," I said.

"It's not enough. One more surprise." Eric handed me a small gift wrapped in gold metallic paper. I opened the gift-an engraved pen. *To the next big thing—Eric.* The flowers and gift must have cost him at least a week's profits. Speechless, I cried.

"Let's go comb the strip—a drink at each hotel. What do you say? My treat. You can treat me once you've sold your millionth book. When you get your cover, I'll post it around the store." Tears ran down my cheeks. He clearly had feelings for me all along. Why did he wait so long to show them? "I am so proud of you. I'm so … Maya, I…"

I thought he was going to tell me that he loved me, but he didn't and it was too late. "Eric, this is all so great…but, well, I…I don't have to quit right now. I can work another month and the next. My book doesn't even come out until July."

"July is only two months away. No, you have a real career now, a real chance. Don't blow this opportunity to hang out in this dump. I could never live with myself for holding you back. My reasons would be purely selfish because I like having you around. Before I get any mushier, I want to clarify drinks tonight. We'll start at the Luxor," he said. I saw the hurt look in his warm brown eyes.

"Well, that's another thing. I am, uh, dating my agent. I want you to meet him. Maybe he could go drinking with us too? He's staying at my place right now."

The dirty deed was done. I officially ended any chance of being with Eric. By the expression on his face, I also broke his heart. I told myself I owed him nothing and he shouldn't have expected anything from me—expectations were just premeditated resentments or so the saying goes.

That night at the top of the pyramid hotel, Eric met Claude and Claude met Eric. Claude was about as warm and friendly as an ice rink. When Claude went to the bar and got us all drinks, Eric said, "I just want you to be happy. Even if it's not with me."

My eyes welled with tears, but I forced them back. Claude came back with three drinks that Eric insisted on paying for. Claude looked in my eyes. I saw his blue eyes darken.

"Well, Eric, if you insist. The round cost thirty-three dollars and I gave her a seven dollar tip. Forty will do."

Forty dollars to Claude was almost nothing, or so I thought by the way he spent money, but to Eric that might be all of his profits on a slow day at the bookstore. Eric didn't flinch and quickly handed him two twenties. That was the tone of the evening.

Tension was heard, felt, seen, tasted, and smelled. Both of these men were jealous of each other. I had never had a real boyfriend, just a string of regrettable one-nighters. Now I had two men who wanted me. On some level, I provoked this while savoring every second of the attention. That was one of the many mistakes I made with both of these men.

With each drink, social filters were shed. By the fifth round Eric couldn't maintain his civility.

"She doesn't deserve you, you fucking phony snake oil salesman. I love her and you're just using her," Eric said as he threw a shot of tequila in Claude's face.

Claude pushed Eric into the wall and calmly said, "I love her too. And you need to go home." He then punched Eric in the gut and dragged me out of the bar.

I should have stayed. The last four years I waited for Eric to say that he loved me and when he did I left with the good looking snake oil salesman.

Two weeks later, I was married on the strip in a very tacky chapel with no friends or family, just two strangers who volunteered to be our witnesses. I wore a white sheath and a crystal necklace my mother left me, the same necklace that upset the famous Jay McCallister. Claude wore a beautiful custom blue suit. He looked like a model and I looked like a schmuck, but I couldn't have been happier. Claude promised that we would conquer the literary world and travel the real world. My life took on such an exciting turn.

A week later, I finally had the nerve to call Eric. He insisted on seeing the pictures.

"You got married here? Why didn't you invite me?" Eric asked, attempting to act like nothing happened since the night at the Luxor.

"I...It's just that you two didn't get along and I..."

"Are you forbidden? Did he forbid you from talking to me?" Silence. I didn't know how to respond. "Listen, just because he won, just because he got you and gets to live happily ever after, it doesn't mean we can't be friends. I know that it's no contest. He's handsome and charismatic and I'm, well, we both know that I'm not a lady's man."

"Eric, stop it. I didn't invite you because I felt guilty. Guilty about quitting, guilty about bringing you out with us, guilty about possibly leading you on, just about guilty for everything. I thought that my wedding would be rubbing it in."

"Please don't do this. Don't end our friendship," Eric said. His voice cracked.

We hung up with a promise of hitting the reset button on our friendship.

Several weeks passed and my release date closed in. Claude was busy lining up interviews on blogs, e-magazines, radio shows, and even Internet TV. He promised me that I'd soon be big enough for day time TV interviews and major magazine book reviews. I entrusted him with all of it. A lot of his time was spent in Los Angeles. He flew back and forth every week. He wanted me to move there, but I wasn't ready for Los Angeles. He had a signing scheduled in one of the city's biggest book stores.

"Sorry, but I promised Eric to sign in his store a long time ago. He already bought ten boxes of books and covered the windows with posters. I can't."

Claude pouted for days, upset because it was the first time I refused to follow his orders and also because he hated Eric. Two days before my first signing, Claude left again. My husband/agent was not coming to my first signing. I began to suspect he had a girlfriend or even girlfriends.

"You aren't my only client, you know. I've got a few nonfiction authors lined up too. I've got to take care of some business."

Some women would have been devastated, but I was relieved, another sign that maybe Claude wasn't Prince Charming. Signs of me not being his one and only were clear from the get go. His phone rang with calls and buzzed with texts at all hours of the day.

Maybe I was just paranoid. In Claude's defense, I did overhear him tell a caller that he was married. Maybe he needed to get the word out that he was off the market. My suspicions could have been insecurity. We both took vows of being faithful. It was not Claude's fault that women liked him. He was a man that turned heads and made women sigh. But I married him without really knowing him. As time passed, Claude seemed to encourage and even initiate attention from pretty women.

My book was released on a Sunday in July. Las Vegas blazed up to 103 degrees Fahrenheit. I wore jeans and a white tee. I also wore my green crystal as a symbol of remembering where I started and how far I'd come.

I didn't remember my parents. I was three years old or so I was told. I didn't remember much before the age of seven. Maybe I was traumatized and suppressed it. I wished I could suppress the next ten years to follow.

At the age of seventeen, I had had it with group homes and foster parents. My life as an independent woman started earlier than my classmates. I dropped out of school and pounded the strip for a job. It was Eric who hired me and gave me direction. He helped me get my G.E.D. and it was Eric who wanted me to attend junior college. I had some of the many brochures in my magazine rack, but wasn't sure about what to do with the rest of my life. All I ever loved was reading. Now I was a writer about to sell my work to strangers.

As I stood out on the sidewalk only steps away from the bookstore, emotion swept over me. Did I make the biggest mistake of my life? This was my moment and Claude was back in L.A. But Eric would be there. It was his store. Did I pick the wrong guy? Claude was now my family, my only family.

I wished I had parents or siblings or cousins or more friends to come and celebrate my release. Eric used to joke that no relatives were a blessing. But his joke didn't apply to his family. Every Christmas he'd drag me to his mother's and stepdad's home outside of Vegas. I saw more warmth and kindness in a few hours than I ever saw as a child.

I looked in the window of the bookstore wondering how the day would play out. Eric was inside waiting.

I checked my appearance through the window's reflection. My memories needed to do me a favor and burrow themselves deep inside. This was my release day and self-doubt and self-loathing were not invited. Eric was in there waiting for me to peddle some books. I was determined to enjoy myself no matter what.

For the first time in my life, I walked into the bookstore as a featured author and not an employee. I noticed the table set up with boxes of my books ripped open and in the process of being displayed. There were book cover posters throughout the store along with the professional picture of me that Claude had photographers take for the inside jacket of the book.

"You look even more beautiful than you usually do," Eric said, almost running toward me from the back of the store.

I held back more tears and gulped. "Had my hair professionally styled for the first time ever. And look." I showed Eric my fancy French manicure with emerald green metallic tips. "My nails are done. I brought a few hundred pens with my name and website on them for swag. I'm here to sell." I hugged him tightly.

"Well, I have six hundred copies of your books." My jaw dropped. "I know, it's more than I usually order for signing. But this way I can keep what I don't sell or order more if we sell 'um all!" His voice cracked. He was nervous.

"Six hundred? You don't usually spend money on posters either. Eric, this is more than you have ever done for all of the authors who have marched through this…"

"Stop. You're not just another author. What do I call you now? Mrs. Kasmersky?"

"Kazinsky. But I use my real name. I happen to like it—Maya Smock."

"Maya Smock is a beautiful name for a beautiful girl. Does Claude like it or did he want you to come up with something catchier?" I shook my head and smiled. Eric was showing his jealous side. "Will the mister be stopping by to kick my ass any time soon?"

"He is out of town, dealing with his other authors."

"You're his only author, Maya. It's fairly obvious." Eric looked down to the floor. "I'm sorry. Still jealous, all right. I guess that's what I deserve for never, uh..."

"Forget it. I'm glad he's out of town. We were best friends before he entered my life, and I'd like to be best friends again. Even if it means not telling him about it. Besides, I have a feeling he's got his own secrets. I made vows to God or Whomever is out there to give this a chance. *Death 'til we part* or something like it. I've always honored my word."

"I'd be honored to be your secret best friend," he said. We hugged again, this time without fear. I didn't realize how selfish I was back then in clinging onto a friendship of a man who was in love with me. How could I have doubted his feelings for me? I was such a fool. And now I wanted my cake .....

My release day began as a slow, jovial morning which quickly turned into a nonstop book sale. At times, I had over ten people in line waiting for me to sign my book. I couldn't believe it. Eric would quietly replenish my iced tea and feed me cookies which he had brought in from the bakery of the Paris Hotel. He spared no expense on this signing. Six hours flew by and most of the books were gone.

"I love Twitter, Instagram, and Facebook," he said as he promoted me through the Internet.

"I hope you made some money after all of your expenses."

He laughed. "Oh yeah. I made some money. And you made more than some money. Did you even have time to check your standing on Amazon's best-seller list? You're number four."

"Number four for science fiction?"

"No, number four of everything. I guess your publisher and Claude know what they are doing. I just hope that..." He stopped talking as another person came up to my table to buy my book. The interruption was convenient, but I suspected Eric was about to make another pot-shot about Claude's integrity.

"The reviews won't come out until next week. My feast may soon become famine," I said once the customer was gone.

"Impossible. I see movie rights in your future. Claude will have a very rich wife. I'm sure he will do everything possible to make the most of your career."

Again, I suspected this was not a compliment. "Do you think that's why he married me?" Eric didn't answer and then more customers came up to the table.

My question had to be put on hold. I signed three books for a young man in a solar system t-shirt and then another four books for a middle-aged woman who said she was buying Christmas presents. The last person in the short line was an old man with white hair tied back in a ponytail, wearing a dirty UCLA t-shirt, with sunglasses perched on top of his head. His jeans were stained with bleach. I didn't recognize him at first. "Who to?" I asked the old man.

"Jay McCallister. You're wearing that same necklace."

I looked up again, startled. It was him. He looked wild and deranged. "Ah, yes." I took a fresh hardcover book and wrote on the inside cover—*Mr. McCallister, you are hands-down my favorite author. The Ides of Mars from the Bent Time series is one of my favorite books. I hope you continue writing as I will continue to buy your work. Maya Smock.*"

Jay McCallister read what I had written and looked angry. I kicked up my purse from the floor and fished around for pepper spray. My head turned side to side, looking for Eric who was busy ringing away endless sales in books. His faded green eyes glared at me as if he knew what I was thinking. "How many books do you have left?"

I counted the remainder of the last box. Surprised I had sold so many, I answered, "Nine."

"I'll take them." I handed him the box. "How many did you start with?"

"Six hundred."

He laughed an evil laugh. His faded green eyes turned to pea green. "Same number at my first signing. You and I are going to be friends. You see, we are just pawns to them. Nothing more…"

Eric left the cash register and dashed over to the table. "Excuse me, are you Jay McCallister?" he asked, oblivious to the deranged conversation we were having. "I'm one of your biggest fans. In fact, it was Maya who turned me onto your work. Are you buying the rest of the books? Oh please review her book. Let me get a picture of you two. Please, for the store."

Jay McCallister's demeanor changed. "Sure. We were just talking. Maya and I are going to be friends. I'd love to have a picture with her in it. Please email me a copy. I think I got a business card somewhere…" He searched his pockets. "Yes, here it is. Email me the picture for my website."

Eric snapped at least five pictures with Jay and me at the table and then by the bookstore sign.

"Maya," Jay said, "I will find you. And don't be afraid." He took the box of books and paid cash and then disappeared into the night.

"I can't believe it! You sold all six hundred, nine of them to Jay McCallister. You are the "it" girl, Maya. It's past closing. Shit. I got to lock the door." He rushed to the front and shoed a handful of customers away. "This is the busiest I've been in months or even years. Can you believe Jay McCallister was here? And he wants to be your friend! How awesome is that!"

"He's out there. Mumbled something about how we are all pawns. I had my hand on my pepper spray. I told you I met him at Love Fest. He remembered my necklace."

"If he reviews your book…What a day! I'm cracking out the champagne, girl! We're getting drunk."

Before Eric rushed to the backroom, I yelled, "You never answered me."

"Huh?"

"Did Claude marry me for my potential earnings?"

He changed directions and walked toward me. "I need to keep my big mouth shut. I'm jealous of the fucker so everything I think about him will be in the negative realm. Forget about Claude. You sold six hundred books today in my store alone. Who knows how many you sold online. And the most famous science fiction writer in the world wants to be your friend. Let me get that champagne so we can bask in this wonderful moment."

I was somewhat reluctant. Claude would not approve, but then he wasn't with me and he wasn't exactly jamming up my voicemail box to find out how my day went. One drink. Then I would go. I was married and didn't want to lead Eric on. I glanced at my phone for the fortieth time. Still no messages and no texts. Maybe two drinks.

# Chapter Eight

General Andreas called in a few favors. With the Secretary of Defense's help, arrangements for the underground expansion of Broom Lake were first priority. Hours after the call, a team of architects came up with an underground observatory design for the aliens found at Roswell. The largest hangar on the base would be renovated to hold the small space craft and the shattered pieces of the large space craft.

Within weeks, the construction was almost done. The general lit a cigarette and admired the progress that quietly took place below him. Outside of the base was a constant convoy of dump trucks, but little sign of construction. People might have talked, but were banned through legal documents from ever exposing the base to the press.

Only a handful of people knew the full story. Engineers, laborers, and even top officials who helped fund the project were told a cover story that was actually true in other parts of the country. The official reason for all of the underground construction was preparation for a nuclear disaster. Many believed Russia and the United States were doomed to get into a nuclear war.

The observatory also called the "cage" was built under Doctor Jaeger's laboratory. The doctor's laboratory was one hundred feet underground. The observatory descended another fifty feet below the earth's surface. The floor of the cage consisted of concrete and natural rock. Steel bars framed the outside of the perimeter of the rectangular cage. Six inch sheets of specially made Plexiglas bumped up to the bars and framed the inside of the perimeter, forty feet long and twenty feet wide.

A deep shaft with a lens connected Doctor Jaeger's laboratory with the observatory, allowing the aliens to be safely viewed from several feet above.

On three sides of the cage were sealed-tight holes with industrial thick rubber gloves that could safely reach inside. Speakers positioned in the corners of the twenty foot high cement ceiling provided an advanced sound system with twenty-four hour recording capability. On the north side of the cage which was also the only side that butted up against a wall was three tier decks for observation.

The observation deck was equipped with a control panel that featured camera screens, temperature control gauges, entrance/exit buttons, heat and motion sensors, and plumbing controls. Most of the gadgets were not available to the public. The tier of the deck closest to the cage held a false panel that hid an escape exit of a vertical tunnel with ladder rungs. The tunnel led straight up to Doctor Jaeger's laboratory.

There were two entrances/exits for the advanced beings or ABs, a term used by Doctor Jaeger. One entrance was hidden in the ceiling. The seam was almost invisible. The other was on the west side and had a built in drawer meant for food exchange. The general and his architects installed a toilet that flushed into a retrievable container, a shower, and a sink despite knowing if these beings would use the human facilities. Chairs, table and beds were screwed into the floor.

The advanced beings remained in their latched coffins. Andreas had them moved from the doctor's laboratory to the storage closet inside of the base's general headquarters. The coffins were locked up and untouched while construction continued underground. The general hoped the secret underground cage could be utilized, but it was hard to believe that the ABs were still alive.

Almost a month had passed since the advanced beings were found, a month without food or water trapped inside of a coffin. The warehouse was empty at the moment, but the general stationed four guards, one on each side, to guard the building around the clock. They spent too much time, money, and risk to pull this off. He took every precaution he had at his disposal.

Andreas finished his Lucky Strike and lit another one. His casual smoking habit turned into a chain smoking obsession since coming home from war. The cigarettes made him cough at night, but they also calmed his nerves.

At forty-nine years old, Andreas was past his prime. Before the war his hair was dark brown with a few strands of gray. Now it was gray with a few strands of dark brown. A few years ago he had faint lines of middle age. His face had weathered over the last few years. He looked older than he was. One of the consequences of surviving hell. At least war hadn't changed his physique. The general kept lean and muscular by religiously lifting weights every morning before dawn.

Andreas walked over to the warehouse. He needed to make some calls. The space craft and the baby craft should have arrived at the base days ago. He nodded at one of the guards and then opened the front door of the office with his keys. He then sat down at the desk by the front door and called the recently promoted Captain Lionel Redding. It was General Andreas who had been behind the man's promotion. He was one of the general's most loyal soldiers. The general was not informed about the delay.

"Captain, General Andreas. You know why I'm calling?" the general asked, recognizing the young man's voice immediately on the other end of the phone line.

"Yes, Sir. This is a secure line?" asked Captain Redding.

"Yes. You must know that I'm calling about a delivery that has yet to come. It was expected at least four or five days ago."

"Yes, Sir. There were problems that had to be fixed. But good news. The delivery has been en route for two hours, Sir."

General Andreas quickly did the math. Roswell was approximately nine hundred miles. Two hours en route would mean the truck would be approximately eight hundred miles away. If the soldiers drove straight through, he would have his delivery before midnight. "I will wait. What happened?"

"The parts of interest have a very strong electromagnetic charge. The pieces merged together like glue. We needed special tools to pry them apart. The first attempt at delivery caused all of the nuts and bolts of the truck to unfasten. The truck fell apart and left the soldiers stranded approximately seventy-five miles north of the original location."

Annoyed, General Andreas then asked, "So then what?"

"We sent several trucks to individually take back each piece. This move, perhaps unwise, cost at least two days of the promised delivery time. Then the pieces magnetized the trucks, again causing them to attract any metal within a few yards distance. Any debris or nearby metal was drawn to the truck, causing a major distraction to other traffic on the highways. I didn't want to worry you. Luckily, we didn't lose anything. General Blanchard brought in a specialist. The specialist, some of my soldiers, and I demagnetized the parts and the trucks."

General Andreas winced. General Blanchard had clearance to Broom Lake, but never found any reason to visit. He was a trusted general of the president, but a political hack to most of the military. "So General Blanchard knows what we are transporting?"

"Yes, he knows. He's known from day one. And now the specialist he brought in also knows or at least figured quite a bit out."

*Shit*, thought Andreas. "Great. What'd you think of the specialist? Of General Blanchard? Are they going to keep their mouths shut and let us do our job?"

"They were professional, but I can't say one way or another if they will keep quiet. At least everything is now demagnetized. The delivery is now packaged and separated into the beds of three cargo trucks. It was the strangest thing. Normally it takes one, maybe two times to demagnetize metal with our equipment. It took five or six times to demagnetize the trucks and at least fourteen times to demagnetize the delivery. Maybe we need new tools," said Captain Redding.

*New tools, my ass*, thought the general. "Captain Redding, you should have briefed me about these setbacks."

"I apologize, Sir. I called this main number at least three times and it would just ring."

The general knew he was difficult to get a hold of, especially with the underground construction project, but the young captain could have called several others. Redding was sloppy. And now another general was in the know—a general that acted as a "yes" man to the President and the Secretary of Defense. His specialist could also ruin their operation. "I'll have someone monitoring the phone from now on. Call this number if there is another problem."

"Yes, Sir." Captain Redding hung up.

General Andreas went outside and approached the nearest guard. "You answer any and all calls that come from the phone in the entryway."

The guard nodded and the general walked back to the other side to check on the day's progress. As he walked, he lit another cigarette. The New Mexico incident was poorly handled. The weather balloon story was thin. He wondered if anyone else saw the bodies. To add to their security problems, army trucks fell apart from the magnetic material. Someone had to have seen the commotion. He had a feeling major damage control was in order.

Almost a half an hour elapsed as the general walked from one side of the base to another, clearing close to three miles on foot. He preferred to walk over driving his Jeep. Walking was another way for him to keep fit while also clearing his mind.

Andreas had been one of the first pilots to fly during the war. His airborne skills, tactical planning, and leadership put him on a career fast track. After the war, he had many options within the military and other outside agencies, but the general chose to run Broom Lake.

The lake was hardly a vacation destination. It was rectangular in shape, only six by ten miles, making it small and inconspicuous to the outside world. Miles of adjacent land were quietly purchased to discourage any unwanted neighbors.

The lake had originally been a mining area. Now it had two runways, an office building which was really a warehouse, three hangars, two scoot and hide buildings for planes, and housing for soldiers and staff. Besides the immense underground construction project, additional tunnels were being built for the purpose of underground travel. The president wanted a network of underground tunnels that would eventually become an underground transit system available to the inner circle of military and government officials.

Once Andreas arrived at the largest hangar, he went inside, found the hidden entrance, and descended down the elevator. When he reached the bottom, he heard a cacophony of jackhammers, motors, hammers, and drills. He covered his ears wishing he had brought ear plugs. The construction crew cleared enough dirt to fill up a hockey stadium. It was hard to believe only weeks ago this gigantic area had been solid earth and rock.

The general walked toward the cage and noticed Doctor Jaeger in a conversation with a foreman of the crew. *What the hell was he doing? He should be in his lab or in his chambers, not down here.* The doctor was dressed in everyday American clothe—jeans, a flannel shirt, and loafers. *Was he giving orders?*

Andreas quickened his pace and interrupted the doctor's and foreman's conversation. "Doctor, how nice to see you. Just couldn't keep away. Is there a problem?"

"No, Sir," said the foreman, looking nervously at the ground.

"I was just touching base," said Doctor Jaeger. "Without my work, I have nothing to do. I am so very anxious to begin."

"Another week, Sir. We will be out of here and you can go about your business," said the foreman. "Excuse me." The foreman must have sensed tension and walked away.

"Don't you have a slide to analyze?" asked Andreas. They both knew Doctor Jaeger was not authorized to be down in the construction area.

"Oh, you are very clever, General. I have already picked up where I left off back in Germany. I do not have a slide yet, but I have a sample and a picture," said the doctor.

*What is he talking about?* The pit of the Andreas's stomach fell even deeper underground than where he was standing. He glared at the doctor's cold blue eyes and tried to read his thoughts.

"A few hours ago I went to the warehouse. One of your men was so helpful. He walked me to the closet where you keep them. With his assistance and back-up, I opened the closest coffin to the door. I had to take a peek. It's all I think about. There was a sticky fluid by its head. I swabbed it. I also snapped a quick pic and had your soldier develop it. He volunteered. I guess there is a dark room somewhere on this base. I wanted to see the advanced being in a still format."

Andreas knew the room everyone used for film development. He was pissed. *Heads are going to roll! Jaeger doesn't have the clearance to go in the warehouse, doesn't anyone know that? I'm going to choke the doctor and then choke the idiot who let him inside!*

Andreas took a deep breath and paused, searching for the right words, but couldn't tactfully convey the magnitude of this security breach. With all of the patience he could muster, the general restrained from assaulting the doctor.

"Are you fucking nuts? Listen, you sick son-of-a-bitch, I risked everything for you, for this, for fucking mankind, and you're aimlessly snooping…" The general's voice trailed off and then he grabbed the doctor's shirt collar, temporarily losing control. Catching himself, he let go, not wanting to cause a scene.

"I know, you must be a little angry. And yes, it was a very stupid move for such a smart man, but what's done is done. I guess I can wait out the rest of the week and do this right. I had to see them sleeping. General, they are alive. They have to be. Look at this picture. Their fingertips are bright. They must run on some kind of battery or electrical current. Look closely at the skin. It's lighter now, almost a grayish white. It doesn't have an actual nose, just two holes. And look around its neck—there are scales. They have a metallic look to them that wasn't picked up in the picture."

"And their clothes? What's that on the sleeve?" Andreas asked, pointing to the embroidered symbol.

"The black uniform is some kind of a second skin, almost impossible to penetrate into. Which is why I believe the AB that was shot is still alive. It fits them all like gloves. I am not sure what is on the sleeve, some kind of emblem perhaps?" the doctor guessed while they both looked at the pictures.

Andreas's anger subsided and he once again fell under Doctor Jaeger's spell. Deception didn't matter when both of the men were on the brink of unlocking one of the universe's biggest secrets. An inner voice inside of his head kept whispering that this was inherently wrong. He swallowed his guilt and studied the doctor's picture. *How high and how far could these advanced beings take us?*

# Chapter Nine

At times, my marriage to Claude was sexier than a porno. On many occasions I would convulse in ecstasy during, after, and even while thinking about making love with him. He was hardly my first. I had at least a dozen others to compare him to, including a couple of women during two separate threesomes I had participated in.

I was never proud of my sexuality. It was more of an experiment to see what I wanted and what I didn't want. My sexual abuse probably contributed to my promiscuity. But Claude knew how to please me and size did matter. He was endowed with an organ that must have had the perimeter of a Coke can. Yes, our sex life was comparable to a porno, at least in the beginning of our marriage.

Hot steamy nights could quickly run cold, the kind of life-threatening cold that required several layers of protection. Hot and cold, nothing in between. How I longed for a day that we could be lukewarm.

I heard once that the lack of money is the primary reason couples fight. The sudden influx of money had the same effect on us. Claude led me to believe that he had lots of money in his own right. Later on, I found out that he had piles of bills.

I never had money. Born in an orphanage and then later shuffled through a parade of foster homes, I broke out of the system at the old age of seventeen. My life was a scramble ever since. It was Eric who gave me an honest job. It was a low-paying honest job, but it was enough to support myself. My novel took me from a paycheck to paycheck lifestyle into a realm of options.

Claude was there to guide me in the right direction, or so I thought. He reminded me that it was because of him and his brilliant public relations and promotional ideas that the book was doing so well. He did like to keep me busy. Within a month of the book's release date, I had racked up too many radio, TV, Internet, newspaper, magazine, and e-zine interviews to count. I ended each interview the same, promising a soon-to-be released sequel. I hadn't had time to write a page let alone a sequel.

Less than a year after my novel's publication I was practically a household name. The critics called me one of the most brilliant minds in the twenty-first century. My work was original, technological, prophetic, and exciting. Enter the movie option, which officially catapulted me into a new income tax bracket. I was wealthy.

My wisdom and youth did not go together, causing some to wonder if I communicated with the very aliens of whom I wrote about. My frequent "temper" tantrums, as quoted from the L.A. Times, over any editing suggestions only added to the mystique. During an interview with a Denver radio station I mentioned how the book practically wrote itself as if I was in a trance. This fascinated the host, prompting him to turn the interview into a paranormal field.

"Did you ever hear of channel writing?" the Denver host asked.

"Huh," I responded.

"Channel writing is when you go into a trance and your hand starts to write. You don't even remember if it was your writing or possibly the writing from the spirts," he explained.

I laughed and assured him that spirits didn't write my novel. However, his explanation somewhat matched my writing process. The interview and my alleged paranormal abilities went viral, giving me more publicity and more sales. My critics deemed me as a diva and/or lunatic. To give Claude his props, he really knew how to play up my idiosyncrasies, creating more than a writer, creating a brand. He was a talented bottom-feeder.

My first extravagant purchase was a pair of matching Lexuses per Claude's request. I didn't even have a car nor a driver's license. Claude taught me how to drive. The cost made me woozy, but, as he reminded me, I could afford the cars because of him.

With the huge sums of money coming in, my dumpy apartment was no longer good enough for Claude. I wanted a better address too. My neighborhood was a little scary. Claude and I argued over how much house we could afford or really how much house I could afford. He wanted both of us to move to Los Angeles, but I wanted to stay in Las Vegas. I won that battle, but promised to later on buy a small condo if and when more money came in.

Claude agreed. He said that was a smart idea per our income. One of the biggest mistakes I made was allowing Claude to handle our finances. Eric's warning replayed in my head too many times. Claude quickly hired a realtor to show us some houses. His name was Sam Marshall. He was young, good-looking, and fashionable. In fact, he looked a lot like Claude.

"Are you two brothers?" I asked as Sam drove us to the first house in Henderson, a suburb of Las Vegas. They both had dark hair and bright blue eyes. Sam looked at least five years younger and was slightly taller.

"Oh no. Just good friends," he replied as he pulled onto the driveway of one of the houses I wanted to see.

"Then why didn't you come to our wedding?" I asked. He fumbled with the lockbox.

"I wasn't invited. I guess Claude wanted you all to himself that day. He called me and told me all about you. I sell real estate in the Los Angeles area, sometimes out of state, and Claude thought he'd pass me some business."

"How long have you been friends?" I asked as we walked up a tidy stone path that led to the double-door entrance of a small Spanish style ranch.

Sam shrugged. "A while. Now what do you think about this house?"

"I love it. It has everything I could ask for!" I said. It wasn't a mansion, but Claude and I could pay cash and it was still close to the strip. There was room to start a family.

"Sam, you know me. This just isn't going to cut it. C'mon, baby, we can do better than this. I want something with some style. Can you show us something a little more luxurious?"

Sam looked at me and smiled. "Well, Maya, it's free to look. You don't have to buy. There's a beautiful gated community a few miles from here and they got some great deals," Sam said. He had the same charming smile as Claude did.

"All right. But I really do like this house," I said.

"We're not ruling it out. Just seeing what else is available," Claude said.

Each house Sam showed us drastically increased in price. We looked at homes that were too immense to clean and required staff to run, homes that cost over two million dollars.

"How are these to your liking?" asked Sam.

I felt sick. We would have to get a mortgage and I wanted to pay cash. We would have to hire a maid, a gardener, and a pool service and I didn't have a title let alone a page written for a sequel.

"We'll take it," said Claude.

Three point five million dollars. I was not a finance expert, but did know that I would need to write a lot of books and Claude would have to represent a lot of successful authors in order to pay for this. Claude, on the other hand, had the utmost confidence that we could easily swing the house.

"Baby, this is only the beginning. Las Vegas, and then LA, and maybe even New York City. Think big. Paris, Rome. If you dream it, you can do it. We qualify for this house. We deserve this house. You're a star! It's time to start living like one!"

Sam echoed the same sentiment and soon had me signing papers. I was apprehensive about taking on this kind of debt, but had to admit that I was swept away. That day Claude made me feel beautiful, accepted, and loved. My life turned one hundred and eighty degrees. My prince and I bought a castle complete with pool, spa, gym, three tiered balcony, elevator, movie room, and too many amenities to list. It was big enough to get lost in.

A few months went by and bigger royalty checks were cashed. Claude was right about affording the house. At first, we had fun making love in all of the twenty-one rooms. We shopped until we dropped, buying truckloads of modern furniture to go with the décor. But our bliss was short lived. Claude started to spend more and more time in Los Angeles.

I went with Claude a few times to Los Angeles and met his boss, Veronica Tatum. She was every bit the hard-ass Claude described, but she treated me like a goddess. Claude claimed he stayed at a residence hotel when he came to Los Angeles and talked me into looking at condominiums like I had originally promised. Once again, his old friend Sam Marshall showed up. Sam was more than ready to show us some of the nicest condominiums in Los Angeles. There was something almost planned about it. Sam was just too available.

"Claude, we just bought a mansion. Now you want a multi-million dollar condominium? We still don't have that kind of money. Sam, you need to show us something much less expensive."

"Didn't you get the biggest royalty check to date just last week? Remember, Maya, think big," Claude said as he rubbed my arm.

"I am thinking big, but it's too much to take on right now. If you really want this condo, then why don't you use your commission checks? You must be rolling in money from my book along with your other authors," I said.

Claude seemed surprised by my comment and then sulked. "All right, Maya, the truth of the matter is I still got bills to pay. I'm almost debt free though. A lot of the bills are your bills. Who do you think pays for the hotel when you go on a TV interview? Who pays for plane tickets or the rental car? Why do you think you're so successful, huh? It's all in the advertising, the promotional tours. You just don't get it. If it wasn't for me, you'd still be making minimum wage at that shithole bookstore while reading other people's work. But maybe you're right. Sam, show us something not so grand."

I didn't want to argue with Claude. In fact, he had a way about him that made me feel guilty about not buying another multi-million dollar home. I had suspected for some time he was in financial trouble.

Sam didn't miss a beat. He had us in a less expensive neighborhood in the time that it took to make a pot of coffee. He didn't want to risk us changing our minds all together.

I did end up buying a condominium, but this time I kept the cost well under a million dollars which didn't go too far in Los Angeles. The place needed to be remodeled and Claude promised to pay for it. *How gallant*, I thought. *A real Sir Lancelot.*

We went back to Claude's hotel and signed off on the papers. At the time I didn't find it strange that Sam didn't have an office of his own. Once Claude and I were alone, I expected a celebration of sorts, maybe even gratitude. Instead I received petulance mixed with anger over the next two days. He wouldn't even look at me. A pattern emerged. Eric's warning was heard in distance. Love may be blind, but it's not deaf and dumb as well. Claude was using me. I left our trip early after being ignored and cried on the long drive home.

I pulled into my six car garage. So far, it only housed both of our Lexuses. Claude probably had a master plan on filling it up by the year's end. The five hour drive gave me time to focus on reality. I should have been on top of the world—a bestselling book, a new husband, a new house, a real chance at having a nice life. All of it didn't matter because none of it felt real. After only one year of marriage, Claude made me feel like a piggy bank instead of a partner.

I shuffled into the house and looked for anything with alcohol content. Under the staircase was a wine cellar partly full. Wine was one of Claude's newest hobbies. I chose a bottle of Bordeaux, one of his favorites. It was expensive and he would be pissed if it was missing. I opened the bottle with a smug sense of satisfaction instantly realizing that I probably paid for it.

One bottle quickly turned into two bottles. The emotional pain began to numb. I thought of calling Eric and searched for my cell.

I found my phone in my car. There were three missed calls from a number that I didn't recognize. Maybe it was Sam Marshall and there was a problem with the financing. *Wouldn't that be great!* I already had buyer's remorse on the condo. Or maybe it was Claude calling from work or the hotel, wanting to apologize. I listened to my voicemail. Jay McCallister called me three times during the last half of an hour.

I laughed. I was as drunk and lonely as he was weird and entertaining. I instantly hit the redial button and staggered back to the wine cellar under the grand staircase. "Hello, Mr. McCallister?"

"Call me Jay," he said. He sounded even older than he was, like he had COPD or some other breathing disease.

"Are you okay? You sound out of breath. And how did you get my—"

"I am out of breath. I'm old and I was pacing my house. Why did it take you so long to answer the phone?"

"I, uh…"

"You're drunk, aren't you? It's okay. Don't pass out on me. As far as your number goes, I have my ways. In this day and age, it's not hard. There is no privacy. Listen, I told you we'd be friends and we are definitely going to be friends. It's been a while since I saw you at your first signing. I just reviewed your book. I read it four times. A five star no-brainer. Brilliant. Did you even write it?"

My good mood soured. "What do you mean did I write it? Are you accusing me of…"

"Maya, you and I have more in common that you could even imagine. What if I told you that I had help when I wrote my novels?"

"Mr. Mc…, Jay, what in the world are you saying? Are you possessed? Do you think I'm possessed? Are you as crazy as they say?" I asked ferociously. The alcohol removed my polite filter. Then I laughed. The conversation was absurd.

"I can hear the booze on your breath," he said.

"Very funny. Was it my slurring that gave me away?"

"Let me guess, your agent and husband is not the man you thought he was. You have overextended yourself in foolish purchases despite your new found wealth. You're lonely and second guessing yourself. And most importantly, you're trapped. You need to write a sequel if your new lifestyle is to survive."

*How'd he know this? Was he stalking me?* I put down the third bottle and opened the refrigerator, opting for a Starbuck ice coffee. His words sobered me up considerably. "Are you telling me this because of your past? Your failed marriages and your drinking problem? Some even say you're senile or just plain crazy."

Jay chuckled and then coughed. "Neither. Let me make a prediction. You and Mr. Gorgeous will not last. Your next book will come out only after you receive an inspiration."

"I could use an inspiration. Right now my life is more like desperation."

"It will come. You're just in a lull right now. Speaking of inspiration, do you know the word comes from inspire or in spirit? Respiration. A spirit or a god breathes an idea into you. Spirit or a god are key to understanding the meaning."

"So we are back to being possessed by spirits who give us ideas?"

Jay laughed again. "In a way, yes, but we are all under a spell. You and I...we deal with it differently. Listen, come up to my home or I'll come down by you. And no, I'm not making a pass. At my age, I don't think a bottle of Viagra would get me in the mood. You're young enough to be my granddaughter. Please, I'm harmless. I have many things to show you, even teach you. You got to quit drinking or at least slow down. It fogs your mind from the truth. I quit years ago and then I could really see the truth."

"Jay, I have one question for you. Who pays for airfare?"

"Huh? I'll pay for your airfare if you want," Jay said.

"No, I mean who pays when you go on a TV interview?"

"The TV station, why?"

"Claude, that's Mr. Gorgeous. He said that he spends all of his money promoting my book, that's all."

"Maya, I'm the last one to give you marital advice. You got to put your marriage on the shelf for a while. Listen, I got a friend who is a producer for the local news here in San Francisco. I'll get you an interview so that your trip to my house looks more like a business thing. Claude doesn't have to know anything and you can figure out what to do later. We have much, much more important things to share. Okay, buddy?"

"Ah, buddies, huh. Okay, buddy or BFF," I said.

"We will become BFFs. I like you very much. You are the daughter or granddaughter I never had."

The declaration made me cry. My whole life I longed for a parent, but all I ever got were users. I was their tool for anger, sex, money, and every other dysfunction.

"Maya, are you there?"

I coughed to cover my quivering voice. "Okay then, get me to San Fran."

# Chapter Ten

General Robert Andreas looked at the doctor's face before looking at the picture. They had only known each other for two years, yet secrets bonded them closer than all of his past relationships. Andreas kept himself distant from his parents, little brother, ex-wife, and two daughters. Sadly, it was Jaeger who knew him best. It was an involuntary kind of closeness with undercurrents of hatred and distrust. But for better or for worse, both of their fates were dependent on each other.

Andreas first met Karl Jaeger who was known to the Nazis as Doctor Josef Handel in Dachau in March of 1945. Dachau began as a prison for the non-conformists of the Hitler regime. Later on it held Jewish prisoners and became a work camp. British intelligence believed that American and British soldiers were being held inside of the camp as prisoners of war.

During the war, Andreas was ranked as a colonel in the United States Army Air Force. He and ten other airmen jumped out of their planes in a covert rescue mission to free the prisoners of war held at Dachau. They never found who they were looking for, but instead stumbled upon something so hellish, so evil, that it could have only have been directed by Satan himself.

By accident, Andreas tripped over something metal that stuck out of a thatch of bushes one mile north of the camp. He and his men tugged at the metal and brushed away the snow and debris. They found a camouflaged door. There were reports coming in from other soldiers about a network of underground tunnels, hidden weapons, and transportation set in place for potential escape routes.

Captain William Lamprey pried the door open, revealing a long flight of stairs underneath the earth.

Andreas and ten of his men stealthily descended, ending up in a long corridor that lead to another door. The door was locked. First Lieutenant Redding fired off four rounds and kicked the door open. As they crept down the long, dark corridor, they heard sounds that stopped Andreas in his tracks.

"What in the hell is that noise? Is that the sound of moaning?" Andreas whispered to Captain Lamprey.

The young captain shrugged and took the lead. A few dozen more steps and Lamprey abruptly stopped. "Shit, shit, shit." He ran his hands through his high and tight blonde hair. There was a sigh. Andreas thought the captain might have been crying and crying was a sign of weakness.

Andreas squinted at the young man in the dark and then shone a covered flashlight down the corridor. They were about to enter the underground prison. A few yards away on both sides of the hallway were iron bars. Several people lay on dirt floor. They looked like skeletons with a thin layer of skin holding their bones and organs in place, or even ghosts or corpses that moved.

"Smith, Johansen, Grant, Newcastle? Anyone here by those names?" asked Andreas in a commanding tone as he forged ahead with his weapon cocked. He rattled off more names. No one claimed to be one of the missing prisoners-of-war. Men and women pinned themselves to the bars and reached through, begging for Andreas's help.

There must have been at least a hundred prisoners held in the secret prison. The other airmen walked by the prison cells and had prisoners grabbing their legs and kissing their feet as they passed by.

"Everyone, please be quiet or your chance at freedom will be lost," Andreas said as the crowd became more desperate. There were several German translations going off throughout the gigantic hallway for the prisoners who did not speak English.

"There are only a few guards who come down here, maybe two per shift. They walked up and down the hallway some time ago. They probably won't come back until dinner. Be careful. Doctor Handel works down here. He has a lab that way," whispered an old man in the cell next to Andreas. He pointed to Andreas's left.

Andreas understood and then motioned for half of his men to open up the cells. Gun shots echoed throughout the hallway as the airmen shot at the locks of the cells.

Andreas and the other five soldiers inched to his left and soon came upon another hallway. At the end of the hall was a large room without a door lit by a dusty, long tube of fluorescent light. Andreas instinctively looked away from the light and into the dark corners. Glass shattered on the floor. Captain Lamphrey blocked the entrance and then slammed the German to the ground.

Andreas found another light cord dangling from the ceiling and then pulled the cord. Two other long, florescent light bulbs hummed and then flickered, divulging one of the most morbid backdrops he had ever seen. The rumors about Nazi brutality weren't even in the same league as the gruesome experiments taking place.

Andreas fumbled around in his bag. "Yes!" he yelled, elated to have brought his camera. "No one is ever going to believe this unless I can prove it." He watched the expressions on his men sour as they processed the grotesque display of body parts of both humans and animals carelessly strewn on top of the metal table.

Andreas took so many pictures his fingers hurt. "Damn! I'm out of film and I only touched the iceberg of this…this…morgue? Human and animal experiments? What the hell were the Nazis up to?"

Andreas's deep brown eyes swept every square inch of the room with the intention of writing down everything he could not photograph. Microscopes, canisters, test tubes, and metal instruments were jammed in the open shelving.

Dead humans with missing skin were propped up like dolls alongside the wall farthest from the entrance. *He must have been using the prisoners as guinea pigs.* A vulture was nailed into a piece of wood and dissected. Microscopic slides littered the floor. On the bottom shelf of the long metal table was large glass canister with a head inside. The head was neither human nor animal. The general knelt down to observe.

"Before you kill me…" said the doctor. He sat on the floor, cowering. His beady, glacier blue eyes were wildly looking in all directions. His skin was so white that even with the poor lighting, Andreas could see blue veins beneath the surface. The man could not have been older than forty, but he had the kind of face that made it difficult to determine his age.

The thin, pasty man looked terrified and harmless. Andreas became more confident that there were no other Nazis in this dungeon prison. The doctor spoke in a thick German accent that made him almost impossible to understand. He must have realized the language barrier and slowed down his English. "That's the head of a creature not from this world. He and his friends showed us life, power….I know things, things that will make America great! Please, I beg of you. My life's work…Take me to America!" the German screamed.

Andreas looked in disgust at the man's yellow, crooked teeth. He understood the doctor loud and clear. He was ordered to arrest or kill all Nazis inside of the concentration camp. He knelt down once again and studied the alien head inside of the glass canister. The head was slightly larger than human but the remains of the neck seemed too small for support. At that moment, Andreas had two choices—defy his order and take the doctor back to the states to continue his hellish experiments or kill him and end all hope of learning about what was floating in the glass jar. *Shit, don't even know what this psycho is working on and I'm running out of time. And what about my men? Lamphrey, Malone, Redding, Bolantano, and Jackson had always been trustworthy, but this...*

As Andreas factored in all of the variables, he came to the inevitable conclusion that he didn't much care about the possible repercussions. He could die for this kind of information.

Looking at the doctor and then the alien head, all that mattered was the ultimate validation that humans were not the only life in the universe. If Josef Handel knew about extraterrestrial life, then so did his Nazi hire-ups. America needed the intel.

As a pilot, Andreas had seen so many peculiar objects in the sky. When he would question his majors and colonels, they'd all tell him the same thing—classified information and he wasn't allowed to discuss. Eventually, he kept his sightings in the sky to himself. He often wondered if the brass and the president already knew about these creatures. His silence was rewarded as he moved up the ranks.

Andreas quickly made a decision and said, "You do realize I am risking my career, the career of my men, hell, all of our lives for you—a piece of shit Nazi that uses Jews like dolly parts for whatever the hell you are doing."

"These things came here years ago. They showed us things that give a more in-depth glimpse of the universe. Please, I don't care about Hitler or the Nazis. This was just an opportunity for me to work. My work is my life and I don't care who benefits. I've come so far in understanding the inner workings of life outside of Earth. Just take me back with you and I'll live somewhere underground, somewhere like this and continue. I have several journals of work and dozens of slides. I'm so close to…Oh, there's no time to explain. The guards will soon come for dinner rounds."

Andreas studied the lost faces of his men. "This information stays among us and only us, understand?" His soldiers looked at him and nodded. "Doctor, you're about the same size as that stiff in the corner. Get his stripes." Andreas pointed at the dead prisoner in the corner.

The doctor raced over and undressed, quickly changing into the dead man's prison clothes. He then took a ratty black sack and stuffed it with journals and boxes of microscopic slides. He clamped the canister of the alien's head shut and swaddled it with a blanket.

Andreas and his men smuggled him out of Dachau and freed the underground prisoners without looking back. A month later the U.S. military freed the rest of the Dachau work camp.

Andreas made sure that all of his men, even the other five soldiers who were freeing the prisoners from their cells, were given the opportunity to work with him after the war. He quickly moved up the ladder. One and half years after Dachau, Andreas became General Robert Andreas. The irony made him smile. Years earlier, he was almost discharged for reporting his sightings.

Andreas was given full command at Broom Lake after the war. The sleepy, tiny base was the perfect location, already complete with an underground lab for Doctor Handel. Other plans for top secret projects were in the works.

Doctor Josef Handel was immediately renamed Doctor Karl Jaeger and given private dialect lessons to shed his German accent. According to Jaeger, some of his research had been stolen by the great Doctor Mengele. The research supposedly centered on eradicating certain genetic traits that cause disease. Andreas didn't believe him, but allowed him to prattle on about his contribution to humanity. Both Jaeger and Mengele didn't care about saving anyone's life.

The new and improved Doctor Jaeger claimed that his original experimentation led him a new direction. Andreas did admire the man. Unlike most of the Nazi doctors, Jaeger was more interested in his work than in his glory.

Jaeger soon explained his research to the general. "What I was working on in Germany and what I am continuing to work on here is the art of creating a super-human, someone immune to disease, immune to injuries, maybe even immune to death. I might be able to do this by piecing different genes together to create the ultimate race. Hitler foolishly thought that we, the Aryans, were as high of a level as it got. You saw my souvenir-the head."

"So you are like the great Doctor Frankenstein, but you won't create a monster. You are creating something new with different genes? How?" the general asked.

"In time, I will explain," Jaeger said.

Andreas shared what little he knew about the doctor's experiment with the Secretary of Defense. Arrangements were made to keep a loose leash on the doctor while giving him whatever he wanted to continue the study. And like that, an enemy became an ally. But this new ally came with a price.

General Andreas wasn't the only general with a pet Nazi. Other career military men stumbled upon physicists, engineers, rocket scientists, and other brilliant doctors with the same ambition. The practice was called *Operation Paper Clip*. These Nazi monster recruits were never to be trusted. They were spared from trials and death in exchange for knowledge. All of them were kept under surveillance and not allowed to leave the secret facilities they worked for.

# Chapter Eleven

Claude had Maya pegged for a basket case from the start. She was very attractive, even beautiful with an exotic, forbidden, witchy look that turned him on. Maya's dark-hair, dark eyes, and dark skin matched her dark soul. There was difference between dark and evil and Maya was just dark or maybe just different. The neurotic, unpredictable sex-pot he met at the writers' convention was changing into a confident diva.

He knew the Vegas mansion was pushing it. Maya told him how poor she had always been. Claude, too, was brought up poor. The difference between them was he wanted everything the world could give him whereas she just wanted a family and a place to call home.

Claude saw how her face lit up when they walked through the bedrooms of their new home. They were decorated for babies and kids. They never talked about having children, but it was obvious that she wanted a family complete with dogs and kids in their big Las Vegas home. Claude had no problem with dogs, it was the kids who scared the hell out of him.

His mother was a low-level scam-artist and his father was a mostly absent sociopath. What if he favored one, or worse, both of their parenting styles? Dysfunctional cycles repeated. Bringing kids into the world would only prolong another generation of assholes. His contribution to society was ending the abuse. He had a vasectomy at the age of twenty-five, long before he met Maya, but he never told her that.

He never told Maya about his past. His childhood was painful and embarrassing. Mom and Dad were in and out of jail, while teaching him and his brother various cons to make a living. The only one who had meant anything to him was Sam. Claude had practically raised him. Sam was five years younger and had a different father than Claude. He was the product of one the many infidelities of their mother.

Both he and Sam looked just like their mom. She gave them her large, bright blue eyes, black hair, chiseled features, and long eyelashes. She was beautiful, but her looks faded as she rotted away in jail for credit card fraud. Her absence was a relief. She was just a thorn in Claude's side, upset with him for going off to college and leaving her alone. Sam had feelings for her. He had always been a mama's boy and her claws were hooked in deep. Because of her, Sam had already done some time.

When Maya told him that she was an orphan and foster child, he was almost jealous. She was free from shame. He, however, wasn't sure when his mom would get out of prison or his dad would drop in wanting something. He never wanted her to meet them.

Claude spared Maya his past because he worried she would opt out of the relationship. He really did love her, at least for a while, but the simple fact was that Claude could never love anyone for an extended period of time. After one year of marriage, the novelty had worn away.

Almost a month went by since they closed on the tiny but pricey Los Angeles condominium. The place had one redeeming quality—it was within walking distance to the literary agency. Claude still wanted a car to keep at the condo, but didn't want to push his expenditures.

The new place slowly grew on him. In time, he and Maya would get a bigger condo in more exclusive neighborhood. This was the first time in their marriage that she had shown some backbone and he didn't like it.

Claude kept his bases covered. Maya didn't know it, but all of the paperwork Sam had her sign wasn't just for the condo. She had signed off on tens of thousands of dollars in home equity loans. The extra money enabled Claude to pay off his debt without her knowing.

Claude had always been a spendthrift, but managed to keep it secret. He knew his looks only got him so far with women. Massive debt would cause Maya to drop him like her twelfth shot of whiskey if she knew how broke he really was.

His finances were a nonissue. Maya's book was on every best seller list. She was on everyone's short list for multiple literary awards. He just sold a six-figure movie option and she had a seven figure advance on the sequel. Claude couldn't help but think big—*Star Wars* big. Books and movies were only the beginning. He dreamed of action figures, costumes, posters, t-shirts, and much more.

At the beginning of their marriage, Claude cast aside all of the booty-call skanks he used to roll with. A couple of them got a goodbye romp. Since he was ending their hookups, he considered himself as a faithful husband. He was officially taking himself off of the fast-paced Los Angeles singles scene. Then he met Allie Calloway.

A few days after Claude moved into his condo, Sam took him out to celebrate. Claude was ushered into a private party held at one of L.A. hippest bars. Amidst the crowd of beautiful people, loud music and dark lighting, he couldn't help but notice a blonde, dressed in gold from head to toe. She wore a fringed bustier, spandex booty shorts, fishnets, and sky-high heels. The gold metallic clothes complimented her long, golden hair that spiraled in soft curls to the middle of her back. She had to be a model or a Playmate or an actress.

"You don't have a chance," Sam said.

"Maybe not, but there's an empty stool next to her and I got nothing to lose," Claude said as he took off his ring and put it in his pocket.

Claude took a seat. "Can I buy you a drink?"

The woman in gold smiled. She introduced herself as 'Allie' and mentioned her career as a lingerie model. Claude feigned interest when she talked about her job and how she longed to make it as an actress. She wasn't exactly an intellectual. But for what Allie lacked in book smarts, she more than made up for in other areas.

Like Claude, Allie shared the same jaded, cynical perspective on human nature. The night they met Claude took her back to his new condominium and banged the shit out of her. It was primitive and all about him, but she seemed to enjoy herself. When it was over, she got dressed.

"Where you going?" he asked.

"I thought I better leave before your wife gets home," she said. He shrugged as if he had no clue as to what she was talking about. "I saw you put your ring in your pants pocket before you sat down next to me. It's all right."

"Okay, you caught me. I'm a louse. But why did you go home with me if you knew I was married?" Claude asked as he watched her squeeze back into the skimpy gold outfit she wore the night before. Her body was sculpted but thin. Her breasts were much too big for her frame and probably fake, but bounced gently as she moved. She was tan. Her golden skin set off her long, golden hair that looked sexy and wild. She bent down, giving him a perfect view of her heart-shaped ass as she put on her gold stilettos. He suddenly became rock hard and wanted her to stay all morning, afternoon, and night.

"I have needs that you fulfilled. I like how you're married. You won't want anything more than I am willing to give. I don't want a relationship. Right now I am focused on my career. That's why I went home with you. But now it's time to go. You better clean those sheets before your wife gets home."

Claude reached for her hand and guided her back into bed. "My wife doesn't live here." He kissed her softly and stroked her large breasts. He slowly took off the fringed outfit. She sat on top of him and inserted his manhood into her. Fifteen minutes later Claude rolled off the bed and whipped up some omelets. This was the beginning to the perfect relationship.

Claude stayed in Los Angeles for weeks. Work was the excuse he gave Maya and he did manage to get an honest day's of work in when in town, but most of his work could have been done in the gigantic library of their Nevada mansion. Allie was the reason he hadn't been home. She practically moved in. One night, after too many vodkas, Allie confessed that she would soon be turning thirty-four.

"I'm old, Claude. Too old to ever break into the big leagues. I'll be modeling swimsuits for old, middle-aged fat women pretty soon if something doesn't come my way."

Claude was surprised. He never asked her age, just assumed she was twenty-something. She certainly could pull it off. Age didn't impact her beauty. Where ever they went, it was Allie who got the stares from both men and women. Claude was used to be being the better looking one in every relationship he had ever had, but he was merely average in her presence. He didn't understand why she was hanging around. She could get herself a rich, old sugar daddy and be set up like a queen. But then Claude was like her sugar daddy, except he was young and good looking.

Their dates were always expensive—the best restaurants, plays, concerts, and wine. Within a week, Allie had him buying her new clothes, jewelry, and even a photographer. *Peanuts*, thought Claude as he raked up the charges. His paltry gifts were nothing compared to what she could net. She was the kind of trophy-wife material that belonged to a billionaire. Nevertheless, Claude would not accept that he was a step down for her. She must have enjoyed being with him. And he enjoyed being with her.

Maya was suspicious. Claude barely called her, claiming he was swamped at work. He did muster up some insincere gratitude over the condo. "It's working out. It's really not all that small." He even had Veronica cover for him after Maya made too many calls at the agency.

By month two, Maya quit giving Claude the Spanish Inquisition. He had her so busy, she didn't have the time. Maya didn't like Los Angeles, but she found the time for a quick visit. Allie left some of her things behind, but Claude luckily found them before Maya did and hid them.

"Like what you done with the place. Great furniture. You have quite the woman's touch," Maya said as she looked around the kitchen and adjoining living room.

Claude panicked. Did Maya find something of Allie's? His alarm subsided. She poured them each a glass of wine and a few minutes later they were in bed. No animosity or jealousy. He was worried about nothing.

It was a godsend that Maya knew virtually nothing about finance. She never asked questions and let him handle the purse strings.

"How much was the last royalty check by the way?" Maya asked as she got dressed.

"I don't know. I'll ask Veronica tomorrow. Sorry, been busy with other writers. Are you going? You just got here?" Claude asked.

"Yes, I'm going. I got a show in New York City that you scheduled." Maya kissed his cheek. "And Baby, you are working way too hard. Relax and enjoy yourself. You seem so stressed out. When this book tour dies down, make some time for us. I love you."

Claude made a quick dinner of chicken tacos and then walked Maya downstairs into the lobby and waited with her for the cab. The lobby area of the high rise was a cozy nook by the doorman's podium. A couple of sofas, winged-back chairs, and coffee tables were elegantly arranged. Usually the seating area was empty.

Allie sat on one of the winged-back chairs, dressed for attention. She wore red sequins and stilettos, looking very much like a hooker who was waiting on her john. Maya looked straight at her and seemed indifferent.

"Babe, is that a lady of the evening? I thought you and your real estate agent said that this was a decent neighborhood," Maya whispered as she and Claude walked past the lobby.

"This is a great neighborhood. Maybe she's got a friend who lives in the building. Maybe she's going to a club. Hey, did you get a chance to go over the talking points for the morning show?" Claude asked. He watched Allie out of the corner of his eye while he walked Maya out of the building to her cab.

Claude waited with Maya for nearly ten minutes which seemed like years as Allie sat a few yards away, reading calmly. As Maya's cab drove off, Claude angrily sat next to Allie in the matching winged-back chair. She acted as if he was invisible and continued reading.

Claude looked at the book. Anger took over. "What the hell? Her book? I can't believe this. She saw you all right. Who wouldn't notice you dressed like that. Damn it, Allie! What are you doing?"

"Keep your voice down. The doorman is watching you. And for your information, I love this book. I almost asked her to autograph it for me," said Allie as she flipped a page.

"You're a real piece of work. I'm practically living here because of you. I shower you with attention and gifts. You are the one I want to be with. Why are you so jealous? You know I don't love her. It's more of a business arrangement than a marriage. And you're fucking with my business arrangement. Now listen, you little c...," Claude said and then paused. He was almost yelling. In a whisper, he continued, "you ever pull a stunt like this again, and I'll..."

"You'll what? Kill me? Dump me? Tell me to go home? Don't be such a drama queen, Claude. Why don't you just kill her? You'd at least get something out of it," she said and then coldly laughed.

The doorman looked at Claude and Allie with judgment and Claude shot him a dirty look back. "Come upstairs, now." He grabbed her arm.

They rode the elevator in silence. Allie didn't want to argue. She pressed herself against Claude as they ascended to his floor. Once the front door of the apartment shut, she ripped off both of their clothes. He mounted her on the living room coach.

Afterwards, Allie threw on a t-shirt, lit a cigarette and sat up on couch. "You're right. I was a bad girl today. I have no claims on you."

Claude poured two glasses of wine and sat down next to her. "Here, a burgundy from Napa. Listen, I can't stay here forever. You can stay here when I'm out of town, but I need to go back to Vegas and play husband. Don't look at me that way. You knew I was married from the start."

Allie put her cigarette out and took a sip of wine. "You never told me what your house is like in Las Vegas. Maybe I could stay there when you and your wife are out of town."

Claude laughed. "You're quite the comedienne. No way. No fucking way. You'll never even see the place. I refuse to give you the address. That is off limits. And the house is beautiful, in a gated community so don't get any ideas. Several of our neighbors are famous. Some are entertainers on the strip."

"Oh, someday I'll get there, babe. I'll be there to rub elbows with you and Maya and the Vegas celebs. Who are some of your famous neighbors?"

"Allie, I don't rub elbows with anyone except you. I'm here most of the time, remember? But Maya's met a few neighbors, just rich ones though. No celebs. Actually she is the only celeb on our block."

"Maybe she'll meet a rich, good looking neighbor and divorce your ass. Then I could have you all to myself." Claude rolled his eyes. "I'll stop. I'm really not the jealous type, but what you do to me…" Allie gently squeezed his genitals and scooted closer to him on the couch. "I can see why Maya puts up with all of your shit. By the way, does she have a sequel written? Don't you have to produce something after receiving an advance?"

"Why all the questions about Maya?"

"I'm her biggest fan," Allie said. "She really is a great writer. She could be another Stephen King or Danielle Steele or…, I think those are the only authors that I know of."

Claude laughed. "Actually, Allie, my wife is way too busy to write. I keep her busy so that I can hang out with you," he said.

"You said option. Will there be a movie?" Allie asked as she primped her long, golden hair.

*Ah*, Claude thought. *An actress angle.* "Don't know yet, but a studio was pretty serious about securing the option to produce. Why? Do you want to star in it?"

"Of course."

"I'm working on it and yes, you will have a part if it goes through. I don't know about the starring part, but a part," he said. He had no problem lying to her. She must have known he and Maya would not cast a potential film. That was the producer's job.

"How many copies of *The Master Race* did she sell so far?"

"Well, I don't know exactly, but the first six months she sold around five hundred thousand copies. A miracle for a first novel."

"When the movie deal is sealed, you could put me in part of your negotiations. Would you do that for me? I need a break before I'm too old. Please, I'm begging you." She looked at him with her giant blue eyes and he gulped.

"Yes, Allie. I would do that for you. I want you to reach your dreams."

"Claude, do you love me? I love you," she said in a breathless, vulnerable way.

"I love you too," Claude said and he didn't regret it. On some level he might have meant it at that moment, but the truth was that he had never loved anyone. His past would not permit him to ever fall in love. His mother made sure of that.

"How much is she or the two of you worth? How much could she be worth?"

Claude had to laugh. *Ain't love grand.*

"So many questions about my wife. Okay, I don't know how much we're worth." Claude stroked her long, blonde hair as she lied in his lap. Her questions were too personal, but he loved talking about the literary business. "Well, to put it into perspective, J.K. Rowling is worth about one billion. She's another author that you might have heard of." Allie shook her head. "Well, she wrote the *Harry Potter* series."

"Oh yes, I know that series."

"Well, Maya doesn't have a movie yet, let alone a series of movies. King is worth over a billion. I know you know who he is. Then there is E.L. James. She wrote the *Fifty Shades of Gray* trilogy. She's a newer author. Maybe she's worth sixty million."

"But do any of them write sci-fi like Maya? You know, compare apples to apples?" she asked.

"Oh, how could I forget, Jay McCallister. He's worth somewhere in the billion dollar range as well. Most of his books became movies or TV series. I'm trying to think, did you ever hear of *The Ides of Mars*?" Allie shook her head. "Yeah, sci-fi isn't my thing either. Anyway, he wrote Maya a five-star review stating that she will be the greatest sci-fi writer of the twenty-first century. That endorsement alone will probably sell another two or three hundred thousand copies. That's how much power he wields in sci-fi."

"Amazing. But how did you know she'd sell anything? Aren't there hundreds, thousands, millions, hell, I don't know, books written each year? What makes her so special?"

Claude had to smile as his mind drifted back to the first night he met Maya at the Bellagio Hotel. "I could just tell that she was in a class by herself. And I happened to be in the right place at the right time."

"So you could be sitting on quite the golden goose?" Allie asked and Claude nodded. "What if she died?"

Claude smiled again. "I think we both know the answer to that."

# Chapter Twelve

Jay McCallister was true to his word. Two months after our phone conversation he booked me on a San Francisco news show as a guest of a news panel. I didn't follow politics, but apparently it didn't matter. They would send me subject and talking points to study a few days before the show.

Jay's review almost doubled my sales throughout the month. Hardbacks were reprinted to include the review. Key phrases of his accolades were part of the summary typically found on the back cover. He nominated my novel for both Hugo and Nebula awards as the year's best new science fiction novel. Jay was the best friend I ever had, with exception of Eric, and I didn't know why.

I decided to think of Jay's interest in me as a gift instead of an omen. He had a familiar way about him, like we once knew each other. I instinctively trusted him. He seemed to want to take me under his wing and warn me about something almost supernatural.

My expensive husband was working away in his expensive condominium that he deemed as pure crap. He told me without a hint of gratitude that the condo seemed to be working out. With book sales at a record high, he was probably looking at upgrades with his good ol' friend Sam. Claude practically lived in Los Angeles full time. I was almost positive he had a girlfriend.

The first clue to another woman was the décor of the condo. The space was modern like Claude preferred, but there were pastel towels, patterned throw pillows, and even a dust ruffle in the master bedroom. The kitchen was packed with various kitchen gadgets like potato peeler, serving spoon, and even a butter dish. Claude didn't cook. He bought ready-made meals and take-out.

Next up, to add to my suspicions, was the Visa bill. Claude insisted on paying the bills with our joint checking account, but I began to take a more active interest. I quickly found that our charges had tripled from previous months of our marriage.

The condo only had four small rooms so there wasn't much to buy. Home goods and furniture were only part of the bill. Jewelry stores, women's clothing, a handbag boutique, and even a photography studio had jacked up the charges to an unsustainable level. If this was a preview of what Claude would average over the course of our marriage, I knew that I couldn't type fast enough to keep our heads above water. I should have been angry, but instead felt guilty, as if I was sneaking around behind his back. I never confronted him about his spending. I chose to keep records of everything, creating a dossier of sorts.

If I didn't have enough circumstantial evidence to dump him before he ruined my life, his absence at our mansion that he had to have validated my deepest fears. Two months passed by since Claude took possession of the Los Angeles condo and he had been home a total of six days.

Loneliness set in. Eric and I had lunch. I desperately wanted to tell him everything, but this wasn't the right time. His judgment was clouded and I was especially vulnerable. Two wrongs didn't make a right. I missed him, the store, and so many parts of my old life. The only reason that I married Claude was because he asked. I loved Eric all along.

I was out of town a lot, but still managed to meet some of the neighbors. They couldn't wait to meet my husband who they probably thought I invented. My San Francisco trip couldn't come soon enough. Maybe Jay would have some great advice about my marriage.

Claude called a few days before my trip. "I'll be home this Monday," he said.

"I'll be out of town," I said. It was not a lie, I would be out of town. "I'm booked on a news show in San Francisco. I'm part of the panel. I think it's called Left, Right, Center."

"Yes, of course. I booked that last month."

Rage flooded me. Claude took credit for a booking I knew damn well was Jay's doing. Did he do anything for my career, or was he just there for the ride? I planned to call my publisher direct. I planned many things in the split second of silence. I held my breath before saying a word.

"Maya?"

I had much to ask Jay about. "Ah, yes, Claude, you must have booked it a while ago. It was on our calendar. Anyway, I got the show and then a few signings. I'll be gone a full week so I won't see you until then."

"Good luck and I love you," Claude said and then hung up.

My thoughts turned from rage to loneliness as I packed for my trip. I wanted to go down to the bookshop and vent to Eric, but I suddenly had the urge to write. Maybe I wanted to channel all of my anger and fear into the sequel that I needed to begin or maybe the writing was like therapy. Jay called these moments inspiration or "in spirit". Whatever it was, I needed it. I sat at the computer for three hours and typed up a prologue and two chapters. Words, characters, and a story line came effortlessly. By the time I was finished, I felt renewed, full of energy and hope. Writing was like a program that went off in my head, or, like Jay said, a spirit was guiding me.

I googled "spirit" and read seven or eight Internet definitions, all of them sounding supernatural. There were so many advertisements for spiritual advisors in the margins of the websites that I browsed. Claims of being able to contact spirits of the dead along with revealing one's future popped out at me. They had to be scams, but then what if they weren't? What if it was possible to talk to my mother? I had her necklace. Maybe that would be enough to talk to her through a medium. The nuns told me she was very sick when she gave me to the orphanage and died soon afterwards. My mother didn't name my father on my birth certificate and the nuns told me that they didn't force her to give out that information.

It was a Friday night and I was once again alone. My flight to San Francisco didn't leave until the next morning. I needed an adventure or even a destination. Las Vegas was overflowing with these so-called spiritual advisors. Not only did I want to talk to my mother, but I also wanted advice about my marriage. After some Internet research, I found a spiritual medium a block off the strip who was highly rated from Yelp and Google—Marvelous Melvin the Medium. I grabbed my mother's necklace and then got in my car. Twenty minutes later, I paralleled parked in front of the business.

*Marvelous Melvin's House of Spirits* was two blocks away from the Las Vegas strip. The business was an unassuming gray warehouse with a neon sign in the window that flashed a pentagon symbol. The words "Marvelous Melvin" blinked yellow, red, and orange. My car was the only one in sight. The blinking sign and the well-lit entry made the place look open for business despite it being close to midnight.

I walked up the cracked concrete path and rang a loud bell. A deep, male voice yelled, "The door is open."

I entered into a large room that glowed with dozens of candle flames. There was an old, French gilded writing desk with a bronze candelabra in the center. An ornate, gold velvet chair looked more like a throne. Gold and red damask drapes hung behind the chair. Three more velvet chairs that didn't match but were of the same style sat in front of the desk. The floor was stained concrete. A large, red Oriental rug covered most of the floor. Stained-glass Moroccan lanterns with candles hung from the ceiling and gently swayed despite no breeze. I smelled sage as I nervously took a seat and waited.

A few minutes later the long drapes that hung behind the chair-throne were pulled back and a man I assumed to be Marvelous Melvin appeared. He certainly dressed the part of a medium. Marvelous Melvin was very tall, at least six foot four, bald, forty-ish, and African American. He wore flashy gold hoop earrings and a bright brocade robe cinched with an orange obi. He looked part fortune teller, part pirate, and part samurai. If this was a scam, I would at least be entertained.

"Thank you for coming to *Marvelous Melvin's House of Spirits*. I am the great and marvelous Melvin whom you've come to see. What is troubling you at this late hour?"

His voice was so deep, hypnotic, like velvet. I looked at his almost black eyes and noticed he wore eyeliner. "Hello. I'm Maya Smock. I'm new to all of this…spiritual guidance?" I looked at him to correct my terminology but he just stared. His eyes seemed to drill holes in my soul. "I'm here because I want to know my parents, or at least my mother. I grew up in an orphanage and was told that she died. I don't know who my father is or if he's alive. All l have is my mother's necklace."

Melvin paused and watched me take off my mother's chain. "And you know for certain she is dead?"

"Well, that's what the nuns at the orphanage told me," I said.

"Nuns can lie. Everyone lies," he said.

"So can you," I blurted.

"The dead don't lie. They don't have to. There is nothing in it for them. Death gives one a release from ulterior motives. If your mother truly is dead, I will try to locate her wherever she may be. Are you open-minded?" I nodded. "Then I need three hundred dollars for my service."

"How can you prove…"

Melvin interrupted me. "Trust and willingness to acknowledge the unknown is needed first. Proof will come after that is established."

I set out three hundred dollar bills which Marvin snatched up and set in his desk drawer. He took the necklace from my hand and stroked the pendant.

"It's a little bit warmer than the room, but not as warm as my temperature. I've seen this before. What kind of stone is this? Not emerald. Not jade…"

"It's moldavite. I took it to a jeweler a long time ago."

"Ah, yes. Now I see. Moldavite crystal. It's beautiful and exotic, much like you, Maya. It almost seems alive the way it glistens. It's associated with religion. I know that moldavite is used by my healing brothers and sisters to help the sick. It's also been linked with angels," Melvin said as he continued to rub my mother's pendant. He reminded me of Gollum and the ring.

"Angels? Moldavite is mentioned in the Bible?" I asked. Melvin's credibility was waning. Religion was both real and fake. I tended to pick and choose the parts that I wanted to believe and follow.

"Yes. One particular angel named Lucifer. Do you know who he was or is?" asked Melvin.

"No, but please go on. All of this lore is interesting," I said.

Melvin laughed. "Remember, Maya, keep an open mind. If you can't believe in an afterlife, then you won't be able to locate your mother. Religion needs to be respected." I shrugged and tilted my head, motioning him to continue. "Lucifer was God's favorite angel until he wanted to be God. Now he's known by other names—Satan, Devil, Beelzebub, the Dragon, the Serpent, and many more. He was crowned in Hell by other angels. That's where the moldavite comes in. His crown was said to be made of moldavite. Moldavite also has links to the Holy Grail. Hindus believe moldavite was the god Shiva's third eye. And Greeks used Moldavite to honor Persephone, the goddess of spring. Why am I giving you a lesson in Moldavite? Because you paid me three hundred dollars." Melvin laughed and I grimaced. "Enough jokes. This is all your mother left you. Kind of an odd choice. Most ancestors leave gold or diamonds or rubies or emeralds, something much more common. Your mother's taste in jewelry says something about her. She believed. I'm not sure what she believed in, but maybe we will find out tonight. Are you ready?"

Melvin grabbed my left wrist with his right hand and clutched my mother's necklace with his left hand and started to chant unknown words and phrases. I immediately thought Latin, but wasn't sure. His words were jumbled and I couldn't even repeat them. His eyes looked at the ceiling which cast shadows of flames from the flickering candles. A few minutes went by and some of the candles blew out. Marvelous Melvin's black eyes disappeared and I could only see his white eyeballs. They bulged out of his face. Melvin and I were not alone. Something or someone was in the room. I felt an energy that gave me goosebumps. Melvin's chants got louder and I suddenly felt tired when I should have felt terror. My head bobbed and I opened my eyes. I thought I fell asleep. Melvin was screaming!

"Defanatus! Defanatus! Who are you? Your mother's not dead! She never lived! Oh it burns!" Melvin dropped the necklace to the floor. His hand was branded in the shape of the pendant. "Here is your three hundred dollars. Go and never come back. I cannot help you," Melvin said. He opened the desk drawer and slid my money across the table. He then stood up and opened the door, ushering me to leave. I reached to the floor and scooped up my mother's necklace. It was glowing a greenish yellow.

"What do you mean my mother never lived? Please, I'm sorry. Are you angry? Listen, I don't know who I am. Please finish what you started. I just want to know my mother," I said.

"Maya, if that's your real name, whoever gave you that necklace wanted you to find out the truth. The spirits are afraid and you need to go."

I left Melvin's place both confused and offended. His warning about the necklace stayed with me. The necklace had been part of my life for as long as I could remember. I must have lost the necklace at least a dozen times and even had a foster parent steal it, yet it always came back like a boomerang.

I got into my car. It was past three o'clock in the morning. Where did the time go? I didn't have any more time to waste with Marvelous Melvin and his spirit friends. My plane would be taking off in less than four hours and I needed to stop back home and grab my bags. Maybe Jay could give me some answers.

# Chapter Thirteen

"Moment of truth, Doctor," Andreas said, one hundred and fifty feet below the earth's crust. He and the doctor were alone. "My men will be here within the hour. I thought you could tell me some more details on what you plan on doing with these ABs as you call them. What do you think of the cage?"

Both men looked around the technological masterpiece. In under three weeks, the most advanced surveillance cage to date was built with the goal of containing four aliens found in New Mexico. They were ready to observe, experiment, and perhaps even communicate.

"The craft is here, right?" asked Jaeger.

"Yes, it's on base. Each part had to be specially packed and demagnetized several times. There's a small craft, like a life boat but for space. It's in pretty good shape. We are in the process of selecting top scientists and engineers to take a look at them," Andreas answered.

"I know quite a few, General. You should have asked me."

"Ah, I'm sure that you do, but we don't want the whole base one big Nazi reunion, Doctor. What do you think about the cage?"

"If this does not hold the ABs, then nothing will. Well done. Quite a feat finished in record time. Did you find my friends, General?"

Andreas nodded. "Two of them are dead and one is still not found. But we got Hans and Wolfrik. They are in the process of being questioned. Like you, they will receive new identities if they prove to be of no threat. Maybe by the end of the week they will be here, if all goes smoothly.

You want to tell me what your plans are. How are these men going to help? I checked out all of your cloning, gene cutting or splicing or whatever you call it, all of your Doctor Frankenstein bullshit. None of what you tell me is remotely possible. I had top professors in the world tell me they are just figuring out what deoxyribonucleic acid even is. Nothing has been published. No one has attempted to clone animals, let alone people. Yet you claim that you are going to clone an alien. Excuse me, an advanced being. Are you telling me fairy tales so that I keep you around?"

The doctor looked down at the ground and didn't answer right away. The silence made Andreas grow angry. The doctor looked into his eyes and said, "No, nothing is published. There are no mainstream theories. But what I know and other Nazis know was classified. Great lengths were taken so that no one knew what we were working on. Just the Fuhrer and whoever he wanted to share the information with knew about my genetic research.

"My work wasn't about credit or glory, it was about knowledge. And Germany had obtained a great deal of knowledge in many things, not just biology. Hitler knew the value of ancient books, artifacts, and art. He knew where to look and what to do. He talked about Germans being the master race, but what he didn't share was why. We both know it wasn't because of blonde hair and blue eyes. Eventually everything that I know will be discovered by someone else. Time is the only advantage that I have. Please, General, let me do my work. Your country will be at least a century ahead of the world in information. I know what deoxyribonucleic acid or DNA is and where to find it. I also know about ribonucleic acid, which is key to genetics. These acids are the building blocks to life. My friends have an idea on how to copy it, even reproduce with it. All we need is time. You've provided everything else. Soon you will have the results that you are looking for."

"You never told me how you knew about these ABs. You saved the head of one. How did you get it? Did you kill it?"

"No, no. I was spying on them. They crashed in a forested area not far from Dachau, before war broke out. I wasn't the only one who saw them. Some of the villagers also saw the crash. I went to the site, but stayed back and watched. I couldn't believe what I saw. It was an aircraft shaped like a saucer. And it was so bright, almost blinding. Some of the townspeople tried to open the craft. A beam shot out and melted the skin right off of them. So controlled, so efficient. The most sophisticated weapon I ever seen. I read about similar accounts in the Bible and the Vedas.

"One of the villagers got away. After he told the Schutzstaffel or, as you say black shirts, about the crash, he was immediately shot down. Soon the forest was crawling with black shirts. Like the villagers, many were killed by the beams from the craft. One of the black shirts took off his necklace and his wedding ring, both gold, set them down, and slowly walked away. He yelled at the craft. He said he didn't mean them harm and would get them whatever they needed. A door opened and one of the advanced beings walked down a ramp and took the necklace and ring. As he walked back inside of the craft, a beam was targeted through the being's neck. His head was lopped off and rolled close to where I stood. His body, if indeed it was a male, disintegrated like ash. I scooped up the head and ran as fast as I could back to my car. I kept the head in formaldehyde solution since then. One of the black shirts saw me. I was just a research doctor back then. He told his superior who told his superior. Anyway, I ended up in Hitler's office in Berlin. He gave me a lab, and then when the war got going and the camps were built, he gave me Dachau. The Jews were at my disposal to use. My colleagues, the ones you sought out, and I believe the DNA of the ABs and humans are not that different. We think they are us, but evolved. We believe that they time travel back here to check on us."

Andreas wanted to believe him, but it all sounded like something a kid with one hell of an imagination would make up. Yet there they were, standing in front a cage built especially for ABs. Maybe a kernel of truth was in there somewhere, but he was in no mood to sift it out. "So Hitler knew about these things or ABs?"

"Oh yes, they left some clues about their space craft behind. Hitler used the technology to advance his air program. Now America is using the technology for their air program."

Andreas wondered how Doctor Jaeger even knew about any air program. He spent his life in an underground lab. There must have been a leak. Someone was keeping the doctor updated on current events.

"Let me get this right, the head that you have, it belongs to an AB that was shot down by its own craft with a laser? Why?"

The doctor nodded and then shrugged.

Their conversation was interrupted by the descending elevator. The shaft echoed like a freight train, causing a vibration as it hit the bottom floor. The doors opened and four of Andreas's airmen exited with two dollies that held two neatly stacked coffins each. They wheeled them out of the elevator toward the almost seamless entrance of the cage. The general walked up to the first tier of the observation deck and opened one of the entrances.

"Put them inside, and open them up with one of the sets of gloves," he said through a microphone. "Good. Now exit the cage." Andreas closed the entrance. The coffins sat inside the state-of-the-art cage waiting to be examined. He opened a top panel of the observation deck and motioned for two of the airmen to walk up to the third and highest tier. The open panels allowed them a clean shot from above if things got out of hand. They nodded at Andreas and had their weapons ready.

"Okay, Doc, we're ready. Open them up," Andreas said, again through the microphone.

Jaeger was on the main floor of the new underground addition. He walked into the cage and hovered over the coffins. His hands were clad in extra thick, synthetic gloves. He opened the first coffin. Inside was an AB who appeared to be sleeping. His or her abnormally long fingers glowed as the rest of the body appeared motionless.

Jaeger pushed the coffin away from the Plexiglas and bars and then opened the next closest coffin. The AB's body had bullet holes all over its torso. This had to be the one who attacked the doctor. The silver box was open and empty. There were holes in the ABs uniform from the bullets, but no signs of blood, liquid stains or shell casings. The uniform must have protected it. The ABs fingers also glowed. It did not appear to be dead, but sleeping or even charging.

Underneath the bright florescent lighting Andreas could see the outline of the cuffs for sleeves and the neckline and pants bottom. There was the strange embroidered symbol which he remembered from the first attack in Doctor Jaeger's lab. He had forgotten to ask around about its meaning. He took out a notepad and drew the image.

Jaeger's facial expression showed his frustration. He quickly opened the next two coffins. The remaining ABs were lying inside like the other two with long glowing fingers.

Through the control panel, the general placed a metal prod into a metal clamp on a track from the ceiling. The prod hovered over the doctor's rubber gloves. Through a remote, he dropped the prod. "Doctor, wake them up."

Jaeger picked up the prod with the thick rubber gloves and poked each of the bodies that lay inside of the coffins. Nothing.

"There's a switch at the end of the prod. It's got an electrical current. Try giving them a zap," Andreas said through the microphone.

The doctor was more apprehensive, but turned on the prod and heard the buzz. Again, he poked them and nothing.

Andreas, the doctor, and four airmen looked inside of the cage for several minutes for movement. From the control panel, Andreas used the camera and took several close-ups of each of the ABs. Were they dead? Maybe the amber yellow light of their fingers would eventually burn out, signifying some kind of extraterrestrial decomposition.

Their grayish white skin was as smooth as polished stone. In the light it cast a faint metallic shimmer around each of their necks where the scaled skin was most prevalent. None of them seemed to show any facial lines, pores, or body hair. Three of the four had silvery stands of hair on their head and one was almost bald.

"They are alive, General!" yelled Jaeger. "We just don't know how to wake them. Maybe they have an internal timer of some kind that shuts them down during shock. But they are definitely alive."

Days went by and Jaeger sat at the control panel, waiting. Andreas brought in the brass, the Secretary of Defense, and even the president. Everyone who saw the ABs were flabbergasted at the discoveries.

Within two weeks after the cage was finished, Jaeger's two Nazi friends were vetted and cleared. Hans Schroeder, a former Nazi biologist from an esteemed university was now Hans Schmidt and Wolfrick Schundler, the head of the maternity ward of a hospital in Berlin, was now Frederik Richtor. They looked much like Jaeger. Both men were somewhere around forty years old, pasty, with blonde receding hair and blue eyes. The only major difference between any of them was Frederik. He was short and chubby, but all three men could have been brothers.

Several weeks went by and the trio of Nazis finally left the control panel and went up to the lab. They continued to observe the ABs, but used the camera from the lab that ran down a shaft and through the ceiling of the cage. While they watched the ABs, Andreas and his airmen watched them.

Jaeger and his two friends spoke in German. Both of the new doctors supposedly knew very little English, or at least that was what they told Andreas. Their conversations had to be translated—another obstacle to clear.

Andreas had Major William Lamphrey watch them the majority of the time. The young soldier's mother was from Germany and he learned it as a kid. Although he was only half German, he looked like the poster boy for the perfect Aryan man—tall, muscular, blonde, blue-eyed, and handsome. The three doctors liked him the most of all of the airmen who had clearance to the lab and the cage. He also spoke German.

Two months went by and the ABs still had not moved. Five guards stationed around the cage were now reduced to two guards. Major Lamphrey only watched the Germans during day-time hours and no one watched them at night. They were recorded, but Lamphrey didn't always listen to the recordings. Much of what they talked about was over the young man's head.

Security had gotten ultra-lax. New information regarding the ABs had ceased. Andreas worried that Washington would start coming down on him. The operation had cost of fortune. But as long as the ABs fingers glowed and their bodies did not decompose, Andreas's covert underground base was in business.

Andreas began to shift focus on the space craft which sat in boxes in the hangar above the laboratory. The space craft and baby craft might have been the keys to waking the ABs up.

On a cool November night, Andreas and four of his airmen began unpacking a few of the endless boxes that were delivered. They needed to be demagnetized again in order to continue working. The force was so great that pieces stuck together.

In the warehouse, Jaeger, Schmidt, and Richtor approached him while he was prying two small parts of the craft apart.

"General, we have an idea," said Jaeger.

Andreas almost jumped out of his skin. "What are you doing here? You're not supposed to be in this hangar."

"So sorry, General, but we need something, we need women. Women who will not be missed to continue our study."

# Chapter Fourteen

Jay McCallister went through wives, money, and therapists like water. At some point in his life, in his early fifties perhaps, he needed to slow down. With exception to an occasional screw-up, Jay went cold turkey. He lived the life of sober bachelor who rarely dated. The gigantic royalty checks were invested wisely instead of being pissed away. Within a short period of time, his new lifestyle catapulted him to one of the highest paid writers of all time. With a clear mind free of dramatic distractions, his writing and imagination sharpened to a new level. But none of it made him happy. He was certain that some kind of force was pulling his strings.

At sixty-seven years old, Jay looked a good ten years older. His face was etched with deep lines and his jowls hung past his jawline. Age spots dotted his face, neck, and arms. His long hair was almost completely white and he usually wore it back in a ponytail. His career began almost five decades ago in his home town, Los Angeles. Most fans did not realize he began his professional writing career straight out of high school.

Jay had written twenty-eight novels, seven movie scripts, twelve television series scripts, innumerous articles for dozens of magazines, and even partnered with other authors for nonfiction books. It was the nonfiction work that made him look insane. His outrageous statements made on talk shows only added to his oddball persona.

His agent told him to stick to fiction, which he agreed upon, realizing the world wasn't ready for the truth. Fiction was the easier and softer way to prepare his fans for the shit that was about to hit the fan.

Jay already had a reputation of wearing a tinfoil hat. He and his best friend, Glenn Lucasek, put up large sums of money to build an alien institution. They named it TAH or T.A.H. for 'They Are Here' Institute. Glenn had been a close friend and his lawyer for decades. He investigated UFO and alien sightings and worked the institution's work into his weekly show.

T.A.H. Institute started small, but soon fans of Glenn's alien show began to contribute to their cause. Both men expanded the institution by relocating to the inside of a mountain once used to be a military safe haven. They became known as the nation's leading alien experts, or, to others, complete crackpots. The institute set out to prove the existence of extraterrestrials. An unintended result of T.A.H. made both men super wealthy and gave both men authority and respect in an otherwise exploited field.

In Jay's earlier work, he suspected that aliens were guiding his plot and characters. Soon he discovered a code embedded in his novels. His fiction was not really fiction. Yet no one picked up on it, no one that he knew of until Maya.

After reading Maya's *The Master Race*, her wording, style, figurative language, theme, all of it, was too close to his own. He knew she was a fan of his, but there was much more depth and symbolism in her novel than all of his put together. Her words were arranged in a pattern, the same pattern as Jay's novels. The odds of her work being pure coincidence and imagination was next to impossible. She must have had help. Was it the same help that he had?

Jay lived in one of the most beautiful homes in all the Bay Area. His mansion was perched on a bluff that overlooked the Golden Gate Bridge and all of San Francisco in the town of Tiburon. He had always lived in the Los Angeles area, but needed a change. Tiburon offered him the convenience of a major city but the peace and quiet of an affluent neighborhood.

Jay employed twelve full-time staff members to keep his compound spotless and beautiful. In addition to grounds men and maids, he had two security guards who worked rotating shifts. He paid his staff handsomely and treated them like family. Their children went to nice colleges and had extravagant weddings with Jay paying the tab. Any health concerns of his staff or his staff's family were taken care of. Some of his staff lived in the servant wing of his fifteen thousand square foot house and some lived in the guest houses sprinkled across the four acres of property. The rest of his staff lived across the bridge in San Francisco.

Jay loved and appreciated his staff and they loved him back. He settled in Tiburon shortly after his fourth and final divorce. Most staff was hired eleven years ago. No one ever quit or gotten fired. No one ever betrayed him by stealing or talking to the media. His home was the only place in the world where he felt safe. He hoped Maya would feel the same way after her stay.

Jay didn't have many close friends, but the few that he regularly hung out with were his family. He would sometimes get moody and not want to leave the house. His doctors called these moods a sign of depression. They were constantly recommending anti-depressants. But he knew that medicine could not fix his deep sorrow. If the world could only see itself for what it was—a zoo and a laboratory for aliens. He knew the world was much like an updated version of Jurassic Park except the humans were the dinosaurs. All of that would change.

Soon humans would not be entertainment to the aliens. They would be forced into working any way the alien ruling class saw fit. But not all human beings were doomed. A few lucky ones would be part of the new ruling class. Some of the world caught on to the master plan.

Politics, media, academics, pop culture, and economics began to shine a spotlight on the face of a world agenda. Yet the concept was too overwhelming for the average mind to conceive. Others, more and more each day, began to believe that something big was about to burst. New World Order was what the conspiracy buffs called it. Those who believed in God said the future would soon spark the End of Days or the Apocalypse. Scientific minds believed a change in Evolution along with a climate change was around the corner. Darwin's Survival of the Fittest would change the landscape of planet Earth. Jay just simply called the future a takeover.

Saturday morning, hours before dawn, Jay sat out on his balcony with a cup of coffee and watched the light traffic cross the Golden Gate Bridge. He thought back to his first novel, *We Are Not Alone*. He was seventeen years old when he wrote it. Like Maya, he had no family and loved science fiction. Writing was a calling. The book did very well, but wasn't a best seller. It was good enough for him to sign a three book deal with a major publisher.

Jay always had low self-esteem. At age seventeen, he lacked the experience to see how the jealousy of others worked. Other science fiction writers had panned his work, calling the book a one-hit wonder with a short shelf-life. The criticisms made him question writing all together, but a nagging impulse to type up bizarre space-age stories trumped self-doubt. One year after his first novel he wrote *The Rise and Fall of a Starman*. This was the break-out book that changed his life. His critics were pressured into praising the book as it rose to the number one on the New York Times Best Seller's List.

Jay wished he had someone to take him under his or her wing. He was thrown into an ocean of sharks who all wanted a bite on both a personal and professional level. Agents, lawyers, and publishers were only part of it. Women were in a class of their own.

Jay was never handsome, just average looking. He never had a date until *The Rise and Fall of a Starman*. As his book sales rose and his book signing appearances increased, he attracted much female attention. Women were flirting with him. When he didn't know how to flirt back, they threw themselves at him.

At twenty years old, he met Brenda, a hot, little blonde who looked like a Dallas Cowboy cheerleader seven years his senior. Sexually speaking, before Brenda he was blind, and after Brenda he could see. She was an expensive wife or so he thought at the time. She turned out to be chump change compared to the others.

Jay racked up four wives before the age of fifty and four divorces by the age of fifty-two. None of his wives gave him children. Two doctors told him that he shot blanks, but he believed there was something more, something that they could not explain.

Jay's third book, *Orion's Belt is Missing*, practically wrote itself. Once finished, he read the book from start to finish, editing the mistakes. As he read the first draft, he did not remember writing most of it. There was a chapter dedicated to Einstein's theory of relativity, a theory that Jay had never studied. The theory focused on time travel and Jay wrote about it as if he was an expert. He became curious as to where the information came from. A day at the library verified everything that was mentioned within the chapter. His background information was spot on and written in a manner that any of his readers could understand while not missing one detail. He was twenty-one years old at that point, still married to Brenda. He asked her what she thought of this odd miracle. She chalked the knowledge up to a television special that must have been watched and/or a magazine article that must have been read. He accepted the simplest answer.

Six months later, after the book was in the top ten of the New York bestseller's list, Jay had an odd symbol blazed onto his front lawn. The incident prompted him and Brenda to move into a gated-community with security outside of the Los Angeles area. But the symbol was also blazed into his mind. He began to see it everywhere, in the cream of the coffee he drank, in the shadows of candlelight, in the stains of his shirt, in the shape of the clouds-everywhere. Brenda didn't know how to handle his new obsession. She stuck it out a little longer, but Jay's symbol turned into an alien manifesto. That's when she split.

Jay didn't blame Brenda for leaving. She was like most of the sheep in the world as were his other wives. Talk of aliens and outer space made them all leave. And they all left with a fortune. They probably would have left anyway. Jay just gave them a really good reason. His first marriage kicked off an insatiable obsession with alien theory. The more knowledge he obtained about time, space, and aliens, the lonelier he became. Three decades later, he became the genius with the tin foil hat. The odder his behavior, the more money he raked in. But all of the women, booze, drugs, and money couldn't make him forget who he was.

After reading Maya's novel, Jay needed to share his thoughts, warn her, and even get to know her. The day before her arrival he had staff prepare the guest suite with new bedding, exotic soaps, and expensive toiletries. A writing desk from another room was moved into the sitting area along with a new laptop that Jay bought for her to take home. He had one of his maids estimate her size and then fill the closet with casual clothes.

Jay thought of how much he could share with her before scaring her away. If he didn't pace it just right, he'd come off as a mental patient and she'd leave, just like his wives. Then again, she might already know who she was. She had one of those chartreuse rock necklaces.

By mid-morning, a couple of hours before Maya's arrival, Jay's rented Bentley and hired chauffeur arrived.

He hoped Maya would get a kick out of the red carpet treatment.

He was nervous. He changed his clothes three times before leaving the house, settling on a pair of jeans and Yoda t-shirt. He pulled his hair back in his trademark ponytail. She had to be more nervous than he was. She was only twenty-two years old. Fame, fortune, and marriage— Jay was about to deflate all of it. Or maybe she already knew that they were overrated.

Jay lined up some fun things for him and Maya to do over the course of the weekend. Her television interview was on Monday, so he would have her full attention for the next two days. He wanted her to have some fun. From what he heard, all she did was promote her book. Her husband had her working like a dog.

Jay didn't know Claude Kazinsky, yet really didn't like him. Like Claude, Jay was from the Los Angeles, and like Claude, Jay went to U.C.L.A. Their paths had crossed before. Jay still had plenty of contacts in L.A., starting with his agent, Barry Ellerbee. When Maya agreed to visit, Jay was even more curious about her husband.

"Barry, it's Jay. You know a lit agent named Claude Kazinsky?"

"Oh yeah. He's a real prick. I hear he fell into it with that new author, what's her name?"

"Maya Smock."

"Ah yes, poor girl. He works a few blocks away for Veronica Tatum. Want me 'ta get ya some details?" Barry said. Three decades in Los Angeles and Barry still sounded like a mobster from Chicago. Although he was an upstanding citizen who dealt with authors and books, Barry was known to bring in the underworld every now and then for a variety of reasons. Jay had made Barry filthy rich and in return Barry kissed his ass twenty-five hours a day.

"That's why I'm calling. Maya is a friend of mine, a new, platonic friend, and I want to know what she's in for."

"Papa McCallister. I get it. You're taking on 'ta role of 'da mentor. I can't compare Claude ta any of your exes. Rumor has it he's a financial mess and a real user. I'll let ya know A.S.A.P."

Four days later Barry called after hiring a tail. "You were right to check on the jag. Mr. Wonderful is practically living with a beautiful blonde in a little love nest that Maya recently purchased. The man's a ne'er-do-well among certain Los Angeles circles. He has 'ta have the best of everything. Before Maya, he hit the jackpot with a bestselling diet book. He pissed away enormous commissions on who knows what.

"Claude's from white trash. His mama is a con-woman and his daddy's missing. He's got a half-brother Sam, five years younger. Ta boys learned early on how ta work the streets. Mom went to work sucking ta dicks of rich businessmen in the city's darkest corners while picking their pockets. She's serving five to ten, credit card fraud. Sam also served some time. Claude's record is clean." Barry paused.

"Anything else? He must have been smart. Tatum's got a great agency," Jay said.

"Despite it all, he finagled himself a scholarship at U.C.L.A. He pulled himself up from his bootstraps, or so he did on paper. He's still at Tatum's agency. Pretty prestigious job. And he manages Maya's money, or shall I say takes her money. None of my business. But she has brought him some other celeb types of clients. The guy's no good."

"Barry, I owe you," Jay said and then hung up. He felt guilty for glimpsing into Maya's private life. He would make sure this week would be fun. Saturday morning Jay slid into the back seat of the beautiful silver Bentley and headed for San Francisco International Airport.

Maya walked out of the terminal and headed toward the curb.

Jay rolled down the car window and yelled, "Maya, so glad you made it." He got out of the car and carried her only bag to the trunk. For a moment he felt very awkward. Should he hug her? Kiss her? He wasn't the touchy-feely type. She didn't seem to be either. He didn't want to give her the wrong idea. "So how was your flight?" he asked.

Maya ignored the question and gushed over the gorgeous car. "Is this yours? And you have your own chauffeur?"

"They are both mine for the week. Thought I'd show you San Fran in style. First time here?"

"Yes. But I've been doing a lot of traveling. Never have time to stop and enjoy the places that I visit. Thank you for this. I plan on having a blast. Your offer couldn't have come at a better time. Again, thank you so much," Maya said.

"The pleasure is mine. Your guest spot is this Monday so we have the weekend without interruptions. I thought we'd do lunch with some of my friends. Very open-minded types who love to talk. They love science fiction and paranormal, anything occult. They keep me around for laughs. I'm like their crazy old uncle who they let out from the basement every once in a while. Plenty of eye rolls." Maya laughed. "I'm grateful for their friendship as I am grateful for yours. Driver, Fisherman's Wharf, Pier Thirty-Nine."

"Lunch already?" Maya asked. It was only ten o'clock in the morning.

"No, lunch is at two o'clock, but I want to show you the docks. There's lots of things to do and see. Like to shop?" Maya nodded. "Good. Me too. We can put our bags in the car and not have to worry about carrying anything."

"I love that! This is so beautiful," Maya said as she got out of the car.

Jay and Maya walked up and down the pier and across the street, shopping and drinking coffee, laughing like old friends. She was easy to be with and his nervousness subsided. Maya bought cups, wind chimes, a rain coat, and chocolate while Jay purchased chocolate. They took a break and watched the seals climb up and down from the docks.

"Where's your necklace? The one with the green stone?" Jay asked as he noticed she wore just a plain gray t-shirt and jeans.

"Would that be the necklace that you tried to yank off of my neck back in Las Vegas? The one that got you posted on YouTube?" she asked playfully.

Embarrassed, Jay nervously laughed. "That's the one."

"I brought it with. It's in my bag. I actually have another necklace story that you are not part of." Maya looked over at a store window in the plaza. "I think I want to get a new necklace, you know, to represent a new start, here with you."

Jay blushed. It was quite a compliment. "Very well then. So what kind of stone was your old necklace?"

"Moldavite. It has attracted too much attention. That jewelry store over there has beautiful things in the window. Come. I've got to tell you about last night at Marvelous Melvin's."

Maya stopped in front of the jewelry store window and stared at the diamond and ruby pendant. "That's the one. I love it. The main stone is red. I need a change," Maya said. She and Jay went into the store and she purchased the necklace without asking the price. It was eleven hundred dollars and Maya proudly charged the item with a gleam in her eye. Something about her expression suggested a sense of liberation.

"Will this be the second necklace in your jewelry box?" Jay asked.

"I don't need a box for two items. But it will be the second necklace on my bedroom dresser." Maya took the new necklace and immediately hung it around her neck.

"'A gray t-shirt and a fancy ruby necklace. Huh. I like the contrast. So I'm bursting with curiosity. Who is Marvelous Melvin and what does he have to do with your old necklace that I once tried to steal? We still got thirty minutes to kill before we're expected at that crab shack across the way."

Maya laughed and then proceeded to tell him about her mother that she never knew, the necklace that her mother supposedly gave her, and Melvin's reaction to the necklace after praying to the spirits. "And then he told me I had no mother. I was motherless and to get out. He gave me my money back and seemed to be sincerely scared. Why?"

*Spoon feed it to her*, Jay thought. He didn't want to scare her. "Well, I'm sure Melvin was scared. One of my friends, Paula, is an expert with paranormal stuff. If you feel comfortable, you might want to ask her about the man's outlandish reaction during lunch."

"Yes, of course. I'll ask Paula, but what do you think? I mean, motherless?"

"Well, were you a test-tube baby?" She shook her head. "You don't need a mother for that."

"Well, maybe you don't need a mother, just the eggs of a donor. But don't you need a surrogate to carry the child?" asked Maya.

*You're way off, but we'll get into that later*, thought Jay. "Well, that depends. What if there was such a thing as an artificial womb? Egg, sperm, artificial womb, a test tube, and even some gene modifications," Jay said as he arched his bushy gray-white brows.

"Modifications? Like soybeans and corn from Monsanto? That's ridiculous."

"Yes, like most of our food. Certain genes that are good could be added to an embryo while taking away certain genes that are bad. Think about it. Were you ever sick? Did you ever have trouble in school, at least academic trouble? How long did it take you to write *The Master Race?*"

"No, never sick to my knowledge. Could have been when I was a baby. I really don't remember anything until age seven or eight. I never had any academic problems in school, but I was bullied and made fun of. I was a foster child. To give you the short version of that, I had lots of troubles. And your last question, hmmm, I think it took me two months to write the novel. I'm including the time it took me to edit the manuscript."

"Two months with edits? Do you think that's the average time it takes a writer to whip up a novel?" Jay asked.

Maya shrugged.

"Most people take at least a year and some take several years. What about babies? Are you and your husband trying to get pregnant?"

Maya's big brown eyes welled with tears. Jay hit a nerve and felt terrible. "Sorry, it's none of my business."

"He doesn't know it, but I've been trying to get pregnant. I want someone to love and who loves me back."

Jay knew exactly how she felt and didn't have the heart to lay on the bad news quite yet. "Hey, it's lunch time. Let's go stuff our faces with some modified food."

Maya wiped away a tear that was about to roll down her cheek. "Yes, I have a taste for some GMO slop."

# Chapter Fifteen

General Robert Andreas officially crossed over to the dark side after ordering Major William Lamphrey, the recently promoted officer, to take four random women of different races into custody for classified reasons. The young ambitious man did not question his order or ask for details. Just a *yes, Sir*.

Andreas's guilt compelled him to explain. "Major, I need you to bring them here. They are part of the greatest experiment of our time. Our German friends need them for their eggs, so make sure they are young. And please do not tell them why you are bringing them here. You also need to make sure that they are not missed. Maybe runaways or prostitutes."

Again, Lamphrey said, "Yes, Sir." The young major looked more like a choir boy than the kidnapper he was about to become. He became indispensable to this top secret operation and would undoubtedly make it all the way up to general within the next decade or two. Both Andreas and his Washington superiors had their eyes on this bright young man.

"Take two others who prove trustworthy. And take your time. The last thing we need is for any of you to get caught."

"Yes, Sir. I will ask Redding and Bolantano." The men William chose were also young stars within the Air Force and recently promoted. All of them were at Dachau when they first met the Nazi doctor.

"Very well. Take a couple of the civilian cars and try to blend in. Bring 'um back here to headquarters."

There was no turning back. Andreas just sentenced the three men to hell and they were only too happy to go.

Not a question or even a sneer. *Where had human decency gone,* he thought. Lamphrey's blue eyes held the same dead expression as Jaeger's.

Years ago, when Andreas was William's age, he would have spat in his superior's face for ordering something so downright evil. Andreas started off his military service as a talented and brave pilot, filled with idealism. He learned Christian values from his parents. But those values were compromised. His marriage vows and fatherly duty was the first to go. He hadn't talked to his ex-wife or two daughters for years. All that was left of his upbringing had vanished. A few decades later he adopted the mindset of the ends justifying the means.

The new generation skipped over the chasm of right and wrong, heading straight for glory and ambition. Maybe it wasn't the entire generation, just the accomplished men the Air Force had been recruiting. Everyone who worked at Broom Lake was fully committed to studying life from another planet. A few dead prostitutes was a small price to pay.

Andreas wasn't sure what the doctors were trying to do and they weren't exactly sharing information. Most of it was very complicated and he didn't have enough of a science background to fully comprehend. The fact that the Advanced Beings had yet to wake up and might even be dead didn't hold any of the doctors back from spending fourteen to sixteen hours each day holed up in the underground laboratory.

Andreas checked on the ABs every morning after rigorously lifting weights. Their body temperatures never dipped above or below eighty-five degrees. Their fingers still glowed a bright yellow-green neon color. Something was going on inside. Whether dead or alive, the doctors made it clear that they would be invaluable to their research.

Andreas lit a Lucky Strike and walked to one of the hidden entrances inside of the hangar. He took the freight elevator to the bottom and headed towards the cage for the second time that morning. No one was there. The ABs were not being monitored. He would have words with his men, but for now he slipped his hands inside of the rubber gloves and prodded the closest alien.

On the sleeve of the ABs upper arm was a symbol that Andreas noticed before. He drew it again in his notepad. There was a familiarity about it, but he needed more information. It was still morning. He changed into civilian clothes and headed out to Las Vegas. It was a good two hour ride, but the town had a library he could use.

The autumn day was cool and sunny. Andreas enjoyed the road trip and chance to get away from the base. He had not left Broom Lake for months. He thought hard about the breakdown of security. He was in charge of some of the most valuable commodities in the world, maybe the most valuable and things were getting sloppy. Improving security was much easier to think about than what Lamphrey, Redding, and Bolantano were doing. *Today it's women. Tomorrow will it be babies?* He pushed it out of his head.

Once at the library, Andreas walked up to the librarian and asked for a book on symbols. She was an old, stout woman with gray bushy hair.

"What symbol are you most interested in?" she asked as she sat behind her desk.

Andreas took out his small notepad and showed her his sketch. A split second later he regretted it. He had just shown her classified information.

"I think you know this one," she said and then smiled. "We've got a few books just on this symbol alone."

"Excuse me?" he asked.

"You're obviously a soldier. I can tell by your haircut and the way you stand, you know, your posture.

You must have been in the war. Look a little closer. This is a swastika worn by our enemies. See the lines. These four dots in corners, just a variation," she said.

"But it couldn't be," Andreas said, exasperated. *Am I losing my mind?*

"Let me get you that book." The librarian got up from her desk and He followed her to the other side of the library. "You see, what most people don't realize is that this symbol has been around for thousands of years. There are some variations to it, but it's basically a hooked cross." She led him into a book aisle and scanned for the book. "Ah, here it is. You can read it for yourself. The whole book is about the swastika. May I ask why you are so interested?"

"I saw this symbol somewhere and wanted to know more about it," Andreas said. He tried to be as vague as possible. The librarian glared at him as if she could sense he was lying. She was much too nosy. "Thank you and good day."

Andreas took the book and sat down at a nearby reading table. With his small notebook, he jotted down some notes as he read.

*Swastika found in Sanskrit tablets.*

*12,000 years ago swastika sign found in Ukraine. Found all over the world. Common in India as well as Navajo Indians.*

*European connection-Ukraine, Troy, Scandinavia, and Germany.*

*In Greece, the sign was used by Pythagoras.*

*Sacred in Hinduism, Jainism, Buddhism, and Odinism.*

*Means "good luck" or "wellbeing" or "permanent victory."*

*Sign inverted to right means Vishnu and Sun, inverted to the left means Kali and Magic. Sign is linked to heaven earth.*

Andreas looked at his drawing again. It's inverted to the left. Hitler's sign was inverted to the right. He continued to read.

*German Volkisch movement-sign was connected to Aryan identification, purity of Germanic ancestry.*

*Hitler writes about the sign in Mein Kampf.*

The more Andreas read about the sign, the angrier he became with Doctor Jaeger and friends. The three men were holding back just about everything. The Nazis and Hitler knew about these beings for a long time, even choosing their symbol for their party. They didn't just happen to land in Dachau and the doctor didn't just happen to pick up a lopped off head of an AB.

On his way out of the library, the librarian caught up with him by the exit. "Aren't you going to check that book out?"

Andreas shook his head. "No, I got the information I needed. Again, thanks for all of your help." *That was one annoying bitch*, he thought. He wished he hadn't shown her the symbol.

The long drive home put the general in almost a trance-like state as he listed off dozens of the questions. Every question seemed to stem from one question that needed to be answered—How long have the Germans been communicating with these Advanced Beings? That would certainly explain their claims to superiority. Should he confront Jaeger and his friends?

The sun set by the time Andreas was back at the base. Broom Lake was invisible to anyone who was unaware of its existence. He quietly drove up to the guard shack and flashed his identification. The guard opened the barred gate and let him in. A few miles down the inconspicuous dirt road another guard opened another barred gate and let him through. A third guard shack would soon be necessary, especially if strangers were to be brought in. The other side of the base wasn't even watched.

A barbed wire fence was put up along the perimeter of their property. All of this had to change. He stopped the car and wrote himself a note about increasing security.

Behind his truck, Andreas saw two sets of headlights. *Lamphrey.* He turned on his parking lights and then got out of the truck. Lamphrey pulled up the sedan with two women bound and gagged in the tiny backseat area.

"You're back so soon," Andreas said. His stomach flipped. Guilt made his hands shake. "Follow me back to headquarters."

Lamphrey nodded and motioned the other car to follow. A few miles down the desolate dirt road was the warehouse they used for headquarters.

Andreas lived in a small mobile home a few hundred yards away. The other half of the airmen lived in the barracks built steps away from the largest hangar on base.

The base was pitch black. Lamphrey, Bolantano, and Redding dragged four women out of the two cars. The men followed their orders perfectly.

Of the four women, one was black, one was white, one was Mexican, and one was Indian. All were gagged and cuffed. The white and black women were dressed provocatively. The general assumed they were prostitutes. They both had that distrusting, violent look in their eyes as if they were immune from crying and could no longer feel pain. The other two women looked poor. They also looked young, like teenagers. They might have been runaways, homeless, or even hitchhikers. It didn't matter. They were hysterical. Their dark brown eyes were filled with terror.

Andreas didn't sign up to mutilate women. He always thought of himself as the hero, the knight in shining armor, the savior. Yet here he was, setting up their worst nightmare. They didn't deserve this—no one deserved this.

The black woman managed to chew through her gag. She spit on Andreas as they were led into warehouse.

"Wow, she got spirit," Andreas said as he wiped his face.

The black woman screamed and then said, "You sons-of-a-bitches! Fuck you all…"

Major Lamphrey hit the black woman's face so hard that she fell to the floor. With her hands bound, the white woman transferred her weight and swung her arms at Lamphrey, splitting his lip. Blood trickled from his mouth.

"You bitch!" Lamphrey kicked the white woman in the stomach several times until she fell onto the floor. "Now get up, both of you, get up! General, I'm so sorry. They have been very difficult and need to be watched closely."

The two women looked like they were used to getting hit and had no problem hitting back. They got off of the floor. Lamphrey pushed them next to the other two women. The four of them were in a line for inspection.

"Okay. Please turn around so that the General can get a good look at you," Lamphrey said.

"You and you," Andreas said to the white woman and the black woman. "What are your names? How old are you?" He would have guessed them both for being over forty years old.

"I'm Billie and this is Sophie," said the black woman. "I'm twenty-eight and Sophie just turned thirty-one." Her beady, black eyes scanned every square inch of the entry and office area of the headquarter warehouse. Lamphrey was right. These two women were clearly survivors and would need to be watched. The other two women were still crying. They would require much less maintenance.

"All right then. Gentlemen, take off their gags. No one will hear them scream. Please feed these women, make sure they shower, get them some clean scrubs, and watch them while they sleep. We will have the doctors look them over tomorrow. And one more thing, don't even think of touching them!" Andreas bellowed.

Bolantano, Redding, and Lamphrey led the four women down the long hallway to the showers. All three of his men wore apathetic expressions.

Voltaire popped into the general's head. *"Those who can make you believe absurdities, can make you commit atrocities."*

It was well past midnight. The general drove out to his trailer, smoked his last cigarette of the day, and slept like a baby, looking forward to the excitement of tomorrow.

# Chapter Sixteen

I was surprised, no, actually shocked by the red carpet treatment provided by my very new friend, Jay McCallister. The fancy car and driver, shopping, and high-powered lunch with other celebrities forced me to pinch myself throughout the day to make sure that this was all real. I was sitting in a private booth in the back room of George's Crab Shack with four of the most interesting people on the planet.

In the corner, closest to the wood paneled wall, was Paula Lynquist, a paranormal expert who wrote books, guested on paranormal reality TV shows, and hosted a syndicated radio show. Until today, I never listened to her show or watched anything paranormal, but I knew who she was. And if I knew who she was, then she was really famous. When Jay mentioned her name before lunch, my jaw dropped. I had a "you know her" expression on my face. With exception to myself, she had to be the youngest at the table. I would have guessed her to be somewhere in her late twenties to early thirties. She was a tall, black, large boned woman dressed in a colorful blouse and skirt. She was so beautiful, like a woman in a painting.

On Paula's right was Glenn Lucasek, a writer and host of the hit TV show *Alien Theories*. Glenn owned my favorite magazine, *Constellations*. He and Jay founded the T.A.H. Institute. He was the leading expert on anything and everything that had to do with aliens. I recognized him immediately. He was somewhere within Jay's age bracket, pasty and wrinkled without makeup, and twinkling blue eyes. He had thinning gray hair and thick jowls. He looked like someone's grandfather in a checkered shirt and green cardigan. I was very familiar with Glenn Lucasek and had been a huge fan of his show for years.

On Glenn's right sat Mercedes Garcia, a famous sitcom actress who was more famous for her tell-all book about the inner workings of the Creationology religion. I saw reruns of her big hit TV show that ran for years, ending a decade ago. With long black hair, large dark eyes, and milky white skin, she looked part Spanish and part white. Television didn't do her the justice she deserved. She was one of the most stunning women I'd ever seen. She had to be pushing fifty years old, but looked to be somewhere in her thirties. I couldn't help but wonder if she had some work done. She wore plenty of makeup and a classy beige blouse, jeans, and boots. I wasn't familiar with designer clothes, but the casual outfit looked expensive.

And then there was Jay, a man who needed no introduction. There I was, some dingy book clerk about to break bread with these giants. How did I get here? Or more importantly, how do I stay here?

I sat next to Paula and Jay sat next to me at the large, private round table. A pitcher of iced tea with lemon was placed in the middle. We were the last two people of the group of five and I wondered if we were late.

"Well, well, well. This is something new. We're on time and all of you are early. Maya, you seem to bring out the best in my old and dear friends. Please let me introduce you to..."

"Jay, I already know who all three of your friends are. Talk about intimidating, I'm sitting at a table of greatness. This could very well be the greatest day of my life," I said.

"Actually Maya, I am one of your biggest fans. Loved your book and if you have the time this week, I would love to have you on my radio show," said Paula.

"I'd be honored, but I thought you were more focused on spirituality, spirits, you know, paranormal happenings," I said.

"It's all related. I'll fill you in later. For now, I'm going to blow off my diet and order some crab cakes and clam chowder in a bread bowl."

I looked at the menu. Everything sounded delicious. Jay recommended the prawns so I thought I'd try them. While we waited for our food, Jay whispered to me about Melvin.

"Do you want to share your medium Las Vegas encounter?"

"Sure, but you do the talking," I whispered back.

"Paula, here's a story right up your alley and the perfect topic for your show. Maya was curious about her mother who is presumed to be dead. She went to medium last night." Jay recited my Marvelous Melvin story in such a way that made it sound even more interesting and mysterious. The table grew silent as we all hung onto each word.

When Jay was finished, I had nothing to add. Paula was the first to comment. Her dark eyes brightened. "This happens to be my area of expertise. So this Melvin guy gave you back your money and appeared frightened, claiming that you are motherless...hmmm.... It's technically possible not to have a mother. You're only twenty-one?"

"Twenty-two," I answered. I watched everyone's facial expressions. "Okay, you all can't bluff. None of you would win a cent in Vegas. You want to tell me what is going on? So Melvin was not out of his mind? Please. My childhood couldn't have been more painful. Nothing that you could tell me could make me feel any worse. Just spill it."

"Maya, I know we hardly know you. But what Melvin was afraid of is the same thing that most of us mediums are afraid of. Sometimes the spirits, well, they don't want to communicate with you," Paula said.

"My mother dumped me off at an orphanage so I already know that she didn't want to communicate with me," Maya said.

"How do you know that the person who dumped you off was your mother?" Paula asked. "I guess what we are all trying to say is this—your mother might have been dead well before you were born."

"How is that? Do you mean I could be a test tube baby? Someone's egg and someone's sperm mixed into a tube? And the person who owns the egg died before I was conceived?" I asked. I was surprisingly calm as they were trying to tell me that I was the result of two anonymous parents.

"The way Melvin reacted, well, maybe your mother did not donate her eggs to science. You might be part of…" Paula mumbled.

"An experiment," I interrupted, "that two people did not consent to?"

"Jay has a similar story," Glenn added. "You are not alone in all of this. Something bigger than ourselves, bigger than this world is taking place. We are just tiny pieces to a gigantic puzzle."

"Glenn, I watch your show every week. I am well aware how you feel. Everything is somehow part of an alien conspiracy. Not sure if I buy into all of it, but your show is so entertaining. I just love it. What you're inferring is, well, purely science fiction. But then again, why am I not surprised based on all of your backgrounds. Do you know how crazy this sounds? You are telling me this based on the rantings of a dime store Vegas medium?" I asked.

"Are we offending you?" asked Mercedes in a motherly way. "We can be a little intense sometimes, and even a little out of line." She shot Jay a dirty look.

"No, I'm not offended in the least," I said. But the lunch kept getting weirder and weirder.

"To throw in another variable to this line of thinking, maybe you have three or four or more parents? With genetic modification, why not?" said Mercedes. "You think that a multi-parent study is a new discovery? Think again. It's been around for decades. Everything that seems new is not new. The elite have known about scientific possibilities for a long time. The discoveries are in fact not discoveries. Just humans taking credit for what the aliens help them with."

The waitress came to the table with platters of food. We all dug into our meals. After a few bites of my fisherman's platter, I was the first to speak. "All right. First, let me say that you all have a truly original way of welcoming me into your little circle. It's like this, 'Great Vegas medium story. You must be created in a lab by aliens. And by the way, you probably have three or more parents.' C'mon, you're scaring the shit out of me."

Everyone laughed like I was the hottest comedienne on HBO. I also laughed. The ice was officially broken and I knew then that I was with my own kind—no walls, no bullshit.

"If you think we're weird now, just wait until the end of the week," said Glenn who laughed between words. "And Maya, I think you fit in with this crazy group perfectly."

"Bear with me. Maya, my interest in you began when I saw that necklace. I too had a rough childhood. Like you, I started off in an orphanage. But I got lucky, at least temporarily. I was adopted by two wonderful people when I was ten. A few years later right before I turned sixteen, I lost my parents in an auto accident. Again, I was alone. At least I wasn't poor. They left me enough money to take of myself for a while. I wasn't old enough to live alone, but cash seemed to get people to stop asking questions. I graduated early. Went to college and dropped out. Before my parents, I lived in a Catholic orphanage. The nuns were decent people. My mother or whoever it was who left me there, was just outside of Los Angeles. She left me with a yellowish-greenish stone necklace. When I was ten, shortly after my adoption, I thought I'd open up the rock, you know, curious kid, that kind of thing. First I pried off of the setting and then, with a chisel and mallet, I split the rock into two pieces."

"Why?" I asked.

"Sometimes the necklace glowed a yellowish color." Jay jammed some of his baked potato in his mouth and paused.

I nearly dropped my fork on the floor. My heart skipped. My rock had also turned yellow for no apparent reason.

Jay continued on. "And sometimes the rock felt hot. Something odd about it. Anyway, after I smashed it in two, the pieces levitated in the air and bonded as if they never were split. I was terrified. My family took me to Venice Beach the next day and I nonchalantly threw it into the ocean," Jay said. "I have seen moldavite and that stone definitely looked like moldavite, but it was different, almost as if it was alive. I think your stone is just like mine. It's probably what scared poor Melvin during your séance."

"So you think the stones, the orphanages, all of it is not a coincidence? Something quite nefarious is going on and the necklaces are a clue?" I asked.

"Well, yes. That's the million dollar question. Okay, here it is. I have this theory. You see, I believe that I was modified or enhanced with an Advanced Being's DNA. I think you were too. But I'm not sure why," Jay said.

"Maya, I can see by the look on your face that you've fallen down the rabbit hole and you want out. It's a lot of information to process and personally I think Jay is doing a shitty job. But hear him out, hear all of us out. Jay didn't write most of his books. He recorded them. It's called automatic writing. Kind of like a spirit or some kind of intellectual energy takes over and inspires you to write," Mercedes said. "Paula has had many shows about it."

"That's how I know Paula. I was listening to one of her shows a few years back and it suddenly hit me. All these years I couldn't tell you how or where I got my ideas. All I would do is sit down in a very relaxed manner and the urge to write would be so strong. Once the pen touched the paper I couldn't stop. After reading your book, I suspect that is how you write," Jay added.

"So how do the stones fit in?" I asked.

Mercedes gave me a warm, protective look and then said, "Well, we don't really know. But you and Jay are not alone. Glenn has interviewed at least a dozen others who came out of orphanages with that same green stone. Glenn ran a show about this mysterious green stone insinuating it must have held extraterrestrial powers. The show aired one time. Out of all Glenn's shows, this show is the only one that won't be repeated. I saw that show and so did Jay. You see, I don't have a stone, but my sister did. I don't know what happened to it."

My head was spinning. Here I thought my necklace was so unique. It was as common as dirt among this crew. "And?"

Mercedes finished her last bite of food. "Well, my sister ran away many years ago. She was sixteen and I was thirteen. A few years later she called me and told me she joined a church. She joined Creationology and she begged me to join which I did and now regret. She later told me that she ran away because she found out that she was adopted. And she found out from snooping around my parent's files. At first I didn't believe her, but my parents admitted it. They gave her a necklace that was left with her at an orphanage when she was a baby."

I pushed my plate to the side of the table. "Mercedes, let me guess, the necklace was a yellow and green color."

"You got it, Maya. I was angry about how they treated her and broke off all ties from them. My sister and I pledged our lives to this church. She became a very successful business woman and I became a very famous actress. Most of our earnings we gave to the church, but they wanted more. They wanted my sister's rock necklace. She refused to give it to them, explaining that was all she had from her natural parents. She tried so many times over the years to locate them and always a dead end. Anyway, she came to me one night, very scared. Saying awful things about the church. She said she was going to quit. I never saw her again. She supposedly hung herself the next day, but I don't believe that. Also, her rock necklace was gone—not in her home, car, office, nowhere. I was furious. A year later I even wrote a book. I've had several death threats and had to hire a bodyguard. I don't have one anymore, but still have home security."

"Security? You and Jay have private security?" I asked.

"Actually we all do," said Paula. "So we are not just delusional, but paranoid as well." She laughed and then winked at me. "We all have our reputations to uphold—complete wackos. But we just wanted to share. You can believe us or not, but we still want to be your friend. I don't have any necklace or alien stories, just a keen interest in anything outside of the proverbial mainstream box. But this is a really heavy conversation. Maybe we could talk about something lighter when you guest on my show. Yes, something lighter like Marvelous Melvin flipping out in Las Vegas."

I laughed. Yes, these wackos were my kind of peeps. After the empty plates were whisked away, we talked for hours. Jay and I stuck with club soda, but his friends shared wine. No one had any filters. Conversation turned away from rocks and towards religion, history, and of course aliens. I saw Eric through them—kind, smart, open-minded, semi-crazy, and curious. I suddenly wished he was with me to share this moment. Claude would probably be looking at his watch, itching to leave. Then I felt guilty. Maybe I wasn't being fair to Claude. Maybe he wasn't the scoundrel I imagined. At this moment, I pushed him out of mind. Yes, this was a merry band of weirdos and I was so happy to be part of it.

We said our farewells and Jay invited everyone to his home Friday night for dinner and a séance. My new friends were determined to contact one of my family members.

Evening had just begun, but the fall months shaved hours off of the days. The black night contrasted with the city lights, making me think of Christmas. Jay's driver drove us across the Golden Gate Bridge. The lights shimmered against the water, giving it a blurry mirrored effect. The full moon cast even more light. The city looked both magical and mysterious. I looked back from the bay with awe and smiled at Jay. He nodded.

"You hungry? My staff prepared all kinds of snacks. We didn't know what you liked so we made a huge variety," Jay said.

I liked how Jay referred to his staff as "we", as if they were all one unit, one team. He must have cared about them like family. "As far as food goes, I haven't yet found something that I didn't want to eat! And since you all went through so much trouble, how could I not sample it all. Plus I am on vacation and calories don't count."

We rode in silence for several minutes once across the bridge. Oddly, it was a comfortable silence that only happens among family or long-time friends. The driver pulled onto a street with several opulent mansions set back from the road on manicured lots full of mature landscaping.

Although it was dark, they were well lit. Through the trees I could see the water which I assumed to be the bay. The car continued to drive on a steep incline, turning off on the top or level part of a bluff.

"Jay, what town do you live in?" I asked. I felt strange asking him a question that I should have known the answer to.

"I live in Tiburon. I'm on the opposite side of the bay. I can't wait to show you the views. I'm very proud of my home. It's my sanctuary."

The driver turned into a cobblestone driveway surrounded by a tall stone fence with ivy sweeping over it. Over the driveway was an enormous trellis that connected the stone wall that was separated at the driveway. Bright fuchsia bougainvillea thickly weaved around the trellis. A black iron gate blocked our path. Next to the gate was a guard house. Jay waved and the gates opened.

The house that sat far back from the gate looked like something out of a story book. The gigantic home was made out of limestone, gray and white stone that matched the wall in front of the house, and patched with dark gray brick done in a European castle style. Green copper turrets extended from a slate roof. There was a balcony above the limestone portico. The house must have been three levels.

Despite its lavish façade, there was something humble about it. The wooden shutters, simple wooden door, and traditional three-tiered fountain that centered the front of the house toned down the grandeur. The fleet of old Toyotas, Fords, and Hondas haphazardly parked around the circular driveway also eased the pretension of the building. Among the fleet of regular cars was a rusty, old Ford pick-up.

Jay saw me staring at the cars and smiled. "That red truck over there, that's mine. See why I rented him and the car? Didn't want to scare you off by picking you up in my rust bucket."

I laughed. The driver parked and opened our doors. He then placed our shopping bags and my luggage at the front door. Within seconds a heavy-set middle-aged Hispanic woman brought them inside.

I continued to soak in the scene. The landscaping was elegant, but not nearly as opulent as the house. There were flower beds all over, each with purple flowers and green foliage. The house emanated simplicity and tranquility.

"This mansion is amazing. Doesn't go with your truck," I said.

"No, but then I don't want anything with GPS or any of that tracking shit. Speaking of mansions, I heard you got yourself a beauty back in Vegas."

"Ah, yes I do, but nothing like this. And if I don't write another best seller soon, the house will belong to the bank and I'll be back at my old, tiny apartment."

Jay looked at me and nodded. "You will write another best seller and it will make more money than all of my work put together. But the money is not why you or I do it. I'll admit money is one hell of a perk. This is the only house that I own. I bought it years ago, after my fourth and final divorce. First time I lived anywhere outside of Los Angeles. It represents a new life for me. Come, let me show you why I bought the property. You've got to see the back."

Jay paid the driver and led me along the side of the house. We followed a cobblestone walking path that matched the driveway. Once in back of the house I looked out from the patio beyond the pool and one of the guesthouses. I could see San Francisco lit up in all its glory and part of the bridge. "Wow. I never want to leave."

# Chapter Seventeen

Doctor Karl Jaeger was in a state of bliss since coming to America. From what could have been the end to his work and his life, turned into the beginning of a new world, a new order, and a new race. Hans Schmidt and Frederik Richtor, their new names per General Andreas, were found with ease which was not surprising to Karl. The United States had outstanding Intelligence and global connections.

Schmidt settled in a small town close to the southern tip of Argentina whereas Richtor had made a home in the middle of the country. Both men were in their forties like Karl Jaeger. Schmidt had a wife and three children back in Germany. They all assumed him to be dead. Although he missed them, they were better off without him. His children would have to wear the stigma of having a Nazi doctor for a father. If only they knew he was working for the United States.

Richtor did not have a wife or children, but supported his mother. Like Schmidt, he thought it best not to contact her again. He was too afraid to even inquire about her to friends of friends. He hoped to ask General Andreas about her in the very near future.

Jaeger had once had a wife, but she lied to him. He found out that her mother was a Jew. Part of him did not care, but Hitler's SS did. With permission of Nazi's highest ranking general, he volunteered his wife as a test subject for Doctor Josef Mengele's work on blue eyes. His allegiance was rewarded.

Jaeger was not exactly friends with the two Nazi doctors, but they were well aware of his research. During the war Adolf Hitler had assigned five doctors to assist him. Each doctor specialized in different fields of genetics. Only two of the doctors were left of his original team.

Back in Germany, Schmidt and Richtor were specialists in genetic research. Unlike Jaeger, they got away as the war came to an end. Maybe they should have been left alone. They both led separate, peaceful lives after the war and had plenty of money to live in luxury until death. But they were very capable, knew the research, and were desperately needed, causing Jaeger to have them hunted down by the United States.

Schmidt came to Washington D.C. first and then a few days later Richtor showed up. Both men had every right to be furious, and at first, they were. After a thorough line of questioning, both men were brought to Broom Lake. They accused Jaeger of being a traitor and threatened to kill him in his sleep.

Jaeger gave them a tour of the underground cage. They stared at the four open coffins for several minutes. Waves of shock and emotion swept over both of them and they cried. Their captivity no longer matter. These men were reconnected for the sole purpose of finishing what they had started so many years ago back in Germany. All three of them embraced, wishing that the other three men who were involved in alien genetics were there with them.

Jaeger and his two German doctors had everything they could ever want at their disposal—lab equipment not yet known to the public, an underground laboratory, the enclosure with an observation deck, and then four trapped Advanced Beings for them to study. The cage held cameras that allowed them observe while working in the lab. Whatever they wanted they got—the sky was the limit. In Germany, they were given time and basic equipment. Their work was a constant struggle.

Before his capture, Karl was shown by an AB many secrets of genetics. Someone or something lopped off its head and left it for Karl to find. He took the head and preserved it. The head later saved his life back in Dachau.

Before General Andreas found him in his laboratory, he and his team of doctors took the alien's knowledge and applied it to human test subjects, using Jewish prisoners during their early trials. Even though they were unsuccessful, they kept getting closer to discovering the secret to creation.

Gene modification and cloning human cells were science fiction to the unenlightened world. Jaeger knew it was more than possible. He and his colleagues had outlined a plan to create a human being and then alter his or her genetic makeup. Schmidt and Richtor each had their own specialties to the process. The only element missing was a woman.

Whatever Jaeger and his doctor friends needed, they got. Food and medical care, only hours away, pharmaceuticals and any medical equipment, a day's wait, human subjects, were on the way. Still, Jaeger had a hard time trusting General Andreas and his men. The general had too much warmth in his eyes which made him look weak. Jaeger wondered if the general could stomach some of the sacrifices that would have to be made.

The three German doctors did not plan to be residents of Broom Lake forever. They scoped out the base in hopes of a future escape. Every morning they were allowed to walk around the base. Soldiers were supposed to escort them during their walks, but sometimes there were none available. Security had gotten lax.

The doctors mapped out the base with the skill set of a cartographer. They recorded the schedules of every soldier on every hour of every day. Weeks of food and water supply were kept in hiding. They knew where the cars were parked and the keys were kept—it would be so easy. For now, they just wanted to finish their work.

One morning in late fall, Jaeger and his colleagues were awakened. The sun had yet to rise, not that they ever saw the sun in their underground bedrooms. But the clock read 5:18 AM. In their bunker stood Captain Michael Bolantano.

"Get up. We have a surprise for you. Christmas came early," said the young captain. He looked like a Greek god, tall, well-built, and dark. Jaeger guessed him to be somewhere in his mid-thirties, single, and Italian. Bolantano lived in the warehouse mainly used for the base's headquarters. The man had a reputation for being ambitious.

The three doctors jumped out of their beds and got dressed. The handsome captain led them into the laboratory. There stood General Andreas, Major Lamphrey, and four women of different races.

Jaeger looked at the women with predatory eyes and then watched his German counterparts do the same. Oddly, none of them had a hint of lust. All four women were somewhat attractive. Being underground with only men for several months should had made him think about sex, but nothing. Jaeger hadn't had sex with an actual woman for years. Every few months, he used his hand to relieve himself. This occasional release was all he needed. Sex had once been joyful during the early days of his marriage, but when he found out his wife was a Jew, the very act was more of a dirty trick. Besides, Karl's work was much more arousing than any woman could ever be.

The women wore handcuffs but were not gagged. The white woman swore profanities under her breath. *Looks like she will be going first*, thought Jaeger. Her disobedience did not go unnoticed. Major Lamphrey smacked her across the face and she stumbled. Of all of the General's men, Jaeger liked William Lamphrey best. He would have made a fine German soldier.

Jaeger gave Richtor and Schmidt a familiar look and then walked over to the cooler. The two doctors pushed the woman against the wall after Jaeger was finished loading up the syringe. There was enough tranquilizer to put down an elephant inside of that syringe let alone a hundred and ten pound woman. He stuck her in the arm.

"You mother fuck…," the white woman yelled and then went limp.

The three other women screamed in horror.

"Get them out of here. We don't need them yet. And watch them like hawks," Doctor Schmidt said in broken English.

Major Lamphrey and Captain Bolantano hustled the women out of the lab, but General Andreas didn't move. Jaeger pointed to a long lab table at the far side of the lab. Hans and Frederik sprayed it down with some kind of cleaner and lined it with several layers of sheets.

"Sorry, General. We did not know you would be delivering us the women so fast. I'm afraid we are a little unprepared. Let us clean up and we will proceed. Do you want to watch or participate in this operation?" asked Jaeger.

"I'll watch for now. But I might change my mind," said General Andreas.

"Then you will need to clean up. Go change into these." Jaeger went into an upper cabinet and handed General Andreas a set of green scrubs. "I think these will fit. Wash up and then put on a pair of these gloves."

All of the men changed into the scrubs and took turns at the sink. The general watched them and then copied their technique.

"Is this room sterile?" asked the general.

"It's sterile enough for us," said Schmidt. He then laughed.

"It doesn't matter. Listen, General, maybe this is too much for you to digest. We are going to take parts from this young woman that will be used for research. You can leave and we will all understand," said Jaeger.

"I want to see exactly what you are doing, Doctor. Are you taking these women apart? Taking what you can use, like an auto mechanic?" Andreas said.

Jaeger looked at his German friends. All of them smirked. "Your analogy is spot on. General, if you insist on observing, then be prepared to see blood. Please help us put her on the table."

The woman was passed out cold. Once sprawled on the metal table, she looked like a corpse inside of a morgue. Jaeger took a scalpel and cut into the woman's lower abdomen. Blood leaked all over the crisp white sheets and onto the floor.

Jaeger hooked up a sucking instrument and began to suck up all of the blood. A few minutes later everyone could see the internal organs. Jaeger began to cut away more skin until the full uterus was in view.

"General, we are taking out her uterus and ovaries." Jaeger instantly saw the general's face drain, making him glow like a ghost under the florescent lights. "Would you like to help? You can do the honors."

"No, I think I'll watch. But what will you use them for?" asked the general.

Jaeger carved around the woman's body until he found one of the ovaries. He cut it out and then held it up for Andreas to see. "Here is one of the ovaries. They contain the woman's eggs, which we need for reproduction. Would you care to cut out the second one?" The general shook his head and shot him a dirty look. Jaeger quit teasing. He dug into the woman's body again and cut out the second ovary.

"You need sperm, right?" asked Andreas.

"Yes. Would you like to donate? If not, one of us will," Jaeger said. Again, Andreas shook his head. "You are right. Sperm is needed and one of us will supply it. Our aliens might not produce the kind of sperm that we use. Perhaps they don't even produce sperm. At this point, humans and Advanced Beings may not be compatible. However, their genes are eighty-nine point nine percent like our genes. We want to make a baby with three parents—our friend on the table, a sperm donor, possibly me or you, General, and our Advanced Being. You don't need to have sex to make an embryo. All I need is an egg, some sperm, and a test tube and like magic, well almost like magic, I've got a zygote that will grow. Then I will cut out the preferred genes from one of the Advanced Beings and fuse it into the DNA strand of the zygote. The ends of genes are naturally sticky, making the process easier."

The general looked confused. "Slow down. Cut out genes? With a scalpel? Scissors? How? It's so tiny."

"I don't use a knife. I use enzymes. I'll show you how it's done." Doctor Jaeger cut away at the woman's skin and discarded unwanted parts in a nearby garbage bag. With Richtor's help, they pulled out the uterus and quickly stored it inside of a tub filled with solution.

All three of the doctors looked at the general. Andreas's white face resumed back to normal. Instead of throwing up, his eyes were bright with curiosity. Maybe the general had finally crossed over to the dark side.

"How will the baby grow without a mother?" asked the general.

"That's why we pulled out the uterus. We need cells from the lining to clone. Hans is almost finished making an artificial womb. It looks kind of like a big bowl with a transparent lid. Frederik has invented an artificial placenta. His gadget looks more like a couple of tubes attached to a filter and nutrient bag. He is anxious to try it out," answered Jaeger.

"I also have figured out a recipe for the amniotic fluid. The key trick is changing the water's chemicals during each trimester of the pregnancy. I need to extract some hormones and antibodies from one of our subjects once we are ready," said Richtor. He rarely talked to the Americans. Up until now, no one but Jaeger and Schmidt knew he spoke English. Jaeger wished he remained silent. It was an extra advantage that was now gone.

"Well, our operation is a success," Jaeger said.

"Are you going to sew up the girl?" asked the general. His tone of voice suggested that he regretted asking such a dumb question.

The three doctors laughed. "And what? Take her back home?" said Jaeger with sarcasm. "She is a liability to us all." He sliced into her jugular vein. More blood leaked out. "She's gone now. We need your men to remove her body. And we'll clean up the lab."

"These ABs, they taught you this?" asked Andreas. He seemed angry.

"Yes, they taught us lots of things," Jaeger said while he began cleaning up. He sensed the general was onto some of the lies that he had told and needed truth. "General, what you and the world does not understand is this: Hitler was not like the Romans or Alexander the Great or even like England when it came to world domination. He was in a class by himself. He knew the truth. He wanted more, a new world. And the only way he knew how to accomplish that was taking over, destroying everything and everyone, and then rebuilding. That's the final solution.

"Hitler saw the world like a big, old, dilapidated house that could be restored into a beautiful mansion. We were responsible for rebuilding the population on the entire planet. A new world can only be accomplished with new people. Specifically speaking, Hitler himself recruited us to dabble with gene splicing. At some point he stopped listening to the Advanced Beings and his leading intellectuals, preferring the vainglorious thoughts of mankind. He, like most powerful men throughout history, allowed hatred and emotion to cloud his judgment. Blue eyes and blonde hair do not make a master race, General. We make the master race."

"How do you know that these Advanced Beings haven't told someone else these secrets?" asked Andreas. "I know that the symbol on their sleeves is some kind of swastika. The symbol has been used since the dawn of civilization. Germany was not the first chosen to be blessed with this knowledge."

Jaeger was stunned. The general was doing his homework. "You're right, General. We are not the first, but I hope that we are the last."

# Chapter Eighteen

General Robert Andreas just witnessed three Nazis cut a woman open, rip out her ovaries and uterus, and then slit her throat. He calmly excused himself from the underground lab, while holding his breath as he went up the elevator. Alongside of the hangar where cars and trucks were parked, he vomited. He needed a break from the doctors. After heaving up coffee and water, he nervously searched his jacket for cigarettes. Only two Lucky Strikes were left inside of the pack. He took both cigarettes out and frantically chain-smoked them to calm his nerves.

As the sun came up, the temperature rose. Andreas hopped into the Jeep and drove to the nearest town for more cigarettes and a pint of whiskey. The twenty minute ride did him good, clearing his head from the bloodbath below the hangar. He was surprised by his reaction. The horrors of war had made him immune to human suffering. But this was different. He had a vague idea of what they were going to do to those women, yet somehow the talk of the plan didn't have the same impact as watching the hatchet job live. *With great advancements come great sacrifices*, he told himself over and over as if that would be enough to wash away the guilt.

Andreas bought a carton of Luckys and a pint of Jim Beam at the local general store. Before starting up the Jeep, he lit up a smoke. He had outside pressure from the new chairman, General Elroy Blanchard, of the newly formed Joint Chiefs of Staff. The man announced he would soon be at the base for a tour of the project.

Andreas barely knew the chairman. He had served as a general in the army, but was well aware of his cutthroat reputation. None of the brass were the least bit astonished to hear that Blanchard got the nod. Besides his ruthless military tactics, Blanchard had always been a kiss-ass.

Andreas used to dream about becoming one of the top advisors to the president. After getting control of Broom Lake, all that changed. He believed that his position was potentially the most powerful position in the world and had no plans for an upgrade in titles.

Blanchard was one of the few who knew most of what went on at Broom Lake. He was in charge of the army base closest to the crash outside of Roswell. He saw the ABs' carcasses as well as the smashed up spacecraft and the baby craft. Now, with his promotion clenched, he wanted a tour. The general wasn't used to outside interference until now. Blanchard had always been curious about Andreas's operation and now he had the clout and clearance to actually see it.

The chairman nicknamed the project Operation Chrome. The chrome was for chromosome. Blanchard thought of himself as clever, but Andreas resented the name. If anyone should name the operation, it should have been him. He remained silent as he did about everything. He was an old pilot who liked to fly under the radar and chose to live his life the same way. Blanchard could name his project anything he wanted as long as the funds remained unlimited. A time table for results did not exist.

Andreas knew how to put on a dog and pony show for the brass. He didn't rise this high within the armed forces because of his intellect and accomplishments. Schmooze put him on the short list. He could be the most charming jag on the planet when he had to. Of course it was a full blown act and anyone who really knew him knew that he was a quiet loner at heart.

Soon the general would be fifty years old, too old to continue the phony small talk and eagerness to please. But his practicality outweighed his pride. He would send

Lamphrey, Bolantano, or Redding, whoever he ran into first, to the grocery store to buy steaks, beer, gourmet coffee, all kinds of booze, cigars, and make this Blanchard's visit as pleasant as possible. He'd show the man the ABs, the German doctors, his new panel of scientists, the rubble from the spacecraft, and whatever else the chairman wanted to see. A day or two, maybe three, Blanchard would be satisfied and then leave. More pressing world problems would come up and interest would wane, or so Andreas hoped, and he could continue on with his project.

Twelve years ago, Andreas almost threw his career away. He had seen several 'unidentified objects' in the sky during flight. Some were round and shaped like saucers, some had wings, and some were a long cylinder shape, but all of them glowed an eerie yellowish-white light. After each sighting, he filed a report. Eight reports later, no one had followed up. He wasn't the only one who had seen the UFOs. Many pilots liked to talk about the strange objects in the sky. It was Bradley Vanderhigh, Andreas's best friend and co-pilot, who filed report number nine. Both men thought it best if Vanderhigh filed the report because Andreas's previous reports might have raised some eyebrows.

Report number nine differed from all of Andreas's previous reports. He and Vanderhigh flew off course for a better look at the bright beams of light they saw at a higher altitude. The craft looked like a huge, clay-colored disc hovering over the Southwestern skies. They slowed down the plane for a better look. Sensing their presence, the UFO shone laser beams at their dash and then proceeded to fly into them. With some amazing reflexes, Andreas dove under the craft and flew back to their base.

Like Andreas's reports, Vanderhigh's one report was not investigated. Vanderhigh raised hell with his superiors. One year later, he was shot down on during a mission over Germany.

At first, Andreas bought the Air Force's narrative, but years later he wondered if Vanderhigh's death was not an accident. He had seen a few more UFOs in the sky since the war, but kept it all to himself. The Air Force along with the world were ready for the truth.

By the end of the war, Andreas moved up the chain of command with the speed of lightning. Through life's irony, he oversaw the extraterrestrial findings at Roswell. He was one of the most potentially powerful men in the world.

But there were casualties during his rise. His marriage slipped away and he no longer talked to his daughters who were now adults in their early twenties. For all Andreas knew, they might have their own children. He wasn't around to play grandpa. His wife would be forty-eight years old in December. He wondered if she met anyone who treated her like the queen that she was. She left him the minute he came back from the war after finding out about a girlfriend he kept tucked away in England. Andreas was good even great at so many things, but relationships were not one of his talents. He did have a guilty conscience. Once a month, he sent his ex-wife half of his paycheck.

Andreas parked the Jeep and then walked inside the biggest hangar on the base located above the doctor's laboratory. The hangar easily housed ten planes, but Andreas had his airmen move the Beechcraft, Boeing, and Douglas aircraft to the other hangars on the base. This hangar was essentially used to store, organize, and study the spacecraft found at Roswell.

Andreas wasn't sure when General Blanchard would visit, but it would be sometime early the following week. The spacecraft came to Broom Lake in seemingly a million smashed up pieces. It took four military trucks to transport everything. The transport was constantly being postponed because of the strong magnetic fields the pieces gave off.

Four scientists and engineers were hired on to put together the space craft. Of the new hires, all had doctorates with impressive resumes. Doctor Kate Costello was the only woman of the small group. She received an Ivy League degree in physics specializing in magnetic fields and gravitational pull. She was probably the smartest of the group. Andreas worried if a woman on a military base would be asking for a headache. The female doctor was no spring chicken. The dates on her resume put her around forty-two years old.

Andreas noticed right away that she still was beautiful despite styling her long, dark hair in tight buns and never wearing makeup. She was thin, but chose to hide her figure beneath sloppy, loose clothes. Her hazel eyes were deep set with crow's feet around the corners. Within less than a week, she found a way to work with men by telling colorful jokes and constantly using swear words. Andreas made it clear from the first day of her hire that she would be treated with respect. Everyone was warned that their careers would be jeopardized if there were any problems.

The other three scientists were equally as impressive. Doctor Ira Kaplan was getting old, but at sixty-one he still dominated the field of electrical engineering. He was short, round, and gray. His hair and mustache were in need of a barber. He could have known the Nazis below. They were all from the same region. Kaplan left Germany a few months after Hitler became Chancellor and served his new country, the United States, in any capacity that he could.

The other two doctors, Doctor Benjamin Jansen and Doctor Herbert Spencer, were well known in aerospace engineering. Andreas hired them to put the spacecraft back together and repair the baby craft. The men worked at Lockheed and were somewhere in their early thirties. They were not related but frequently mistaken for brothers. Neither seemed very friendly.

The four scientists had clearance and ranking above any of the airmen on base, meaning they had authority to get their assistance at any time of the day. They immediately used four men to get them thick sheets of mu-metal, a metal made up of mostly nickel, and then built a maze of eight-foot high walls within the hangar.

Alike pieces of metal from the recovered space craft were methodically placed within these mu-metal-made cubicles. The mu-metal walls didn't fully block the magnetic field each piece of the craft gave off, but prevented the pieces from piling up into one gigantic heap of metal. This helped, but the magnetization problem was still not solved.

Within each makeshift mu-metal cubicle, the pieces clumped together into small heaps of metal. The scientists demagnetized each cubicle by using an instrument that would heat the metal fragments to Curie point. Each piece would then be pounded with a metal hammer. The magnetic charge would temporarily disappear for one full day, allowing them time to run tests.

Andreas walked through the metal maze for several minutes and finally found the four scientists in their own cubicle, studying some of the metal panels from Roswell. "Hello." They looked at him and nodded and then quickly looked back at the long table they had set up for experiments. He wasn't sure if they were being rude or just absorbed in their work. "I don't mean to disturb you. All of you are making tremendous progress. But if you have a moment, I need an update on your findings."

"Of course, General Andreas," said Doctor Kate Costello. She was the only one of the four scientists who had any social skills. "Well, as you can see, we have everything separated in a somewhat logical fashion. Right now we are trying to figure out this metal's properties. As you already know, we use alloyed aluminum for our aircraft. This is very different than aluminum. The magnetic problem is sort of under control. The coercivity of this metal is…"

"Whoa, stop right there. Sorry, I should know this, but what is coercivity?" asked Andreas.

Kaplan answered, "A resistance of a magnetic material to change its magnetism. This metal doesn't resist, but then it doesn't fully demagnetize either."

Doctor Jansen said, "We don't know that much about this material, but it has many of the characteristics of most metals. We believe that somewhere through this pile of rubbish, there must be some kind of power source. A battery, some kind of fuel, something that the smashed up metal panels are reacting to. As you can see, we have divided the pieces into partitions, forty-six partitions to be exact. You probably had to walk through at least fourteen of them to get back here."

"Yes, probably more. I got lost a few times," Andreas said. All four of the scientists laughed. "General Blanchard will be here early next week. He is very important to our project. We need to impress him to keep the funding coming. Tell him all about the magnetism issues. But if you find the power source, please do not share that information with anyone except me."

They all nodded and then looked at each other anxiously. Andreas was just about to walk away, but then crossed his arms and cocked his head.

Doctor Costello was the first to blink. "We think we found something," she said. The other scientists looked relieved. "We were just running some tests. Here." At the end of the table where Andreas originally found all four scientists hovered around was a sheet of paper on top of an object. Costello lifted the paper. There were shards of lime colored crystal rocks that changed into yellow. A few seconds later, the rocks were back to lime green.

"This was found over in cubicle four. We labeled each of the tiny rooms in the upper right corner. One begins on this side of the building. Four is right over there," said Doctor Jensen. That might have been the first time Andreas heard his voice.

Andreas walked through a few cubicles and found Cubicle Four. The scientists were behind him. Inside the partitioned room was a pile of smashed up alien metal panels, all slightly curved as if they were once soldered or screwed together. None of them were sticking together like most of the other pieces in the other cubicles. The doctors stood behind him and waited for his reaction.

"Why aren't these pieces sticking together?" he asked. "Were they just heated or hammered?"

"No. All of the pieces look the same, right?" asked Doctor Jansen. Andreas nodded. "Well, most of them are the same. We randomly picked one piece to study. It was the top piece on the pile of metal. We pried it off the pile, then heated it and then hammered it. In the middle of the piece there was some kind of pocket. Inside this metal pocket or compartment were crystal pieces. Kate had the crystal in her hand and ran back in the cubicle to get another piece. Not realizing she was holding the crystal, the whole pile came undone. The magnetic field was gone. We think this crystal acts like some kind of charge or even an energy source."

"General, take a piece of crystal inside of a different cubicle and see what happens," said Doctor Spencer. He handed Andreas a shard the size of his hand.

Andreas took the crystal and walked across over to the cubicle marked number seven. The four scientists followed him. There was a pile of metal that was clumped together in the middle of the makeshift room. The moment he was all the way inside of Cubicle Seven, the panels fell apart. "That's weird. I would expect them to be attracted directly to the crystal. But then I just fly planes, I don't build them."

Doctor Kaplan smiled. "General, you are much too modest. But your question is the very same question we are trying to figure out."

# Chapter Nineteen

I was given the grand tour of Jay's castle. It was enormous, at least three times bigger than my new Vegas mansion. I knew I'd get lost a few dozen times before getting the layout of the property. The interior of the house was as opulent as the exterior. For the most part, Jay stayed true to his Old World motif. Through all of the fancy antique furniture and artwork, an easy, lax style was still prevalent. The house was formal without feeling stuffy. Instead of crystal chandeliers, Jay had iron chandeliers hanging in every room. Puffy leather sectionals were placed in the living areas instead of heavily brocaded settees. The walls were either stone or paneled mahogany. Beautiful paintings and sculptures were scattered all over, yet the house did not feel like a museum.

One thing stood out—Jay's passion for technology. Each room had a large mounted television and video game console. Laptops sat on end tables, buffets, breakfronts, and counters in almost every room.

After the tour, Jay's maid prepared a feast of appetizers for us in the dining room. I sensed a bar food theme going as Maria brought out each platter of food. We pigged out on nachos, buffalo wings, egg rolls, quesadillas, and potato skins. I could feel my ass expand in the medieval looking chair, but continued to gorge myself silly.

Maria was warm and friendly. When we finally couldn't eat one more bite, she cleared the table and ate what was left in the kitchen.

"She could have eaten with us. Now I feel bad," I said.

Jay laughed. "Actually when I'm home, we all eat together, but since you're my guest she and everyone else thought they would act like my staff. But my staff is like my family. They and my friends are all that I have. Tomorrow I will tell her and whoever else is working to join us since you don't mind."

"Oh, of course not! Please don't change your routine because of me. What a great cook! I am stuffed." Although I never had a real home, I imagined this was what it felt like.

"It's been a very long day for you. Let me show you to your suite," Jay said. I followed him up the double staircase and then down a long hallway dimly lit with gas lanterns that hung on the wall. He led me through a double doored room where my bags sat on the small couch in front of the marble fireplace.

"Wow. I don't know what to say. The room is incredible—possibly one of the best rooms that I ever seen. It looks like Princess Diaries meets Game of Thrones," I said as I soaked in the canopy bed draped with velvet and the two story hand-painted dome ceiling of the night sky. "What constellations are they?" I asked as I pointed to the ceiling.

"That one up there is Orion's Belt. See the three stars in the middle? That's how the pyramids were laid out. The one next to it is called the constellation of Taurus. You can see Pleiades or the Seven Sisters in it. And that one there is Canis Major. The brightest star right over there is called Sirius or the Dog Star."

I was impressed. "Jay, you certainly know a lot about astronomy."

"You have no idea. Maybe later this week I will take you to the top of my house where my observatory is. I have one of the most private sophisticated telescopes in the world. You can see just about anything up there."

"Ever see a UFO?" I asked.

"Oh yeah. But that's a story for another day. That door over there leads to your bathroom and that desk has a brand new laptop on it. That's my gift to you. I hope that you can find some time to write your sequel."

"But, Jay, you already have been so generous. I can't."

"But I want to. I hope you like the laptop. It's an Alienware. If you like video games, it's one of the best laptops out there. It has Windows and works like all the other kinds of computers."

"I don't know what to say. It's like Christmas right now and you're Santa. I did start my new book. Something came over me and I was inspired. I brought the flash drive that I started working on," I said.

"Well then I won't disturb you. Good night and look forward to tomorrow."

Jay left and closed the double doors behind him. I went into my bathroom and almost screamed with glee. Everything in it was some kind of onyx or marble. Jay had the bathroom stocked with expensive soaps and shampoos. The towels were thick and fluffy. I filled the tub and took a long bath.

By the room's entry door was a small cart with a silver pot and teacup. There was a plate of homemade peanut butter and chocolate chip cookies still warm from the oven. The tea was hot and I poured myself a cup. The fireplace looked too inviting. I searched around the mantle and quickly found a switch. With my tea, cookies, and phone, I sat in one of the oversized winged-back chairs with my feet propped up on the matching ottoman and sighed. This had to be a dream.

I sipped my tea and stared at the fire. A surge of energy swept over me. I played with my phone and thought about Eric. I wished he was here with me on this wild adventure. I wanted to call and tell him about my wonderful day. The phone seemed to be egging me on. As I scrolled through my contact list, it vibrated. Claude's picture appeared on the phone screen. I answered.

"Hi, Babe. It's me. Just checking in with you, hoping your flight and hotel check-in went well," Claude said.

"Where are you?" I asked. "L.A.?"

"Ah, yeah. Miss you. So tell me more about San Francisco. Where are you staying? Where's your book signing? What show are you going to be on again?"

My head rushed with anger. He never asked me where I was or what I was doing. He also said that he booked me on *Left, Right, Center Show* when I already knew that Jay was the one who booked it. "All of that is written down on my itinerary and I'm just too tired to get up. You booked the show. Don't you remember?"

"Yeah, not offhand. But where are you staying?" he asked.

He had lied to me many times and now it was my turn. "Four Seasons."

"What room number? What street? I thought that I might fly up there and we can make a romantic getaway out of it," he said.

Part of me wanted to believe him, but my intuition told me he just wanted to check up on his golden goose. "I'm in Room 205 and it's on Main Street. Listen, I appreciate the romantic gesture, but I think that I am going to catch an early flight after the show and fly home. I'll see you in a few days. It's really not worth you coming all the way out here. I just want to get this done with and come home, take a few weeks off from promoting, and start writing my sequel. Listen, I'm really, really tired. I love you and goodnight."

"I love you too," Claude said and then hung up.

My urge to call Eric was gone. Life was too messy right now to get him involved. I wanted to escape. The shiny, new computer beckoned me over to the hand painted writing desk. After another cup of tea, I felt wide awake. I slipped the flash-drive into the computer. My fingers raced all over the keyboard as if I was on auto-pilot. The words just flowed onto the pages. A floating feeling came over me. I seemed to be watching myself from the painted ceiling of constellations. It was if I was someone else whose hands were on fire. I didn't know that I could type so fast. I watched myself work until two o'clock in the morning and then fell from the two-story ceiling into my body. One hundred and eighty-five pages on top of the thirty-four pages I had already typed. I was about one-third of the way through with my second novel.

# Chapter Twenty

Allie danced around the idea of murder, but that seed had been planted for some time. Maya's windfall success kept the seed from sprouting. If Claude held out a little longer, if Maya wrote another book or two, if her novel became a series, if the series became movies, if, if, if… Her wealth could easily become monumental wealth. In a divorce, Claude would lay claim. All he needed to do was wait. He had everything he wanted.

Tonight was one of the few nights that Allie wasn't at the apartment. She slept at her place on the other side of town that she shared with three other roommates. She had a lucrative modelling assignment and she needed to be at the beach by dawn. Her apartment was at least forty minutes closer. Claude was relieved she was gone. Their last conversation was about Maya. She was clearly jealous and started to push. She was like the female version of him, except not as bright and not as ruthless.

Allie assumed that Claude was wrapped around her little finger. With her incredible looks and bedroom talents, part of Claude was whipped. He wanted her around all of the time. But when push came to shove, Claude had always put Claude first in every relationship. Maybe it was because of his hopeless childhood that forced him to survive. Or maybe he was just like his sociopathic father. If Allie wanted to believe that he would kill Maya for her, then so be it. The idea turned her on. But the simple truth was he thought about murder since the first royalty check was cashed.

Although he was rich by most people's standards, that wouldn't last. He sensed that Maya was pulling away. First there was the fight about the condo and now, after calling her in San Francisco, she seemed distant. He imagined Maya was tired, but she had never been too tired to talk to him. She also shrugged off the idea of him joining her in the city. His looks and charm were not enough anymore. Even their sex life had waned. Maya didn't seem as enthusiastic as she once did. He wondered if she knew about Allie. She had to have been suspicious.

After talking to Maya, Claude couldn't sleep. He needed to be more attentive, more romantic. At three o'clock in the morning he jumped on the computer and found an online florist. He ordered several bouquets of a variety of flowers, complete with heart-shaped balloons and candy. *To the love of my life*, he typed in the text box that went with the order. It was time to enter the shipping address. Maya told him that she was staying at the Four Seasons on Main Street. He typed in "Four Seasons, San Francisco". The only one that showed up in the search was Market Street. Something wasn't right.

Claude looked up the phone number of the hotel and called. "Hello, I wanted to send flowers to my wife, Maya Smock. Can you confirm her as a guest? She said she was staying in Room 205," Claude said to the woman who answered the phone.

"Sir, I'm sorry, but we don't have a Maya Smock checked in nor do we have a Room 205."

Claude was speechless. He dropped the phone and stared at the wall for a few seconds. He heard the woman's muffled voice on the floor and then the dial tone. "Fuck!" He thrashed the phone at the wall. The iPhone smashed into countless pieces. His tantrum didn't stop there. Taking a bottle of men's cologne on his bedroom dresser, he threw it at the mirror. Shards of glass were all over the floor. The dresser reeked of Tom Ford Noir. "Fucking whore!"

Destroying anything and everything within sight was the only way Claude knew how to release anger. Flashes of his mother only added to the rage. He pictured her laughing and then saying, *Did you think a girl like that would stick with scum like you?*

An hour and several broken household items later, Claude poured himself a huge glass of vodka and sat on the couch. He was losing control. Maybe the seed needed to grow.

Claude thought about the how, when, and where. Allie was obviously on board and Sam would help out in any way that was needed. The most important part of his rough draft of a plan would have to be an accident. Claude remembered Maya telling him about her horrible childhood of orphanages and abusive foster parents. A staged suicide might work. If only he could hold on for another novel and another movie option. A third novel and a movie would be even better. But timing was everything. Even a whisper of divorce would put him behind bars, like mother, like son.

The first thing Claude needed to do was take off a couple of weeks from the agency. He was currently on Veronica Tatum's 'agents who walk on water' list, an ever-changing list to be on, and knew that she would grant him the time off. He quickly emailed her with some bullshit on how he was helping Maya with her sequel. Veronica ate that shit up.

Maya claimed to have a few signings and a TV show booking. That would be easy enough to check on. Once his nerves were calm, he jumped on the computer again. Her picture was on one of San Francisco's morning shows. She wasn't lying about that. He thought of going to San Francisco.

First, he checked the flights. But then he didn't like having a record of his whereabouts, plus he intended on following her without her knowing.

The sun hadn't come up, yet Claude called Sam. "Hey, I need a favor now. I need your car. Will explain later. You can have my Lexus."

Sam was too groggy to argue. A half an hour later, Claude was at his half-brother's door. Sam had new black Buick Enclave, a nice and roomy low key car that would go undetected. The car was purchased last month. Claude helped him out and gave him the cash. There was no way that Maya would recognize it.

The first stop after picking up Sam's car was the Apple store. Claude patiently waited in the parking lot until it opened and then quickly bought a new phone. By late morning he was on Interstate 5. The ride would take six or seven hours, depending on traffic. He'd be in the city well before Maya's TV interview.

As he drove, Claude rehashed his options. If Maya was sick of him, there was hope. But if Maya had a new man, he was fucked.

Claude pulled into the Bay area by dinner time. He booked a room at a Holiday Inn, which was within walking distance of the TV network that Maya was scheduled to guest on. He checked his phone for the ninetieth time. No texts or calls from Maya. And when he called her, he was dumped into her voicemail. Allie, on the other hand, left four texts and one phone message. Her texts started off with "great day at work, got another modeling gig", "what do you want for dinner?", "Where are you?", and then finally "I'm worried." And then there was the voicemail. "Claude, I haven't heard from you all day. Are you all right?" Funny how his wife was acting like a disinterested girlfriend and his girlfriend was acting like a nagging wife.

Once checked in the room, Claude thought of getting something to eat, but was too exhausted to order food. He wondered what Maya was doing.

Claude called the television network and found out that the morning show was taped at seven in the morning. He would be outside of the studio by 5:30, waiting. He wasn't sure of what he'd see. Maya claimed she had a couple of book signings later on. Claude seethed with jealousy. What did she need the whole week in San Francisco for? Did she have friends? Was she with that loser, Eric? Were they on a romantic getaway? Claude wanted to kill the skinny fucker from the moment that they met. It was obvious that the geek was in love with her. Was she in love with him?

Claude poured himself a few more drinks from the mini-bar and Googled San Francisco's most popular hotels. He called Omni, Donatello, Fairmont, Drisco, and the Argonaut. No Maya. Where could she be staying?

Claude lay in his king-sized bed in his junior suite and let his head spin. After several more drinks from the mini-bar, he began to relax. Eventually he fell asleep. A few hours later he woke revived, sober, and famished. The all night room service sent him up a burger. He showered, sent Allie a few texts about a last minute business trip, and then started walking. Ten minutes later, he was in front of the studio. There were front and back entrances. Claude chose to stake out the front.

He sat on a bench across the street from the studio, drank coffee, and waited. Almost an hour and a half later, a Bentley pulled in front of the building. The car's driver was dressed like a chauffeur. He got out of the car and opened the door. Out came Maya. She was dressed to the nines in a stylish gray wool suit and crisp white ruffled shirt. Claude guessed it had to be new. She had nothing that nice in her closet. The car, the clothes…his taste for the finer things was finally wearing off on her. She certainly looked gorgeous, like a million bucks.

Claude wanted to believe their marriage was as strong as it was on their wedding day. Maybe she wasn't lying. Maybe she just didn't know the hotel that she was staying at. She traveled all of the time.

Once Maya entered the building, Claude looked at his watch. She had forty minutes before the show would air live. He fiddled with his new iPhone and found the Internet link to the broadcast of the *Left, Right, Center Show*. Commercials were aired and then the show began. Maya was on a panel with other famous people, talking about politics. She was asked all kinds of questions about the news and then asked about aliens and conspiracy theories. Her panel was very smart. She surprisingly held her own. Claude had no idea how well versed she had gotten in current events. Her questions were answered with the kind of polish, confidence, and expertise that usually came from experience.

Who was this girl he met a year and a half ago in Las Vegas? Claude doubted his standing in their marriage even more. After all, what did she need him for? Her fame had multiplied exponentially as did her money. If she found out about what a shit he was, game over. The seed needed to grow. Ending everything on his terms was his only option.

Once the interview was finished, Claude expected her to exit the same way that she came into the studio. His blue eyes fixated on the entrance. The Bentley pulled up and waited. This time the chauffeur was not alone. There was a man who sat in the back seat. He wore round sunglasses and had his long, white hair pulled back into a ponytail. Claude nonchalantly snapped a picture once the street was cleared of cars. The man was at a distance and it was hard to see. Claude looked at the photo and zoomed in. He knew this man or at least knew who he was. Could Maya be having an affair?

Maya was young, pretty, and rich. Why she would cheat on him with an old geezer? The Bentley suggested some kind of sugar daddy set-up. Claude took another picture, this time of the back license plate. He had to leave his bench for the picture and hoped the driver and passenger did not notice.

Maya walked out of the building's revolving door. The old guy in the backseat hurriedly got out of the car and opened the door for her. Claude got an even better look at the man. He looked more like an old hippy than some rich tycoon. He wore khaki pants with a zillion pockets and a faded Hawaiian shirt. Claude had him pegged for some kind of creep who ran a crystal meth lab. Nonetheless, this rival had a face that was too familiar. Claude was sure he knew him from somewhere.

After the car drove off, Claude dialed Sam's number. "Hey, can you do me a favor?" No small talk. Straight to the point.

"Go ahead, but hurry. I got a showing in an hour. Shoot," Sam said.

"That's all the time it will take. I am going to text you a pic of a Bentley license plate. I need to know who the owner is or lease holder or whatever. Still friends with Officer Friendly?" Claude asked.

"More like Officer Expensive. He doubled his prices, but I gotcha. Let me track him down and I'll call you once I got some answers," Sam said. Click.

Claude had one more call to make. "Maya, you finally picked up. I was getting worried." Claude estimated they weren't too far from the television studio. "I saw your show. Saw it on the Internet. You were amazing. You have come so far in such a short amount of time. So impressed!"

"Thanks. And I did try to call, but the call didn't go through," Maya said.

"Yeah, ah, I had some phone problems. Just got a new one. But now it's working fine. You know, I love San Francisco. I got some time off from work and would love to join you for the rest of the week. This could be like a honeymoon. I know you're busy, but if…"

Maya interrupted him. "I got another interview on a syndicated radio show. Paula Lynquist. I think the show is called *The Sixth Sense*. It's live and syndicated. I'll get you more information. I've also picked up another signing. This week is really turning into a lot of opportunities. Not much time. I'm coming home in a few days, Saturday morning. Maybe we could spend next week somewhere. I'd love to go to an island, sit in the sun, and finish my book."

"Finish? Didn't you just start?" Claude asked.

"About three quarters through. I can't wait for you to read it. Listen, I gotta go. Love you." Click.

*Three quarters finished? What the hell?* Who was this old timer she was hanging out with? Claude walked down the block and found a café. He sat at the counter and ordered pancakes. The food was cold and he wasn't really hungry. He gulped down several cups of coffee and worried. The phone rang. Sam came up on the I.D.

"Hey, Officer Friendly asked about Mom. I told him she was good lay, but he said that he already knew that. I told him to visit her when he had a chance and he promised to bring her flowers." Both brothers laughed. "No problem. He ran the plates. CBJ Luxury Car Rental. He also called the rental agency and gave them some cop bullshit about this particular Bentley. The stupid ass girl who answered the phone told him the man who rented the car was Jay McCallister. Isn't he some rich author?"

# Chapter Twenty-One

I hung up the phone. Claude was oddly talkative and curious about my whereabouts. I felt guilty for cutting him short and leaving out the incredible friendships that I had made. Wasn't marriage supposed to be about sharing? The word sharing made me think of Eric and not Claude.

Jay's driver pulled to the curb of an amazing historic lavender and gray Victorian on top of a hill that overlooked the bay.

"Are you all right?" Jay asked. His green eyes held a grave expression as if he could read my mind. He probably was the best person in the world to talk about a disappointing marriage, having been divorced four times, but for the moment I wanted to keep my problems to myself.

"I'm fine," I said. "Fine as in freaked out, insecure, neurotic, and emotional."

Jay laughed. "One of my favorite acronyms. Maya, we all are fine, fucking fine."

"I need a break from Claude. Our marriage is...not exactly what I signed up for. His name gives me a queasy feeling in the pit of my stomach. The worst part of it is that, well, I don't think he loves me. But that's a novel in itself, one that I don't know the ending for. Right now, I am with you and we're sitting in front of a gorgeous dollhouse in the heart of San Francisco. I think I'll concentrate on the glass being half full today."

"Yes, the glass is half full, but it's a very *fine* glass that we all drink out of. You're not alone, Maya. We all got hurts. Let's forget our troubles and see Paula. She's standing on the porch waiting for us." Jay told the driver to take a long lunch as we got out of the Bentley.

Paula was a large woman, but looked tiny from the street as she stood on the immense wrap around porch. I remembered her striking face from a few days ago. She was one of the most beautiful women I had ever seen, even more beautiful than Jay's actress friend, Mercedes.

Paula wore her hair in a thousand braids swept up in a high bun perched on top of her head. Her deep brown skin was flawless. She didn't need makeup, yet artfully played up her high cheekbones with bronzer and accentuated her huge, dark eyes with lavender eye shadow. She wore a hundred strands of purple and white beads and stones around her long neck and wrists. Her shirt was denim and her long broom skirt was a tie-dyed composition of purple and white. Stunning and Unforgettable.

"Jay and Maya, my two favorite people," Paula said. She leaned in to give me hug. It was very awkward for me. I wasn't a touchy-feely kind of girl, but I appreciated her warmth. "Please come in. I cooked. A rarity, but I think everything is edible. Hope you like chicken noodle and homemade bread. Come."

Paula led us into her ornate two story foyer. Creamy white hand-carved molding was everywhere. The furniture fit the style of the home. I felt like I was time traveling into the 1800s. I followed Paula and Jay down the long hallway into the kitchen and sat down at the table. The kitchen was beyond charming. The décor stayed with the Victorian theme. Kitchen appliances were made to look old. Copper pots hung everywhere. Accents of hand-painted tiles of Wedgwood blue were used for the backsplash. Paula quickly placed two iced teas in front of us along with some wine cheese and crackers.

"The bread should be ready in a few minutes. Catch me up on your stay. I saw you this morning, wow! You sound like you've been doing this forever. My questions will be a little more ...,"

"Provocative? Personal? Strange?" interrupted Jay.

"Well, yes. I like to give my listeners something to listen to. My show is about provocative, personal, and strange happenings. It's about anything that is outside of the normal realm. And you, Jay, are way out of the normal realm. Maya, I can get very personal. And I don't like my shows scripted. If I get out of line, give me a signal. Even though this is radio, it's televised for the Internet. How about this?" Paula took her right hand and scratched her head. "Can you do that if you become uncomfortable?"

I nodded. The gesture seemed to be a reasonable way out of a tough question. Paula served us her soup and bread.

"Good. Hope you're not talked out from this morning. Jay will also be a guest, since he's here," Paula said and then winked in between bites of bread. "He's one of my listeners' favorite. The two of you can debate whether or not you believe in the extraterrestrials. You can also talk about life, religion, anything spiritual. If you want, you can include the story you told me a few days ago, the story about Marvelous Melvin. I want it to be off-the-cuff." We finished our lunch and Paula quickly cleared the table. "My brother Joel is upstairs in the attic, Tweeting, Googling, Instagramming, Snapchatting, and who knows what. Lord knows that I can't keep up with it. He's my producer, PR agent, assistant, secretary, you name it. He also lives here. It's just us two. I would have had him eat with us, but he's the busiest before the show."

Lunch was phenomenal. Before the last bite, Paula herded us out of our seats. We followed her up the first grand staircase and then down a long hallway to another staircase, less grand, more narrow with very steep steps. On the way up there was a landing with a window seat and built-in book shelves. I saw my novel sitting on the window seat. Paula grabbed it.

"Maya, I must have your autograph before you leave," she said as she led us up the final eight stairs. "Ah, finally here. Great workout."

Paula's studio was a fully finished attic with high ceilings and more intricate molding that fit the Victorian era. The furniture was a neutral gray velvet matching loveseat and sofa with an oversized leather tufted chair. The furniture was arranged around a large floral printed ottoman with gold rope fringe. The room was very girly and warm. Scented candles gave off a floral smell. The equipment was minimal, a couple of computers, speakers, microphones, and cameras were stationed around the room. A cordless phone with a zillion switches and a board sat on a desk in the corner.

"Joel, you know Jay. My other guest is Maya Smock," Paula said to Joel. The good-looking, young, black man looked up from the computer and waved. He had the same eyes and mouth as Paula. "He'll be more social after the show. Don't take it personally. Again, my show is taped for the Internet so you will be on camera. Do you want to freshen up?"

*Was that a question or a suggestion?* It didn't matter and I shook my head. I was still fixed-up from the morning show. There was already too much primping for the day. My hair still looked good from morning. I wore my new suit—the one I bought specially for the morning show, and new necklace. My mother's necklace, if indeed it really belonged to my mother, was left untouched in my carry-on bag.

"All right then. Jay, Maya, have a seat," Paula said. She took the oversized leather chair, I took the sofa, and Jay took the loveseat.

"In five," Joel said. He pressed some buttons and advertisements for car insurance, vitamins, and wrinkle cream played. "Go."

"It's Paula Lynquist on *The Sixth Sense*. I am so excited. I got Jay McCallister with me as promised."

I saw lots of buttons on the board that sat on Joel's desk light up.

"I see the callers are reserving their spots for questions. Don't worry, there will be plenty of time for that. But Jay is not my only guest. At the last minute, I talked an amazing new author to come on the air. Some of you already know her—Ms. Maya Smock. She's hit the literary world by storm with her new novel *The Master Race*." Paula continued to rattle off a very flattering review of my book and then showered Jay with compliments on his esteemed writing career. "Maya, your novel, *The Master Race,* is science fiction. I don't want to spoil anything, but the master race in your book is not from Germany. It's from another planet. We all know how Jay feels about aliens. What about you? Ever see an E.T. or a UFO?"

"No, but I believe that we are not alone in this universe," I said. So far, I hadn't had the need to scratch my head.

Now it was Jay's turn. "Paula, as you already know, not only do I believe that aliens are real, I believe that they created us through genetic modification and are breeding us to evolve into what they are now. I believe they time travel back and forth from the future to check up on us to make sure that we are progressing at a satisfying pace," he said.

"Maya, care to comment?" Paula asked.

"Well, I've heard the theory before. And Jay has influenced my writing more than anyone. I can't help but wonder where God fits into all of this. If Jay believes that aliens created us through genetic modification, then who created the aliens?" I asked, not sure why I was bringing up religion. I wasn't exactly a Bible thumper, but maybe the nuns from the orphanage had some kind of impact after all. I still did not use the hand signal.

Jay smiled at me and rolled his eyes. "God? C'mon. I guess you are still very young, so I won't hold that against you. God is, well, He's a nice bed time story, a neat and clean way to explain how we got here. But he's not tangible. I'll focus on what I know rather than an easy, simple explanation. Life is confusing enough."

"But the simplest explanation is most often correct, Occam's razor, I believe." I had no idea why I said that or even knew that. "As far as tangible, we have several writings left behind by God as well as a bunch of historical sites that are mentioned in the Bible. So God is tangible, at least part of Him is. What did the aliens leave behind? Where is their book?"

"Their book is imprinted inside of us, it's in our DNA. You want to get into history, they left behind dozens of clues, the Great Pyramids, Machu Picchu, Stonehenge, crop circles…"

"Maya?" Paula interrupted.

"Maybe you are right. Maybe there is no God. But you really don't know and neither do I. I'm not an expert. The ancient alien theory you seem to buy into just adds another level onto the age-old question of how we got here. No matter how many questions you want to tack on to it, we all had to start somewhere. There's got to be a Supreme Creator."

Paula looked at Joel and nodded. Joel wrote on his dry erase board the name Gary Brockaway, Chicago. He then pushed a couple of buttons and the speakers came alive.

"Hello there," said Paula, "Gary from Chicago. Thanks for listening. What questions do you have for our guests?"

"Hi, yeah, been listening to your God discussion and no offense, Jay, but Maya makes a great point. I've often wondered if aliens and angels are the same thing, just called different names by different cultures," Gary from Chicago said.

Jay and I looked at each other and he motioned for me to answer. "Hi, Gary from Chicago. I was there a few weeks ago in the NBC building. Great question and one that I had not given much thought to until now. Angels and winged beings are found in all kinds of tablets, holy books, and wall writings. I've only scratched the surface in learning about them. But from what I have read, it appears that angels come to Earth when they are ordered to come to Earth, ordered by God. I guess my point is this, someone, some Supreme Being or God is calling the shots here on Earth, in Heaven, wherever that may be, and the Universe for that matter," I said.

"Maya, I have read many of the ancient texts and writings, but not because I'm religious. To me, these writings were written by very primitive people who recorded what they saw. And not all angels who visited earth were told to visit earth. For example, in the book of Enoch we got a group of angels called The Watchers, or, as I believe, aliens, who came down to earth to visit Enoch. They took him up to the seven Heavens. Sounds more like an alien abduction to me. That's only the beginning of odd stories that sound more like E.T.s than divine beings."

Gary the caller interrupted Jay. "Thanks, Jay, but I have a hard time believing that we were so primitive that we couldn't tell the difference from divinity and another species from another world. Still love you and love the show." Click.

"What a great debate we are having. Gary, thanks for the call. Onto another topic—the writing process. I've known Jay for a while. Listeners, you know that Jay says that he blacks out, floats outside of his body like an out-of-body experience, and gets really hung up on certain word usage despite what his editors say. He has implied many times that he has some kind of inspiration, which he believes is an external force not from this world. Because he writes about aliens and science, he believes this force that he is channeling is almost like an alien muse. Now Maya, explain to our listeners what you undergo when writing."

*Out of body experience? Had two of them since I stayed with Jay.* My stomach dropped. *Was this man drugging me? The tea, the cookies, did they cause me to get in such a hypnotic state?* Distrust covered me like an old familiar blanket. I had my hand close to my head, ready to give Paula the sign. But I didn't.

"When I write, I, too, am very particular about certain words even when told it's bad writing. For example, my editor mentioned all of the adjectives that I overuse. Or some of my sentences are awkward and could be clearer if written another way or when I repeat something on the same page. Bad writing. But I refuse to change certain things. I'm not sure why, they just make more sense to me. As far as an out-of-body experience goes, Jay, what are you smoking? Are you drinking some kind spiked tea? Eating up some hash cookies?" I asked, secretly accusing him of drugging me. And he got the undertones. He shook his head and had that soft, caring look in his eyes. Maybe I jumped the gun. "Paula, to be honest, something really weird happens when I write. I've started my sequel and it's coming along even faster than the first novel. So yes, like Jay I feel as if there is a force using me to record parts of the story when I write."

"They are using us, Maya. Our work is meant for something much more than entertainment. And one day I hope to have figured it out," Jay said.

"Do you think that this force, whatever it may be, is using other people in the world for some kind of an agenda?" Paula asked.

"Yes, absolutely. Writers, scientists, politicians, the media, even you, Paula. They will use whoever they can to carry out their agenda," Jay answered. "Our world is not advancing fast enough for them, it's not turning into the world in which they need it to be in the future."

"So a real conspiracy is going on. Like New World Order with an alien twist. Could the aliens be the inner circle?" Paula asked.

I felt more like an embroiled listener than a guest at this point. Jay and Paula went into New World Order conspiracy theory, a theory that I only knew by name. They both were well versed on how this world will give up its borders, cultures, languages, wealth, and resources, only to become slaves to the inner circle. A few callers had questions about reptilian aliens who looked humans and how presidents and kings were all related. The discussion was becoming too unbelievable. I had nothing to contribute.

Jay finally wrapped it up, claiming he believed aliens were behind a one world government. "Paula, we've hashed this out before. Even though we disagree on some key points, we both know it's coming. These beings have some kind of time line that they don't want us to screw up. I don't have all of the answers yet, but you know that I'm working on it."

"Those two hours went by in the blink of an eye! Big thanks to Jay McCallister and Maya Smock. Great show!"

Jay, Paula, Joel and I hung out in the attic and chatted about the show. I told them all how stupid I felt when it came to many of the topics they spoke about and they all reassured me that I was terrific.

"Maya, don't worry. We'll brainwash you with our paranormal conspiracies in no time," Joel said. "This is a hard show to guest on. Paula and her listeners are quite the intellectuals. I also read your book and you're well on your way."

"Well, I got a lot to learn. Aliens and New World Order, wow, blew me away," I said.

"You're as smart as whip. Next time, you'll out debate all of us. I like what you said about God. I'm not positive that He exists, but have faith. No one can argue that evil exists. But I am positive that we go somewhere when we leave this earth," Paula said. "There are forces of good and evil. Something is out there, something or someone who can save us, save our soul. You and I got to bring Jay around."

"Here we go again—the attempt at conversion. I guess it's time to leave," Jay said. He texted his driver who arrived in less than five minutes. We rode mostly in silence on the way back to his home.

"I never drugged you. The tea is chamomile and cookies are homemade with food as the ingredients. I know that you don't know me very well and I know you had a rocky childhood, but I mean you no harm. This force that I talked about on Paula's show, I believe it's with me and also with you. We act as its receiver. Don't be afraid. Let them use you for now. I have a plan. You see, you and I are more than alike. We are family. I'm almost positive that we had the same mother or the same father."

I felt sorry for him. He was losing his mind, like a harmless old man on his way out. "Not sure how that is possible."

"We were part of seventy year old experiment," Jay said.

*** 

Jay's comments got weirder and weirder as the week wore on, but I strangely got used to his eccentric if not out and out bat shit crazy views on everything, not just our alien heritage. As crazy of a week that I had, it was also magical.

I miraculously finished my sequel or at least had a very rough draft to clean up once home back in Las Vegas.

I wasn't quite sure how the story went, but there were four hundred pages inside my new Alienware computer. My "brother" Jay might have been cuckoo, but he was also kind, generous, intelligent, and fun. He, his friends, and even his staff had become like family.

The last time I felt this much at ease was at Eric's parents' house during the holidays. I suddenly missed Eric. I thought of him more and more. One thing was certain. Once home in Vegas, I would edit my manuscript and then ask Eric to read it, just like he read the first book. I needed his input. I needed him. During my last breakfast with Jay before I flew back home, he caught me smiling at my Eggs Benedict.

"You look goofy, like a woman in love. Do you miss Claude?" asked Jay. He had a dour look on his face when he asked, the same look he always had when talking about Claude.

"No, not Claude. You don't like Claude, do you?" I asked and he shook his head. "I love my old boss at the book store I used to work at. We were always friends. He is the one who encouraged me to become a writer. He took me in without wanting anything in return. In a way, he is my savior. One problem. He never made the move and I got sick of waiting. Claude was just a gorgeous man who I met at a writer's conference in Vegas. In fact, it was the same conference where I first met you. He's kind of like a trophy husband. I think I fell in love with him because he is the kind of guy who dates supermodels. You know, someone completely out of my league-gorgeous, cool, charming, and charismatic. I will say this—he is really, really great at publicity and promotion. I will give him credit where credit is due. He put me on the best sellers' list."

"Yeah, I'm sure that's what he wants you to think. Listen, I don't know Claude, but I've seen him before. He's been around the biz for some time. He's a Los Angeles boy. That's where I'm from, where I got my start. He's obviously a lot younger, but we do hang in similar circles. You know, six degrees or some shit like that," Jay said.

"So why don't you like him?" I asked. Jay's green eyes darkened. "Please, at this point, nothing would shock me. Like I said, I think he is using me."

"Then there is nothing left to say," Jay said. "Of my four wives, I think all four of them used me. Don't feel sorry for yourself. This Eric fellow sounds like the real deal."

"Don't change the subject. Spill it. I'm your sister, remember? C'mon, you bared your soul to me with all of your wild conspiracy theories of the world, of the universe, and now you're holding back on this?"

Jay laughed nervously. At this point I knew him well enough to tell he was omitting something. "Well, to be honest, I made some calls about Claude. Like I said, he and I live within the same circles. He's from a family of grifters, jail birds, and who knows what. He's clean, though. He has a little brother who did some time and his mother also has done time, and is currently doing time right now. He could be dangerous. Be careful, that's all."

*Sam*, I thought. I needed a lawyer and needed to review all of the papers I had signed. "Thank you. I had my suspicions. So you were checking up on me?" Maybe I should have been pissed, but instead I was moved. I fought back the tears. Jay had become my protector. Eric also warned me long ago.

"Maya, take it from an expert like me, divorce is messy. He'll want at least half of everything if not more. He'll want half of your sequel royalties and any other income the two books might generate—movies, a third book, who knows. He'll probably claim that if it were not for him, you'd still be working at the book store. Listen, my first two lawyers were terrible. It's amazing I'm not living under a bridge. But my third lawyer was decent. You actually know him. It's Glenn."

"Glenn Lucasek? But I thought he just did..."

"The TV show? He started off as a lawyer, still is a lawyer, just my lawyer. I guess Mercedes also used him and was satisfied with the work that he had done. Maybe I'm overstepping. I'm sure Vegas has some outstanding lawyers or maybe even marriage counselors."

I hugged him right there, in the middle of breakfast. "Give me his number before I leave. And thanks for having my back."

"Promise me this—you'll come here for Christmas. You can bring your savior," Jay said. "Love to meet him."

"You celebrate? I thought that you were not religious?" He rolled his eyes. "Of course I'll be here with or without Eric, with or without my husband. You know that I think you're crazy and that I am not your sister, but now that I know you, you are family. You told me a few weeks ago that we'd be friends and you're right—we are friends, and I hope we are friends forever."

Jay looked moved this time. His green eyes lightened. We finished breakfast and spent the rest of the day lying by the pool. I began the tedious task of editing the first draft of my sequel.

This was my last day at Jay's castle by the bay until Christmas. He spoiled me every moment of my stay—the Bentley, the house, the staff constantly waiting on me, the view, the trips to the city—shopping, dinners, comedy club, a musical, his friends, and of course Jay—kind, quirky, and real. This was the best vacation I ever had.

My life was a mess. Claude needed to go, no matter how much money it cost. Tonight would be spent with Jay and his friends. He was throwing one last dinner party in my honor before my Saturday morning flight. Jay agreed to let Paula finish where Marvelous Melvin left off.

Evening came on quickly and Jay's friends whom I also considered my friends came by. Maria, Jay's cook, prepared another delicious meal of Frito pie and Spanish rice which we all scarfed down, leaving the pie pans and rice bowls empty. I hoped Maria made extra for herself and the staff.

Jay's friends, the same friends that I initially met on the wharf, were filled with questions about my stay in San Francisco. Paula and Mercedes looked exquisite. Both women had a flair for fashion—Paula in a long red blouse dripping with bright, chunky jewelry, and Mercedes in simple, classic black pants and a royal blue silk blouse. I felt so unsophisticated and homely next to these two stunners, but that was my fault and my insecurity, not theirs. I thought that I might attempt to be more stylish and attractive in the future.

Glenn Lucasek looked very ordinary. Like me, he wore plain clothes and had a no-fuss look about him which was different from his TV show. His voice was deep and velvety, like on his show. I looked at him with a different lens. Could he get me out of my marriage? Would he be my divorce lawyer? I planned on asking him once we were alone.

After dinner Jay insisted on continuing the party on his roof. He led us up the stairs and then up another flight of stairs hidden behind white molding panel. This was the first time I had been on the roof. He had it decked out like a patio with furniture, fireplace, outdoor kitchen, and bar. It was our little roof top party. The view of the bay was even more spectacular than it was from the backyard. On one side of the rooftop was one of the copper turrets that gave the house a castle feel. The turret wasn't only there for aesthetics. It was cleverly used to hide Jay's observatory.

"My pride and joy. I worked with an architect and an astronomer to get this right. I wanted it to blend in with the look of the house yet also be on the cutting edge of astronomy. Maya, I was holding out on you, saving the best part of the house for last. Come inside. Everyone else has already seen it," Jay said.

I walked towards the turret. A panel flap had moved to the side, allowing a narrow entrance into the dome-like structure. Jay pressed a few buttons off of some kind of handheld device and opened up the panels that were located on the top of the turret, allowing us to see the night sky. Inside the dome were several telescopes on stands. In the center must have been the most expensive of the collection. It was massive—with a scope at least five foot in diameter held in place by a metal stand with an attached leather seat.

"Don't know a thing about astronomy, but all of this looks like it cost a fortune," I said.

"Actually it cost more than a fortune—a whole 'lotta dough for some lenses and mirrors and worth every penny. I keep on trading in old telescopes for newer and better ones. My observatory rivals most planetariums in the area. My gardener gets up here and trims back all of the trees so that I don't have any obstructions. On a clear night I can Jupiter, Venus, Saturn, hell, most of the constellations, asteroids, solar eclipses …"

"Aliens?" I interrupted. I had a feeling that aliens and UFOs were the point of this extravagance. Jay was the real deal—crazy enough to put his money where his mouth was.

Jay laughed. "You think I'm nuts, don't you," he said. "You've never been to T.A.H. This telescope is garbage in comparison. For your information, I might have seen something of an extraterrestrial nature." He winked at me. His green eyes twinkled. "But I do love to gaze."

"This is one bad ass set-up. Please teach me what is in the sky so worth staring at." He motioned me to one of the larger telescopes that sat on a tripod stand. After adjusting it to my short height, I looked through the lens. Complete awe. The stars sparkled like diamonds. "Wow, I guess this is worth a look. Really makes me feel small, like an ant."

"That's Taurus you are looking at. The seven little stars all bunched together are Pleiades. Now come look through this one." Jay led me to the biggest one in the dome, the one with the chair. He sat down first, and with a joystick, adjusted the scope. "Now sit. You see it? That's Mercury."

I sat in the comfortable white leather chair and stared in astonishment. My eyes misted with tears. I had seen pictures in books, but this was different. I understood. Maybe Jay wasn't as crazy as I thought. Something bigger than us was definitely out there.

"I'm dumbstruck whenever I come out here. Not sure what happens when we die. That's more up Paula's alley. But I do believe. In the Universe, other races or species, maybe even God Himself. You're right about one thing—none of us really know until we're dead. And then it's too late. Maybe your mother is up there, maybe our mother. Let's find out."

Jay and I joined the others at the long iron table. Someone had started a fire and lit candles around the rooftop deck. The dim flames and the bright stars provided just enough light to give off a soft glow. The evening was cool, but the fire made it comfortable. Lively chatter was replaced with solemnity. Everyone got up and took a turn inside of the dome to see the constellations.

"Maya, we can clearly see the Pleiades constellation tonight. That has an effect on our séance. The Pleiades represent seven sisters or cows or even goats. The constellation is mentioned in the Bible so maybe this is a sign that your mother is up in Heaven, ready to reveal herself. Pleiades is part of Taurus, the bull. Many cultures worshipped the bull, tried to tame it. There is even an advanced being or alien link with the bull. The Atlanteans were once considered to be the most superior of all extraterrestrials. They worshipped the bull. In mythology we have the Minotaur, or half bull head and half human body. Taurus even has links to Egyptology. At any rate, we have a lot going on tonight. It's in the stars," said Paula.

I was surprised at how knowledgeable she was on astronomy and astrology. "Paula, here." I handed her the stone pendant and chain that my mother supposedly left me. "I haven't worn it since the Melvin episode. I used to wear it every day since I was little."

Mercedes picked up the necklace and nodded. "Maya, this is the same one my sister had." She then handed it to Jay.

"Yup, it's the same one I smashed and then threw in the sea. It's a symbol or maybe an artifact of some kind. Someone left them for us to make some kind of connection, to find one another. Oh Mercedes, I wish your sister was here," Jay said.

A tear dripped down Mercedes's cheek. "We all have questions, Paula. I pray that you ask the spirits the right ones. I pray that we all finally get the answers that we seek."

"Then let's get started. Glenn," she yelled, "come and sit down with us." Glenn exited the dome and joined us at the table. Everyone joined hands. Paula bellowed out something in another language for several minutes. Maybe French, maybe Latin. Her dark eyes lightened to green, the same shade as my mother's stone pendant. My heart beat like a drum.

"Lam, Lam," Paula yelled. Her eyes rolled in back of her head and she began to convulse. "He's here with me now," she said a few seconds later, seeming to be back in the moment. "He knows about the stone. But this necklace does not belong to your mother, Maya. It belongs to your father, to Jay's father, to Mercedes's sister's father. It belongs to the father of change, of evolutionary change. They are here. They have arrived. Lam, Lam, tell us more."

Terror set in. This was no show. Something was very wrong. The fire in the fireplace had burnt out and the candles' flames were snuffed simultaneously. I began to shiver. We sat in darkness with only light coming from the stars. Paula let go of Glenn's hand and reached for my mother's pendant.

The stone glowed the same weird chartreuse color that I saw at Marvelous Melvin's shop. Paula looked distorted, deranged. She rose from her chair and then stepped over to the fireplace, grabbed a poker, and then walked back to the table, almost floating like a possessed spirit. Like a maniac, she beat on the necklace again and again and again. The iron table chipped from the blows. Each swing stronger than before. Several swings later, the stone cracked. We all screamed, wondering where the pieces were.

A noise with a sound of a thousand flies made me cover my ears. But it wasn't flies. I smelled Sulphur. And then I saw what was making the loud sound. Chips of my necklace whirled in circles above the table. They automatically connected back together by some kind of super-magnetic force three feet above the table and then dropped in front of me. No silver pendant setting, no chain. Paula fainted.

Jay was the first to the ground, checking her pulse, her breathing, heartbeat, all of it. Within a minute her eyes, back to their deep brown color, opened.

"What happened?" Paula asked.

"You contacted a spirit called Lam. I know who he is," Jay said.

# Chapter Twenty-Two

Weeks and then months flew by. The crisp, cool air of autumn and winter was soon replaced with the blare of the sun. Nevada was unusually hot for spring with temperatures soaring well over ninety degrees. The lack of humidity and cool climate of the underground laboratory made it somewhat bearable.

Progress at Broom Lake occurred at a snail's pace yet Andreas's airmen, engineers, and scientists were decades, if not centuries ahead of the world in scientific knowledge. Andreas liked working with the small crew of geniuses inside of the hangar. They rebuilt a quarter of the craft that landed outside of Roswell. Using the baby craft for clues, each piece that they demagnetized and put into place sped up the process.

Like most top secret operations, the general's engineers were not sure what went on underground and the German scientists underneath the earth were not sure what went on in the hangar. Both sets of recruits were not allowed to mingle.

Andreas's experience as a pilot caused him to be much more interested in the craft than the ABs underneath the earth. The ABs were probably dead, but the spacecraft had all kinds of potential for the future of aviation. He guessed the craft had something to do with the mysterious foo fighters that he and so many of the pilots had seen during the war.

The Nazi scientists disgusted him more and more with each passing week. Their work was important and he tried to withhold all judgment. However, the group of scientists was constantly pushing the envelope. Andreas was tempted to break Jaeger's jaw after another request for more women. He had seen one of the women murdered, but never asked about the other three. They were expendable parts to their research.

The general was in way too deep. It was all or nothing. He asked Lamphrey and Bolantano once more to round up some more test subjects as he liked to call them.

The Nazis might have been repulsive, but they produced results. In complete awe and amazement, Andreas was shown the completed artificial womb and the manmade fertilization process.

"General, can you believe that we can create a baby by a test tube?" Jaeger said with pride. "You are looking at the future. Sex will be a thing of the past. It is now possible to reproduce by inserting and deleting certain gene sequences inside a laboratory."

Andreas was more than impressed but their success came at a price. "Doctors, great work. But I would rather reproduce the old fashioned way with lust, passion, and even love."

The three doctors laughed as if lust and love were for the naïve.

The next morning, right before dawn, Andreas was already caked with sweat as he faithfully worked out inside of headquarters. One of the empty offices was changed into a gym. Sometimes others on base would join him, but not today. He was the most disciplined soldier on the base when it came to staying in shape. He had just turned fifty, but refused to give in to old age. At six foot one, two hundred pounds, there wasn't an ounce of fat on his muscular frame.

About halfway through his routine of dumbbell curls and squats he was interrupted by Doctor Jaeger. The doctor's presence startled him. None of the Nazi doctors had ever used the weight room.

"You look startled, General. I have wonderful news. Our friends have finally awakened! Even the one who was shot! Come, come. They are very groggy, but crawling."

The sun had not risen. Dressed in shorts and a sweat saturated t-shirt, Andreas followed the doctor to the hangar, hopped into the elevator, and descended one hundred and fifty feet below the earth.

"I am not sure what to give them. We slid a bowl of water and a plate of dry cereal in the cage. They have not shown interest yet. Oh, what a day!" The doctor yelled. He babbled on in a state of euphoria, but Andreas too was too excited to listen. The wait had been long and he had almost given up in believing this day would come. The elevator doors opened. Andreas rushed out to the cage.

There they were. Magnificent. *Should I bow? Or should I show force?*

Their pale, grayish skin was now a chalky white with hint of pink in their faces, almost like the albino skin of a human. Their necks were made of thin, half circles that shimmered like an opal. Andreas thought of iridescent fish scales. Their extra-long fingers no longer glowed. The two holes in the middle of their faces were no longer flat. A three dimension triangle protruded, resembling a human nose but with sharper lines.

They looked alike, but not identical. One AB was bald while the others had light colored strands of hair on their heads. None of them had eyebrows.

Their eyes stood out from all of their features. The size took up almost a quarter of their faces. The eye colors were different in each of them. One had eyes paler than the sky while another had a greenish tint like an aqua color. The other two had deep gray-blue eyes, so dark that they almost appeared black if not seen in the light. All of them had gray pupils instead of black.

Their faces were void of expression, but Andreas assumed they must have been both terrified and furious.

The hair on the back of his neck stood on end as he watched them crawl around like spiders in their new cage.

Like the scales on the ABs' necks, their uniforms also shimmered a color that the general had never seen before. At a basic level, the color was a blueish black metallic, but there were more hues and brightness in the uniform they wore that Andreas could not describe. They glowed a dark color. The uniforms had a subtle swirl pattern to them that moved in random directions, almost as if the uniforms were a separate and living entity. He guessed that underneath that uniform their bodies glowed like their fingers did when they were asleep. The emblem on the sleeve did not glow or swirl, but was embroidered with metallic silver thread. There was no doubt it was some kind of version of Hitler's swastika. The Germans must have known the ABs for some time, studied them, maybe even learned their language.

"Aren't they amazing!" cried Doctor Schmidt. "I thought that I'd never see one again! This makes it all worth it!"

Andreas couldn't read Jaeger's mind, but noticed the tight lipped, ice cold glare that he gave Hans. The look could only mean one thing—*say one more word and I'll kill you.* Hans immediately quit gushing.

"So you've all seen these things, these Advanced Beings or ABs?" Andreas asked, knowing full well there would be a lie to follow, but was more curious about the body language of the three German doctors.

"Hans was with me when I saw them. Remember, I told you about it," Jaeger said. Without missing a beat, the doctor instantly changed the subject. "If we can just figure out a way to communicate, they might tell us how to map out their desirable genes, identify them, even show us which ones would benefit our manmade embryos. We can create the perfect hybrid, who knows, maybe even a modern day chimera. This could be what our Egyptian and

Roman brothers and sisters were talking about through their myths and lore! We will take our research to the next level!"

Andreas was mesmerized as he watched them move. Would this cage contain them? They appeared to be so agile, quick and graceful. The moral sacrifices were forgotten as he stood in awe with the three doctors. The kind of secrecy and power all of this wielded was the ultimate aphrodisiac.

Trying to contain his exhilaration, the general asked, "And what makes you think they will help us? Hell, what makes you think they will ever be able to communicate with us?" The Germans continued to stare at the ABs as they crawled around their cage. Their silence looked more like omission. "Why do I get the feeling that you know much more? C'mon, gentlemen, we are a team."

The doctors and Andreas watched the ABs in silence for several minutes. They crawled like spiders around the cage, one of them getting high up the Plexiglas wall and then falling several feet to the cage's floor. He or she, the general wasn't sure if they even had a gender, seemed to bounce as if made of rubber. Soon they were all upright and walking towards where Andreas and the doctors stood. Their enormous, weird eyes with gray pupils just stared back and tried to mimic everyone's stance. *Were they joking with us? Learning our mannerisms?* Still no expression on any of the ABs' faces. Did they even feel hatred or fear or anger? What other kinds of feelings could they have? They were in a multi-million dollar cage being studied yet Andreas felt like he was on display.

Doctor Jaeger broke the silence. "They know who we are. Let's not guess who is the smarter species. They are. Give them a chance. As you know, General, we can watch them in my laboratory. Please, let us show you our progress. We are on the verge of creation."

The general followed the three men to the elevator and then into their lab. He was still in his workout clothes. No uniform and weapon made him feel vulnerable. These men were as trustworthy as three rabid, hungry wolves. He had to know what they were up to and how the ABs were going to help.

The lab looked different, more cluttered. Andreas had more or less given the three men carte blanche in expanding their equipment. They had instruments that he had never even heard of—electron microscope, 3-D imaging, and a calculating machine were just some of the stuff Andreas saw them use. These men seemed to match each machine that they were given with one of their own creations. The once enormous laboratory felt almost claustrophobic. Soon they would need more space.

"Over here are the artificial wombs. We have four of them, each made with the cells of your donations," said Schmidt. "With your new donations, we will soon have three more." *Donations. Interesting word choice.* "The embryos in each of the a-wombs, as we like to call them, are ready to go. We successfully fertilized four eggs and then spliced a few of the ABs genes into each one of them. A lot of guesswork. Do not know what kinds of genes we are infusing into the fertilized cell or if it will even be accepted. Some of our embryos have perished before inserting them into the a-womb. Our gene combinations must not have been a good mix. But with our friends alive and well, well everything has changed!"

Andreas and the doctors watched them through a camera that ran from the lab and into the cage. They sniffed the food and water left behind.

"How many genes do these ABs have?" Andreas asked, trying to get some kind of statistic on how long this could take.

"Not one hundred percent positive, but we think they have the same amount of genes that we do," said Doctor Richtor.

"And how many genes do humans have?" Andreas asked. "I know we have forty-six chromosomes, twenty-three pairs, right?"

"Very good, General. We are turning you into a scientist," said Jaeger with a smile. "No one knows for sure, but many supposed intellectuals believe we have one hundred thousand genes because we are so complex. Genes are hard to count. They are part of a DNA strand. You have to match up sequences to name each gene. We believe that number is somewhere between nineteen to twenty-four thousand genes total as do our new friends. Now this is the hard part, figuring out which gene goes with what trait."

Andreas had been reading up on genetics. None of what the doctors told him had been published. Every time he visited them he learned something new. "Okay then. I can see through the window of those a-wombs that something is growing." He studied their revolutionary contraptions. The a-wombs were large bowls big enough to hold a twenty pound baby. The bottom part of the bowl was made from some kind of metal and the top part was made from clear glass. He looked in and felt queasy. There was some kind of cellular sheet of pinkish tissue that lined the bottom part of the bowl. In the middle, floating in each of the a-wombs, were small non-descriptive masses of cells slightly smaller than a ping pong ball in dirty, muted colors.

"Those are the new generation. As soon as they reach a point of development, we will hook them up to the manmade umbilical cord and feed them. Right now they float in a homemade concoction of amniotic fluid. This is as far as we have gotten. Hopefully these embryos won't die. We must have inserted an incompatible gene in the others. Right now, we have all four of the wombs in use. We want another three wombs to try different combinations of genes," said Karl. "If you can get us more women, we can make more wombs. One hundred wombs will take a decade without help, but one thousand wombs, well, maybe a few years. With their help," he said as he pointed to the camera connected to the ABs' cage, "we could give birth to our first generation of a new species."

Andreas's stomach turned. Did one thousand a-wombs equal one thousand women? Couldn't they clone cells for a uterus? Maybe that would take too long. Their operation could never remain secret. "The three women that you asked for will be the last three women that you will get. So figure out a way to make do. Clone some more uterus cells, extract more eggs from the ovaries, or figure out something new, but this is it. I'm not building you another concentration camp of women for body parts. Doctor Jaeger, you better hope you're AB friends will help you. Let's give them a few months to adjust. Maybe, just maybe they will cooperate."

"In exchange for what?" asked Doctor Richtor. "Their freedom?"

"Of course not, but if you have to lie to them, go right ahead," said Andreas. "If I remember correctly, you said that you needed male sperm to fertilize the eggs before inserting AB genes into the embryo. Which one of you is the father?"

None of the men admitted to being the sperm donor. "General, you will be the first to know once we have an infant."

"I have a right to know," Andreas said.

"All right. No one is the father. You cannot be a father if you do not have a baby," said Jaeger.

The general silently boiled over Jaeger's flippant answer as he walked by the camera and watched the ABs. They finished off the water, but the cereal was still in the cage. Their mouths were moving. "Hey, do you have sound?"

Jaeger nodded and reached for a button. Their voices were high pitched, sounding more like chattering birds than an intelligent species. They were clearly having a conversation.

"God forgive me," the general mumbled. He knew in his heart that the world was about to change.

# Chapter Twenty-Three

Claude was on his fourth cup of coffee at the diner down the street from the television studio. His mind was spinning. Jay McCallister? Maya was with Jay McCallister? Claude was on the verge of getting dumped for Jay McCallister? He had to be at least sixty if not one hundred years old. It was no secret that Maya had issues with family, specifically men. She opened up to Claude and told him about some of her foster daddies. But Jay McCallister was grandfather territory. Maybe, just maybe they were friends. This could be a misunderstanding.

Sam's cop was, as usual, a wealth of information. Within less than two hours after initially calling Sam, Claude had Jay's address, his phone number, his truck, his driver's license, hell, his life story.

Claude couldn't remember Maya's schedule for the rest of the week, but none of that mattered anymore. Jay McCallister and whatever his intentions were with another man's wife were what mattered. He hung out a little longer at the diner, using his phone to research the rest of Jay McCallister's life. He was almost surprised to read that Jay was only in his sixties. He seemed to be around for at least a century. But then, like Maya, he began his career at a very young age.

Claude studied up on the plethora of masterpieces Jay wrote over the last four decades. He recognized the titles. They sat in a bookcase in Maya's living room. It suddenly occurred to Claude that Jay had been her favorite writer, a detail that helped explain the attraction.

Jay obviously liked women—four wives. No kids. Maya was young and pretty. The whole 'let me take you under my wing' bullshit was probably the line that was used to get her up to his house. And then there was the money. He reportedly was worth over one billion dollars. Jay's fans saw him as a mentor, a leader, and maybe even a prophet.

Claude suddenly remembered something about Jay visiting her at Eric's bookstore the day of her first signing. She had a picture of them on one of the bookshelves in the living room. Was that the beginning of their affair?

Claude finished reading the bio on his phone and then left fifteen dollars on the table, unsure of what the bill was. He quickly found a sporting goods store at the end of the block. With cash, he purchased a Nike track suit, new sunglasses, a map, and a *Giants* baseball cap. The clothes along with Sam's Buick were enough to drive around the Bay area incognito.

Claude retrieved the car and headed out towards Tiburon. He had never been there, but was well aware of its affluence. Cautious of the car's navigation feature, Claude chose to map out Jay's home on paper.

Once Claude was over the Golden Gate Bridge, the city landscape changed into a playground for the rich. He envisioned a weirdo like Jay to live in an underground bunker somewhere in the middle of nowhere, alone, wearing a tin foil hat while praying to Osiris. But Jay was not off the grid, he was in the heart of luxury. Was Maya impressed? The more Claude drove around, the more worried he became.

Jay's street was high up on a bluff. The street had high fences and enormous trees, making the homes hard to see. Gated entrances, guards, and cameras were everywhere. Claude was familiar with the layout. Years ago, he convinced Sam to rob a few homes in Beverly Hills. Their night of local heists proved lucrative. Unfortunately, his brother went on a few more without Claude's guidance and eventually got caught. Luckily Sam was a kid, seventeen, and only served a year. His record was sealed.

Claude turned off the street, parked a mile away in a large sports complex, and got out of the car. He didn't have much of a plan, just to watch the street and see if Maya was staying with Jay.

With a new tracksuit, hat, and sunglasses, Claude jogged through the neighborhood. It was a beautiful day. So many people were out, jogging, dog walking, roller blading, or biking. Claude blended in well. After a mile run, he headed down Jay's street. The slow jog gave him time to scope out the security. Two cameras were pointed at the entrance just before the gate. So far, not much of a challenge.

Just before Claude passed Jay's gated entrance, a car pulled out. Not the Bentley, but a Nissan. Claude assumed the woman in the car had to be staff. He caught a glimpse of the guard shack. One guard. Claude was surprised. A colossal manse like Jay's should have had much better security.

Claude jogged around the block again. A small park with a jogging trail was a block away. He sat down on a wrought iron bench and fiddled with his shoe laces. From his vantage point he could see the main connecting street, Jay's street, and the entrance to his home. Perfect place to rest, watch, and wait.

Claude looked at his watch. The afternoon had flown by. Dinner time was near. While he waited, he noticed Jay's neighbors' security cameras. They were even more lax. Claude smiled. If he and Sam were still robbing houses, this would be the hood.

Down the busy road of the intersection, the Bentley sat at a stoplight. Even in this neighborhood, the car stood out like a sore thumb. He started jogging towards Jay's home. The car would eventually pass him once the light changed. He suddenly got nervous, almost feeling exposed.

Was Maya in the back seat? He couldn't see. If she was, would she recognize him? No, he thought. Just paranoia trying to get the best of him.

As the car neared the gate, Claude slowed down his gait. Maya was definitely in the back seat with Jay. He watched the car pull into the driveway, watched the gate open, and watched them drive into the estate. His stomach sank. Maya was undoubtedly staying with Jay. That's why she lied about the hotel. That's why she didn't want him to join her in the city. And that's why she avoided his phone calls. Maya was having an affair with Jay McCallister.

Claude raged with jealousy. He worked hard for his new lifestyle. Maya was his wife. Jay had no right.

Claude drove back to Los Angeles the next day. He was done following Maya and Jay around. He knew all that he needed to know. Hours later, now Tuesday night, he pulled into Sam's underground parking. Sam buzzed him into his apartment building.

"Want a beer?" Sam asked.

Claude nodded and reached across the kitchen bar as he took a seat on the stool. Sam handed him an ice cold Dos Equis. Claude was more of a wine kind of guy, but anything cold, anything alcoholic would do. He twisted off the top and gulped down half of the bottle.

"That bad, huh?"

"I thought the skinny, pasty geek from the book store would do me in. Little did I know she has a thing for senior citizens," Claude said.

"You got Allie. It's not like you love Maya. Divorce her, take half of her shit, and move on. You'll be rich. And sought after. After Maya's success, every author will want you to represent them. Claude, this doesn't have to be a bad thing."

"You don't understand. Women don't dump me, I dump them. And what would I get out of this? A few mil? Big deal. Maya's on her way to being the next J.K.

Rowling. And with that geriatric disaster by her side...You know he's a billionaire? A fucking billionaire! Mother Fucker! With his dough, he could get anyone. What the hell is he doing with her? Fuck him! Fuck this! I'm not about to let this happen!" Claude took the beer by the neck of the bottle and broke it on Sam's granite counter. Beer and glass fragments splashed all over the tile floor.

"Take it easy, bro! What the hell? You mad? Then go trash your own apartment. There's nothing you can do about this, so be grateful for the millions that you will walk away with."

"You made off pretty well too. We got her to sign off on that equity loan. If only I could somehow ride this out a little longer. She finished the fucking sequel. That should double her worth. He has to go."

Sam looked in a few cabinets until he found a small broom and dustpan. As he swept up Claude's mess, he asked, "Are you suggesting killing off the old man? You nuts? He probably has enough staff to convert into an army if need be. How are you going to pull that off? It's a bust. You'll end up in the building next to Mom for life all because you're fucking greedy. You've always been greedy."

"You in? I'll give you two hundred thousand to help me. Just like the old days, Sam." Sam shook his head no. "Think about it."

# Chapter Twenty-Four

My smashed necklace put itself back together as if it had a life of its own. Our séance was cut short due to Paula's dizzy spells and need for rest. She had been calling out the name Lam during the séance. Who was Lam?

After everyone left Jay's home, he asked me to have some tea with him out by the pool before my flight. It was well after midnight, but I wasn't the slightest bit tired.

Jay's staff had gone home or to bed. The house was completely silent as I waited for him. Eerily silent. I almost couldn't wait to get on my plane and felt guilty for all of the wonderful things Jay had done for me throughout the week. These people were my friends now and I felt a sense of loyalty towards them. Yet my fear was real. Darkness. It felt like wet air and smelled like burning leaves.

Jay came out to the pool with the tea. The orange spice in the tea took me out of the moment. He sat next to me at the pool.

"You okay? Paula's séances are usually low key." He set the tea on the side table between our large, wicker chairs.

"Yeah, I'm okay. Scared. I know now that you've been telling me the truth. Your version of the truth, but nonetheless the truth. Something is out there. I don't know what. And you're right. We were brought together for a reason. I'm glad you invited me here. I'm glad that I got to know you. But something…"

"Something what?" he asked.

"I don't know. I am sensing something very evil is about to happen."

"Paula can get really heavy sometimes. Lam. Do you know who Lam is?"

"No clue. Who is Lam?" I asked.

"Some say Lam is an alien and some say he is a demon. I believe Lam is a type of being from a dark force. So does Paula and she is terrified of these kinds of beings. She once had a few cult members who follow Lam on her show. Maya, I'm not as in tune as Paula is, but I can say this—your mother is not some poor young woman who had no choice but to give you up. Your mother is something more abstract."

"I had a feeling after that freak show. But this feeling isn't really about my mother. Jay, what I am trying to say is that something very evil is going to happen to you. Here. I can feel it, almost see it, like a cloak over you. An omen. Would you like to hang out at my house for a while?"

"But I'm indestructible." Jay smiled and then sipped his tea.

I also smiled. We stared out at the bay. The water glowed against the big, full moon. The silence wasn't awkward, but comfortable, as if he were my father or even my grandfather. The dark presence went away. I was eager to get home, even more eager to see Eric and tell him every detail about this trip that I would never forget. Divorce was suddenly on my list of things to do.

"You know, you're writing in code. Do you even realize that?" he said after several minutes.

"Even the sequel?" I asked and Jay nodded. "No, I don't realize that. When I write, something just takes over, especially now, especially here."

I can't remember what else we talked about, more or less rehashing the week. Jay told me all kinds of personal stories of Paula, Glenn, and Mercedes. He wanted me to know exactly what I was getting into. We talked until the sun came up.

That morning with my bags packed, my new necklace around my neck and my mother's necklace tucked in my wallet, I left Jay's mansion with a heavy heart. He changed me forever. We were destined to be friends.

"Christmas, you and that man you're in love with need to come up and stay with me," he said.

He hugged me like a father and I hugged back. Would I make it back here? Would he uninvite me? Tears filled my eyes. What should have been joy felt like impending doom.

The short flight gave me some time to stop and think. I needed to clean up my love life. Claude didn't love me. I was not entirely sure if I ever loved him. Theoretically, divorce should have been simple.

I didn't hate Claude, in fact I was grateful. He got me to know myself and what I really wanted, who I really needed. I was prepared to offer him half of everything, and considering it was I who earned everything, my offer was more than generous. I was probably worth a few million at the moment. Two, maybe even three million was a lot for Claude to walk away with. It was time to cut both or our losses.

Eric was always in the back of mind. I shot him a quick text while on the plane.

*Have much to talk about. On way home from Jay McCallister's. Can I take you to dinner? An all-you-can-eat buffet on the strip? I want to eat and talk all night. I miss you.*

Within a few minutes Eric replied.

*Hanging out with THE MAN????? And all-you-can eat? I'm in. And you're rich. I have a taste for all-you-can-eat lobster and steak.*

I smiled. Despite all of my mistakes, he still talked to me.

*Name the place and time—I'll be there solo.*

He texted back a smiley face back. I wanted to text back those three little words, but chickened out.

The plane landed and it was still morning. I wasn't in any rush to get home. Las Vegas was unusually cool for late October. I told the cab driver to take me to the strip and drop me off at the mall. I felt like stopping in the book store to say hello. I bought Eric a few touristy gifts—Ghirardelli's chocolate, a t-shirt, and a seafood cookbook. He loved seafood and loved to cook so I thought the gift would be hit. I lugged around my large carry-on bag, which was much heavier. The gifts, new clothes, and laptop doubled the weight.

With my giant purse and carry-on bag, I wobbled through the mall, shaking the closer I got to Eric's bookstore. I saw him through the window ringing up a customer. Our friendship was strained after Claude and I got married. We texted and occasionally spoke on the phone, but I had only seen him a few times over the last year.

With a deep breath and a gust of courage, I walked into the store. There was a pretty girl behind the second register. My replacement. I wondered if I was possibly interrupting something. They looked like they were having a moment, both smiling as he came to her register to correct some sort of mistake. I wanted to cry. So this was jealousy—now I knew how he must have felt when I married Claude. Unlike Claude, this girl had a look of decency, like she would never hurt him.

At that moment I had realized how arrogant and thoughtless I had been. As if I was the sun and Eric was supposed to revolve around me. But then he saw me. I must have looked ridiculous standing in the middle of the store with two enormous bags, just staring at the register counter. He smiled, said something to the pretty bitch and walked out from behind the counter.

"Maya, the bags…You left him?" he asked.

"No, but I plan to. Just got off the plane from San Fran…"

Eric took me in his arms kissed me, right there in the crowded book store, in front of at least twenty people, and I kissed him back. My insecurity attack was in vain. This man loved me and I loved him. This was the happily ever after part in a movie.

He held me in his arms and said, "I should have done that years ago."

We never did go to an all-you-can eat buffet. Instead, Eric introduced me to Lauren and then told her to lock up at six o'clock. She gushed when hearing my name. *Oh, I have to have your autograph....Oh, I can see this becoming a movie. Please, please, please do a book signing here....*

Lauren was definitely pretty and sweet, but I wasn't jealous anymore. She might have been my age or she might have been in high school. It didn't matter. Eric had just swept me off my feet.

Eric bought champagne and a bouquet of flowers at the closest liquor store and then we went to his apartment. He poured us each a glass, we toasted, and then a few seconds later he kissed me again. He carried me to his bedroom, stripped us both down, and kissed every inch of my body. His tongue inside of me made my eyes roll in back of my head. Had I known he was this skilled, I would have never married, much less looked at Claude.

Once he inserted himself inside of me I felt excited, but peaceful, loved. He looked at me with much more than desire. He looked at me like I really was the sun after all.

"I love you," he said after he came inside of me.

"I love you," I said. And then I cried. Sex with Claude was always good, but our sex life had an animalistic element to it, like two people in heat wanting a release. With Eric I felt cherished. I felt like I mattered.

"I never want this day to end," Eric said. "You hungry? You know I love to cook. How about something Asian? Or maybe French? Anything you want."

I shrugged. Eric routed around his kitchen. "Oh, I know. Italian. Veal Parmesan. I'll be back in an hour. Don't leave. I want everything to be perfect. I've dreamt of this for so long. I love you." He kissed me a raced out of the apartment.

While Eric was gone, I took out the souvenirs that I had bought for him, placed them on the counter, and then checked my phone. Claude had called twice and wondered where I was. Again I was reminded of the mess left for me to clean up once I got home.

I couldn't muster up the courage to call him back. My voice would have given me away. Regardless of what he may or may have not done to me, I was committing adultery and disrespecting my vows to God. Religion was never my specialty, I did believe something out there was greater than all of us. I did believe in God. My view of Him was distorted, even dysfunctional. In my warped perception of sin, I believed that sleeping with someone when unmarried was okay, but sleeping with someone when married was not. I picked and chose which commandments to follow. What I was doing with Eric made me feel ashamed. I had to end my marriage in an honorable, amicable way.

I texted Claude back, preferring the less personal type of communication.

*Sorry. I'll be home later. Got caught up shopping and had my phone off. Didn't realize you'd be home until later.*

Lies, all lies. He was very clear with me that he'd be home Saturday afternoon right after my flight came in. That night I ate an amazing dinner and then called a cab to take me home. The expression on Eric's face was the same dejected expression he wore when I got married.

"I got to tell him it's over. You driving me home, well, it would just aggravate the situation." I kissed him. "I love you. I always loved you. Just didn't know it until it was too late. Let me clean up my mess."

That night the cab driver pulled up in my driveway. Every light in the house was on. I opened the garage door while balancing my bulky bags and slipped inside through the laundry room, avoiding the front door. My covert efforts were for nothing. Claude was in the living room watching a sit-com. I could hear the canned laughter from down the hall.

"Maya?" he called.

So much for my stealth entrance. "Claude, it's me. Let me put my bags in the room." I took a brief refuge in the bedroom, washed my face, and held my breath. I just wanted him out—out of the house, out of my business, out of my life. Maybe I should have been afraid, but exhaustion and numbness set in.

I probably smelled like sex, but no longer cared. I walked into the living room and sat down at the bar next to Claude. He got up and tried to kiss me as if I was missed. His touch made my skin crawl and, by reflex, I backed away.

"What's wrong?" he asked.

"I...I...Well, I...I want a drink," I said. He readily poured me a large glass of one of his fancy wines which I gulped down in record time. After an awkward moment of silence, I just blurted it out. "I want a divorce. This is not working. I know you don't love me. I don't love you. We need to go our separate ways. I care about you and want to leave as friends. You can have half of our net worth. I think we are worth somewhere in the neighborhood of four million after my last advance and royalty check. If you want to keep this house or the L.A. apartment, then we'll just subtract the equity from the net worth and..."

"Hold on! What the fuck, Maya?" Claude was drunk and I was rambling. My timing was off. "Have you been talking to a lawyer? Net worth? Equity? Since when have you been interested in bean counting our assets? I don't want a divorce. I want you."

"Claude, let's be honest for just one minute. I know that I am not your one and only. I don't want to fight, I just want to start over." I was actually aggravated with his reaction, as if announcing that I wanted a divorce would be enough for him to go away.

Looking back, my naiveté could have got me killed. Claude's gorgeous blue eyes brightened into a manic, pale hue. My heart rate doubled. I remember thinking this might be the end of everything, including my life. For the first time in our marriage, I caught a glimpse of the monster behind the movie star mask. But it was too hard to believe. Trying to rationalize it all, I kept telling myself that the fear was all in my head.

Claude screamed while breaking every glass in the bar. He called me a whore and demanded that I admit to having an affair in San Francisco. I admitted nothing, but San Francisco was way off base. After his temper tantrum, he balled up in the corner of the living room and cried. The monster now looked like a helpless infant who needed a mother.

"I can't lose you, Maya. You're the best thing that ever happened to me. Please, I'm begging you, I have no other reason to live. You want me out of your life? I could slit my wrists or turn on the car with the garage door closed. You're right, I've been a shitty husband, but that's going to change. Please, please at least promise me some counseling. At least give me that. I'll give you some space for now. But I need you to promise me that we will at least get some help before you throw all of this away..."

He dribbled on for what seemed forever, but all I heard was 'I have no other reason to live'. Suicide? Was Claude going to kill himself over a divorce? I couldn't bear that kind of responsibility. 'Thou shalt not kill' came to mind. Maybe counseling wasn't a bad idea. I could tell the counselor in private about his depression. I didn't want to destroy him, just leave him.

"Okay, we could see a counselor. Monday I'll call one. I'll look through the White Pages. You're not going to do anything rash, are you?" He shook his head. "For now, why don't you sleep in the guest suite?" He nodded.

I slept with one eye open and the door locked. The next morning, Claude's car was gone and his bed looked untouched. I should have been curious as to where he went, but all I could feel was relief. Throughout the day I called Jay and then Eric. Both men told me to get out of the house and at the very least check into a hotel. Both men warned me that Claude was crazy. Both men reminded me that it was in Claude's interest to inherit the whole enchilada of assets instead of splitting the fortune and going our separate ways. But they didn't know him. They didn't see him helpless and desperate and vulnerable, claiming to end it all. I couldn't just walk away without getting him the help that he needed.

That evening, Claude still had not come home, but he called and said he drove up to Los Angeles and was staying with Sam. His drive became a road trip and thought that I would prefer to be alone until we started counseling. I asked to speak to Sam.

"Maya, Claude is fine. He's with me. No need to worry," Sam said.

"You've been friends with him for a while, right?" I asked. I had always been suspicious of their relationship, yet chose to play along even after Jay told me Sam was his half-brother. Claude never spoke about his parents and claimed to be the only child.

"Yeah, we go way back," Sam said.

"Is he suicidal?"

"Never been suicidal and I don't think he is that stupid. I'll keep an extra close watch on him, though. I've never seen him so sad. He drove here last night, drunk.

Lucky he didn't kill anyone. But he's coming back tomorrow. He's hoping to start counseling. Give him another chance. He loves you so much."

I didn't love him at all but with Sam's assurance, I calmed down. Feeling a sense of security, I continued proof-reading my manuscript to get my mind off of things. Late Sunday night or early Monday morning, I turned on the television and tried to get some asleep.

After flipping through five or six channels, I ended up settling for the midnight news. "The Middle East...Another senseless shooting...Riots about court ruling..." Blah, blah, blah. I went to the fridge for a bottle of Starbucks coffee and some yogurt, and then lay back in bed. The next news story woke me up like a cold shower.

*Best-selling author Jay McCallister was found dead this afternoon in his Tiburon home. Details are still sketchy, but his death appears to be the result of foul play. Any information connected to Jay McCallister's death, please call the Tiburon police. Jay McCallister will be remembered most for his enormous contribution to the science fiction genre. He wrote dozens of novels adapted for film and television. He cofounded T.A.H., an institute devoted to proving life on other planets. Privately, he was known as a charitable eccentric and intellectual among the alien-believing community.*

My bottle of Starbucks crashed to the floor.

# Chapter Twenty-Five

Less than a year after waking up, the ABs figured out a way to communicate with the German doctors and General Andreas. Their natural voice was as high of a pitch as the ear could handle, yet they lowered it to a comfortable level, learning the English language with ease. Maybe they knew it all along. Andreas suspected the Germans had been communicating with these kinds of ABs for some time.

The ABs didn't seem too angry about their captivity. But then their expression remained neutral on everything. They rarely drank or ate. Every few weeks they requested cereal, grains, or other plant based foods and water. None of them seemed to excrete the water or food, making Andreas wonder if every molecule they consumed was used.

One of the aliens, seemingly the leader of the four with the least amount of hair, asked the general when they were going home. He didn't have the heart to say never, but did tell them that they were putting their craft back together.

"Here, let me show you some pictures of my engineers' progress," Andreas said. He slid the photos in a drawer that emptied into the cage.

The ABs greedily eyed up the photos and chattered like birds in their native tongue. Their gray pupils darkened as they talked. He stared at the symbol on their sleeve, the swastika. The German doctors obviously knew of this race, but for how long?

"Can you take us to it?" the bald AB asked in his high, screechy voice.

Andreas initially walked away from the Plexiglas wall. Later, when the Germans were in their lab diligently working on more of their enhanced embryos, he visited them alone and gave all four of them an answer. "Soon you will see your space craft. The baby craft is damaged, but still intact. Will that help the engineers?"

The four ABs nodded. For the first time Andreas saw their eyes dance with life. They were clearly excited.

"Will you help the engineers?" Andreas asked and they nodded. "I need you to answer some questions. Did you know the doctors before? Back in Germany?" Again, they nodded. "How?"

Before answering the general, they chattered in their bird-like language. The bald leader of the four turned, looked Andreas straight in the eye, and said, "Vaa rilly, va rill."

"Huh?"

The alien repeated, "Va rill, va rill."

"You were in a group together? Here, on earth? What kind of group? Did you meet on a regular basis? Was there any kind of hierarchy, any rules for belonging to this group?" The bald alien shrugged his shoulders. The scales on his neck fluttered almost like feathers. Andreas wasn't sure if he was pretending or really didn't understand what was being said. One tidbit was confirmed. They had some kind of relationship dating back to Germany.

"All right. One more question. Did you show the doctors how to make embryos?" They nodded readily. "What about embryos with your genes, your DNA?" Again they nodded.

The bald leader asked, "Now you will take us to our craft? Then we can go home?"

"I'm working on it," Andreas answered.

Andreas realized that the doctors could have heard every word that he and the ABs uttered. There was a camera in their lab that allowed them to watch the cage while working. *Oh well*, he thought. *Va rilly or va rill, some kind of group back in Germany? A group of what? Nazi doctors who wanted to play God?*

Andreas rode the elevator up to the doctors' lab. Since the aliens had woken up, their progress on both fronts, genetics and reverse engineering, had spiked.

Several embryos died or were destroyed during the doctors' trial and error methods in gene manipulation. With the ABs help over several months, ten more artificial wombs, a total of fourteen, were built without abducting more women for parts. The doctors learned a faster way to clone cells. Thousands of eggs from the original four women plus the last three that Andreas had given them were frozen on site.

By the middle of 1949, test tube embryos had lived past the first trimester of development. Richtor tested out his manmade umbilical cord. There were a few glitches to the contraption, but easy fixes. His umbilical cord allowed them to provide a solution chalked with nutrients for the growing embryos. The three men looked like proud fathers as they doted on each one of the A-wombs.

Andreas couldn't get past the hypocrisy of it all. None of these men had an ounce of respect for human life, yet revered the lives that they worked so hard to create. A classic example of how the ends justified the means.

The German doctors skipped over the ethics and produced incredible results, the kind of results that attracted attention from the world's most elite players. General Blanchard brought the President, other generals, and some select heads of state to the site to show off "his" project. Every accomplishment whether big or small was because of the brilliant decisions made by the incredible General Blanchard.

Andreas let the man take all of the credit. He only knew a fraction of what was really going on. The tight-lipped team of Germans were doing what they did best— not talking and he wasn't exactly volunteering any more information than asked. Judging by their limited questions, General Blanchard nor anyone in his political circle understood the science involved in genetic engineering, reverse engineering, or space-aged energy.

His hire-ups let him down. He had expected them to do some homework. He had spent endless hours reading up on all of it. Even though he considered himself both intelligent and well-informed, the information the doctors were using was not even published, let alone imagined in any scientific circles around the world. Their work was as revolutionary as scientific breakthroughs got. As a result, Andreas's budget tripled.

"Security, security, security," said General Blanchard like a broken record. He was right. Andreas was in charge of not one, but two of the world's greatest wonders. He was constantly adding more levels of security to Broom Lake, but it was not enough.

Andreas took some of his gigantic budget funds and gave the security of Broom Lake a makeover. The first step was to monitor the comings and goings of the base. Next, he insisted the government buy up thousands of acres of nearby property to permanently keep it off the market. Isolation was the only way secrecy could continue.

Seventy-five more soldiers were added to the payroll. Andreas bought fighter planes, tanks, and artillery. He had walls, fences, and guard shacks built around the base. More runways and hangars were added. Cameras and security control rooms came shortly after. He even had his airman patrol the base from the sky.

Some soldiers lived on base, but most lived in Las Vegas. The out-of-towners flew into work each day. This must have drawn attention to the private Vegas runways, but for now the arrangement would have to do. Besides, Andreas didn't want everyone to live on the top secret base.

The Roswell spacecraft was almost finished. Some of its special features were given to General Blanchard. The engineers explained how the United States could use these concepts for their own benefit. The spin-off technology would put the United States at the forefront of the world in terms of advanced weaponry.

Again, the engineers only tossed Blanchard a bone, and it was a pathetic bone at that. This little think tank had intrigued Andreas from the start. They were his kind of people. One of the engineers, Doctor Kate Costello, had especially impressed him. She was a sheer genius when it came to magnetic fields and gravitational pull. Her brains were not the only part of her that Andreas noticed.

The beautiful doctor was equally impressed with the general. By New Year's Eve, their professional relationship had turned into a romantic one. The engineers invited Andreas to a party in a Las Vegas hotel. He took the time and enjoyed himself over the course of a long three day hiatus. On the last day, New Year's Eve, Costello challenged him to a drinking contest. They drank one shot after the other and then took the party upstairs to Andreas's room. They both did not know it at the time, but the other engineers had placed wagers on when the two of them would start to date.

Costello was forty-two years old with long dark hair, an occasional strand of gray, large hazel eyes, and a full sensuous mouth. She tried to tone down her looks, but Andreas had noticed her voluptuous body from the day he hired her.

Andreas did not want a relationship. The last one he had did not work out too well. But Costello couldn't have walked into his life at better time. She was one of the only people he could talk about his work with, making her extra special.

As their affair heated up, the general broke down and told Costello bits and pieces about the aliens below the hangar she worked inside of. She wasn't surprised. Most of the engineers assumed the species that created the spacecraft had to be nearby either alive or dead. She had seen the German doctors several times.

"One of them likes to spy. He had blonde-gray hair, receding, and glasses and…" Costello said.

"Yes, that's Karl. He's from Germany. I brought him here," Andreas said as he interrupted her.

"But Robert, why is he so interested in the craft?"

"I think they promised them something," he answered. "Probably told them they would go home after their Frankenstein baby experiment was finished. And if he is spying on all of you, then I'm going to guess he wants to make good on the promise."

"Please, Robert, please. Can I see these beings?"

At first the general refused her requests and soon she stopped asking. She and the other engineers were trying to piece together the control panel of the craft. Andreas watched them, knowing they had the configuration all wrong. The ABs could never reach the knobs. The tallest one was only five feet tall.

Costello asked him again, this time in front of Doctor Kaplan, Doctor Jensen, and Doctor Spencer. "We need to know their size, Robert."

Andreas caved. Costello did have a valid point. He took the four engineers to the underground doctors' laboratory. The three Germans were busy looking at something in a microscope. They barely lifted up their heads as the general and four engineers walked through to the elevator.

They all descended another fifty feet below the lab. The elevator doors opened. Andreas looked at each of them and watched their jaws drop. He remembered feeling the same kind of awe the first time he saw them. They approached the cage.

Andreas cautioned them to stand back. "They are not used to you yet." He approached the cage first and then tapped on the glass. The balding leader came forth.

"See these people with me?" the general asked and the AB nodded. "They are the ones putting your spacecraft back together. They work for me, not Karl nor the other German doctors. They've got questions about your control panel. Like me, they speak English. They are not here to hurt you. Can you or your friends help them?" The AB nodded. Andreas turned to the doctors and waved. "Slowly, okay?"

Within a few minutes the doctors were five feet away from the glass wall of the cage. Doctor Kate Costello was the first to ask them about a lever with gray handle. Doctor Benjamin Jensen asked them about a white needle. Doctor Herbert Spencer asked them about fuel and the crystal they had found. Costello then asked them more specific questions on pressure gages and propulsion.

Two hours went by. Although everyone was speaking English, the general could barely understand them. Then he realized the German doctors could hear every word that they said. *They probably don't know a damn thing about any of this*, he thought. *They were too busy with human genetics to be well-versed in rocket science.*

"We are done for now, Robert. And thank you. You just saved us five or ten years of work, gave your government a few more spin-off weapons, and most of all, gave us all the thrill of a life time," she said. She smiled. Her teeth were perfect. He wanted to kiss her right then and there, but chose to keep his feelings for her professional in the presence of others. They had already gotten too casual by calling each other by their first names.

"The ride is not over." He took the engineers back up to the lab. "Hello, Doctors. These are the engineers who have been slaving over the craft, but something tells me you already know that." After a brief introduction, Andreas took his crew over to the artificial wombs or a-wombs as they were now called. The three Germans looked pleased with themselves.

"See these machines?" Andreas asked as he pointed to the clear plastic over the bowl of liquid. "Look inside. Those are babies. Babies made with a woman's egg, man's sperm, and special genes from the ABs. Still foggy on how they were created. Somehow they cut out the genes with some kind of enzyme and fused it into the fertilized egg." Andreas was under the impression that the Nazi doctors wanted this little field trip to be over. "Their goal is to make a hybrid."

"So if we have the technology to make our own beings, wouldn't it benefit the government to make a super-soldier?" Costello whispered as she looked over at the other side of the lab, watching the doctors.

"I'm sure that's one of the things they are considering with each new discovery, but for right now we are seeing if it can even be done," Andreas said.

Kate was too smart for her own good. Maybe the general shouldn't have shown her much less of this than the other engineers. But the time had come to share some secrets. Besides, the Germans seemed to be well-versed in the advancements the engineers had made with the spacecraft. After several minutes of bewilderment, the general escorted the engineers back to the hangar. Secrets on both sides were shared.

Later on, well into the evening in the general's bedroom, Costello told him a few of her own secrets. She picked up her jacket from the floor, routed around in the pockets, until producing several chunks of a yellowish green crystal.

"Remember the small chunks of crystal we showed you a few months ago?" Andreas nodded. "We found two enormous hunks the size of small boulders along with more shards, rocks, and pieces dispersed through the heap of metal. They were everywhere—in the crevices and folds and knobs, all over. We showed you their magnetic powers. I'm keeping these as a souvenir or maybe just to prove this is all real and not a dream. You want one? That craft had to be powered by something. We all think the crystal was the main power supply. You won't find it on any of our reports because we still have a huge pile of metal to go through."

Andreas took a piece and gazed at the chartreuse color. It seemed to glow like the ABs fingers glowed when they hibernated. "You can't keep these. They are classified. They belong to the government."

Costello snatched up the pieces, leaving him one piece. "The hell I can't. I didn't have to show you any of this. Who do you think you…"

Andreas kept one of the stones on his nightstand. He grabbed Kate's shoulders and kissed her on the mouth. The kiss was long and intimate. "There," he said. "That got you to shut up." He smiled at her. "Don't tell me about your souvenirs. I don't want to be the asshole. But do keep me in the loop. Kate, I love you."

"Likewise, General."

Andreas kissed her neck and then her breasts. For the second time that night, they made love. She made him feel like teenager. Was she worth it? He wondered as he thrusted into her and climaxed.

Their relationship made the general slip up from time to time, sharing things she did not need to know. She also told him too much. Keeping the crystal was technically stealing classified information. But love was blind. Was Costello the love of his life or was she his Achilles Heel?

"There's a guy over at NASA—Braun. Do you know him?" she asked as they lay in bed sharing a cigarette.

Andreas was well aware of the famous man. "No, who is he?" he lied. He wasn't sure why he lied about such a trivial thing. Maybe it was an effort to start lying to her. She knew way too much.

"A Nazi who NASA recruited. He has designed intercontinental missiles. He can build a rocket that will make it to the moon. A friend of mine who works with him told me that his work wasn't entirely his. He said that *they* influenced his work and *they* were the true architects of his designs. When asked who *they* were, he said *they* and then looked at the ceiling. Someone asked if he was talking about aliens and he nodded and then changed the subject." Costello paused, took another drag of the smoke, and then said, "Robert, I think the Nazis have been communicating with these things for some time."

Andreas didn't tell her how right she was. It had been obvious. The modified babies, the spacecraft, and now the rockets, hell, all of their revolutionary advancements were supposed to happen at this point in time one way or another, whether Germany won the war or not. They had an agenda and he was playing right into it. Maybe Kate was right. A super-soldier was the end game.

# Chapter Twenty-Six

"You ou owe me, Claude. That old geezer was one tough mother fucker to kill. We almost fucked the whole thing up. You could have got me life. Two hundred thou ain't gonna cut it," Sam said as they headed back to Los Angeles.

"He's a lot stronger than I thought he'd be, but we were in and we were out. No witnesses, nothing left behind. It's done. Two hundred is more than fair," Claude said as he sat in the passenger seat, chain smoking in Sam's Buick. He rarely smoked, but the stress got the best of him.

"You're insane. I shot him three times and nothing. He had me in a choke hold. We had to hold him underwater for ten, twenty minutes until he stopped struggling. For one hundred years old or however old he was, he was strong as a bull. If you weren't there, I couldn't have pulled it off. Yeah, you almost got me life, asshole. You better figure on some kind of bonus. And it's still not over. Never hung around to get the shell casings."

Claude yawned and then said, "Who cares about the shell casings or the bullets inside of him. The gun's untraceable and you know it. Sam, I will take more than care of you like I always have. What's done is done. I need to get home by tomorrow. Maya and I are starting counseling. It's all going to work out, bro. Next year, maybe next two years, you and I will be rich. We will forget about our past and all of this ugliness. Think about what is to come. What you and I been through, we deserve this."

"Do we, Claude? Do we deserve this? I don't know. This plan is…it's evil."

Claude didn't respond to his brother's comments. Life was much too short for guilt, resentment, and regret.

Sam still did not understand that in life you make your own destiny.

The men came from less than nothing. Their mother was a self-absorbed, wicked little whore and thief, maybe even a murderer. Although Claude and she had plenty of differences, he admired her survival skills. The biggest and only difference between him and his mother was education. She was small time and stupid. He wasn't. Sam was on the fence somewhere between stupid and smart. He didn't have the backbone or confidence that Claude had. In time, Sam would thank him. He'd write him a big check once the dust settled.

As they drove in the dark and Sam bitched, Claude drowned out his brother's voice. Relief set in. His romantic rival was eliminated. Now Maya could focus on her work, make more money, and eventually have an untimely death. Judging by Sam's whining, Allie might be a better recruit for the next murder Claude would have to commit.

By the time Claude picked up his car in Los Angeles and then drove back to Las Vegas, it was late morning the next day. Monday. The day he and Maya were supposed to start counseling. He was surprised how mushy she got once the word suicide was mentioned. If the table was turned, he'd encourage her to end it, thus leaving him with the entire estate. Not Maya. Her brown eyes lit up with fear. Guilt was the only weapon he had left.

Claude stopped at one of the best bakeries in town, bought everything in the store, and went home. It was almost ten o'clock. Maya was probably just waking up.

As predicted, she sat in her robe at the kitchen table glued to her laptop. Her eyes were swollen as if she had been crying.

"Good morning, Beautiful," he said as he set the bag of goodies next to her on the table. "Let's pig out." He got himself a cup of coffee and sat down.

"Thanks, that was very kind. Let me see here, streusel, pound cake, Bismarck, Danish, coffee cake, *kolache,* oh my, you cleaned out the store. So much for my diet. I've got to try some of this."

While they ate, Claude tried to read her mind. Did she know Jay was dead? Was she interested in marriage counseling? Did she still care for him?

"Did you make an appointment yet?" Claude asked.

"I emailed a few local psychologists and counselors. Let's see who is available," Maya said.

"Are you finished with the sequel?"

"Yes, I'm proofing it before I send it to the publisher. Hey, did you hear on the news that Jay McCallister died?"

She knew. That meant that everyone knew. That must have been the reason for her tears. "Jay McCallister the author? How? Who would want to kill him?"

"I don't know if he was murdered. The details are sketchy. It was on the news last night. I would like to go to the funeral," she said.

"Why? Were you two friends?"

"Yes, we were friends. I didn't know him for very long. But he did a great deal for my career. His review of *Master Race* alone must have sold a half of a million copies. I really need to go to the funeral."

"I'll go with…"

"Claude, let's work on marriage counseling first, okay?"

And just like that, Maya had suddenly gotten the upper hand in their marriage. He felt trapped. This wasn't going as smoothly as he had planned. He kept telling himself to just hang on a little bit longer. He'd get what was due to him and the bitch would end up just like Jay. One year, maybe two, and Claude would be sitting on four or five times more than a shitty divorce settlement would get him. He was up to his neck in blood. It was too late to wimp out.

Claude looked at Maya's plate of pastries. She barely ate a thing. Was it the stress of losing Jay or the stress of divorce? Maybe she didn't trust him, even with food. It could have been all of the above or none of the above. He was finding it increasingly hard to figure her out, but then she had always been unpredictable.

"Yes, you're right. A marriage counselor is definitely the first step. I am hoping and praying that he or she will help us patch things up." Maya was staring at her computer as he spoke. "You seem busy. I'll let you work." Claude got up from the kitchen table and tried to kiss her head. She jerked away. "I'll be out by the pool."

"Claude, I got an email, Doctor Walter D. Fidell. He's not a marriage counselor, but has experience with couples. He's a therapist. If you are interested, he can see us today at two o'clock. We could wait it out for another response if you don't want to see him," Maya said.

"Of course he will do," Claude answered. "Thank you for doing this, for trying. I'm so sorry. This whole thing is my fault. I fucked this up. My folks, well, they didn't give me much to go on when it came to being a good spouse. I'll be out by the pool. Two o'clock."

It was early November, but felt like June. Las Vegas was in a heat spell. Exhausted, Claude relaxed by the pool, periodically dozing off. He spun different versions of how all of this would play out. Maya wasn't as naïve as she was when they were first married. Who the hell knew what Jay, her boyfriend, had told her. Maybe Jay had turned her against him. His death felt that much sweeter.

Maya was bluffing about looking for a marriage counselor. He'd be willing to bet everything that she just emailed psychologists, therapists, and psychiatrists—no marriage counselors. Their marriage would end as soon as Claude was "well". She wanted to get out guilt free.

Claude had some experience in psychology. It was his minor in college, a minor that served him well in his personal life. He knew what buttons to push, how to turn on the tears, all of it. She wanted to play games, he could play games. Her sequel was finished. Soon it would be published. He was almost there.

That afternoon Claude and Maya drove together down the Vegas strip. The office building was a few blocks away from the mall. The building and the waiting room were plain and depressing. An attractive young woman behind a large reception desk checked them in.

Doctor Fidell came out from his office and escorted them back in. The therapist was an overweight, middle-aged, graying black man with a face devoid of expression. He asked general questions and wrote everything down. Claude forced himself to cry, claiming he was going through depression. The doctor offered nothing in terms of sympathy. Instead, he wrote Claude out a prescription for Zoloft.

"Okay, this is just an initial visit. Please take one of these every day, Mr. Kazinsky. I'll see you both tomorrow?" They both nodded. "Mr. Kazinsky, I need a moment alone with Maya. Please wait outside."

Claude sulked on his way out of the office. What the hell did the headshrinker want to talk to her about? Did he lay the lovesick depressed/suicidal pussy on a bit too thick? Claude thumbed through some boring magazines about golf and then watched the receptionist as she talked on the phone. He knew that he shouldn't be checking out other women at this time, but he couldn't help it. The woman looked a lot like Allie. Not as pretty and not as thin, but the same type. He missed Allie. Short phone calls and texts weren't enough. Once Maya ran off to Jay McCallister's funeral, he would go back to Los Angeles.

"Mr. Kazinsky, I need to ask you some more questions," said Doctor Fidell as Maya walked out of his office.

Claude followed him back into the office and continued to act like the love-sick husband who just wanted to make his marriage right. The therapist seemed to be convinced.

# Chapter Twenty-Seven

I saw a shrink once. The state of Nevada forced me to go after I told them that my foster father was molesting me. I only went a few times and swore that I would never return. Doctor Fidell's office could have been the same office that I sat in when I was sixteen. Six years later, my life went full circle. Only this time I wasn't being molested, I was being mentally abused, neglected, and robbed. Always the victim. Oh God, I missed Jay. He would have had the best advice.

Eric told me to leave him and move in. I wanted to so much, but I needed to know that Claude wouldn't do something rash. I couldn't live with the guilt. I wanted Doctor Fidell to give me a yes or no answer—Was he suicidal? I knew it wasn't that simple. My plan to divorce Claude was also not as simple as I hoped.

Claude looked so desolate when he told the doctor about how much I meant to him. He claimed to have nothing left but our marriage. I believed him. The doctor didn't seem to be too sympathetic. He nodded and scribbled what both of us said in his notebook. Once the hour was almost up, he handed Claude a prescription.

"Thank you for seeing us on such short notice, Doctor Fidell," I said as we both got up from the plain, upholstered chairs that sat across from his desk.

"Ms. Smock, I need a moment alone," said the doctor.

I looked into his dark eyes and tried to read them. I sensed some kind of urgency. "I'll be right out, Claude," I said.

Once we were alone, he proceeded to ask me more personal questions. "Is your husband suicidal? How would you describe his mental stability? Does he have a history of mental illness in his family? Is he violent? What kind of family did he come from?" He must have asked at least twenty questions. I didn't know what to make of it.

"Doctor, I'm a little confused. Do you think my husband is suicidal or not? In truth, I have no intention of repairing our marriage. He might not have been the best husband, but I am not the best wife. I just want to move on. I just want someone to say it's all going to be okay. Claude will go away quietly with half of my money and I can start my life over."

"Do you think he is trying to manipulate you into staying married? Using guilt as a means to get you to stay?" he asked, still writing frantically in his notebook.

"I certainly wonder. My husband came from nothing, hell, less than nothing. His mother and brother are criminals. Please don't tell him that. He doesn't know that I know that. My friend found all of this out." And then I started to cry.

"Is there anything else that is going on?"

I looked at the plain white walls. No pictures, no art. The only warmth in room was a wall of built-in bookcases, which held a few knick-knacks, a series of framed degrees, awards, and lots of books. "Doctor, my husband might have loved me once, but it certainly didn't last. His life will go on with or without me. What he loves most about our marriage is my money. I offered him half for an amicable divorce, but evidently that's not enough. Now his life is over. Did you know that you are one of the eight therapists whom I've emailed for a consultation? I just want him to get the help that he needs."

"Yes, you are very clear about that. Maybe you could stay with family or friends for a while," Doctor Fidell said. He fiddled with his double chin. For the first time during their session, he looked nervous. His dark eyes were filled with caution.

"Is that wise? What if he tries something? Who will save him?" I said.

"We'll come up with some kind of plan, some kind of schedule. Right now everyone is highly charged. I know you want to do the right thing," he said, again with a nervous, cautionary look in his dark eyes. "I'll see him now. Please send him in."

I didn't know what to make of all of this psycho mumbo-jumbo. Was the doctor warning me? Or was the doctor being professional, wanting both of our separate story? And what was Claude going to say to him in private? My simple plan continued to get more complicated.

Later on, Claude and I had a quiet dinner and then I went into my room. With each passing minute, I felt more uncomfortable in my own home. Paula called me around eight o'clock.

"Maya, I'm going to assume that you know Jay was...Jay was murdered. The police are calling it foul play, but I know someone killed him," she said.

"Who would want to kill him? He was a quiet man who kept to himself, had a small circle of friends...I just don't understand."

"I don't know either, although he is, I mean was, considered to be a controversial figure. He spent his life talking about aliens. Did you know he got a lot of hate mail?"

"What? He didn't have much security. Just a guard at the front gate and a bunch of cameras," I said.

"And a safe room. And a stockpile of weapons. He was a paranoid man. But I guess not paranoid enough. His security was a Monday through Friday type of thing." Paula paused. I could her voice break. I also wanted to cry, but the tears weren't coming out. "Do you want me to handle his funeral arrangements?"

"Why are you asking me that? I am of course going to come to the funeral, but what can I do to help?" I wondered what kind of funeral it would be. Jay was clear with me that he didn't believe in God.

"I want it to be small, intimate, and no later than the end of the week. His closest friends, some of his colleagues, his agent and publisher, maybe some directors and actors he worked with, and of course his staff. Jay toyed with the idea of one Creator. I consider myself a Christian, not in the traditional sense. Jay and I would get into it. I don't know if I ever convinced him. You also got into it with him on my show. Remember?"

"Yes, of course. Then throw him a Christian funeral with some kind of clergyman. What can I do? I only knew him for a very short time. I wish I knew him better. He had quite an effect on me. I was invited to spend Christmas with him, with you, with all of you. Oh Paula, I can't believe someone would kill him because of his beliefs. Could one of his wives have wanted him dead?"

"All four of them are still alive, but he paid each and every one of them very handsomely after each divorce. The last wife he still sent maintenance checks to. I doubt she'd want him dead. I guess we'll learn more as the week wears on," Paula said.

"Can I come up to San Francisco? I could stay in a hotel, maybe help you make the arrangements?" I said.

"I would love nothing more. But one condition. You will stay with me and Joel. A hotel is out of the question. You've been in my house—it's huge. Come on up whenever you can."

The tears started to stream full force. I wiped my eyes and smiled. Paula couldn't see my face and my voice hadn't broke, but I paused. "I would like that very much. My husband and I are getting a divorce and things are a little bit awkward right now."

# Chapter Twenty-Eight

It was the spring of 1950. Almost three years ago, Andreas was given command of Broom Lake. The sleepy, little airbase that no one had ever heard of was now attracting attention. The space craft was almost complete. The aliens were awake and communicating with Andreas and his staff. Security had to be amped up to unprecedented levels.

The general drove around the entire base, which now expanded twenty miles to the west of the lake and ten miles from the east. Property on the north and south side was not for sale but currently and quietly under negotiation with the United States government. Landowners of worthless desert were about to become rich like the landowners to the east and west of the lake. This and growing security attracted more attention.

No one wanted some yahoo to stumble upon one of the biggest mysteries in the world. All who were in the know were well aware of the unconventional research techniques that the doctors underneath the earth were using. Millions of dollars were invested in keeping everyone who didn't belong out and everyone who did belong in.

Andreas took a long drive around the base in his Jeep and took it all in. The tiny airstrip had turned into the most secure airbase in the country. The soldier patrol, high fences, tanks, cameras, and armed guards in watch towers and guard shacks sent a very clear message. Even a simpleton could speculate that something very secret and valuable was being contained beyond the fence.

The first phase of the project was almost finished. With the ABs help, Costello and the other three engineers assembled the craft. The next step was getting the disc-shaped object up in the air. Andreas didn't want that happen. He had fallen in love Kate Costello and didn't want her to leave. Time was running out—shit or get off the pot.

Andreas had never been a romantic, but Costello had softened his heart. He wasn't skipping around reciting poetry, but did plan an intimate vacation, which Costello agreed to go on.

Being the General of the Air Force had a few perks. Andreas flew Kate out of Broom Lake in a Boeing B-50.

"Is this champagne?" Costello yelled in the seat behind Andreas as he jetted off the runway. Once a mile up in the air, Andreas straightened the plane and headed southwest.

"Yes, that's champagne. But before you start drinking, want to drive?" he asked.

The look in Costello's big hazel eyes said it all. The plane was definitely a nice touch. He crawled out of the seat and helped her get situated, showing her the controls and the steering.

"I can't believe this! I'm flying!" Kate said as she flew over the Nevada/California border. "This is amazing! I feel like I'm on top of the world."

"That's how I feel every time I fly. This is a real short flight, maybe one hour. We'll be there in less than thirty minutes. I have a week of even more surprises." He watched her as she looked out of the cockpit window. *She knows how to put together a spacecraft but never flew a plane. What a woman,* he thought.

"We're landing at a naval base. I'll show you boats and subs like you've never seen before. They're almost as cool as airplanes."

"I can't wait! Robert, this was such a great idea. I haven't had a break let alone a vacation in years. I'm so happy to be here with you."

"Well, I'm going to ask you to move. It's almost landing time."

Andreas landed the plane. Some navy officers pulled the plane into a hangar. A Jeep was given to the general to use for the week. He was considered a king within the military community and took full advantage of royal treatment. His goal was to impress Costello and then ask her to marry him. She was beyond impressed.

"General, Sir, will you be spending some time on the base?" asked one of the naval officers.

"I plan on showing this wonderful lady all of San Diego. We will end our stay by the fifth day of our trip. If you have any vacant barracks or..." the general said.

The navy officer interrupted. "General, Sir, I am under direct orders to give you and your friend the finest living quarters we have to offer. The admiral will be staying in the barracks. We will have it ready for you in five days when you get back from your vacation, Sir."

Costello nodded and smiled. "At ease, Commander. We will be back in five days then."

They drove off from the base to the city.

"General Andreas, Sir, what do you have in store for us this week?" Costello asked in a flirtatious tone. "I do believe that young man wanted to impress you with the admiral's lodging. My, my. You are kicking the admiral out of his home."

"And I'd be insulting him if I didn't stay there. I can't wait to show you their subs. But for now, it's all about the beach. I booked the most beautiful suite right on the beach. Now that's romance, right?"

"Yes, that's romance. I have a feeling you're going to get lucky tonight," Costello said and then winked as Andreas drove alongside the beach. He pulled into a parking lot of an enormous hotel. "Wow. This place is gorgeous. A five star hotel, a private ride on military aircraft, a gorgeous man at my side...Am I dead right now? In heaven?"

The weather in San Diego could not have been more perfect—warm with no rain. They spent four days hanging out on the beach, shopping, eating expensive dinners and making love. Time was passing by too quickly. Andreas wanted to introduce Costello as his finance by the time they got back to the naval base. He brought with him a three carat round diamond set in platinum.

*Get up your nerve. What if she says no*, he wondered. They had been sleeping together for months and she had never once put any pressure on him to marry her. Maybe she didn't want to get married.

Their last day on the beach, Andreas took her to a seafood restaurant recommended by the hotel's concierge. It's now or never. Andreas told her to dress up. He donned a gray suit, the only suit he owned that wasn't military. She wore a floral sleeveless long dress and had her long hair braided into an ornate bun. Beautiful. After lobster and cheesecake, he got down on his knee. Before the words came out, he dug in his pocket for the velvet box.

"Yes!" Costello yelled before he even asked. She threw her arms around him and kissed him. The ring fit perfect. "Oh dear, this is huge. My hand hurts from wearing it. Oh, Robert, it's absolutely gorgeous."

Andreas's two part goal was achieved. He and his fiancée spent the rest of their vacation at San Diego's naval base. He bragged about her accomplishments to anyone who would listen. She was so much more than a pretty face.

The naval base was quite familiar with Broom Lake and its rumors. Andreas only told them his cover story—designing new kinds of aviation and advanced weaponry. The story wasn't exactly a lie so it was easy to say with a straight face, but judging by all of the questions from the navy's top brass, everyone seemed to know the project had something to do with aliens and Nazis.

As the general and his lady said their goodbyes, he asked, "Do you think we have a leak? I mean aliens and Nazis—talk about hitting the nail on the head."

"Maybe, but the heightened security just a few years after Roswell and the unconvincing weather balloon story, well, many people saw the UFO that night. And many people also believe that we took the most brilliant Nazis back here to use. That's why so many of them have never been found."

"You're right. And what does it matter anyway? I'm about to marry the most beautiful, charming, and intelligent woman in the world. Oh, I forgot kind. You are so kind and so good-hearted. So when is the day? Do we get hitched at Broom Lake, Washington D.C., Boston by your family?"

"Robert, I love you with all of my heart. But before we get married, there is one thing I have to do."

"And what's that?" he asked, nervously.

"I have to get that spacecraft up in the air."

Andreas understood that Costello wanted to finish what she and the other engineers had started.

Once back at Broom Lake, Andreas learned that the doctors 'gave birth' to two babies. Once the first baby reached maturity, the doctors cut the cord formed from the baby and lifted him out of the a-womb. He survived on formula for a full day. They repeated the process with the next baby. The doctors wanted the children to study, but didn't want the work that went with two babies. Soon there would be five more ready to take out of the a-womb. The general went down to the lab and held each of them. Both were boys, one white and one black. Both appeared healthy.

Andreas mentioned the miracle to his new fiancée, maybe because she was a woman or maybe because she would soon be his wife. She didn't say a word. Her thoughts about this kind of experiment were hard to read.

Did it disgust her or was she indifferent? He regretted telling her, but soon she and everyone would know. Two babies were hard enough to hide from everyone at the base, let alone seven crying babies.

Costello buried herself in her work. She leaned on Andreas for more access to the ABs, consulting them on just about everything. Their input had reached a plateau. Never once did she ask to see the babies. Did she hate kids or worry that she would have to stop her work and care for them. She was the only woman on the base.

The space craft was Costello's first love. Andreas, too, loved his work more than anyone or anything. They were the perfect couple. And then the day everyone had been waiting for came. The endless piles of metal were soldered together, the control panel was up and running, and the crystal was used as a battery for the controls. The baby craft was repaired and inserted within the space craft's undercarriage. Most of the partitions inside of the hangar came down.

In the middle of the hangar was the oddest flying machine anyone had ever seen. It was round, but not perfectly round with a forty-eight foot diameter. The center of the dark gray disc was raised. Around the raised part were small rectangular windows made with glass or some kind of material that was clear.

Doctors Costello and Kaplan approached the general once he made eye contact. He pointed to the space craft and they nodded.

Andreas climbed inside of the cabin, which was the raised center of the craft. His head brushed the ceiling. Quarters were tight. There was enough room for eight maybe nine adults, but the ABs were considerably smaller. At least twelve ABs could fit.

A panel of controls wrapped around the cabin just below the rectangular windows. There was no seating. The general guessed that they stood up during flight. He hunched over the joystick. This must have been used for steering the craft. "Well, you did it. You put the craft back together."

"We didn't have all of the pieces, but we had enough to patch it back up. We used some aluminum, plastic, magnetized nickel, and other material to fill in the holes," Kaplan said as he showed the general the control panel.

Kaplan then lowered one of the huge chunks of crystal into the bottom compartment. The panel board lit up like a Christmas tree. There were a few similarities between a space craft and jet plane, but this was beyond anything the general could imagine.

"The power—is this all from the crystal? This is better than electricity. I don't understand…What the hell is this?" Andreas asked as he fidgeted with the levers and buttons.

Costello took the crystal rock out of its compartment. "It's like Superman's kryptonite. We know that it's electromagnetic. It might be part of a star, but it's not used for fuel. We aren't sure yet on what they used for fuel. Although there is a small tank that we patched up on the side of the craft. Something liquid was used. One more hurdle to go. The ABs want you to let them out so that they can have a look."

Andreas took the crystal from her arms. It must have weighed at least forty pounds. There was another one about the same size. "Do you think the other rock is a back-up? Like we use back-up batteries?"

Doctor Kaplan interjected, "General, you are exactly right. Again, the ABs are no longer cooperating. All of us are a little nervous that we missed something essential. Oh my, forgive me on my terrible manners. Congratulations. I hear there will soon be a wedding. You two make a fabulous couple."

"Thank you. I just need to get a date from the bride, but first she's determined to get this thing up in the air. Once you figure out what kind of fuel is needed, I'm assuming you plan on flying this."

"We have something else in mind. Still too soon to tell. Once we figure out the fuel, we'll need a pilot. Robert, General Andreas, will you do the honors? It has to be you. Maybe you could talk to the ABs and learn the controls," Costello said. "We could go flying together again, only this time in space."

"If that's what it takes to get a date out of you, I'll talk to them." The three of them laughed. "Kate, snap a few pictures and I'll bring them down with me as a reference. This is really a spectacular day for us and for all of science. This could not have been done without you, all of you. The best think tank in the world. Your findings have paved the way for an American space program. I knew I hired the right team for this and I couldn't be prouder. This little airbase has proven to be a beacon of knowledge to America, maybe even the world. Now excuse me. I will be back to admire your handiwork later on." The general kissed Costello on her head and descended into the earth to check on the new babies.

When looking at the black and white baby boys, Andreas thought of the prostitutes his airmen nabbed. Who was the father? If he had to place a wager on the father, he'd guess Jaeger, but he didn't know. Maybe they alternated paternity. There were five other babies that would soon be ready to take out of the a-wombs. The doctors wasted no time. The a-wombs of the first two babies were already in use with new embryos from the test tubes.

Andreas thought it cruel to raise babies in a laboratory, but they needed to be studied. The two boys were not named, just simply called baby one and baby two. The Nazis' lack of compassion festered like an open sore.

He stuffed his feelings. The project promised the impossible. His star was rising higher than moon. Washington's finest tossed the entire base too many accolades to count.

Within a week another baby was taken out of the a-womb, a boy called Boy Three. The morning after the third baby was born, Andreas must have run ten miles around part of the base. He then went into the weight room, prepared to burn off steam. Jaeger was sitting on the weight bench. The sun had not risen.

"General, I thought you'd be here much earlier," Karl said. His voice sounded hollow.

"I went for a run before my workout. Doctor, what is it?"

"The new baby is gone."

# Chapter Twenty-Nine

I called Eric and told him about Jay's funeral. "Do you want to go with me?" I asked.

"More than anything. Have you talked to a lawyer yet? This whole marriage counselor..."

"Therapist," I corrected.

"Whatever. This is pure manipulation. He's not going to kill himself. It's all bullshit. Listen, I want to be with you more than anything. I wanted this for so long. But is it wise to show up at a funeral of a very famous man with your boyfriend before you are even divorced? You'll look like the asshole even though Claude is the asshole. Maybe you should go alone and if anyone asks, say you're separated."

"I guess you're right. I never thought that..."

"You are famous now. You have a reputation to think about. The press could spin it like you made your way to the top and then dumped the man who helped you get there while he was having a breakdown, etcetera, and etcetera."

"Eric, since when did you know so much about public relations?" I asked.

"I read a lot, and not just science fiction. You know how much I love biographies. Don't let the press cast you in the role of the villain. I'll be here for you always. Let's do this the right way."

Against my better judgment, I left my depressed and suicidal husband home alone. I called Veronica Tatum, his boss, and told her everything. It was the ol' 'pass the buck' routine. And she was more than willing to let me 'pass the buck.' She promised to keep him busy by giving him some new manuscripts to sell.

"I'll have him on a plane by the end of the day. He'll be too busy to think about killing himself," Ronnie said. She made good on her promise.

This was my first taste of power, the power of celebrity. Others would clean up your shit because you made them money. No wonder they called it a trip, a power trip. I had been helpless for so long. This new power encouraged me to change my life for the better. I wanted out of my marriage. The guilt of Claude killing himself vanished. In fact, I almost wished he would end it.

I was on a plane once again, headed to San Francisco. I had just landed in Vegas a few days ago, high on friendships that I made. Now I was returning to say goodbye.

Once I got off the plane, I saw Glenn Lucasek at my gate. He looked like a kind grandfather, wearing jeans and a flannel shirt. He greeted me with a hug.

"You need to get your luggage?" he asked as he took my carry-on from me.

"No, just the one bag. Thank you. What brings you to the airport? I would have just rented a car," I said.

"Paula told me your flight details and then told me to come and get you. She's not taking this well. When she's depressed, she cooks. And she's been cooking for the last two days," Glenn said as I followed him through the airport. "And don't worry about renting a car. You can use mine."

I followed him to the parking lot. The older man moved like a young athlete. I had a hard time keeping up with him. Many people were staring at us and I felt self-conscious.

Glenn must have sensed my insecurity. "We are famous. That's why everyone is staring. You'll get used to it. C'mon. I know a short cut to the parking lot."

Glenn continued his run-walk pace. I had to break into a jog to keep up. We cut across a huge parking lot before reaching his car in the outer parking lot. I panted from the exercise and vowed to get in shape. Glenn laughed. "We're here. Out of breath? We'll have to start running together. You're too young to be this tired. Here's your car for the next few days, weeks, or however long you want to stay. Hope it's up to your liking." Glenn put my bag in the back of the enormous cream-colored SUV.

I got in the front seat and sank into the leather. The walnut interior and sophisticated dash made me think this had to be expensive. "Glenn, this car is beautiful. What kind is it? I'm afraid to drive something this nice."

Glenn laughed. "It's definitely a nice ride. An Escalade. You can fit a lot of people in the car too if you need to. Did you ever ride in Jay's truck?"

"No, but I saw it parked in the front of the house."

Glenn weaved in and out of lanes as we sped out of the airport. "Now that's one piece of crap. He liked it because it didn't have GPS or any computer chips in it. He was so paranoid about some things, but not paranoid enough in others. I'm going to miss that guy."

"I just began to get to know him. It's not fair."

"You might not have known him for long, but you knew who he was and what he was about. You shared a bond with him that will never be broken." Glenn was on the highway, patiently idling through a traffic jam. "Maya, did you know I was a lawyer?"

"I think Jay mentioned it. You are his lawyer, right?" I asked.

"Well, yes. Part-time lawyer. I handle legal affairs for my friends, mainly Jay." Traffic cleared up. Glenn sped up the car. His cloudy blue eyes looked troubled with grief along with something else. "I represented him in two out of his four divorces, real estate deals, business matters, problems, and now I handle probate." Tears ran down his cheeks. "Oh God, if You really do exist and I sure hope You do, may Jay be up there with you right now. I'm sorry, just a little emotional. I don't know if Jay was religious. Paula was working on his spirituality. He never left anything in writing or mentioned what kind of funeral to have. We are guessing—burial or cremation. With his money, we could freeze him. I think it is called cryogenics? Anyway, you, Mercedes, Paula, maybe even Joel, and I are going to gorge on Paula's cooking and discuss how we want to handle the arrangements. He had no other family but us. He had a ton of business associates, Hollywood actors and writers and directors, and even some fans who will get an invite. Figure on five hundred people showing up for this."

I was beyond flattered to be included in Jay's funeral, but felt like that I hadn't known him long enough to have a say. We were off of the highway and Glenn began to slow well below the speed limit.

"We're almost at Paula's. I need to tell you something. There is no easy way to say this so I'm just going to blurt it out. You're probably questioning why you are so involved with the funeral arrangements or why you were invited to help out instead of just being a guest. Maya, you're Jay's heir, his sole heir. Everything is yours. He had me print up a will, which he signed the last night you were his guest. In fact, he signed it on the roof, right before the séance."

My head was spinning so fast that I thought it was going to fall off of neck. "Pull over now!" I opened the door in the nick of time. Orange vomit came out of my mouth like a waterfall. I saw the Slurpee I had at the airport, the toast, and even that bag of peanuts I had on the plane gush onto the cement road. After everything was up, I sat back in the car with the door open.

"There's more. You might want to keep the door open for this one. Okay, here it is. He didn't want to tell you because he thought it might scare you away. Maria, his maid if you remember, went into your bathroom and rummaged through your personal stuff and…Well, he wanted items with your DNA so he could run a test and compare it with his. He wasn't joking about being your brother. And I'll be damned, he is your brother, half-brother. I don't know how. You both must have been part of a laboratory experiment, I don't know. You're his family, his only family. He never had any kids."

Just when I thought my stomach was empty, I heaved some bile mixed with more orange Slurpee. "What? That's impossible! What did Maria take?"

"She took hair from your brush and a couple of used tampons in your garbage. I brought you the results. Do you want…"

"This is just crazy, fucking crazy. Just drive. I'm done puking."

We rode in silence. I couldn't believe he was my brother, my flesh and my blood. I thought about the money. Jay must have been worth a billion, give or take. What did I know about high finance? I could barely manage the small fortune that was recently earned from my novel. I could fuck up an empire.

A few minutes went by and then my stomach dropped down to the center of the earth. "Glenn, am I a suspect? Talk about motive. Once the police find out I had what? A billion reasons to kill him?"

"Actually one point three billion reasons, but no, you're not a suspect to my knowledge. And if you need a lawyer, I'll help you out and find you the best."

"I thought you were the best."

"Ah, not for murder. But they aren't sure if it was murder and I am assuming you had an alibi," Glenn said. "You didn't even know about the will until this very moment. Besides, they aren't saying there's even an investigation. He drowned in his pool. Maybe it was an accident." The tone in his voice didn't sound too convincing. "But there is even more to tell you. Maybe I should spoon feed you on this."

"That ship has sailed, Glenn. Keep it going," I said, prepared for anything.

"I assure you it's not a dream. I don't think Jay accidentally drowned. He was a great swimmer, swam almost every day. Maybe someone drowned him. This isn't the first time someone... Look, years ago there was an incident. Someone tried to kill him. He had written a book badmouthing the government, claiming that they were covering up something on a global level. It was called *And They Knew*. On TV and radio interviews, he spouted all kinds of conspiracy theories. Threats of libel and defamation were tossed around. Book sales tanked.

"Jay was too drunk and stoned to really care. He had just divorced Number Three. Someone took a shot and a bullet went through his head while he was out bar hopping down at the Wharf. The bullet wound was healed in hours. Doctors said they never seen anything like it. They never found the bullet. But going by the wound, it grazed his brain. Jay thought it was a gun for hire by his ex. I begged him to get security. He was still in Los Angeles at the time and made somewhat of an effort. He moved into a mammoth estate, almost like a fortress. A couple of armed guards patrolled the place around the clock. Then after Number Four, he moved here. No other attempts were made and he scaled back on his security. It wasn't an ex. It was the government. Only problem is I can't prove it."

I was flabbergasted. "So this swimming accident is really the government finishing what they started?" Glenn nodded and pulled up in front of Paula's house. I remembered the house. The Victorian was hard to miss— one of the prettiest homes I had ever seen. "Do you have a copy of that book? The nonfiction one about the cover-up?"

"Yes, but you also have a copy. Jay kept all of his work in his library. His house is now your house. Please keep all of this quiet for now. The press will be all over you soon enough."

"Glenn, I'm about to file for divorce. Will Claude be entitled to…"

"No, not in Nevada, not even in California. But if you die before the divorce…then that's another matter. I don't know your husband, but divorce can get ugly and again, security would be wise. Maya, one more thing. The TAH Institute—T.A.H. It stands for They Are Here."

I knew exactly what he was talking about. "Yes, yes. You talk about it all the time on your show. You've got experts who prove that aliens are here on Earth besides roaming through the skies. It's kind of like SETI or MUFAN."

"It's a little bit different than those two organizations. We do some work with UFO sightings and abductions, but we've been investigating certain inner circles for years. Now that Jay is gone, I will need someone to continue his work. Would you be interested?"

"Do you need money to continue?" I asked, not sure where he was going with this.

"Oh, no. It's funded by like-minded people. Rich people. Important people. We employ dozens of scientists and doctors. We also have dozens of volunteers. I don't need money. We have plenty sitting in a trust. What I need is you. Jay and I were making some amazing progress. And now he's gone. Will you help me? You're pretty and young and now you're famous. Think about it."

Before I could answer, there was a knock on my window. Paula stood outside of the door. I heard her yell, "You two coming in or are you going to sit in the car the whole damn day?"

Glenn and I got out of the car. Before entering the house, he put his index finger to his lips, motioning me to keep quiet. I suddenly thought of Claude and again wished he would pull the trigger, slit the wrists, start the engine with the garage door closed, or whatever way he wanted to leave this world. He had one point three billion more reasons not to leave.

Glenn and I followed Paula to the door. This was the first time I saw her without makeup, dressed in loungewear with her hair pulled back in braids. She was still beautiful, but her large brown eyes were puffy and lined.

Paula led us into the kitchen. Mouth-watering smells filled the air and suddenly I was hungry. Mercedes was seated at the table, looking every bit the gorgeous actress that she was. Not a hair out of place or wrinkle to be seen. But beneath the put together, stunning exterior there was a break in her voice as she said hello and stood up to hug me. Paula's brother, Joel, was the only one missing from our little clique, but then maybe he was not part of the clique, just a brother who worked with Paula. Again, I didn't know everyone that well.

I excused myself and made a beeline to the bathroom. I washed my face, rinsed the vomit out of my mouth, and gargled with the mouthwash that was underneath the sink. I sat on the toilet and cried. My brother, my blood was gone. All my life I wished I had a real family and just when I miraculously found one, it was taken away. Fate was ruthless. Several minutes must have went by. There was a knock at the door.

"You okay, girl?" It was Paula.

"Yeah, I'll be out in a minute," I answered. Sheepishly, I opened the door and wiped my eyes once more. I followed Paula back to the kitchen. Jay might have been gone, but I was still part of this little family. The only one missing for me at this moment was Eric. He should have been here by my side. The hell with what anyone thought.

"All right, y'all, I've got quite a spread going. Fried chicken, mac and cheese, homemade onion rings, seven cup salad, coleslaw, and loaded baked potato skins. That should clog up your arteries. And desert, well I'll tell you about that spread later. Let me set up my island like a buffet style restaurant. Be just a few minutes," Paula said in her attempt to sound upbeat.

We stuffed ourselves and talked mostly about Jay. He was truly the most remarkable man I had ever known. I even laughed when Glenn talked about some of the trouble they both had gotten into. I learned quickly that Glenn had known him the longest, almost thirty years. Mercedes shared that she used to date Jay. His track record and idiosyncrasies ended the romance, but he was too special to her and her to him to completely end it. They promised each other to be friends and they both kept that promise without regrets.

I'll never forget that meal, almost like our last meal before everything changed. During desert we discussed the funeral. I had no idea what an event it would be. Jay, the eccentric billionaire author, had few people in his life who knew him well, but his list of acquaintances was endless. The funeral was more about being seen than saying goodbye.

Mercedes wanted a classy funeral, one with Jay inside of a casket in a prestigious Catholic church. She wanted him buried in a Christian cemetery despite his shaky religious beliefs. With a few modifications to this basic plan, Paula agreed.

Glenn, on the other hand, wanted the funeral to have a circus-like atmosphere. He laid it all out, "None of us are certain on how Jay felt about God, so let's take church out of the equation. If he believed and made it into Heaven, then how we throw his last party is irrelevant. I was thinking of something more unconventional, maybe a huge wake, catered in one of the finest hotels in the city. Forget about a burial, cryogenics would be the way Jay would want to go."

A friendly debate that bordered on a heated argument began. I sat back and listened to both sides, and knew in my heart that I was the only one who could legally make this decision.

"First, we aren't even sure how he died. The police aren't broadcasting anything. So based on that aspect alone, cremation has to be out of the question. If new developments occur, then the police can't exhume the body for answers. I am in favor of having his body frozen. It's eccentric, scientific, and might even be practical for the police if they need to reexamine the body. After the wake, we can host a dinner at one of the best hotels in the city with five hundred or so of his favorite acquaintances. We'll have an open mic and let the guests say something about Jay. As far as where the wake takes place, maybe we could all compromise. If Glenn gets his way on the cryogenics, then maybe Mercedes and Paula should get their way on the location of the wake," I announced. Did Paula and Mercedes know I was his sister?

"We could make it work if the church was at least nondenominational. Catholic Church insinuates that Jay had a religious preference and we don't even know if he believed in God. Let's not be too hypocritical," Glenn said.

I looked at the women, hoping they would cave. It took a few more minutes of bantering back and forth, but we now had a loose plan.

# Chapter Thirty

Claude's mind was a whirl. He and Sam had just pulled off the murder of the century by drowning a man after they shot him. Foul play? Did the police completely miss the bullet wounds? Or were he and Sam the luckiest bastards around?

His ringer went off. "Hello."

"Claude, I need you here in Los Angeles. Got a line wrapped around the block of hot new authors who only want to work with you," Veronica Tatum said.

"They want Maya Smock's husband, not me," he said.

He heard Ronnie sigh in annoyance. "What difference does it make?"

It made all the difference in the world to Claude. He was just about finished with working for a living. Soon, he would be sitting on a beach, drinking cocktails and reading books for fun. He would be fucking Allie, playing bigshot, and vacationing all over the world. All he needed was a little more time and patience.

Sorry he picked the phone, Claude said, "Veronica, I don't know. I'm going through quite a funk right now. Doctor's got me on Zoloft. Maya and I are seeing a therapist. I just don't…"

"Pack your bags and keep yourself busy. I know Maya is out of town."

Claude thought about it and he really wanted to be in L.A. He also needed to talk to Sam and feel him out. "Maya called you, didn't she?" There was an uncomfortable pause on the phone. "All right, but just until she gets back."

"You won't regret it. I'm handing you on a silver platter a tell-all book about the former Speaker of the House. This new writer interviewed his girlfriend, former wives, politicians who were fucked over, everybody. It's a sure thing," Veronica said.

"That's quite a bone to toss me. I really appreciate it. You've always stuck by me—all of my highs, my lows, you were there. I should have married you, Ronnie."

"I would have said no. Now quit feeling sorry for yourself. You and Maya are going to work it out." Veronica hung up.

Claude was already weary of Vegas despite only being there a day. Ronnie's offer was too good to pass up. He called Sam and Allie to tell them he was driving in. Several hours later, he arrived at his apartment and found Allie stretched out on the sofa wearing thigh high leather boots, pasties, and a garter belt without panties. She belonged in Playboy. Claude pounced on her with raw, animalistic emotion. He missed her, his love den, his Los Angeles life.

Afterwards, Allie lit up a joint, took a toke, and handed it to Claude. As they got high together on the sofa, she asked, "Did you kill Jay McCallister?"

Claude coughed so hard that phlegm spewed all over the coffee table. "For Christ's sake! Are you fucking nuts? Why in the world would you even think that?" he yelled. His fantasy sex slave was full of surprises.

Allie got up, still in her sexy lingerie, and walked over to the fridge, helping herself to a chilled bottle of wine. As she uncorked it, she poured two glasses and sat back down next to Claude. Smiling, she said, "C'mon. She's up in San Francisco right now, isn't she? Was that where you were last week? Spying on her? Was she stepping out on you?"

Claude needed a break. His apartment had always been his refuge. How dare she accuse him of spying, of killing, of being a jealous husband. He stood up from the couch and hit her. Wine spilled all over the floor. She winced in pain, but was not afraid. She glared at him with those bedroom blue eyes.

"Clean it up!" he yelled.

She laughed and strolled into the kitchen for some paper towels. "You hit me because I'm right." She threw the roll onto the floor and stared as it absorbed the dark red liquid. She was wasted.

"You need to shut your fucking mouth right now, Allie. You don't know what you're talking about!"

"I know exactly what I am talking about. And don't worry. I'll help you kill her when the time comes. You see, Claude, you don't need to pretend with me. We're cut from the same cloth. We want the same things. That's why we are so perfect together."

Claude set his wine down. He didn't know if he wanted to kiss or kill her. He opted on the kiss, which led to a second round of sex. This time she leaned over the ottoman and Claude took her from behind. They both exploded within minutes. He fell asleep for the first time in days.

The next morning, Claude went into the office and met his new client. The author was impeccably dressed in preppy clothes and round glasses. He wore a bow tie and looked like someone who saw himself more important than he actually was. Nevertheless, Veronica knew he would make the agency a lot of money with his unauthorized biography on the Speaker of the House. Timing was essential before the story died down.

The author rambled on about how important his book was, even mentioning distinct literary awards that were expected after publication. After a few hours of listening to all of the man's demands, Claude was certain that working for a living was not for him. Soon he would be able to tell Ronnie to fuck off, but for now he nodded and assured the man that his book would be published and then on the best seller's list by the next month.

After Claude gently shuffled his new author out of the agency, he called Sam. "Lunch?"

Sam grunted something that sounded like a yes and then said, "Mellidano's. I'm starved and they got fresh homemade pasta."

Within thirty minutes, the two half-brothers sat inside of the Italian restaurant and studied the menu. Claude wasn't reading the meal choices.

As soon as the waitress took their order, Claude got straight down to business. "Looks like we're in the clear. They are calling it drowning. The incompetence is almost scary. How the hell did they miss the bullet wounds? Or the shell casings? Or are they covering something up? Was he involved in some top secret shit?"

"I killed for you, Claude. And I feel just terrible about it. Can't eat, can't sleep…"

"Really? You ordered yourself appetizers and one of the largest meals on the menu," Claude said, half expecting some sort of shakedown. He was prepared to negotiate.

"This is the first time I ate since we, you know. I haven't been to work since. Saw Mom yesterday. Drove all the way out to Chowchilla and back just to talk to her for an hour. She misses you, you know. She said you never write or call, let alone visit. How could you be so cold? She's our mother. She raised us the best that she could," Sam said.

The waitress placed two platters of appetizers in the middle of the table and set down two plates. Had they not been in public, Claude would have strangled him.

Once the waitress walked off, Claude said, "You weren't stupid enough to tell her, were you? Please tell me you didn't tell that cunt about Jay." Claude grabbed his white linen napkin and twisted it tight around his hands.

"No, of course not. But I told her that you could have got me sent away. That you had your own plans, your own get rich scheme. She told me that if I had to get my hands dirty, then I also should get half of whatever you benefit from all of this."

Claude knew his brother well. Sam was clearly lying. He was a real mama's boy despite all of the shit the bitch put both of them through. When she got out of prison, he worried that he'd have to cut her in as well. *South America, new name*, Claude thought. With his greedy fucked up family he always had to be thinking of his next five moves as if life was a real game of chess.

"Sam, what do you want? I've got my own problems. As you know, Maya wants a divorce. The only reason she's still around is because Jay is now out of the way and I am playing the suicide card. You want me to divorce her now? I'll get tops two million, that's a million for you if we split it, which I'm not willing to do. This was my plan, my idea, and Mom is not gonna fuck it all up like she fucked up her life. You want more than what was promised, then you'll have to wait. Maya is done with the sequel. She's just cleaning up the manuscript as we speak. Hold on a little longer and I'll have a whole lot more than two million to walk away with."

"You gonna kill her too?" Sam said as he stuffed his face with calamari and bruschetta.

"Yeah right. Where did you get that idea? Mom? That would probably be her next move. Please tell me you never told Mom that I got married." There was a pause in the conversation. Sam wouldn't look at him and continued to stuff his face. "Okay. You never told her that I am married to someone rich, did you?"

"No, but I told her your wife's name. Is that okay?"

Claude's food was set in front of him. He had a strong urge to stuff it down Sam's throat, kind of like the way livestock farmers stuffed food down the throat of geese. It was a mistake to get Sam involved. Their mom had her hooks in him from little on. As sure as the sun rose in the east, his mother would have had someone Google up Maya's name. She undoubtedly knew the exact amount of money Claude was sitting on. But she had another five years at least, and that was with good time. She was only forty-nine years old, so he couldn't count on her dying any time soon.

"Sam, I am really disappointed in you. After everything she has done to both of us. I was more of a parent to you than she ever was. Go ahead and stuff your face. Just remember, you fuck this up, you get nothing. If I go down, you'll go down with me, and that's a promise." Claude threw a fifty dollar bill on the table and left.

A few days went by and everything calmed down. Jay McCallister's death was reduced to a freak drowning accident. Claude talked to Maya a few times and she told him about the funeral arrangements and how she'd be home soon. She seemed to be one of the people organizing the whole thing while never explaining to Claude why. But Claude already knew why. She was fucking him and now had the nerve to play grieving widow. The whole thing made him look like a cuckold. That was the part he'd play, the desperate, pathetic, mentally unstable wimp who wanted to save his marriage. She would be the whore who was stepping out on him with a billionaire.

The weekend came and Claude lay in bed with Allie while watching the news. Jay's funeral was scheduled. Claude wondered if it would make the news. He knew that many celebrities would be there. It was a real dog and pony show. He saw Maya in the front pew of the church, dressed in a simple gray suit. She looked like she had been crying.

"Was Maya fucking the guy or what? Look, she's got tears in her eyes. And the cameraman keeps putting the camera on her. There's like thirty or forty celebs there and it's Maya who gets all the attention. Why? Kind of weird that you're not there. She's sitting in the front row, as if she's his wife or something. This is really fucked up, Claude," Allie said in a slurred voice.

Claude had an uneasy feeling. Was it public knowledge that Maya was with Jay? Was there something else that he had missed? Allie continued to goad him on. He tuned her out and turned up the volume on the television. There were at least three cameras, one pointing at the closed casket set before the church's lavish altar, one pointed at the pews, and another camera that zoomed in on celebrities, especially Maya.

The beautiful Asian reporter was live on the scene. "Jay McCallister drowned last Sunday in swimming pool. He was sixty-six years old. He will not be buried or cremated, but frozen shortly after the service. His net worth is estimated over one billion dollars. He leaves behind no wife, no children, and no known family. Who will inherit the McCallister fortune? Some believe it will roll into the T.A.H. Foundation, which was co-founded with long-time friend, Glenn Lucasek. Others believe author Maya Smock will be the beneficiary. This is Suzanne Lu reporting from San Francisco."

Claude looked at Allie after the segment. Her expression was a mix of adoration and joy. The news program broke into a commercial break.

"Did I hear that woman correctly?" Allie screamed. She stood on the bed and started to jump. "Maya might inherit one billion dollars. One fucking billion dollars! Claude, you're gonna be one of the richest men in the world. One billion dollars!" She jumped and laughed like a child.

"Stop it! You don't know that. You heard the reporter. It's an unconfirmed rumor. The money will probably go to his foundation. Please keep it down. You're really loud," Claude said. She ignored him and ran into the kitchen, filling up their wine glasses.

Maya inheriting this prick's fortune certainly put a new spin on things. Claude wanted to join Allie by jumping and screaming and carrying on, but he needed more information. Should he call Maya and just ask her? The phone rang.

"Hey." It was Sam. "Did you see the news? Your wife might inherit one billion dollars. You owe me, asshole." Click.

Claude ignored the threat and hoped Sam didn't run off to Chowchilla to tell Mom. He could only imagine the hell that the two of them would inflict if the rumor was true. Claude stayed up a little longer, drinking and fucking Allie. His mind raced with possibilities, the kind of possibilities that come with unlimited funds.

Allie passed out around one o'clock in the morning, but Claude was wide awake. He logged onto his computer, looking up T.A.H. or *They Are Here*, Jay's foundation. There were all kinds of links that led back to Glenn's television show, *Alien Theories*. The "about us" page explained T.A.H.'s origins and goals. Glenn and Jay put some of their own money into its birth, buying a world class observatory and office in Nevada. Their goal was to prove the existence of aliens and their influence on major world events such as politics, science, culture, religion, entertainment, media, and academia. *Conspiracy crap*, thought Claude.

He continued reading the website. T.A.H. had raised over eight hundred million dollars over the last twenty-five years. *Who the hell would donate a cent to this bullshit let alone eight hundred million dollars?* He continued to read. There were all kinds of UFO sightings, crop circles, artifacts, and claims of alien abductions. Jay and Glenn even built a museum inside their headquarters that contained some of the "evidence" that proved alien existence.

According to the website, they were in possession of top secret artifacts that proved alien involvement of the world. Other tabs had astronomy photos taken by some of their telescopes of constellations that supposedly meant something to the future of the world. There was even more nonsense that was spewed by doctors and scientists who volunteered to work for T.A.H. The more Claude read, the more he understood why he got away with Jay's murder. Jay was poking the proverbial bear.

Jay spent his life as a thorn in the side of the world's superpowers. Part of the website posted a manifesto of sorts, claiming a cover-up on alien findings by the inner circle of the world. The website had a testimonial page. Surprisingly, at least one hundred celebrities and credible people wrote praise over the T.A.H. Institute. If Jay was declared murdered, it would only add fuel to the conspiracy.

Claude moved on to some legal sites and looked up Nevada divorce law. Quickly he learned that he would not be entitled to a cent of Maya's inheritance unless she comingled the money. At this point, he doubted that she would be that stupid. Plus, she had Jay's smart friends helping her. *It was probably fucking Glenn who wrote the will*, thought Claude. It said on the T.A.H. website that Glenn had once been a lawyer.

The sun was about to rise. He planned to call Maya later on. Maybe she would tell him the truth. If divorce was her goal, and Claude believed that it was, he had to be ready. There were a lot of *ifs* to think about. The biggest *if* was *if* Maya really did inherit a billion bucks, she would have to die.

# Chapter Thirty-One

"One of your babies is missing? Where are Hans and Frederik?" Andreas asked, not especially alarmed. He thought the security around the base was almost perfect. Apparently not.

Jaeger sat on one of the weight benches in the general's weight room. "They are roaming the base right now. The baby was changed, fed, and then put down in his crib at midnight. When I woke up at five o'clock this morning, he was gone. That's when I woke up Frederik and Hans. General, this is not an outside job. Someone with clearance, someone who knew our routine kidnapped the baby. I went through the camera tapes inside of the lab. Nothing but a black screen. This is very intentional. Whoever took the baby, knew exactly where the cameras were mounted. A cloth was draped over every camera. We can only hear footsteps and baby sounds. Didn't see a thing. General, you might not want to hear this, but…"

"Who is watching the other babies and embryos right now?" Andreas interrupted. Jaeger looked down at the ground. "Are you nuts? This could be some kind distraction. You need to get back down to that laboratory now. I will assign a few more men to guard the perimeter. What are you thinking leaving the lab unattended? No wonder it was so easy…"

"General, please, I was just about to return." Jaeger stood up from the weight bench and rocked on his feet.

"What? Then why are you still here?" yelled Andreas.

"Your fiancée, Doctor Costello. She has been in our lab. You took her there several times. She, well, she always seemed like she didn't approve of our experiment. Could you at least question her?" Jaeger asked.

Andreas wanted to choke him. *Of course it had to be Kate*, he thought with venom, *she's a woman and finds creating babies in laboratories offensive. As if she were the only one on the base who might think the German doctors' methods were unethical.*

Andreas stepped close to the doctor, close enough to make him flinch. "I've just about had it with you and your Nazi buddies. How dare you accuse her? Just about everyone at this base who knows what you are doing does not approve. You are altering human life. And you will be judged for it, in this life or the next. You, Frederik, and Hans go against God. But I will question Kate along with all of the airmen, engineers, scientists, soldiers, and laborers after I review the tapes. We will find out who took the baby and we will get him back. Now please, Doctor, get back down to the laboratory and guard your genetic empire before it's all gone."

Doctor Jaeger silently left the weight room. Andreas cut his workout short, called Major Lamphrey, and explained the situation. The sirens rang. There was a breach on the base.

The general quickly changed out of his workout clothes without showering. There were four large trailers around the base. Each trailer served as a camera room and break room for the security guards posted around the perimeter of the base. Andreas headed for the eastern trailer by foot. It was only a few hundred yards away from headquarters.

The walk gave him time to cool off. How dare Jaeger insinuate that Kate had something to do with any of this? But then if Jaeger was thinking she took the baby, then others probably did as well. About halfway to the security shack, Andreas turned around and headed back to his trailer. She would be there. He found her in the bathroom, brushing her hair. She looked at him and smiled.

"Forget something?" Kate asked. Andreas shook his head. "Sirens woke me up. Is everything all right?"

"No, we have a serious problem. Stolen property."

"Oh no. You've got cameras all over the place. I hope you find the thief." Costello seemed oblivious to the problem at hand. She was either the coolest cucumber he had ever seen under pressure, or she didn't have anything to do with it.

"I will. I'm headed to one of the trailers to review the tapes. One of the doctors' babies was stolen," he said, examining her face, looking for signs of stress.

"What? Oh no! That's terrible! What can I do? Maybe we could help comb the area, organize some kind of search party," she said. Her voice sounded surprised and sincere.

"Maybe. I'm working on it. You should keep your radio on. I'll give out instructions after the tapes. Probably won't find much. It was clearly an inside job. Whoever took the baby knew exactly where the cameras in the doctors' lab were."

"Maybe it's for the best. Whoever took the baby might have wanted it to have a normal life." Costello sat down and tied up her sneakers.

"Maybe. Karl Jaeger actually thought it was you. He said that you look at him and the other two doctors with scorn. And you are a woman. Although he didn't specifically give that as a reason."

Costello stood up with her hands on her hips and yelled, "Do you think I took the damn baby? Am I being questioned here? Is that why you're here? Time is ticking and you are here asking me about the baby?"

"No, I just came back here to see if..." Andreas couldn't come up with a reason quick enough to explain his pit stop back home. "I just wanted to grab an extra radio..."

"Bullshit!" Costello exclaimed. "So you think that just because I have shared with you how Karl and his Nazi friends are a bunch of mother fuckers… You think I must have waited for you to fall asleep, snuck into their lab, and then what? Took the baby? Okay, where's the baby then if I took it? Or did I give it up for adoption in the last few hours?"

Costello's hazel eyes raged, but she had a point. Was it even possible for her to have enough time? If she was involved, could there have been another person helping her? Andreas didn't want to believe she had anything to do with it.

"I'm sorry. You're right. Just keep your eyes and ears open. I'm going to try and solve this mystery. Karl was the one who put the thought in my head and I should have known better. He could even be involved, who knows why. Please forgive me. I am an asshole. This time I really am going to the trailer."

Costello didn't kiss him goodbye, just stormed out the front door. Andreas felt guilty for accusing her of something so sneaky, but no one, not even she, was above suspicion. Morality wasn't the only motive for stealing the baby. Money came to mind, lots of money. The baby was evidence of aliens, genetic engineering, cloning, fertilization without sexual reproduction and so much more. The baby was face of progress.

An urge to snoop came over Andreas. He went through Costello's toiletries in the bathroom and then the dresser she kept some things in. Nothing. His trailer was too small to hide anything, yet Andreas combed every square inch of the room. He felt better. She had to be telling the truth.

Too much time was wasted. Instead of walking, the general jumped into his jeep and sped up to the east trailer of the airbase. Three guards were inside of the trailer rolling camera tape.

"You know what we are looking for?" Andreas asked. The three men were young, maybe twenty years at most, all too young to be part of the war.

The skinny blonde man was the first to answer. "General, Sir, we were told that one or more people on this base stole part of a top secret operation. We have been running the tapes since twenty-three hundred last night. So far, we have not seen anyone come or go. We are now viewing the tapes of the base's perimeter starting 0100 hours, Sir."

"And you name?" Andreas asked. Impressed with all of the men's initiative.

"Isaac Godfrey, General."

"Got your radio?" asked the general. Isaac nodded. "Good. Radio me the second you find something."

Andreas drove around the lake beyond the small mountain range to the far western trailer of the airbase. There were two soldiers inside reviewing tape from 0200 to 0300 hours. One of the men he knew.

"Captain Redding, surprised to see you here," Andreas said as he climbed into the trailer.

"General Andreas, I just got here. This is First Lieutenant Charles Avignon. He might have found something, Sir." Redding pulled up a chair to the cameras and the general sat down. "General, at 0242 hours there is something a little out of the ordinary. See this?"

First Lieutenant Avignon replayed the tape. Andreas saw a dimly lit still of a gravelly area. Several seconds later he saw a shadow. It passed over the gravelly area in less than a second, almost as if it or he or she knew exactly where the camera was.

"What camera is this?" Andreas asked.

"It's about seventy five yards that way, General," Avignon answered.

"This could have been so easy to overlook. Good work, Lieutenant. Let's take a ride. I want to see for myself."

In less than a minute Andreas, Avignon and Redding were standing in front of the camera that caught the shadow.

"So this is the gravelly area," Andreas said as he walked around the camera, up and down the area, and then into a grassy area beyond the gravel. The three men combed the area for several minutes.

"General, Captain, I found a pacifier!" yelled Avignon. He stood about eight yards away from the security camera in the grass, facing the side of the camera, away from the lens. Another twenty yards away was a wall with barbed wired on both sides.

*Fuck, fuck, fuck, fuck*, thought the general. About half of a mile past the wall was a public road. He couldn't call the Nevada police.

"General, the thief had to have climbed the wall, and then cut the wire with a baby in tow. Not saying it's impossible, but it would have been much easier to do if an accomplice helped the kidnapper escape through one of the checkpoints. Maybe we should be questioning the guards at the exit posts inside of the wall," said Redding.

"I agree. Lieutenant, you stay here. I'll get you a partner. We are on high alert. Captain, take me to the closest exit from this trailer. And get me a schedule of whom was supposed to be working between 0200 and 0300 hours."

Just as the general sat down in the jeep with the captain, his radio went off.

"Go ahead," Andreas said.

"General, it's gone. They're gone." It was Major Lamphrey. His voice had lost all military decorum in his radio etiquette.

"Not sure if I read. Repeat." Andreas was losing his patience.

"General, you're needed in the hangar now. Radio unsecure, Sir," yelled Lamprey.

Irritation turned to sheer panic. Could they mean the ABs? Could it mean the space craft? Was the missing baby a distraction? He looked at Captain Redding and said, "I've got to go now. Please check out that guard shack for me." Andreas peeled away from the trailer and headed back to headquarters.

# Chapter Thirty-Two

I went shopping with Mercedes the day before Jay's funeral. She, Paula, Glenn, and I set up every detail, made hundreds of phone calls, and went through dozens of photo albums and videos. People who either worked for or worked with Jay sent us pictures.

We agreed to run a slide show during banquet hall dinner after the wake. Jay's body would be shipped to a cryonics clinic in Southern California. Once he was set in ice, he would then be sent to the T.A.H. Institute to be stored.

Mercedes and I bought large electronic picture frames for every banquet table, each loaded with dozens of digital photos of Jay. Sutton Wycliff, one of the many directors Jay had worked with, offered to put together a movie collage of all Jay's novels that were turned into movies. Everything was coming together. He would be remembered.

"The press is going to eat me alive," I said. "I'm going to be cast into the role of the young hoochie mama who stepped out on her suicidal husband to gold dig on one of the richest men in the world. What should I wear? Mini-skirt? Bra-top?"

"No. Be easy on yourself. You were his friend, not his whore. Get some thick skin. Yes, everyone is going to whisper. But who cares. Saks Fifth Avenue is right down the street. Let me buy you a smashing suit that says 'friend' and not 'grieving girlfriend'. You're going to be on the news and probably the entertainment shows as well. Be ready and look like a serious woman. Don't look like a poor slob."

Before I could argue with her, she led me down the street straight to the glitzy department store. I had heard of Saks, but never shopped there. Mercedes quickly picked out three suits each in a size 6. One was gray, one black, and one was a mustard dress with matching jacket. I tried them on and modeled them for her.

"No black. Too much like a grieving widow. The gray Alexander McQueen. Here. A simple navy shell to go on underneath the jacket. Shoes will be some sort of gray heels. Done. You can wear that necklace you always wear, you know, the one you bought with Jay. The ruby one. It's gorgeous and would go."

Mercedes picked out the shoes faster than the suits and then threw in a gray clutch. The bill was over ten thousand dollars. My jaw dropped.

"Mercedes, this is too much. Please…"

"Maya, I'm rich. Not as rich as you are, but I can afford it or I wouldn't offer. Trust me. You want to look like you've got your act together. Now we will go get our nails done and then call it the day." Mercedes handed me the bags. "You get to carry this."

I carried the bags back to Glenn's Escalade and then drove to Mercedes's favorite salon. A manicure cost about five times more than the going rate, again the service was her treat. The place looked more like a five star hotel lobby with marble floors, a bar, library, wide screen televisions all over, and nail stations. She and I got basic French manicures and talked about all of the details.

"This funeral will do Jay justice," she said. "Do you feel like you know him better now that you've seen all of the photos and videos?"

I started to cry. A few moments later, I calmed myself down. "Yes and it makes me sadder. He was such an amazing person. You know I have no family. My marriage is in shambles…"

"Claude will soon be gone. You mentioned there was someone special back in Vegas. Tell me about him."

"He saved me in a way that is so hard to explain. You see, I never told him about my childhood, but I was an orphan and then a foster child. I was molested. He took me in without any strings. He was my friend when I could no longer trust." I started to cry and she gingerly held my wrist. I told her almost everything as we waited for our nails to dry. I wished Eric was with me.

"Eric sounds pretty special. And he's right. He would only make you look, well, like a cold, heartless man-eater. In a very short time, you will be able to live how you want to live. Get divorced first. Maya, did Glenn tell you about T.A.H.?" Mercedes asked as she motioned for us to leave. The manicurist tested our nails and nodded.

"Yes. It stands for They Are Here. I watch his show, so I am somewhat familiar."

"It's not a gimmick. It's real. Everything about it is real. In fact, Glenn downplays most of what goes on there. He wants you to fill Jay's shoes. They started the organization together and he doesn't want to run it alone. I'm not sure he can run it alone."

"Are you part of it too?"

"Sort of. I am a board member. Paula is too. Her brother helps out and acts as an employee. My point is this—the organization is worth hundreds of millions, maybe even another billion. Our donations ballooned over the last ten years. Like politics, donors who donate large sums of money expect certain things in return. Glenn probably did not tell you everything. Some of our donors, well, I'm not sure they have the organization's best interest at heart. They want T.A.H. to work as propaganda. Glenn doesn't much care as long as the money keeps coming in, but Paula and I are concerned. You need to be very careful. After Jay's wake, you need to go there. It's nothing like what you see on TV."

"The show says it's in an undisclosed location," I said. "Nevada?"

"Yes, Nevada. It's in the mountains."

I should have just signed away whatever claims I was entitled to right then and there. T.A.H. sounded more like a cartel than a foundation. She wanted to tell me more, but something was holding her back. She spoke in riddles that I couldn't decipher.

Jay's wake was held in one of the most beautiful churches in San Francisco, the Wooden Cross Community. As we agreed, the church was nondenominational. His body lay in a cream casket with matching velvet lining. He wore a beige three piece designer suit with pale blue shirt and red and blue silk tie. His long white and gray hair was tied back in his signature ponytail. A gold cross necklace was placed within his hand.

Glenn was irked. "None of you told me about that detail," he said before the wake started.

"It's my cross and he won't be buried, I mean frozen with it," said Paula. "He was coming around, coming over to our side." Paula put her arm around Mercedes and gave Glenn a look that would freeze water.

Droves of people piled in once the pastor opened the church's double doors. All of the pews on both floors of the church were filled. Late comers stood against the back wall and in the aisles as the pastor recited the eulogy that I personally wrote.

"…what many people didn't know about Jay was his kindness. He treated his staff like family and his close friends like royalty…."

I sat in the front pew with Mercedes, Glenn, Paula, and Joel. Maria and the rest of Jay's staff were also seated in the front row on the outer edges. Actors, directors, his agent, television stars, other writers, scientists he interviewed for research, radio personalities, critics, publishers, editors, his first and third ex-wives, and even the mayor of Tiburon were there. People who had no connection at all were there, too many people. I wasn't sure if they came to pay their last respects or to be seen by the entertainment world.

The media was also there, but not to see Jay. They set up cameras to film per an agreement we made with the church's elders. Part of the deal was that they would leave us all alone at the invite-only banquet.

The pastor continued the eulogy. "…Jay was not known to be a religious man, but in recent weeks he had a change of heart. I pray for him. May he be saved."

"Amen," said almost everyone in the pews.

"Jay was responsible for numerous good works. He was such a humble man when it came to generosity, but he donated and even created charities for the poor, the orphaned, and the disadvantaged. He was a very private man. Most of you know him as the eccentric writer who loved to create controversy with his alien beliefs. But those who knew Jay…"

I looked like a strong, classy woman. My new clothes, nails, even hair screamed sophisticated. But deep down I felt like a little girl again who had another setback that tore me apart. Tears rolled down my cheeks. Mercedes sat next to me and pinched my leg.

"Not here, not now. I will keep digging into your leg until the pain stops the tears, understand?"

Mercedes's long nails almost ripped my skin, but she was right. The tears stopped. I wondered at that time if the camera had caught my grief in those few seconds that I lost control.

Once the pastor was finished, those seated in pews formed lines and got up in single file to see Jay one last time. I made small talk with a movie star and a director and then spoke to Maria. I wasn't sure if she and the rest of the staff knew that they now worked for me. I didn't say anything.

I spoke to Barry, Jay's agent, a bright and upbeat man, who came off as a high-class used car salesman. He asked me personal questions about my contract with Claude's agency. Fans and more fans wanted to talk to me. Apparently, I was expected to fill Jay's shoes in the science fiction world of writing. I could never fill his shoes in anything. He was truly larger than life, larger than Earth, larger than it all. I could feel the tears well and sidestepped my way to the restroom.

In the church lobby, one of the reporters was talking into a microphone with her cameraman. She was a beautiful Asian woman who I recognized from the national news.

"Maya Smock, can you confirm or deny being the sole heir of Jay McCallister's estate?" she asked. I kept walking to the ladies' room. "What kind of special friendship did you and Jay have?" The door was only steps away. Mercedes told me this would happen. "Were you..."

I made it into the bathroom. It was a single bathroom with a lock. Gratitude filled me as I locked the door. Several minutes passed as I cleaned the smeared mascara off my face. I hoped the reporter was not waiting for me.

I opened the door. As I walked out of the bathroom, more reporters swarmed around me. Multiple camera flashes made me see nothing but white light. Out of nowhere a hand grabbed me and led me out of the pack of wolves.

"Is it true Jay McCallister left you one billion...Was Jay McCallister your lover...Are you pregnant with Jay's..." And on and on it went. Someone leaked something. All I could think of was Maria. She now knew that I was her new boss. Maybe she knew all along and leaked it to the press. I wished Eric was there with me. Even Claude would have come in handy. Anyone to show that I was already in a relationship and we were just friends.

Once I was out of the limelight, I saw Paula's beautiful face and cried. She hugged me and stroked my hair. "It's gonna work out. All of this will be old news by the end of the week. The pastor showed me a secret way out of here. Follow me. Glenn is getting the car and we'll go straight to the hotel. These vultures aren't allowed in our private ballroom."

I followed Paula upstairs to the church organ and then into an elevator. The door of the elevator was paneled to blend into the wood paneled wall. Down we went into the basement, which led out to underground parking. I wanted to kiss the pastor. He and his elders were too busy distracting and threatening the press in the church lobby.

The banquet dinner hosted one hundred and fifty people, most of whom were close business acquaintances of Jay's. The food, the digital pictures, and the movie montage of Jay's greatest scenes were a spectacular ode to a spectacular life. This funeral was the nicest funeral I had ever been to, but then I never lost a loved one. I never got close enough to anyone, even Claude.

And then I met Jay and his merry band of misfits. Suddenly I had confidence and a sense of security. I began to believe that maybe I deserved more than what I was getting. In one fell swoop, I took a chance and found something real, something that I had all along with Eric while ending something I knew wasn't working. All of it was because of Jay.

I felt relaxed as grief changed into gratitude. Maybe it was the wine, but I even laughed and enjoyed myself throughout the banquet.

Glenn passed around the cordless microphone for everyone who wanted to tell a story about Jay. The wacky stories and the amazing deeds only made me love him more. He was the brother I almost had. I got to meet him, stay in his house, hang out with his friends, and inherit his fortune. His legacy and influence lived on through me.

I looked over at Paula as the producer, Harvey Sodenburg, stood up with the microphone and talked about Jay's first novel that became a movie. He described Jay as being a blast on the movie set, talking about the elaborate pranks he pulled. I never saw that side of Jay and now I never would.

I heard Paula laugh so hard that she snorted. An idea popped into my head—maybe she could conjure Jay up in the near future. His spirit could tell me what to do with his money, his charities, and most importantly, his institution.

The stories went on until way past midnight with half of the guests already gone. By two o'clock in the morning, the hotel manager gave us the boot. I drove Paula back to her house, relieved that the press made good on their promise. By morning, they surrounded her hilltop lavender Victorian.

Glenn called me on my cellphone. He wanted me to sign some papers. "I'll come by, take you up to Jay's house so we can talk. You've got a lot on your plate, but there are some things that need to be taken care of now. You inherited a fortune but you also inherited a lot of responsibility."

"You said the money is safe from Claude as long as I don't mix it?" I asked.

"Yes. It's called co-mingling. I'll set everything up so it's separate. Pick you up in an hour."

Glenn pushed his way through the crowd and then dragged me through. We headed off to Tiburon with a few reporters on our tail. "I live in the same neighborhood as Jay did. We're practically neighbors. So glad Jay's house is gated."

"I'm a little spooked. He died in his pool. We talked for hours at that pool. Do you believe in ghosts?"

"He was murdered. Someone held his head down until he stopped moving. I offered one of the investigators a few bucks, well more than a few bucks, to give me some more information. There were shell casings found by the pool. Jay had a bullet wound in his head."

"What happened then? The news isn't reporting anything."

"Again, Jay's body could heal itself without medical assistance. The police couldn't explain how the wound disappeared. They wrote the whole thing off."

"And the shell casings?" I asked.

"Lost. All I have is the word of the policeman on the scene. The Feds came in and took over. They filed a report the next day, claiming it was an accident. Maya, Jay pissed off a lot of people." Glenn pulled into the entrance. The same guard that Maya had just met was inside. She no longer trusted him or anyone.

"So you think this was an inside job?" she asked.

"No idea. Do you want to keep this house?"

"Yes, but I want to re-staff it," I said.

"Smart girl. Make sure you pay everyone a nice severance check and then change all locks, codes, and passwords again." Glenn parked the car and then opened the door with a card key.

"Again? Looks like no one has been here since…"

"Yes, again," Glenn said. I had started to drift off into a day dream. All of this was too much to digest. "Per Jay's instructions, I changed the locks and gave everyone some time off with pay. But that is no longer my responsibility. You will need to do this again. I am here to guide you through all of this, explain what you have. This is now your house."

I looked around the two-story foyer, at the walls and art, at the furniture, at the statues and pictures and knick-knacks. "Glenn, I think I will eventually have an estate sale, but for now, I'd like to keep this house, make it my own. I certainly don't need all of this stuff, but some fans would love it. Maybe sell it and give it to one of his many charities."

"He would love that idea. Listen, I brought you here for two reasons. First, I wanted you to clean out his safe. He had some very valuable belongings that I do not want your old staff or your new staff to have. They might know more than Jay thought they knew."

"Glenn, Jay loved them. Some of them even lived here."

"They don't live here now," he said. "And they don't love you."

"Understandable. A year's salary for severance?" I asked.

"More than fair." We sat down in the dining room and Glenn opened up a briefcase he brought inside of the house. "Please sign all of this."

I was careful, reading every document, afraid this was some kind of scam, but it was not a scam. I was the sole heir and everything was mine. I looked around at the mansion and its contents and felt like a fraud. He shouldn't have left me this.

Once I was finished signing, Glenn walked up one of the double staircase and I followed. The house really was amazing. I remembered Jay telling me this was his sanctuary. Looking out the window as I walked up the stairs I could see the bay. This house was a piece of him that I didn't want to let go. I thought of Eric. Would he be jealous? Did he believe that I was Jay's girlfriend? "Glenn, what should I tell Eric?"

"Oh Maya, I know you love this man and it sounds like he loves you. Please, I'm begging you, just give it some time before you tell him all of this. And if you get married, you have to get a prenuptial."

"A prenuptial? I don't think that is necessary." Glenn looked at me with pity. "We'll talk about that when and if the time ever comes. Glenn, who would have gotten all of this had it not been for me?"

"How do I say this, Maya, Jay rewrote his will fairly often. He was always changing it until he met you and proved that you both were related. He always wanted to leave plenty to the poor, plenty to some kind of science foundation. They would change often. But he would have left the bulk of his fortune to T.A.H. He and I started it and he didn't want to let go. We have so much invested." Glenn took me into the upstairs library and opened a gold-framed oil painting up like it was a medicine cabinet. There was a built-in safe behind the portrait.

Glenn punched in code on the keypad. "The code is currently your name, Maya. I advise you to reset this immediately."

The safe's dimensions were around four feet high and three feet wide. The first item he handed me was a brown envelope. "This is your DNA and his DNA test results. It proves you really are brother and sister. Also, there are samples he left you in case you wanted to run a test on your own."

I opened the envelope and looked at the baggy of hair, fingernails, and flaked off scabs from healing wounds. I thumbed through the paperwork. All of it was codes, bars and graphs. I didn't understand the results. The next page was written. We matched at a 30% rate. "Glenn, why couldn't I have been his daughter? Couldn't a father and daughter have around the same results?"

"Yes, but Jay couldn't have children. It was impossible. If you're thinking of spinning the results to a more favorable view, don't. They'll find out that you lied and then you'll be forced to explain the match. He was your half-brother. Don't worry, it will all blow over," Glenn said. He continued to dig out more of Jay's secrets and treasures. "This is really important." Glenn handed me a three dimensional looking credit card. But instead of numbers, there were symbols. "It's a key for T.A.H. I have one too. There are only two keys like this for the institution. Yours and mine. It opens every room. We are the only ones with full access. You will need to get into the system for security purposes. I don't fool around. T.A.H. is built like a fortress. We'll have more work to do once you're there."

I felt the key. It was made from a different material than plastic, maybe metal, I wasn't sure. But I had never seen anything like it.

"Ah, here they are. No one knows about this. Jay and I split up this little treasure. You cannot tell anyone, not even Mercedes or Paula. Not even Eric." Glenn handed me a small men's jewelry box.

I opened the wooden top. Inside were large shiny gold coins with weird symbols on both sides. The coins seemed to be the same size, but different designs imprinted on each one. "Beautiful. They look old."

"They are very old. Do you know who Solomon was?"

"King Solomon from the Bible. King David's son, right?" I answered. "No, these cannot be part of his treasure. No…."

Glenn shrugged his shoulders. "One day I'll tell you how he and I got them. They really belong in a museum, but we just couldn't part with them. Now they are yours."

I kept grabbing them in handfuls and then let them slip through my fingers. They were hypnotic. "Do you want them? As something from Jay for yourself?"

Glenn laughed. "Oh no, my honesty must seem very odd to you. I know you had it rough. Jay and I made a pact with each other long ago when we found these coins. He wanted you to have them and I will honor his wish. These coins can be very dangerous. They have a power and strength of their own, like your mother's necklace. Maya, we are dealing with forces that go beyond this world, this universe. Jay and I only scratched the surface. Now it's you and I. Together, we will finish what was started twenty years ago."

Glenn insisted that I look inside of the safe. It was officially empty. We cased the rest of the house and loaded up the safe with new treasures that weren't as important as the ones that he gave me. I put the coins and keycard in my pocket and Glenn put the paperwork in his briefcase. The day had turned into night by the time we were finished.

"Before you go home, I have one more stop that we need to take care of. Get some sleep. I'll pick you up tomorrow morning and take you to T.A.H. We'll fly there. I own a jet. From T.A.H. I can take you directly back to Las Vegas."

"Will you represent me? I mean for my divorce?" I asked.

"I would be honored. You are making a very wise decision. We'll get him out of your life," he said.

The next morning, I said goodbye to Paula and Joel and then took off to a small, nearby airport outside of the city. I had never flown on a private jet before. The plane's interior was like an upscale living room. Leather sectional loveseats, recliners and sofas lined the plane with coffee tables and large televisions. There were two bathrooms, both big enough to throw a party inside of, and both equipped with spa-like steam showers and Jacuzzi soaker tubs. There was a decent-sized kitchen at the back of the plane.

"No chef today. It's a very short flight. But a chef will be on board for longer flights. Jay would fly commercial or charter a jet. I just broke down and bought one. But Jay has or had a helicopter. It's now yours. It's parked at T.A.H. He used it for the institute, but it was his."

"Private jets, helicopters, Solomon's coins…Glenn, this is too much. All because we share the same DNA? I still am not comprehending all of this, but thank you for helping me."

"Please stop thanking me. In time, you will see how important it is that you, and nobody but you, continue Jay's work. T.A.H. will blow you away. There's plenty to see, but don't worry, I'll fly you home tonight. Once we get the security worked out, you can come here anytime you like, with or without me. It's maybe a seven hour drive from Vegas." Glenn flipped through papers from his briefcase as he talked. As soon as the plane seemed to get high enough in the air, it began to descend. "We're almost there, on the north side of the Ruby Mountains in a little town called Cattenberg. No one but us and maybe a farmer or two are in the whole town. We are literally in the middle of nowhere."

We landed on a small runway at the foot of the mountains. There was a black SUV waiting for us the minute the door opened. Out of nowhere, stairs were wheeled to our entrance and we walked down from the plane.

I felt excited and terrified at the same time. I didn't know Glenn that well. Because of my past or maybe because of common sense, I immediately suspected he wanted something from me and I hadn't a clue as to what it could be. All he did was give, give, give. He could have buried Jay's new will, the test results, well, everything and ransacked the house. He could have taken control of T.A.H.

I recalled Mercedes trying to warn me, which only added to my suspicions. But the funny thing about fear was that it was reduced to a minor annoyance when faced with the perception of reward. The logical side of my brain told me to take the billion dollars and the house and then run. Looking out at the imposing snow-capped mountains and what lay ahead compelled me to stay.

The driver in the SUV was an Asian man, somewhere between forty and fifty years old. He had a

287 • The Best Seller

thick accent. I could barely understand him, but he was friendly and attentive. He knew who I was—Jay's replacement. He drove slowly up the icy and snowy passage carved around the mountain in a steep spiral pattern. There were no rails or medians. Inches of road separated us from the mountain and death. The look down made my stomach drop. We were halfway from the summit and then stopped going up, just around the mountain.

"I'm a little confused, Glenn. Where is this institute? There's nothing but trails up here." Once again I wished I had taken the money and ran, refusing to fill Jay's shoes at the T.A.H. Institute.

"Ah, scared of unknown," said the strange Asian man. He was smiling and nodding at Glenn as he turned a hairpin corner of the mountain.

I screamed. The Asian driver increased his speed and headed straight into the side of the mountain. I screamed again and closed my eyes.

My head was light from the altitude. A sound that sounded like a garage door opening came from nowhere. The side of the mountain opened up. I was inside.

# Chapter Thirty-Three

Andreas stepped on the accelerator as he drove his Jeep to the other side of the base. Major Lamphrey radioed him a cryptic message about something that happened inside of the hangar.

Andreas pulled up to the entrance and jumped out of the car. "Holy shit!" he screamed. He stood in front of the entrance in disbelief. The metal hangar doors and part of the exterior of the hangar were destroyed. The metal part of the structure curled outward as if something inside had run straight through it. He ran through the new opening. Major Lamphrey was there with Captain Bolantano.

"Major, explain now," Andreas whispered. Lamphrey was assigned to the hangar's security. The two men stepped outside of the hangar and walked behind Andreas's Jeep.

"Sir, you're not going to like this," Lamphrey said. He fumbled in his pockets and took out his cigarettes and lighter. "You want one, General?"

Andreas nodded and waited for Lamphrey to hand him one. The young major lit both of their smokes and then he said, "The space craft is gone. It accelerated right through those doors."

"By itself?" asked the general.

"Well it appears that the engineers figured out what they could use for fuel." Lamphrey pointed to the entrance. "But there's more. The aliens are gone. They somehow got out of the cage or someone let them out. Maybe that's why they hung around for so long. You know, waiting for us to fix their ride. All or most of it should be on tape, Sir. Plus Doctor Costello, Doctor Kaplan, Doctor Janssen, Doctor

Spencer, and Captain Bolantano saw the whole thing. No one could stop them. They're gone."

*I will burn twice for this—first on a stake by the United States government and then forever in Hell.* His stomach felt like a block of lead swishing around. Andreas took a long drag from his cigarette, inhaling almost half of the Lamphrey's Camel. "What about the babies?"

"Just the one, Sir. The same one you pulled the sirens on two hours or so ago."

"I was just over at the western trailer…We talked about…Well, the baby was the distraction after all," said the general as he stepped on his lit cigarette.

"Sorry, General?"

"It's over. We're over. I'll go down for this, ruined. The greatest project the United States ever took part of will now go down the shitter. Save yourself. Find another job, a good one if you're smart. The Joint Chiefs of Staff will… Maybe the Nazis could continue their research at a university…I might as well pack my bags," Andreas mumbled, his words as his thoughts were all over the place without organization.

"General, may I be allowed to talk freely?" Lamphrey said.

Andreas laughed a little too loud. "Of course."

"You're a valuable player in all of this. You know how these ABs communicate, what they eat, how they work, even how they think. You know how they create and how they travel. You know how the doctors made those babies. It's not over yet, Sir. And your fiancée knows how that space craft works. How do you know you're not needed elsewhere? How do you know that these things won't land on earth again? Plus, you still got the babies and you can make more of them. I'll bet the Nazi doctors have plenty of the ABs' DNA to use. If you think about it, Sir, you are an asset."

Lamphrey was definitely cheering him up, but he had too many doubts. The major wouldn't stop talking.

"General, we've got a lot of work to do. We've got to find out how, why, and who. You can salvage this disaster. Please, General, I don't want to work for anyone else. This work, it's revolutionary. You assembled the greatest think tank on this planet to study and even create a different species from another planet."

"Lamphrey, that's enough bullshit, really. I am well aware of how the military works." Andreas didn't know if the young man was his biggest ally or biggest adversary. Time would tell. "Listen, they name and blame scapegoats. About the only thing I have going for me is this place is top secret. But if insiders are sabotaging our work, then our operation is still at risk. The baby was a boy, white with blue eyes, but that doesn't mean anything. Most babies have blue eyes. The color could change. He will hopefully grow up normal, smarter than average, and have a chance at being a productive citizen. Or..."

"Yes, General?"

Andreas paced back and forth behind the Jeep. "I think you already know. He could have been taken to study like a lab rat."

"No different than here. As long as the Russians didn't take him," Lamphrey said.

Now there was a real company 'yes' man. *As long as the Russians didn't take him...* Andreas could see him more clearly. This would be his replacement in years to come. He shrugged off the icy comment. "You're right. I need you to begin searching and questioning all of the engineers and doctors who worked on the space craft. Bolantano will investigate the hangar. I'll go look at the tapes in the cage. Whoever took the baby might have let out the ABs. This whole stunt could not be the actions of a lone wolf. Give me something before I call Blanchard. "

The general disappeared behind the hidden entrance inside of the hangar and descended all the way down to the underground cage. The elevator doors opened. The cage looked damaged. There was a large rectangle cut out on the side adjacent to the control panel. The cut made within the Plexiglas was perfectly straight as if cut by a laser. In the cage was an empty black uniform lying on the floor.

Andreas stepped through the glass and picked it up. Once again, the swastika emblem on the uniform's sleeve caught his eye. Was this meant to be a souvenir for the doctors? His mind raced, calculating all of the possibilities of how the escape played out. He needed to view the camera tape.

There were four cameras mounted in the cage, each one equipped with new technology of motion sensors. Andreas could access the feed inside of the control room. He quickly rewound all four tapes starting at midnight, the time the doctors supposedly put one of the babies to bed.

He watched them screech, chirp, and even sing to each other for at least an hour, fast forwarding parts of each tape until around four o'clock in the morning. That's when all of them became silent, using only body language.

The balding AB who came off as the leader took off his suit. This was the first time Andreas had seen one of the aliens naked. It was without breasts or a penis, just sexless. He still wasn't sure how they urinated or had a bowel movement, but then they barely ate or drank. The naked AB faced the wall and glowed an eerie yellowish green. The scales around its neck tapered down to its chest and shimmered white, green, and yellow. Its overall color was the same color as their fingers before they woke up.

The alien glowed so brightly that it was difficult for Andreas to see what was going on in the tape. Once the being's light dimmed, it lifted its left hand. With its index finger, it drew a rectangle in the six inch thick Plexiglas. The glass pushed out of the wall perfectly, as if cut by a laser. The ABs stepped out of the rectangular hole. That was the last of their actions caught on the tape.

Reality tumbled down like an avalanche. Was the cage nothing more than a hotel room? Their stay had obviously been voluntary. They must have been waiting for their space craft.

Andreas cringed. Besides telling Blanchard that the whole operation was completely fucked from the beginning, the tapes would show the power of the ABs. He smiled at the cruel irony. Years of money and sacrifice for nothing. But then he thought of Lamphrey's heart to heart chat. Maybe the young man was on to something.

*I could take the tapes, maybe hide them...* On impulse, Andreas took the tapes out of the camera attachment and put in blank tapes. He stood with four tapes, one from each camera angle, and thought of his next move. And then his radio went off.

"General Andreas, copy," he answered.

"General, we might have a lead on who took the baby. We need you in the hangar, Sir," said Captain Bolantano.

"I'll be there soon," the general answered. In almost a state of panic, he routed around the control panel's cabinets until finding a binder with side pockets. He stuffed the tapes inside of an empty binder, propped it up next to some old manuals, and then raced towards the elevator.

Andreas purposely stopped the elevator at the doctors' laboratory before reaching the hangar. He wanted to see what they were up to. Frederik was alone, watching the two remaining babies.

"Where is ever..."

"They are being questioned by your men, General," Doctor Richtor said, cutting Andreas off in mid-sentence.

Andreas didn't appreciate the disrespect Frederik exuded. He became bolder as time wore on. "When are you being questioned? Or were you already?" Andreas asked.

"I'm sure I am next. Although, why would I sabotage our experiment?"

"There's a lot of *whys, hows, whats,* and *wheres.* About the only thing we sort of know is the *when.* Something more than meets the eye is going on here. And we will get to the bottom of it, Doctor. Even if we have to resort to Gestapo tactics." Andreas watched the doctor sneer at him and got back on the elevator.

Once Andreas was inside of the hangar, he found at least twenty airmen with Captain Bolantano in command. The general did not like to play favorites, but Bolantano was probably his most trusted officer. He didn't kiss ass and knew how to take charge of a bad situation.

"General, we got a few being questioned inside of headquarters, Sir," Bolantano said.

He saw Jaeger and Schmidt, both un-cuffed, escorted back to the hidden elevator by two soldiers. Their faces were beaten to a pulp.

"General, these men aren't saying anything. However…" said Bolantano. He paused as if he was uncertain.

"Yes, Captain?" Andreas asked.

"We found something. Captain Redding, could you please show General Andreas what we recovered?"

Redding led Andreas across the hangar to where the space craft used to be. He stood in front of the cheap desks the engineers used while working on the craft. Redding looked ill. "General, I found these items inside one of the desks, inside Doctor Kate Costello's desk, Sir." He opened a drawer then took out a bottle, a few cloth diapers, and a can of baby formula.

"You found this in Kate's desk?" Andreas asked in disbelief. "How do you know someone didn't put it there to frame her? How can you say with certainty this is hers?"

"Well, I found the items in her purse. She had her purse in this drawer, General. But someone could have put the items in her purse, Sir. After she came to work. I started searching the premises one hour ago and I was told she was here almost two hours ago."

The general wanted to strangle the punk. Who the fuck was he, Sherlock fucking Holmes? "Who gave you permission to search the premises, Captain? I sure the fuck didn't! I asked all of you to roll through the tapes, not to play amateur detectives!" Andreas slammed his hand on the wooden desk and stepped closer to the young man who was now shaking. He was close to hitting the airman until Captain Bolantano approached.

"General, Sir, I gave the orders. I took it upon myself, Sir, to search the premises. I apologize, Sir."

Andreas switched gears and almost hit Bolantano. The young man whom the general had once respected was now someone he wanted to kill. Andreas's hands shook as he thought about wrapping them around the captain's thick neck. But he took a deep breath instead and frantically searched his pockets for a cigarette. Once found, he lit one up. "All right, Captain. I will question her. You and I will question her together. Now."

Bolantano motioned for the general to follow him out of the hangar and then into their headquarters. Andreas had chain-smoked three cigarettes in less than five minutes on the short walk. Costello and the other engineers were tied and bound to chairs inside one of the offices. Two airman watched them. All four engineers were under suspicion.

"Get rid of the other three for now. I want to ask her some questions," Andreas ordered. He was filled with a quiet rage. They had an argument only hours ago after he brought up the missing baby. More and more Kate's integrity seemed at stake. She looked strangely younger than she did this morning, like a frightened little girl who got caught with her hand in the cookie jar. All love he had felt for her evaporated. He felt like a fool who'd been played. Maybe if her name was cleared, maybe if she could prove she was framed...Maybe. *Who ever said that love was conditional was full of shit. Love in itself was a condition—I love you if you don't completely screw me over.*

Once the room emptied out, it was just Costello, Bolantano, and Andreas. He began with the first questions. "Kate, why were baby items found inside of your desk?"

"Isn't it obvious? I was framed. Robert, I didn't take that baby," she cried. He knew that would be her first claim.

"If you tell us what you did, how you planned it, who else was involved, and where the baby is, maybe, just maybe you can go back to Boston with your career untarnished," Andreas said quietly.

"How can you...Robert, look at me! I'm going to be your wife! You don't trust me? You don't believe me? When would I have had the time for all of this? I've been with you in California and then here and you know..."

"Stop! We both know how smart you are and we both know you thought the doctors were pure evil," the general said.

"So I guess that's it. I don't even get the benefit of the doubt, nothing. How dare you! I was framed and you just stand there accusing me in front of your lackey! Is this for show, Robert? Or is this the real you?" She paused but he would not answer and looked at the floor. "Well, maybe I knew all along what a son-of-a-bitch you are. That's why I subconsciously wouldn't set a date. I bet your ex has plenty to say..."

"Where is the baby, Kate? You can tell me, tell all of us now, tell us the easy way, or you can tell us later, the hard way." The general looked at Bolantano. It was the look both men knew all too well—no more playing around.

Andreas had participated in a few enhanced interviews, but this was different. This was the woman he just gave a ring to and wanted to spend the rest of his life with. As angry as he was, questioning her further was something he could not participate in.

"Captain, I want her and all of the head engineers questioned. Keep me in the loop. Anything from the Germans?"

"Jaeger and Schmidt seemed to be telling the truth. We have no reason to believe they were part of the baby's disappearance. But I wonder about the craft. We let them go back to the laboratory to care for the babies."

Andreas lit another smoke and coughed. His pack was empty. He left the hangar and headed for the closest guard tower located by the eastern camera. As he drove, he looked at his watch. *Hell, it was only 0900.* The day dragged on forever. Part of him wanted to cry, but he pushed back the tears. Crying was something that cowards did. He might have been a fool, but he was not a coward. Maybe Kate was framed. It was more than possible. If she was, he had lost her forever. He had drawn a line in the sand. Now it was a matter of pride. He had to be right.

Captain Malone was at the guard tower reviewing tapes as Andreas entered. The same guard who worked the graveyard shirt was still there. Malone caught him before the shift change.

"The log said Captain Bertrand left at 0205, General," said Captain Malone as he hunched over a very nervous looking kid who couldn't have been more than eighteen years old.

The system they had in place wasn't fool-proof. The guard checked identification and clearance, wrote it down in the log, and then let whomever out of the gates.

Andreas looked at the vehicle. It was not a jeep, but a truck, the kind of truck the civilians on the base had access to. "Do you have the plates?"

The boy, barely a man, nervously reeled the tape and then wrote them down.

"Do a lot of people leave the base at this hour?" Andreas asked, forgetting that most of the people on the base did not live there.

"Well, no, but it's sort of steady, on average maybe a car every hour or so during the night, General," said the boy. "But last night it was only the one truck during my shift." Andreas didn't bother asking his name.

"Captain Malone, I need you to run a search for this truck now," Andreas said. He guessed the truck left through one gate and then came back to the base by entering through another gate. The baby was probably passed on to someone outside of the base.

Andreas drove around the base, stopping at every guard tower. He had a feeling the western tower would be the entrance that Captain Bertrand or whoever was using his name drove through to get back inside of the base. His theory became fact. The same truck came back thirty-eight minutes later.

"General, copy?" Andreas's radio went off. He recognized Malone's voice.

"Go ahead," Andreas said.

"Bertrand is not on the base. He's out of town this week and last week. Death in family, Sir. Someone got a hold of his identification," said Malone.

It was a bad idea to speak so freely over the radio, but the general wasn't feeling like following the rules. He wanted answers as soon as possible.

"Copy, Captain. Thanks. This whole thing was well-planned. Let's take a second look at those tapes. Maybe we'll get lucky and get a shot of his or her face." Andreas drove off and thought about Kate. *What kind of techniques were they using? Were they torturing her?* He felt dizzy and needed a break.

Andreas aimlessly drove around the full perimeter of the base, listening to the radio and answering it from time to time, contemplating his next move. A few hours went by. He needed to inform the Joint Chiefs of Staff. The longer he waited, the more upset the man would be. Maybe the general really could turn this around. He was on his way back to headquarters, rehearsing what would be said to Blanchard.

Lamphrey radioed him. "General, Sir, we got some of the answers you were looking for. Where ever your location, we need you at headquarters."

Andreas was less than a mile away. He sped back to the base and jumped out of the jeep. Bolantano and Lamphrey were waiting for him by the entrance.

All three men lit up cigarettes. Bolantano was the first to speak. "You're not going to like this, Sir."

"How involved was she?" the general asked as he took a drag off of the captain's cigarette.

"She still denies taking the baby. But with some hard questioning, we found out that she, Kaplan and Jensen had struck a deal with the ABs a while ago, shortly after you introduced all of them," Bolantano said.

"What about Spencer?" Andreas asked. He was the fourth scientist originally hired.

"We have no proof either way. His name never came up. Although the man was always aloof with everyone. All he did was work," Bolantano answered. "From what we could glean, the engineers, with Jaeger's help, promised to rebuild the aircraft once the ABs gave them information on how the space craft worked. The engineers wanted fuel sources, time and space secrets, and who knows what else."

"What exactly did they confess to?" Andreas asked.

"Doctor Costello formulated an anti-gravity fuel source with alien help. Something to do with mercury. Doctor Kaplan took parts of the spacecraft and fragmented pieces of crystal from the hangar and gave them to NASA. Jensen was the one who told the ABs that their space craft was finished."

"Kate mentioned she was working on the fuel. Mercury, huh?" Andreas asked calmly and Bolantano nodded. "Who took the baby?"

"We are not sure. Still a mystery. Nonetheless, we have a serious breach," Bolantano said.

"I am about to call Blanchard. Wish I knew more," Andreas said as he walked inside. He could smell himself, a body odor with an metallic edge. He smelled like that during the war. It was the smell of fear.

Major Lamphrey called out to him before he picked up the nearest phone. "General, remember what I said. You have the power. Don't let them take it away."

# Chapter Thirty-Four

I pinched myself a dozen times as we entered the inside of the mountain. The walls were granite, but smooth as if cut by some kind of a laser. Metal poles and concrete pillars were everywhere. The tunnel was lit with single hanging bulbs every few feet.

The Asian driver who called himself Chuck drove very slowly. I jostled in the back seat and wondered if we were driving over rocks instead of a paved road.

After several minutes inside the tunnel our route ended in front of a stone wall. Glenn got out of the car and went up to some kind of computer. He put his hand on the screen and looked inside an eyepiece. Once again the wall slid sideways, allowing us to enter. He got back in the car.

"The key I gave you is not enough to get inside. Fingerprints, handprints, and retina scan are also part of the security clearance. We need to get you set up in the system A.S.A.P.," Glenn said.

Once we crossed through the opening, the pavement changed from rocky to smooth. The area was lit with long florescent bulbs and spotlights making the enormous room bright. As the car idled, a woman with red hair and a white lab coat motioned for us to turn to the right. Chuck slowly turned and then parked.

We got out of the car and I again pinched myself. "So this is TAH. Am I dreaming? This looks like some kind of secret government bunker."

"Actually it was. Jay and I bought it fifteen years ago. It was a major step up from our old location. You should have seen this place. It was a complete wreck. Slowly, we built it back up and added our own modern day touches," Glenn said. He and Chuck looked at each other

301 • The Best Seller

with a smile. I wondered what the hell I was getting into. A nagging feeling of fear tickled down my neck.

I followed Glenn and Chuck through an enormous space into a hallway. The entrance area had jagged walls and was sparsely finished. The hallway was much different. The second I stepped foot in it, I expected a tunnel, but instead I got a sense of luxury. The hallway was very wide, wide enough for at least ten people to comfortably walk side by side. It was also long, endlessly long.

On each wall there were built-in curios that ran down the hallway. Each cabinet was filled with strange artifacts. I immediately became curious and distracted. "Wait up," I said as I paused at several displays inside of the cabinets. There were crystal skulls, curved bones, gold coins, tablets, a metallic black uniform, and so much more. My mind couldn't process all of the objects without slowing down.

"This is part of our museum. Everything inside of the cabinets is authentic and probably priceless. Again, this is a collection that Jay and I started the same time as the renovation for this mountain. You can look at it later. We have much more to see and do," Glenn said, waving his arm for me to keep up.

We briskly walked down the long corridor and through a set of double doors into some kind of office waiting room. There was a reception desk and waiting chairs, but no one was there.

"Come." Glenn darted around the huge reception desk into another door that was paneled on the reception side, but heavy and metal on the other side. I walked into a pure white room. The temperature immediately dropped. Chuck waved and disappeared down another hallway in the refrigerated area.

Glenn kept walking straight. Everything was such a bright white that it was hard for me to see where the walls and floor met or just how the ceiling was. Glenn approached a set of vertical rubber strips, white, the kind you see in a meat locker, and waved them open. The new area was even colder. I could see my breath.

My eyes tried to process and then I screamed. Before me was a glass capsule with a well-preserved corpse inside of it. Two smaller capsules were next to it.

"Calm down. One of them just got here. It's Jay. Look inside." Glenn pointed to the first one on my right. "See, he was shipped immediately after the wake like we all planned. He's frozen solid. Chuck was the one who lugged him up here. If we keep him capsulated and chilled, he won't decompose. Plus, we can study his DNA if needed."

Terror bubbled inside of me. Is this why Glenn brought me here? To have me frozen by Jay's side? To compare and contrast our cells? He must have seen the alarm.

His blue eyes were blank. I didn't know if I should run or scream my head off. He might have been old, but Glenn was at least a foot taller than me. Plus, I had no idea how to get out of this secret place. All I had going for me in terms of survival was hope.

"I am not the enemy, Maya. I can see, smell, and almost taste the fear you're emitting. Please. I am not going to kill you or freeze you, none of it. We own this institution and we are entrusted to keep it going. But I haven't been completely honest, either. There's much left to reveal."

"Who are they?" I asked as I pointed to the smaller capsules. The bodies inside of them looked inhuman.

"Those are two bodies of extraterrestrials. They are dead, frozen for our research, but dead. I'll explain later. I'm just not sure how much more you can take," he said. His blue eyes teared up.

I took several deep breaths and studied all three of the bodies. This room made a funeral parlor look cheery and warm. "You said Jay and I have a distinct chromosome? What do you mean? I thought we had twenty-three pairs or forty-six chromosomes. Half from your mother and half from your father?"

"Yes, Maya, very good. You were definitely paying attention in biology class, but what Jay and I theorized is that, well, you all were engineered. Maybe by one of them." Glenn tapped on one of the capsules next to Jay. "You laughed when he first told you, didn't take him seriously and he didn't push it. But it's true. Come with me."

Again, I followed Glenn through a series of tunnels and rooms, some finished, some looking like a cavern inside of a mountain. I was so lost. Without Glenn I would never find my way back to the car. We eventually walked up a few flights of rock stairs and entered some kind of laboratory. There were a man and a woman looking through microscopes together.

"Let me introduce you, Maya. Doctor Lori Blacksmith and Mister Daryl Everly, meet your new boss, Maya Smock. Maya, this is Doctor Blacksmith and Mr. Everly. They are scientists who volunteer a few weeks, sometimes more, of their time each year to helping us understand extraterrestrial life. We were talking about the extraterrestrial chromosome that you both are very familiar with. Can both of you please show Maya?"

I shook their hands. They stopped what they were doing and hurriedly filed through several slides in a box. Doctor Blacksmith turned on a large projector screen which was hooked up to the microscope so that we could see what she was looking at.

"This is a nucleus of a human cell. Notice the "X" like parts of the cell?" I nodded. "That's chromosomes. Notice the shape. All are some kind of floppy looking "X" and each chromosome is numbered for our purposes of identifying it. For instance, this chromosome is labeled number one and contains around two thousand genes. It holds the most genes of all of the chromosomes." The doctor had a charming English accent, dark brown hair peppered with gray, and warm hazel eyes. I guessed to her to be somewhere in her mid-sixties. She looked like she was once a beautiful woman.

"Okay, Doctor. I follow." I nodded at her to proceed, wondering where she was going with this. "Humans have around nineteen thousand, maybe twenty-four thousand genes, right?"

"Smart girl. Yes, Ms. Smock. Let me switch slides. Please bear with me." Mister Everly handed her the next slide and soon it was up on the big screen for us to see. "Anything different?"

It looked the same to me. I shrugged.

"Here's a hint. Look at the shapes of the chromosomes really closely. One of them is slightly different." Doctor Blacksmith smiled. I wondered if she worked as a professor when she wasn't volunteering inside of a mountain in the middle of nowhere.

I looked again. The task of finding something different was too much for my brain. "I give up. What makes this slide different than the first one?"

Mister Everly smiled. He was a tall, thin, middle-aged black man with a southern accent. "First of all, it's a slide of you. If you look over here…" He took a yard stick and touched the screen, pointing at one of the chromosomes in the middle of the cluster. "See. This one is not an "X" nor a floppy "X", it's a hooked "X". Can you see it?"

"Oh yeah. Now that I look at it. It looks kind of like a Nazi symbol. A swastika? Right?" I asked, unsure of what the symbol was called.

Mister Everly answered, "Yes, a swastika. And no, it's not a coincidence this gene that you and Jay have is shaped like a swastika. Chromosome Eight. On a side note, eighty-eight or eight and eight is a number associated with Nazis. Heil Hitler. "H" is the eighth letter in the alphabet.

And that's not the only connection. You see, Ms. Smock, we believe the Nazis chose the hooked "X" symbol because they knew it was a chromosome that certain extraterrestrials carried. In that chromosome, in your chromosome, is a gene of many genes that take us to the next level from an evolutionary standpoint, speeding everything up. The Nazis with extraterrestrial help, conducted their own experiments. Hitler knew about this chromosome as did other cultures before him, cultures without any scientific backgrounds."

"Show her the *slide*." Doctor Blacksmith was beaming.

Everly inserted the last slide in the microscope. The projector screen displayed a cell with all hooked "X" shaped chromosomes. Everly said, "This is a cell from a hand of one of the aliens next to Jay. We think that you and Jay are related. You see, he wasn't crazy after all."

"So what are you saying? A handful of people in the world used genetic engineering to create a new species? A new race of people? For what? To advance civilization faster than evolution? Why?"

"We don't know why, but we are starting to learn how. Jay was full of theories. And Glenn, well if you watch his show…" said Doctor Blacksmith.

"Yes, I watch his show. I find his show fascinating, but only watched it with half an open mind. Right before Jay was killed, we were on a radio show together. He went on and on about New World Order. Is that one of his theories? Somehow these aliens and an inner circle of the world want to, I don't know, take over?"

"You catch on quick, Ms. Smock," said Doctor Blacksmith.

"Maya, I know you must have a multitude of questions, but I still want to show you another key part of this institution. And you must get set up in the system," Glenn said.

We said our goodbyes to the scientists and headed up more stairs. The stairs never seemed to end. After twenty flights of steps, my calves burned. "No elevator?" I said in between breaths.

"We're almost there. One is in the process of being built."

Another ten more flights of stairs and we were on top of the mountain. The peak was flattened out to be more of a landing. There sat a shiny helicopter on a large, flattened surface. Thirty feet away were several telescopes pointed in four different directions. The cold temperature made my hands cramp. The howling sound of the wind made it impossible to hear Glenn. He pointed at telescopes and then went back into the stairwell, through a corridor, and into a room that must have been just beneath the telescopes. The room was cold, but nowhere as cold as the top of the mountain. The walls protected us from the wind and I could hear Glenn when he talked. The room was set up similar to Jay's observatory, but on a much grander scale.

"You can see through the telescopes from here, like you could at Jay's."

"What about the helicopter? Won't it freeze?'

"The helicopter lowers into the mountain. Someone just raised it out of its structure. The scientists and doctors sometimes use it to get in and out of here. It's your helicopter. We'll have to take a ride in it. I'll give you a list of numbers on who to call when you need something."

"And the telescopes? Won't they crack from the cold?" I asked.

Glenn laughed. "Not these. They are much more powerful than Jay's. They have at least one hundred times the amount of magnification plus we are on top of mountain. You can use them during the day. We have seen and documented several unidentified flying objects throughout the years. They are here, Maya. But their existence is not what is in question. It's whether they are here to be our friend or our foe. Jay always perceived them as a threat and I concur with that belief. My show is not a spoof or a joke, it is real. Jay's antics were not an act or a sign of insanity, they were a logical reaction. I don't know where you stand, and you probably don't know either at this point. But one thing is certain, we must continue to run this institution. It's all that is left in private research."

Against an almost dark sky, I looked through each one of the four telescopes and saw planets and stars. My problems seemed so microscopic compared to this empire that Jay had left me. I wanted to share it all with Eric.

"Mercedes and Paula know about this, right?"

"Most, but not all. Jay and I held onto some secrets that they will never be part of. The more you come here, the more I will show you. Again, please don't discuss this place with anyone who is an outsider, at least not for a while. Not even your new boyfriend, and certainly not your husband."

"All right. For now. What about Mercedes or Paula?" I asked.

"So far, they've seen everything that you have seen. They are safe to talk with. Now come. One last stop for today. I want to get your retina scan and prints for security reasons. You will then be allowed to come and go as you please."

I descended the same thirty flights of stairs and then walked through a maze of tunnels and rooms until reaching the cooler where Jay was kept. I felt as if I was in a futuristic haunted house. Each corner that I turned, I was half-expecting an alien to abduct me.

Once we were back in the freezer, as Glenn called it, I looked more closely at the beings next to Jay in the smaller capsules. I shuddered at the sight of them.

"Are these two the same species?" I asked.

"Yes. Jay and I called this group the Grays for lack of a better name."

"There are others?" Every hair on my body stood erect and I shivered to my spine.

"Oh yes. But this is where the collection of actual bodies stops."

We walked through the endless museum corridor. My head turned to catch the artifacts, but Glenn was on a mission to get me security clearance. I saw a crystal rock the size of my fist in one of the display windows. "Glenn, wait! This is the same crystal as the necklace my mother gave me. Remember, the same one Paula used at the séance."

"I do believe they are the same. You'll have to bring it in for further testing, though. We found it at a crash site from an anonymous tip. There were no signs of an unidentified object, but whoever cleaned up the site had to have missed this. We took it back here, and then had a geologist take a look. It's not from this planet, but that's all we know for certain." Glenn answered. He then motioned me to follow him. A few hundred feet later we were by the reception area.

Behind the gigantic reception desk, he took out some equipment, pressed both of my hands and then finger tips on the touch screen and then pointed a beam of light at my eye. My retina appeared on the screen and he saved the file.

"Okay, we are done. Now you can explore or go home. We've been here for five hours already," he said.

I nodded. "Glenn, one thing before I leave. Will you represent me? I mean for my divorce?"

"Yes, of course. Maya, you don't have to go back to Las Vegas. Jay's Tiburon home is your home. You never have to step foot in Las Vegas again. I have a list of Jay's assets. You can start spending your inheritance now, if you'd like. Take a trip, buy another home."

"Eventually I will, but I want a few things from my house. First is the computer Jay gave me. It has my sequel on the hard drive. Then there's my mother's necklace. I might be scared of it, but I saved it anyway. Jay also bought me some clothes. Those are sentimental. But that's all of the stuff. My real reason for going back is Eric. I want to see him and tell him that I have a lawyer and then explain to him face to face that I was never Jay's mistress."

Glenn looked uneasy. "Please don't tell him the whole truth, at least not yet. If you love this young man, then you cannot get him involved in all of this right from the start. Jay might have been killed because of this. And now you are at risk. I beg you to hire some kind of security. Chuck will drive you back to the jet. I am going to stay here a bit longer." Glenn flipped through the computer screen and then wrote down a number. "Here is a security company, all former C.I.A. and Homeland. Please, Maya, call them and get a bodyguard."

# Chapter Thirty-Five

Claude stared in the mirror for what seemed like forever. Instead of admiring his chiseled features and crystal blue eyes, he concentrated on his next move. He had to have a master plan, a back-up plan, and then even another back-up plan. That was always Sam's and his mother's downfall—the lack of having a plan. Both of them relied on instinct.

Jay's murder was fool-proof, or so he thought as he and Sam meticulously waited for the staff to leave, dismantled the cameras and the alarm, and waited. He did not factor in his rival's ability to repel bullets. Impossible. Was he even human? Claude dismissed the idea. He and Sam must have been a terrible shot. Jay saw them, but it seemed no else did. An endless supply of luck rained down on him. Luck ran in streaks. At least that's what he told himself. He wasn't quite out of the woods yet. And it sounded a lot more appealing than quitting while ahead. The logical side of his brain pleaded to walk away. Take half of what Maya earned in their short marriage and live happily ever after with Allie.

Maya the billionaire. It was almost laughable. She earned every cent of it from fucking that age-spotted, shriveled old crone. Her new fortune upped the stakes. Crying suicide was not going to work anymore. She would attract the best lawyers in the country. Their divorce was inevitable. The only way to get at her fortune was to kill for it. He had to stage an accident or make it look like someone else did it. No mistakes. Maybe he should negotiate with her, ask for ten or twenty million and go quietly. That would be enough to retire.

Claude snapped out of his daydream when the phone chimed. "Hello."

"It's Sam. Forget about lunch the other day. I know you'll do me right. Our friend called."

"Go on." Claude left his bathroom and sat on his bed.

"Turns out our other friend had a lot of people who hated him, a lot of people in high places. There were other times when, you know," Sam said.

Claude hated it when Sam talked about illegal stuff on the phone, but had to admit he was getting better at coding the conversation. "So the official story is just a nice and neat way to put the whole thing to bed?" he asked.

"Exactly. He called me because we called him before, you know. He just thought it was an interesting coincidence, that's all. He wanted to share some extra talk."

"Does he have a friend up there?" Claude asked, wondering if the cop was just sharing rumor or getting ready to put his hand out for part of the take.

"Yeah, he does. Our other friend had pissed off quite a few. The elite, you know."

"Yes, Sam. I get it." Jay McCallister had either pissed of the government or a criminal syndicate and the former made the most sense with his constant rhetoric about the existence of aliens. It was time for Sam to shut up. "Okay then. Listen, I've been thinking a lot. Why don't you come over if you don't have any showings today?" Claude asked.

"I'll be by in a few hours." Sam hung up the phone.

Lady Luck kept on coming. Fuck a divorce settlement. Claude made up his mind—the whole enchilada and no turning back.

Claude made a few calls, cleared his schedule, and told Allie he had some major business to attend to. He added that he was in marriage counseling and would probably be getting a divorce. She didn't sound too convinced and came over after her photo shoot. She practically lived with him and it was her home. Later, Sam stopped by and looked nervous once he saw her in Claude's living room.

"Allie, do you mind running out and picking up some take-out? Maybe Chinese?"

"Trying to get rid of me?" Allie's eyebrows raised. "Bullshit. You're going to kill Maya. I knew it. Once the news announced she might inherit all of that author's money. You're gonna kill her before she dumps your ass."

Claude would have hit her again if Sam was not around. He was growing weary of her mouth.

"Shit, Claude, why'd you tell her? You get down on me for talking to Mom, well she at least is family," Sam said.

Allie looked Claude in the eyes and smirked. "I already know you two knocked off that old writer. Now you're going to finish the job, aren't you?"

"No, we're not. You got it all wrong. Now please, get us some dinner. I need some privacy," Claude said, but it was too late. Then again, maybe he could use her. One billion dollars was a lot to go around. No need to be too greedy. And if things went south, she'd make the perfect patsy.

"No, not until you let me in on your plan. I've wanted to kill the bitch since I met you. Don't deny me that, baby. You need me. She doesn't know me. She knows you and she knows Sam. You can't do it. You need an alibi." She sat down on a bar stool at the kitchen island, crossed her gorgeous legs, and smiled. Allie had a dark side and made no apology for it.

"Sam, do you think you could work with her?" Claude asked and then Sam nodded. "All right then. Let's pack a bag. Maya should be back in Las Vegas in another day or so. We'll talk about the details in the car. To be clear, this is my wife, my plan, and my idea. If this is performed correctly, you will each get paid in installments. I'm offering you each ten million dollars. If we fuck this

up, every man or woman for himself or herself. Deal?"
Claude put out his hand and Sam covered it with his hand.
Allie did the same. A pact was made.

# Chapter Thirty-Six

$M$y woman's intuition told me to leave, but T.A.H. was so much more than a television show. I was wide awake and wanted to see more. "This place looks so small on your show," I said.

"We don't want to compromise our location and some of the sensitive material. Jay and I would have arguments about it. He wanted the world to see everything. I'm more practical. We spent a fortune on this place and the information within it. Too much information in the wrong hands could be very dangerous. Maya, let me show you the library."

There was a door that blended in with the cabinetry of the museum corridor. Glenn led me through. On the other side was an enormous room about the same size as a basketball court. The collection of books, manuscripts, tapes, videos, and media was extensive. I was surprised to see my novel on a shelf next to Jay's wall of works.

"My book isn't worthy to be here." I took the book down from the shelf.

"On the contrary. Your novel is not just a novel. It's a code, a DNA code. The code begins with Jay's first novel and then continues with your book. My researchers, I mean our researchers, don't think it's finished. That's why Jay gave you the computer and time to write the sequel. Once you're edits are complete, once you tell your editor not to change too much as you did last time, we can continue matching the pairs of words. You see, you and Jay have a pattern."

"A pattern? What is it? Jay alluded to that, but I didn't understand. I do like words that start with the letter "C" though. Don't know why."

"You and Jay both love words that start with "C"", "A", "G", and "T". You purposely use them starting on page eight and then on every page that is a multiple of eight. It has to be intentional. The odds of it being a coincidence, well, that's not how writers write. In DNA strands, cytosine bonds with guanine and adenine bonds with thymine. They form the code for DNA. The different combinations are what make us humans. But you and Jay have a different code with a different chromosome than the rest of us. His novels and now your novels are giving us the code for one of your parents. At least that's what we think."

"But why through a novel? Why not just write the code down in a notebook and study it?" I asked

"The books become best sellers. Science fiction best sellers. Millions of people read them. A lot of people who work in science like to read best sellers. It's one way to reach a certain group of people without being overt and advertising to the world. It's out in the open while being hidden at the same time, easy to write off as crackpot conspiracy. But I am speculating. In time the truth will reveal itself to all of us. So please, in honor of what we started here at T.A.H., put your novel back. I'm going to check on something. I'll be back in an hour? You've got to be getting hungry by now."

"Huh? Completely forgot about eating. Too excited. Don't worry about me. I'll be quite entertained within this library," I said.

"There's an intercom switch right there. If you want something, anything, staff will bend over backwards to accommodate. Enjoy."

I found some paper from the printer and a pen in a drawer then immediately began writing down the base codes that were supposedly hidden within Jay's books. Sure enough, on page eight, the eighth word and then the sixteenth word and then the twenty-fourth word and so it went were words that began with "A", "T", "C", and "G".

It was like a puzzle. Odd though. The publisher could have changed the format or fonts. So many variables. I felt like a kid learning how to decode. I kept up my decoding until page eighty when I realized that I could ask someone for the code. But I spot-checked each book, and sure enough there were the "A", "T", "C", and "G" words right where they were supposed to be. Amazing. My brother wasn't crazy, he was ingenious.

The library was filled with originals and copies of ancient manuscripts in languages that I couldn't read. I hoped there were English translations available. The hour was up much sooner than I had figured. Glenn was back.

"Okay, you have my full attention. Actually you had it when the side of the mountain opened up, but now I'm on the verge of a panic attack. All of this is real. I can't just file it in my memory as something that's interesting, but probably bullshit. I'm overwhelmed, exhausted and hungry."

"It's past seven o'clock. Do you want to eat here or on the plane?"

"On the plane would be great. Just want to get home. I will leave it to you to get my divorce finalized. I'm going to stop at my house, pick up a few items, and then stay at Eric's apartment. He must be worried. I can't seem to call or text…"

"Bad cell service inside of a mountain, but we're working on it. You'll be fine once you're out of this mountain range. Let me walk you back to the car and drive you to the plane."

On the way out of the library, I heard a loud drumming sound that caused the floor to vibrate. "What's that?"

"That's something new that we are working on. Tell you what, once I get your divorce filed, I'll give you another tour. Next week? Will you be living with Eric or will you move into Jay's house?"

"I'll call you and let you know. I got a lot on my mind," I answered.

"Of course. There is much more to see. But I am getting tired too."

"Will you be flying with me?" I asked, inquiring if Glenn was staying at T.A.H. or going back home.

"Only if you wish."

I shook my head. "Just get me on the plane."

Within an hour of walking through mazes and then riding down a narrow mountain road with no rails in the dark, I was on the Gulfstream jet, ready for take-off. Within minutes I was up in the air with a plate of chicken Alfredo in front of me. Was there a cook on this flight? I didn't know and didn't bother to ask. Just enjoyed my dinner and liked the added luxury.

After dinner, I checked my phone. Claude called seven times in the last two days. He must have heard how rich I was. Divorce would be more difficult. Eric called twice. I listened to my voicemails, quickly deleting Claude's. All he wanted was to know when I'd be home so we could continue our counseling. I already regretted the therapist. I should have called his bluff right then and there and moved out. Eric's messages were puzzling. He sounded distant.

I called him back. "Hi. I'm on the way home. Just going to grab some of my things and then, I don't know, maybe come over?" I suddenly felt vulnerable. What if he didn't want to see me?

"Maya, the news said that you and Jay were lovers. Is that true? Were you sleeping with him? Did he leave you everything?" Eric sounded angry.

"No! We were just friends, I swear! Please, I have so much to tell you. My life has drastically changed. I know it looks like we had something going, but you've to believe me, Jay and I were only friends. I know it sounds strange, but there's so much more to it. I'm getting a divorce. Glenn Lucasek, the Glenn Lucasek from *Alien Theories*, is my new lawyer. Claude might get everything I've earned for the last few years, maybe everything that I will earn once the sequel is published, but none of that matters. I'm a billionaire."

"What? That man was worth a billion dollars? I can't believe the luck you are having. Claude will want his cut."

"He isn't entitled to my inheritance. Listen, my plane is starting to descend and I'm starting to fade. Would you pick me up? I want to stop off at the house, get a few things, and never look back."

"Stay with me. You can stay forever. I love you and I am sorry for accusing…"

"Stop, Eric. You have every right to question me. It's weird. The whole thing is weird. If you only how weird…" My voice trailed off. I wasn't supposed to tell him too much. I would wait for now, but I didn't want to lie to Eric. "Anyway, I would love to stay with you. I feel better about it now that I have a lawyer who is working on the paperwork as we speak. I'm almost single, and will be completed separated by tonight. That's not adultery is it?"

Eric laughed. "You have such a unique set of morals. But I don't trust Claude. Maybe you could wait until morning when you know the house will be empty?"

"I have a gun. It's in my sock drawer. I'll be in and out. Pick me up at the private airport just outside the strip, you know the one?"

"Oh yeah. Where all of the high rollers land in their private jets. Wait, do you own a jet? Shit! I'm in love with a woman who owns a jet?"

I laughed so hard my stomach hurt. "No, it's my lawyer's, but I do own a helicopter. You got to meet Glenn and Mercedes and Paula. They're new friends I met through Jay who feel like old friends."

"Can't wait. Right now I just want to see you."

Within twenty minutes, I was on the ground. I saw Eric's Ford beyond the fence, waiting. Once the stairs were in place, I raced down them and ran to his car. He got out of the driver's seat and took me in his arms, kissing me softly on the lips. He smelled like Obsession cologne, which he only wore on special occasions. This was my soul mate, my happily ever after. How did everything get so screwed up?

In my driveway was the Lexus I bought Claude from what seemed like a lifetime ago. The car wasn't even two years old, but it represented my first big royalty check. My Lexus was in the garage. Surprisingly, Claude never asked me for another expensive car. He had to have a ton of miles on it from constantly driving to and from Los Angeles. I stared at the car for a few minutes, remembering the beginning of him and me. Now it was the end. Maybe he wasn't even home. He could have flown back to Los Angeles.

"Want me to come in?" Eric asked.

"If he's home, that's going to set him off. Give me twenty minutes to get my stuff, tell him we are separated, and then tell him that I will be staying at a hotel. If he asks, I'll explain that the car in the driveway is my Uber ride. If I don't come out, then maybe. He never hit me or did anything crazy like that."

"Twenty minutes. Then I'm coming in and calling the police."

"All right. Twenty minutes." I got out of the car and went inside the front door.

Claude was definitely home. He sat in the family room with a glass of wine while watching the news. "Maya, so glad you are back. How was the funeral?"

"Sad. Very sad. Thanks for asking. How was Los Angeles? I heard you picked up another very important client. A tell-all book about a politician?" I asked. My hands were sweaty and I suddenly felt nauseous.

Something wasn't right. Claude wasn't acting like the suicidal, heartbroken, jilted soon-to-be ex who was desperate to hang on to whatever was left.

"Yes. So the news says you were fucking that guy. That's why he left you one billion dollars." Claude took a sip of his wine and seemed oddly relaxed.

I wasn't sure if he was stating a fact or trying to start an argument. "We were just friends. Listen, maybe we could talk about this at counseling. That's tomorrow, right?"

Claude nodded. "Actually it is therapy meant for my benefit."

He sounded angry. "Well, I was just going to grab a few things and check into a hotel for now. I got a car in the front waiting for me." I walked toward our bedroom. Before I got up the first step of the staircase I felt something long and heavy, maybe a baseball bat, crash into my head. The next thing I knew I was in the back seat of a Lexus, my Lexus.

# Chapter Thirty-Seven

"Tie her up. Shoot her once you get up the mountains," Claude said. Sam and Allie nodded as they wrapped silver duct tape around Maya's hands, feet, and mouth. "We got a problem though. She said there's a car waiting for her. Look carefully through the blinds. Don't let the driver see your face."

Allie rushed to the front window and snuck a peek out front. "Claude, there's a man in an SUV, a Ford. She said Uber. I don't know. Should I pay him and maybe that will be the end of it?"

"Fuck no. Let me think, let me...Okay. You and Sam take her into the garage and use her car. This will work out even better. Tie me up, gag me. I need bruises. Here." Claude grabbed a couple of cans from the pantry. "Hit me." He handed Sam the cans. "C'mon, in the face. I know you want to. I need a black eye, something to show a scuffle."

In the kitchen, Sam pounded him several times in the face. "Damn it! Okay, that should leave some bruises. Fucking A. That hurt." His handsome face dripped blood all over the floor. "Now tie me to the chair. Hurry. Before this Uber asshole drives off. Carry Maya into her car in the garage. She probably has keys in her purse, but another set hangs on the key hook over there." Claude looked by the refrigerator.

"Remember, stick to the plan. Now gag me." Claude sat in a chair in the hallway off of the kitchen, bound with electrical tape, bruised, and gagged.

The kitchen chairs were tipped over, the rug was bunched, and all kinds of utensils were on the floor, giving off a ransacked look. Claude nodded and then Sam and

Allie dragged Maya's limp body through the hallway and into the attached garage. Seconds later, Claude heard the garage door and tires squeal off the driveway.

He was alone now. All he needed was the Uber driver to come into the house or at least open the door. The front door might be open. Claude took the chair and scooted toward the front door. Within a minute, he saw the knob turn and then started grunting. Standing in the front door was the last person in the world he expected. Eric, skinny, geeky, loser Eric from the bookstore.

"Uhh, uhh," Claude grunted as he scooted down the hall. His heart was racing. Would Eric think this was a set-up or a real break-in? And why was he even there? Did Maya call him for a ride home? *The old goat just dropped and she was in the process of dumping my ass*, thought Claude. Where did Eric fit in? Jay's replacement? *That whore will get what's coming.*

Eric had a peculiar look on his face as he ripped the duct tape from his mouth. "Where's Maya?" he shouted.

"Eric? Uh, uh, I don't know. I came home, went out in the yard, enjoyed the pool, and then got beat up while I was asked a dozen questions about Maya and her role with T.A.H. When I couldn't answer, they bound…"

"T.A.H.? What the hell is that?" Eric said.

"It stands for They Are Here. It's that alien institution that is a backdrop for that UFO show Maya likes."

"Yeah, I know the one," Eric snapped. "What does that have to do with Maya? Who are they?"

"I don't know who," Claude answered emphatically. Eric didn't seem to suspect him in Maya's disappearance.

"Well, where is she? I just watched her walk through the front door. She said she was coming right out and then your garage door went up. That was her car that raced off. Was she inside of it? Were the people who beat you the same ones who took her? Oh my God! We've got to call the police," Eric said. He was on the verge of tears. He grabbed a knife from the kitchen and cut through the duct tape that bound Claude's feet and hands and legs.

Claude's Plan B story seemed to be working. He didn't count on feeling jealous. Jay and now Eric, or maybe both at the same time. She got around. He didn't know why he was so surprised considering how they met. "Eric, why are you here? Do you know that Maya and I are in counseling? Our marriage is about to collapse. I thought Jay McCallister was the reason. Yet here you are, picking her up from the airport. Are you two still friends or is there something more?"

"Listen, you aren't stupid. You know I've been in love with your wife for a long time. Truth is I am not sure how she feels about me. I heard that she and Jay were involved. It was on the news. But she said that wasn't true. You want to tell me what's going on before I call the police?" Eric asked.

"According to the news, she just inherited everything, including some kind of special position with T.A.H. The people who broke in, there were two of them, men, at least they were strong like men. I am only guessing. They wore ski masks. I don't know what they looked like. They tore through the house looking for something, taped me up, and then grabbed her right after she walked in. I don't know what's going on, but it must have something to do with this alien institution. It was mentioned during the funeral. Apparently Jay will not be buried, but frozen and stored in the museum. Do you know where it is?"

"Not exactly. But I watch the show. Somewhere in northern Nevada. I'm guessing the Ruby Mountains. Jay has always been controversial and outspoken. Could he have been murdered because of T.A.H.? Claude, we need to call the police now. Before they get too far."

"Make the call."

*Luck keeps on coming*, he thought. *Now I have an alibi.*

# Chapter Thirty-Eight

It was time for General Andreas to make the dreaded phone call. In his mind, it was the end of everything. General Blanchard could and probably would end his career. But that wasn't all he lost. Kate, beautiful Kate with long dark hair, fair skin, and dark eyes, would hate him forever. She was his superwoman. They were going to change the aviation world forever. She broke his heart. Being his wife was nothing more than a strategy. She never admitted to stealing the baby, but did admit to making unauthorized deals with the ABs.

The engineers had little tolerance to pain. They individually admitted to dozens of new discoveries that guaranteed American superiority in defense for years to come. At least the general had something positive to say when making the dreaded phone call. That would never make up for losing the ABs and their spacecraft. There was no sense in lying about it. Blanchard visited too often not to notice his prized extraterrestrial life and technology was gone.

To add nails to his coffin, Andreas would have to mention the missing baby boy, one of the three babies who was successfully born in an artificial womb with a mother, father and spliced alien genes. The baby was beyond priceless. He was scientific proof that ABs exist. *Fuck!* If only there was another way. He had to make that call.

Doctor Richtor was down the hall from Andreas's fiancée as she was being questioned. Of the three German doctors, Richtor was the only one of the Nazis who verbalized his hatred for the general and all of America. Andreas joined Lamphrey. He had a few questions before making the call.

Richtor sat in a chair in the middle of the room with his hands cuffed. His icy blue eyes were gray and flashed with anger. Enhanced questioning might not work with him. But after watching the tapes inside of the observation deck, the general already knew he had nothing to do with the aliens' escape. Logic also helped their case. Why would any of them want to sabotage their experiment?

"Major, give us a moment," Andreas said.

Lamphrey nodded, briskly walked out of the room, and shut the door. The young major might as well have clicked his heels. He looked more like a Nazi than Richtor with his full head of platinum hair and blue eyes. The major had proven loyalty time and time again. Still, the general wondered if he was involved in any of this mess. Maybe Lamphrey's little pep talk was meant to save his ass.

Andreas grabbed the keys off of the desk. After a couple of tries, he found the right key and unlocked the handcuffs around Richtor's wrists. "You hurt?"

He shook his head with a look of indignation.

"I know you didn't let them out. And you are very clear about your feelings for me. Relax. I'm not going to hurt you. I just need to know a number. How many babies will you have by the year's end?" Andreas asked.

"That's all that you want? You could have asked me that in the lab," Richtor said. "We still have the two babies. The a-wombs have new fertilized cells in them. We'll have four more babies right after the New Year in January and February. The ABs isolated some of their genes on a DNA strand. We want to create the perfect human."

Andreas was both aggravated and intrigued. "What is the perfect human? An Aryan, perhaps?"

Richtor shrugged. "We both know better, General. The ABs narrowed down thousands of possibilities of perfection, but we still have plenty of work. I am sorry about your engagement, General."

"No you're not. It's over. I'm over it. It's time to move on. And my personal life should be of no consequence to you. Who else knows the details of your genetic discoveries?"

"No one but you, me, Karl, and Hans," Richtor said. "And your president. The chairman.

"And the babies?" Andreas asked.

"Us and then the engineers you escorted into our lab," Richtor said with a hint of irritation. "Some of your officers, perhaps."

Andreas cringed. The truth stung like a giant wasp. But a lightbulb inside of his brain went off. Maybe Lamphrey was right. He could still salvage his career. "Do you like working here?" The Nazi nodded. "Would you all like a little more freedom?" He nodded again. "We started a little program. Some call it 'hide-the-Nazi.' You wouldn't have to live here, underground. You could live in an actual house and come to work each day like many others who work here."

"I'm listening."

"I will need a few things from you."

"We understand each other perfectly, General," Richtor said.

"First off, no baby was taken. Engineers will take the blame. We found the baby by the spaceship before it escaped. The ABs escaped from the cage with the help of the engineers."

"General, do you know how the ABs escaped?" Richtor asked.

"Don't play me for a fool, Doctor. You know how they got out of the cage. You probably knew the cage wouldn't work from day one. But we'll keep that little tidbit to ourselves. In case you're questioned by General Blanchard, what will you say?"

"Very few people know what we do here and I think we understand each other." Richtor paused and smiled crookedly. "And everyone knows the baby was found by the spacecraft. He was found right before the ABs were set free. But that's all I know. I spend all of my time in a laboratory." Richtor's face was filled with smugness.

"We understand each other," Andreas said. "You may…"

"General," Richtor interrupted, "You and I are not as different as you think."

Andreas nodded. The Nazi doctor was right. He looked down on the Nazis as if he was morally superior. But in the end, self-interest prevailed.

Andreas now had his narrative down. Most of the plot's holes were plugged with convincing lies that could not be proven or disproven. He was ready for the dreaded phone call.

First, he had Bolantano, Lamphrey, and Redding circulate a rumor that the baby was found in the hangar. The ABs were going to take the baby with them, but Captain Bolantano managed to save the boy just before the ABs got on board. There was no camera in front of the spacecraft's entrance. That lie was safe. None of the guards ever saw a baby inside of the car that left from one entrance and then shortly came back in another. Another lie that was safe.

Andreas's only real problem was the four engineers who had rebuilt the space craft. One of them was going to be his wife. He didn't want to kill any of them, especially Costello, and he didn't want them punished. Yet they needed to serve as sacrificial lambs. Costello was already thought of as a user. Now she was a traitor as were the two other engineers. Because of the highly sensitive nature of their project, the general requested that they be quietly discharged and allowed to back into their old lives as civilians. His request was granted.

# Chapter Thirty-Nine

I was wet and cold. My head hurt like hell. I ran my fingers through my fine black hair and felt a lump the size of a tennis ball on the crown. I panicked, running my fingers of both hands through. I was surprised to find no blood. My name. At first I couldn't remember it. Several moments later, it came to me—Maya, Maya Smock. My mother left me at a Catholic orphanage when I was a baby, or so I was told. My head throbbed. A chirpy-ringy sound interrupted my thoughts. My name faded away and the rest of my memories were wiped clean. Maybe no memories were better than bad ones.

My instincts took over and I stood up. Hesitantly, I took a few steps, terrified I would find more ailments that threatened my survival. I scanned my surroundings, all unfamiliar. I stood on the bank of a lake, soaked to the bone and covered with mud. As the material in my sweatshirt fanned out, a shell casing dropped to the ground. A bullet? Was I shot? Sheer panic took over. I searched every centimeter of my skin, looking for an entry wound, but nothing. My head hurt and there was a lump, but no holes or scabs. I put the casing in my pocket.

It was still dark, but there was a hint of daybreak. I wasn't sure which way was west or east. I would figure that out as soon as the sun rose. There was a lake and a never-ending mountain range in the distance. The cold temperature chilled me to the core. If I didn't get help or at least shelter, I would freeze to death in the middle of the mountains.

I turned a full 360 degrees taking in the scenery. I looked out at the lake. Not a house or dock or boat to be seen. Most of the trees were pines, but a few trees had red, orange and yellow leaves. Fall. Then I remembered it was November. Thanksgiving would be coming up and then Christmas. I was invited to Jay's for dinner. Jay, who was Jay? My boyfriend? Flashes of a face, a handsome face came to mind. Blue eyes, square jaw, and Roman nose. Claude. Was he my boyfriend? No, Claude was my husband.

My thoughts slowed down to a pace that I could process. The thought of Claude made the pit of my stomach drop and the lump on my head throb. I needed to move. I walked up a steep hill through the trees and the brush. The sun began to rise up in the sky like a bright yellow orb.

My movement countered the cold weather. I guessed it must have been around thirty degrees. My clothes were wet and I didn't have a coat. A wave of panic made me dizzy. I stumbled a few feet down the hill. I rolled over to a tree, sat up, and hyperventilated. *Count to one hundred.* The voice inside of my head wasn't mine. I kept counting, obeying the familiar voice.

I screamed and then sobbed while clutching a tree. All of this had to be a nightmare and soon I would wake up. This lie that I told myself calmed me down to a rational state of mind. I had no idea where I was but knew Claude was responsible.

Hours, maybe only minutes, went by. I got up and continued to move. At the top of the hill, I found a gravel road and walked alongside of it. About one mile later, I tripped over the metal stem of a green road sign. The sign's post was bent as if a motorist had mowed the sign down and no one repaired it. It read 'Hidden Lakes, Ruby Mountains'.

My innards felt like they were doused with hydrochloric acid. I knew about the Ruby Mountains. But how? I kept moving for several miles. My clothes had sort of dried as the temperature rose. I was still cold, but my teeth stopped chattering. Hunger set in.

I heard the whishing sound of a car in the distance. The gravel road led to a paved highway. I heard the same sound a few minutes later and then broke into a jog. Soon I was standing along a route or highway. There was a pickup truck driving toward the sun. I threw myself in the street and hoped he saw me. Could this be my savior? Or was it a serial killer prowling for victims? I took a chance. As the truck came closer, I waved my arms. The driver honked and pulled over.

"Where you headed?" the driver asked. He was older, maybe sixty and well-built. He wore a Mariners baseball cap and a flannel shirt. I wasn't afraid.

"I don't know. Civilization. I think my husband tried to kill me."

The driver looked at me with both pity and disbelief. He probably thought I was crazy. "So I guess you're having a bad day."

"You could say that. Where am I?"

"You're in the Ruby Mountains of Nevada, darling. I'm Jim. And you're name?"

"Maya. Does anyone live around here?"

"Yes, but not many. This is God's country. A lot of people come up to hike and camp. I live around here, lived here all of my life. It's very quiet here. Maybe that's why your husband left you for dead. It's a good place for that sort of thing."

Ruby Mountains made my brain light up like pinball machine. I ignored the comment about being left for dead and asked, "Jim, what else are the Ruby Mountains known for? I know this place."

"Ah, well maybe if you watch that alien show. There's some kind of institution that uses telescopes and studies alien sightings. I don't know where it is. The host doesn't exactly give an address."

"They Are Here. T.A.H. That's it, isn't it? Glenn Lucasek. I have to talk to him," I said.

"Why? Did you see an alien?" Jim asked. I didn't know if he was being a smart ass or trying to be sincere. "You can use my phone. Here. I don't have good reception out here, but you can try. When we get to the gas station you can also try their phone. Hey, you said you're name was Maya? It's not Maya Smock, is it?"

I nodded. Jim's phone had no reception. I handed it back.

"The gas station is right up the road. Miss Smock, you're all over the news, little lady. You were Jay McCallister's girlfriend. Hell, no wonder your husband tried to kill you." He laughed.

I didn't feel like disputing the claims of the media. I would wear my scarlet letter for now, knowing full well that when the time was right, I would prove to the world that Jay was my brother. We rode for another ten minutes in silence. A gas station, grocery store, and diner were on one side of the road and a hardware store and tavern were on the other side.

Jim pulled into a tiny gas station. "Here you go. I'll wait with you until you get a hold of someone. Someone who doesn't want to kill you."

I began to get Jim's sense of humor and was in no mood for jokes, especially ones at my expense. But I was just grateful to be safe. The cashier let me use the phone. Glenn Lucasek was not listed. I tried to think of who else I could call. Paula Lynquist popped into my head. I called information. Within minutes, I had her on the phone and then she had Glenn on another line.

"I'll send the helicopter out. You're not too far," Glenn said. It was nice to be rich, but then being rich is what got me in this situation.

Jim was still there waiting with me. Several minutes passed. He told me about his job as a forest ranger and he continued to crack jokes. Seeing the chopper land seemed to dry out his sarcasm. "Well, Miss Smock, it's been a pleasure."

"You saved my life, Jim. Please give me your address. I would like to send you something for all that you have done."

"That isn't necessary. And I'm sorry if I offended you. I tend to play around…"

"Please, Jim," I interrupted, "I must look like a crazy lady coming out of the woods. I would still like your address."

He wrote it down on the back of a credit card application. I hugged him goodbye and walked in back of the gas station. The chopper was waiting for me.

The inside of the chopper was warm. The pilot held out his hand and I shook it. He seemed to yell something and had to repeat it because the noise from the propellers was so loud. "I'm here to take you anywhere you want to go, Ms. Smock. Glenn is still at T.A.H. if you want to meet him."

I nodded and then sat down in the front passenger seat. The pilot handed me headphones and motioned for me to strap myself in. There was a small cooler on the floor under the dash. I opened it up and smiled. Water. I took a bottle and chugged it. The pilot began to ascend. With his free hand, he opened up a compartment in the dash and pointed. Candy and chips. I quickly scarfed down two candy bars before we leveled out in the air and then I grabbed a bag of chips and slowly munched while taking in the beauty of the majestic mountains. I saw a couple of lakes and wondered which one was the one that Claude dumped me in.

Ten minutes high in the air and we were already descending. I saw the flat area at the top of the mountain, the same area where the telescopes were placed. The chopper landed and the pilot helped me out. Glenn greeted me at the helipad. Everything hit me at once. I broke down and cried. Claude wanted me dead. I knew he was greedy and a cheat and a liar, but a murderer? He would have had millions just by signing the divorce papers.

"You're back already! Maya, what happened?" Glenn asked. He tried to sound upbeat, but I could see the pity in his eyes. "You didn't say much on the phone. How did you get here? Did you get lost?" He led me down the stairs from the observatory as we talked.

"I flew home yesterday, at least I think it was yesterday." Glenn nodded. "Eric picked me up at the little airport and then I went home to pick up a few things. Claude was there. And then I...I got hit in the head. Next thing I know, I am lying on a bank of a lake. This good Samaritan type, Jim was his name, picked me up after I walked a few miles to the road and took me to the closest gas station. There was a sign while I was walking, Hidden Lakes." We went down twenty flights of stairs and still had many more to go. I wished there was an elevator.

"Yes, Hidden Lakes is one of the many lakes along the mountains. It's pretty close. I'm so sorry. I should have...I should have made you get security the second it came out that you inherited all of Jay's money. Claude had over a billion reasons to kill you. People will kill for a paltry insurance policy. Which, by the way, I wouldn't be surprised if he had one out on you."

"Come to think of it, I signed quite a few papers when I bought our house in Vegas and then a condo in Los Angles. You win. I will hire a couple of bodyguards by the end of the day. Glenn, here." I handed him a shell casing. "I think I was shot, but can't for the life of me figure out where."

We reached the bottom of the stairwell and entered into the part of the institute that Glenn showed me the day before. "Well, Jay was shot before. Same thing. No entry or exit wound, just healed skin or bullet proof skin. But yes, you need to hire security and you need to call the...Wait. No one knows you're here, right?"

"Well, Jim the good Samaritan who drove me to the gas station saw me get into the chopper."

"These mountain folk don't meddle in the lives of high profile people. You got his address. We'll send him a very handsome reward. But Eric, does he know?"

"No. But Paula knows. Then there's the gas station attendant, but I never told her my name. And then there's the pilot."

Glenn led me through a maze of hallways that looked vaguely familiar. "Paula doesn't count. She's with us. The pilot doesn't count and the cashier doesn't even know. Claude assumes that you're dead. He's going to want your body found so he can collect. But if you don't come forward right away...Oh, look at the time. It's only noon. I want you to see the rest of this place."

Glenn asked if I was hungry, which I was, but I shook my head. Curiosity called. I wanted to see the rest of this labyrinth. He led me down another hallway which seemed to take us deeper inside of the mountain. He had a certain mad scientist look in his normally kind blue eyes. We passed a room which he briefly showed me. Inside were metal hunks that were stuck together. "This is a work in progress. Part of a space craft that we recovered. The pieces need to be demagnetized. We received them a month ago and haven't gotten around to it."

I wanted to study the parts, but Glenn hustled me out of the door. We went through a set of double steel doors and then a long unfinished hallway with a dirt floor which led to another set of doors. Before they opened, Glenn pressed his eye into a silver box mounted on the wall. It had a blue ring around it. The box clicked and the doors went open.

"The retina scan?" I asked. He nodded. We both walked through. I felt a rhythmic beat pulsing in the floor. "What is that?"

"It's a centrifuge," Glenn answered as we continued to walk and go through another set of doors. This set also required a retina scan. "You try. I want to see if your scan was uploaded in the system."

I looked into the device mounted before the doors. It flashed and the doors opened. So far I counted three sets of door, two with required retina scans. "Don't they use centrifuges for nuclear weapons?"

"Yes, but we are not enriching uranium, we are creating an anti-gravitational force." He brought me into a round room. I could feel the centrifuge but still could not hear it.

In the middle of the room was a large tube with a larger circle dug into the floor that curved around the tube's circumference.

"No gravity? Like in space? I am lost. Why are you trying to get rid of gravity," I asked like a scared little girl and I was a scared little girl. My body froze as I looked at the bizarre machine.

Glenn looked at the ceiling. "You'd have to ask Chuck, my Asian friend you met yesterday, that question. He's the leading expert in the anti-gravity field. Jay recruited him from China last year. We were at a standstill. Knew that time could bend, knew how worm holes could be created, but couldn't figure out how to bend time and then travel ahead of it or behind. Two months before Jay was murdered, and I've never been more certain he was murdered, he disappeared in that chamber for six hours. I tried to disappear. Our experts and scientists tried to disappear, but to no avail. It was Chuck who put two and two together. Jay has different DNA than we do. Something happened to his body when he was spun at a certain speed and temperature. A vacuum of air rushed inside of the capsule and then he disappeared."

"I'm confused. So Jay disappeared inside of that tube once you started spinning it?" I asked, not sure if I believed him.

"Yes. Centrifugal force, electromagnetic fields, anti-gravity, all of it are just some of the components needed for creating a bridge between time and space. Some call it a worm hole. In Einstein's theory of general relativity a worm hole could be created by man. On one opening of the worm hole there is extreme movement, some movement as fast as the speed of light, while the other end or mouth of the wormhole is still. One could manipulate the passageway and go forward or backward. We figured out how to travel backward. Some knew about wormholes long before Einstein. Jay proved this when he traveled. He wasn't sure where he went, but it was definitely backwards. No cars, just horses and carriages. He assumed that he was in Europe. The people that he'd seen were white. But it wasn't England. He didn't recognize the language. And he stood out from everyone. He had to steal someone's clothes to fit in. He didn't wander too far off for fear of getting lost from the opening of the wormhole."

"What happened when you tried to go in the tube? Or, time machine?" I asked.

"I spun around and breathed in icy air, threw up all over the inside and was dizzy and sick the rest of the day. Basically, I felt like a kid on one of those spinning carnival rides. That's how everyone felt after five to ten minutes inside of the machine. Jay didn't feel nauseous. Let me show you what happened."

Glenn led me into an adjoining room with a giant desk for at least five people and several computers. He clicked the mouse a few times and brought up footage of them all trying the time machine. I saw sprays of vomit after each person came out. And then Jay went. In less than three minutes he was gone, disappeared, just like Glenn said.

"So you see for yourself, his body chemistry is different. Something in his DNA is made to withstand high speeds and then convert into tiny light particles instead of staying one piece of mass. I think you could do it too, Maya. I know you've been through hell. And I am so sorry your husband tried to kill you. I promise you, he will get what is coming. But you're technically missing right now. Knowing Claude, and I will keep an eye on what he is doing, he called the police and reported you missing. He's probably chomping at the bit, waiting for the police to find your body. Right now you've got some time without having to deal with all of that. Please, we need to know who created the wormhole on the other side and why."

I couldn't believe what he was asking much less believe this was real. The thought of going back in time was something right out of one of Jay's novels. Was time travel his ultimate goal? Was this his moment to find himself? I wanted to try, to go into the unknown, but what if I died? I had so much to live for. What if I couldn't figure out how to get back?

"Glenn, what you are asking is ridiculous. Does anyone besides you and me and the people who work here know about this machine?"

"Paula and Mercedes know. They don't approve. They also don't like Chuck, but not because of his competence. They don't like him because of his backers who are now our backers. They say that Chuck and his friends have ties too close to corporations. Regardless of the economics and politics, Chuck's the one who figured out the final step on how to time travel. Please, Maya, this is important to the world. You'd be like an astronaut of time. Jay wanted to go back. We had so many plans that only you can continue."

"But Eric? I love him, Glenn. I always have. He's going to get worried."

"Do you trust me?" Glenn asked.

I did trust him. He seemed to have nothing but altruistic intentions. As I stared at the capsule, I imagined all of the places and time eras that it might take me to. I was under its spell. Years and years of reading about time travel in novels, and here I was about to live it. Claude, Eric, my fortune, hell, everything that I had in this world could be put on hold. I nodded as if I was in a trance. "What do I do?"

Glenn smiled. "Wait here. Let me get you some clothes." Ten minutes later he had me wearing a men's dirty white peasant shirt and a pair of trousers that were too big and too long. Glenn gave me his belt to keep the pants from falling down. It was neutral enough to blend in.

"These are what Jay brought back with him. You might need new clothes, but this will give you a start. Wait here." Glenn ran out of the room.

I was alone with capsule. Suddenly I remembered the gold coins that Glenn gave, the coins from Solomon in the safe. The key he gave me was also missing.

The floor thumped but then quickly changed to a pulse. Glenn must have sped things up. While I waited, I dreamed of what it would be like to go back. I could pass for white, but looked more Mexican or American Indian. Would I stand out? Glenn walked back into the room.

"Glenn, the belongings from Jay's safe, they were in my pockets. Gone."

The look on Glenn's face suggested he was worried. "Claude?" I nodded. "I forgot about them. We will get them back. I want you to have this." He gave me a bag of gold and silver coins.

"Thanks. I promise not to lose this."

"Unless someone knocks you out and tries to kill you. Please, don't worry. The coins should work as currency. Hold them close to your skin. Maya, thank you. Wait, do you want to leave anything behind? Here, how about this?" Glenn handed her a hundred dollars in different American bills. "The dates are on them. Maybe you will find whoever built the other mouth of the wormhole. Please ask how it was built. Let me get the camera."

Glenn grabbed a tripod from the adjoining room. Chuck and four others came in. I had a little audience. What if I couldn't pass through to the other side? I guess I'd throw up like everyone else. I stepped into the cylinder. There were thick nylon bands which I assumed to be a harness. Glenn opened the door to help me strap in. He then shut the door and locked it with heavy duty clamps. Too late to back out now. There was a loud deafening noise. I smelled a perfumed chill enter the chamber and wondered what was mixed into the air.

The tube shook so hard my bones vibrated. It then turned sideways and spun like the propellers of the chopper I had just rode inside of. I didn't feel dizzy at all, just calm despite the noise and the spinning. And then I felt like I was floating, almost like when I wrote my sequel in Jay's guest room. In fact, I was floating. I was weightless. This must be the anti-gravity kicking in. I tried to look at my arm, but could only see bright speckles in the air. Was this me? A few million light particles floating through space? The feeling was so unexplainable, maybe like a wave of peace that came from a religious revelation. Was this another form of an out-of-body experience? Pure transcendence.

Time did not seem to pass. And then I felt heavy. I looked down and saw my white shirt and trousers. I wasn't strapped in the machine but there was a strap. It was different than Glenn's, made out of brown leather. The spinning and the pulsing slowed down and then came to an abrupt stop. The tube went from a horizontal position to a vertical one. I was now standing on the floor. Gravity returned. I opened the door. The top of the machine was smoking. I coughed from the exhaust. Was I still in the Ruby Mountains? Was this all of a gag? It had to be. Too ridiculous to be true. Must be some sci-fi geek prank. I walked around and called out Glenn's name. No answer.

The capsule I walked out of was different. The room I was in was not the same. It looked like the inside of a barn. I walked through the hay on the ground and out of the doors. There was a young boy with blonde hair pushing a wheel barrow filled with manure. His clothes were similar to mine. He saw me and looked frightened.

"Hello," I said.

He screamed. "Engel, engel!"

# Epilogue

As Andreas rambled off his story to General Blanchard, it occurred to him that Lamphrey had been right all along. The young man was not a threat, but an ally. If he came out of this major fuck-up completely unscathed, Lamphrey would be named his protégé. Operation Chrome could easily run for at least three decades if not more.

After the dreaded phone call, General Blanchard, the President, and Secretary of Defense flew into Broom Lake that afternoon. Their questioning was light, but they later sent in one of their own to establish an inventory and heighten security. Andreas's space craft project officially ended, but the hangar was used for the construction of special crafts the military wanted to keep secret.

The crowning jewel of Broom Lake would always be the genetic research. The Nazi doctors proved to be invaluable. Over the years, their secrets slowly leaked out to friendly corporations who helped fund their operation. The same concept the Nazis discovered was used to modify food and maximize crops. Organs were cloned to prolong life for those willing to pay. And humans could breed without having intercourse. The medical breakthroughs alone absolved the general of much of his guilt.

He would occasionally visit the doctors in their underground laboratory. They used the caged area that was originally dug out for the ABs to expand their artificial wombs. There were twenty-four artificial wombs filled with embryos created with various combinations of alien DNA. The eggs used were from the original women who were sacrificed at the project's earliest stage. The sperm donor or donors were still unknown, but the general suspected all of the doctors of spreading their seed. Their egos needed the stamp of recognition.

Each baby had useless genes for body hair, wisdom teeth, and appendix extracted out of their DNA chain and then AB genes for cognition, protection, health, and survival inserted. With each generation, the Nazi doctors created a life more superior than the next. All of them were starting to age. Two younger doctors were brought in to train and continue the project. The Nazis were very particular, almost insisting on replacements with German sounding surnames. They settled on a woman and a man, both American, with some German descent.

By 1970, Andreas was old, but still physically and mentally fit. He took a backseat to running Broom Lake, passing the torch to General Lamphrey. Part of his project placed the manmade babies in the homes of the American and European elite. They were raised with wealth and privilege and groomed for the future.

The current United States president wanted the hybrid baby program to phase out by the end of the century. There would be enough babies in place by then. Two hundred eighteen and counting were already settled all over the United States, Canada, Mexico, South America, and Europe. Occasionally a baby would die or get lost out in the field, but Andreas kept track of most.

The project ran like clockwork. Despite losing the ABs and spacecraft so many years ago, the United States had a monopoly on technology and weaponry. There were always other sightings, whispers of groups who had seen spacecraft and aliens. Andreas knew there were more races of advanced beings out there. Someone was probably studying them. Was this what the world was coming to? An intergalactic battleground of some kind? Was his soul worth it? Was his life worth it? No longer was he sure.

Retirement was around the corner. Despite being over seventy years old, Andreas received multiple job offers within the private sector. He had no idea what he was going to do, but it was nice to be wanted.

A few months before his official retirement, Andreas picked up his mail from the base's headquarters. In the stack of junk, there was a bank statement, *Time* magazine, and a letter with no return address. There was something familiar about the handwriting. He went inside his trailer, the same one he had lived in for over twenty years, and opened the letter.

*Dear Robert,*

*I am writing you because we are both at the end of it all and we have much unfinished business. I think about you from time to time and try not to be angry. I try to remember the warm side of you that I fell in love with. After you used me as a scapegoat, I thought that I would be killed. Thank you for sparing me.*

*If you are wondering, I ended up working for the government overseas and then landed a job in an international corporation. I still live overseas and will leave it at that. If interested, you are a very powerful man who can find out in a phone call. And if you ever wanted to talk, I wouldn't hang up.*

*I did end up getting married to a mild mannered professor who died recently. He was a wonderful husband and father. Yes, father! I had a little girl about two years after you sold me down the river. I was forty-four. For your information, the baby was not created inside of a test tube. She will soon be eighteen years old, beautiful, bright, and just a light to the darkness I had been through.*

*Anyway, I wanted to tell you that I truly am sorry. I admit to making a deal with the aliens. It was the same deal that gave you undetected weaponry, stealth capability, and anti-gravity technology. The deal also gave you alternate power sources.*

*I'll admit to taking several shards of the crystal found in the heap of pieces, but I think I told you that a long time ago before everything fell apart. For the record, I didn't know the aliens would escape. In hind sight, I should have known. But that is as far as my disloyalty to you and my country went. I had nothing to do with the missing baby. I understand why you lied, disappointed, but understand. Broom Lake was your life and I could have been a part of it, but I would never take its place.*

*But I am not writing you this letter to tell you that I forgive you or to try to convince you of the truth or even out of spite. I am writing this letter because I think I know who took that baby and why.*

*My daughter, Lori, wants to be a teacher, probably a science teacher. She is like me in so many ways. She loves children and volunteers every Thursday at the local orphanage. She watches the babies and toddlers after secondary school. A baby was just dropped off at the front door. This in itself is not unusual. Some mothers just don't want to talk to anyone. They put the baby in some kind of container or basket, ring the bell, and then leave. What makes this baby special is that he came with a green-yellowish crystal pendant, the same stone that I took from the spacecraft all those years ago.*

*I have shown my daughter the crystals many times. So when she saw the new baby boy with the same crystal set in a silver pendant setting, she wanted another look at the ones I took so long ago. It was a match. That baby is one of yours.*

*The supervisor, Lori, and I went door to door, asking anyone if they had seen a baby being dropped off at the door. Two people saw a man in his late forties, maybe early fifties, tall, with dark hair that was starting to recede. I know it's been several years, but that sounded like Captain Bolantano. Let's just say I have some connections at the nearest airport. Michael Bolantano had departed back to the states the same day. Does he still work at Broom Lake with you?*

*Why would he take the babies and leave them with such an odd crystal? I can only speculate. Maybe he's leaving his mark. Maybe he wants someone to trace the babies back to the experiments at Broom Lake.*

*I hope this letter gives you some kind of peace of mind. Again, I am not angry. The second part of my life turned out to be something special. I will always love you despite everything and hope your dedication to whatever you want to call it was worth it in the end.*

*Kate*

**To Be Continued in The Sequel...**

## About the Author:

Author Dina Rae has written The Best Seller, Halo of the Nephilim, Halo of the Damned, The Last Degree, and Bad Juju. Her novels range from science fiction to horror, weaving history and research throughout the plots. Her short story, Be Paranoid Be Prepared, is a prequel to The Last Degree, focusing on the James Martin character. Big Pharma, Big Agri, Big Conspiracy is Dina's first nonfiction work.

Dina also freelances for various entertainment blogs.

Dina lives with her husband, two daughters, and two dogs outside of Dallas. She is a Christian, an avid tennis player, movie buff, teacher, and self-proclaimed expert on several conspiracy theories. She has been interviewed numerous times in e-zines, websites, blogs, newspapers, and radio programs. When she is not writing, she reads novels from her favorite authors Dan Brown, Stephen King, Brad Thor, George R.R. Martin, and Preston & Childs. She also enjoys reading about religion, UFOs, New World Order, government conspiracies, political intrigue, and other cultures.

## Social Media Links:

Blog: www.dinaraeswritestuff.blogspot.com

Twitter:
https://twitter.com/HalooftheDamned @haloofthedamned

www.ingramcontent.com/pod-product-compliance
Lightning Source LLC
Chambersburg PA
CBHW072317020726
47501CB00002B/545